Storm Peak

STORM PEAK

A **JESSE PARKER** MYSTERY

John A. Flanagan

BERKLEY PRIME CRIME, NEW YORK

THE BERKLEY PUBLISHING GROUP
Published by the Penguin Group
Penguin Group (USA) Inc.
375 Hudson Street, New York, New York 10014, USA
Penguin Group (Canada), 90 Eglinton Avenue East, Suite 700, Toronto, Ontario M4P 2Y3, Canada
(a division of Pearson Penguin Canada Inc.)
Penguin Books Ltd., 80 Strand, London WC2R 0RL, England
Penguin Group Ireland, 25 St. Stephen's Green, Dublin 2, Ireland (a division of Penguin Books Ltd.)
Penguin Group (Australia), 250 Camberwell Road, Camberwell, Victoria 3124, Australia
(a division of Pearson Australia Group Pty. Ltd.)
Penguin Books India Pvt. Ltd., 11 Community Centre, Panchsheel Park, New Delhi—110 017, India
Penguin Group (NZ), 67 Apollo Drive, Rosedale, North Shore 0632, New Zealand
(a division of Pearson New Zealand Ltd.)
Penguin Books (South Africa) (Pty.) Ltd., 24 Sturdee Avenue, Rosebank, Johannesburg 2196,
South Africa

Penguin Books Ltd., Registered Offices: 80 Strand, London WC2R 0RL, England

This is a work of fiction. Names, characters, places, and incidents either are the product of the author's imagination or are used fictitiously, and any resemblance to actual persons, living or dead, business establishments, events, or locales is entirely coincidental. The publisher does not have any control over and does not assume any responsibility for author or third-party websites or their content.

Copyright © 2009 by John A. Flanagan.
Cover design by Brad Foltz.

PRINTING HISTORY
Random House Australia Bantam book trade paperback edition / 2009
Berkley Prime Crime trade paperback edition / February 2010

Library of Congress Cataloging-in-Publication Data

Flanagan, John (John Anthony)
    Storm peak : a Jesse Parker mystery / John A. Flanagan.
        p.   cm.
    ISBN 978-0-425-23525-6 (pbk.)
    1. Ex-police officers—Fiction.   2. Ski patrollers—Fiction.   3. Skiers—Crimes against—Fiction.
4. Murder—Investigation—Fiction.   5. Steamboat Springs (Colo.)—Fiction.   I. Title.
    PR9619.4.F63S76   2010
    823'.92—dc22   2009045782

PRINTED IN THE UNITED STATES OF AMERICA

10 9 8 7 6 5 4 3 2 1

In memory of Edwina Rochin,
who guided me onto my first chairlift

PROLOGUE

WHEAT RIDGE,
DENVER, COLORADO
JULY, 2003

On the day Detective Jesse Parker killed Detective Tony Vetano, they had been partners for nearly two years.

They had been slumped in the front seat of an unmarked department Chevy for over two hours, watching Number 1153 Alston Road, while a string of drug dealers arrived to collect their supplies from their distributor. There were seven men inside the ordinary looking suburban house and it was time for the bust. Tony had just called the squad for backup. Seven armed drug dealers were more than they'd bargained for—and a little too many for two cops.

That was when it all started to go to hell.

A Denver PD patrol car turned the corner, moving slowly along the street toward 1153. As it approached, its lights fell on the late model Pontiac GTO belonging to one of the dealers. The car was canary yellow, with the hood decorated in leaping flames. The suspension had been lowered and the rear wheels were shod in fat rubber. In a quiet suburban street like this, it stuck out like a two-dollar whore in a convent.

The black-and-white eased to a stop and the officer climbed out and walked slowly round the GTO to check the tags. He was young, they could see, and on his own. He should have had a partner but departmental budget cuts had been playing hell with the duty roster in the last few months. He moved back to the patrol car, still watching the house, and leaned in the driver's side window. The two detectives heard the muted sound of the police radio.

"Oh, Christ. He's calling it in," Jesse said.

"Maybe the plates are clean," Tony Vetano whispered.

"Maybe he'll move on," Jesse said hopefully.

"Maybe there's a Santa Claus," Tony muttered back.

The radio burbled again as the dispatcher came back with a report on the GTO's tags. The young cop looked at the car again, then at the house. The front porch and windows were in darkness, with no lights showing. Then he hitched up his service belt and began striding toward the gate set in the low brick wall that fronted the property. He could have stepped over it with comparative ease, but he was a meticulous man. He leaned down, unlatched the gate and went into the front yard, then turned to fasten the gate behind him.

"I'm going to have to warn him off," Tony said. "One sight of him and they'll head for the hills."

Before Jesse could stop him, he had the door of the Chevy open and was crossing the street in long, hurried strides. They'd parked a few houses down from the target house and he had quite a bit of ground to cover. Tony called softly to the patrolman but the uniformed cop didn't hear him. Tony lengthened his stride. In the car Jesse moved uneasily. He didn't like the way this was panning out.

The patrolman was marching up the front steps of the porch now. He lit his flashlight, looking for a doorbell. There was a button on the left-hand side of the door. He pressed it. Nothing.

He rapped sharply on the wooden door with his nightstick. Still thirty yards away, Tony Vetano stopped. He looked back to where he knew Jesse was watching, made a small negative gesture, then kept going, moving toward the shelter of a large chestnut tree set in the verge of the road, just before the grassed sidewalk.

On the porch, the patrolman raised his nightstick for another assault on the door. Then he paused as a light went on in the front room. As it did, the young cop made his last mistake of the day—and his life. He began to slide the nightstick back into his belt again. It snagged on his uniform jacket and he looked down to free it and slip it into place. His eyes were down when the door opened, his attention elsewhere.

Consequently, he never saw the Ingram 9 mm—an ugly, boxy little submachine gun with a firing rate that sounded like ripping cloth. Three slugs from the eight-round burst stitched into him, in a diagonal line that took in hip, chest and shoulder, and bowled him backward down the porch steps.

Tony stepped out from behind the tree, his .38 in his hand.

"Police!" he yelled. "Throw down the gun, motherfucker!"

The flickering muzzle flash of the Ingram lit up the front of the house once more as the shooter fired. Chunks of bark flew from the tree beside Tony. He was caught by surprise, not expecting the gunman to react so quickly. He dived headlong away from the tree, sliding into the meager cover provided by the curb. He flattened himself there, trying to force himself lower to the ground as another burst ripped over his head, a few inches above him.

"Christ!" Jesse said to himself. He came out of the car, keeping it between him and the shooter. His .45 Colt 1911 model came up and he thumbed back the hammer. There was already one fat round in the chamber and a full load of seven in the magazine. It was a long shot from where he was, but he had to take the heat off Tony.

For a fraction of a second, he considered calling a warning. To hell with it, he thought, the guy had been warned.

He slammed out three rounds from the .45, knowing he was too far away to hit anything. All he'd hoped was that he'd catch the gunman's attention and he succeeded. The Ingram's muzzle flash lit up again and bullets clanged off the metalwork of the Chevy, ricocheting and whining around him. There was a dull report and the car subsided suddenly to the right as the front tire blew. Jesse ducked behind the hood. It was damned unhealthy out here, he thought.

He duckwalked to the front of the car, peering around the grill. He couldn't see Tony and the porch had gone dark again. There was no sign of the gunman but he let another two rounds go in the general direction of the porch for good luck.

"Tony?" he called. "You okay?"

Another burst from the Ingram erupted in return. The headlight a few inches away shattered, spraying broken glass onto the road. Hurriedly, he pulled back into cover.

"Jess? I'm in a bad situation here," Vetano called. His voice was pitched higher than normal. Jesse could read a trace of panic in it. Jesus. Who wouldn't be panicked, stuck in the open like that with a machine gun trying to chew you up? A short burst rattled out toward Tony's position in response to his voice.

"You hit?" Jesse called. He flinched, expecting the gunner to open up on him but no shots came.

"No. But I'm pinned down. Can't move."

Once again the gunner opened up at Tony's position. Jesse, peering cautiously over the top of the hood, saw strikes on the top of the house's front wall. He realized that the low structure was shielding Tony from the gunman's fire, providing a shallow wedge of dead ground. For the moment, his partner was safe—although safe was a relative term in this situation.

"Stay there!" he yelled. "Don't move!"

"Jess? Get me out of here, man!" Tony was definitely on the edge of panicking, Jesse realized.

"Hang in there, Tony! You're cool," he replied, as another burst tore chips off the brick wall. Tony, his nose pressed to the ground, trying to force himself lower and lower behind the shallow curb, couldn't see that he was sheltered. So far as he was concerned, the gunman was just a lousy shot to keep missing him.

Mind you, all that would change if the gunner decided to move closer and change the angle of his fire. Jesse had to stop that happening and he had to do it fast. He'd need to get closer himself. There was a Dodge cargo van next in line, then a Ford pickup. That was where he needed to be. He took a deep breath, gathered himself and launched out from behind the Chevy.

The gunman reacted a fraction too late. A burst of fire ripped the air behind Jesse, shattering another headlight and punching more holes in the Chevy's hood. He crouched behind the van, felt it rock as more rounds impacted the far side. Then he was running for the shelter of the Ford.

More bullets whined around him but the gunner was shooting too high. The Ingram pulled up when it fired and he wasn't allowing for the fact. If he didn't hit Jesse with the first two shots, the others sailed harmlessly overhead.

Bent-kneed and crouching, Jesse shuffled along the side of the truck till he reached the hood. It had gone quiet now that the Ingram wasn't shooting. The guy knew where he was. He'd be waiting this time. Jesse thumbed the magazine release, dropping the depleted magazine out of the Colt's butt. He jammed a fresh one in and worked the action, pumping a round into the chamber.

"Jesse? I'm getting out of here, man!"

"No, Tony! Stay put! Don't move!"

But a sudden burst from the Ingram, and a grunt of pain that accompanied it, told him that his warning had been too late. Tony had finally lost it. Jesse stood up behind the Ford's hood, pistol gripped in both hands, feet wide apart to steady himself. He saw Tony lurching and spinning as he fell to the ground in the middle of the street. He heard him crying out in pain and fear and knew he was still alive. For the moment. But now he was helpless and exposed.

The Ingram had fallen silent. Gunner must be changing mags too, Jesse thought, and knew he had to stop him before he could reload and zero in on Tony. He could see a dark shape moving in shadows on the porch.

Jesse fired—carefully and deliberately.

Once.

Twice.

Three times.

The gunman had seen him. Bullets from the Ingram slammed into the truck. The windshield shivered apart under a hail of slugs, showering him with pebbles of broken safety glass.

Four times.

Something was moving in his peripheral vision. Something between him and the porch. He ignored it, locked in a fatal duel with the machine-gunner, his upper body completely exposed. Totally outgunned.

Five times. A shape, moving, blurred, indistinct. Ignore it.

Six. A shrill scream.

Seven.

The Colt's action slammed back and locked open, the magazine empty. Jesse stood, pistol still leveled at the porch. Vaguely, he realized he should drop back into cover, rejected the idea.

He stood, waiting for the return fire but there was none. The drug dealer was dead. Three of the heavy caliber .45 slugs had hit him.

Only one had hit Tony.

But when Jesse reached him he was just as dead as the drug dealer.

ONE

Sheriff Lee Torrens shook her head as she gazed down at the dead body, surrounded by trash.

"How the hell did he get in there?"

It was a rhetorical question but Patrolman Paul Onorato, who'd been first on the scene with his partner, Dale Carruthers, wasn't the sharpest chisel in the town police toolkit.

"Guess the killer put him there, Sheriff," he said helpfully. Lee turned a baleful eye his way.

"Thank you for that," she said coldly.

Onorato shrugged, missing the sarcasm.

"There" was the big rectangular container that rode the cable car down to the bottom station at the Mount Werner ski fields. It carried the trash and detritus from the restaurants up on the mountain and when the on-mountain traffic wound down at the end of each day, the operators at the top station would stop the cable car for five minutes or so while they wheeled the big steel container into position. Then they'd clamp it onto the heavy cable and start up again, sending the trash container sailing off down the valley into the gathering darkness.

When the container swooped out of the darkness into the bottom station, slowing as it detached from the main cable to the unloading circle, the bottom station attendant had noticed something odd. About two-thirds of the way up the unloading hatch, a glove was jammed between the hatch and the frame. Leastways, he'd thought it was a glove.

Right up until he'd noticed the glove had fingernails.

The container was open-topped so that trash could be dumped in from above. To unload, one of the sides was hinged at the bottom and held in place by dog clamps. As the attendant looked more closely, he realized that the upper dog clamp on the hatch hadn't engaged properly at one end, leaving a narrow gap through which the hand was protruding.

That had been enough for the bottom station attendant, a kindly old man named John Hostetler. He'd taken one look and run for the phone, faster than he'd moved in maybe forty years. Onorato and his partner, Dale Carruthers, had been cruising in the area and they'd arrived within five minutes. It had been Onorato who had released the other clamps, despite Carruther's warning cry not to corrupt a crime scene. The hatch had fallen open and the body had rolled clear, along with a small avalanche of Dixie cups, soda cans, wine bottles and remnants of half-eaten fast food.

Round about that stage, Onorato realized he was in over his head. The town police attended to minor crime within town limits—disturbances in Steamboat's many bars and restaurants, arguments in the lift lines, drunks, lost children, traffic offenses, crowd control and the like. They were the equivalent of the uniformed branch in a big city police force. They weren't expected or equipped to conduct investigations into serious matters. That was left to the sheriff's office, which had jurisdiction over the entire county.

A dead body in the trash container was definitely a serious matter, so the two patrolmen had put in a call to Lee.

She hunkered down beside the dead body. The corpse stared up at her with sightless eyes. He was male, aged in his early thirties.

"Guess you'll never make it to your late thirties now," she muttered to herself.

"Say what, Sheriff?" Her deputy, Tom Legros, had stepped into the control room out of the wind to make a call and she hadn't heard him returning. She shook her head.

"Nothing, Tom. Just talking to myself is all."

There was a small, circular incision under the chin, and a considerable amount of blood had soaked down into the collar of his parka. A considerably greater amount had collected underneath the skin around the chin and lower part of the face, creating a huge, blue-black edema that looked incongruously like a five o'clock shadow in Lee's flashlight beam. The eyes were wide open. They looked surprised. She guessed they had every right to be.

"Is Denny Walters on his way?" she called back over her shoulder to Tom.

He nodded. "Should be here in five, ten minutes, Lee," he told her. "Doc Jorgensen too."

Lee grunted. Jorgensen was the county medical examiner. Denny Walters ran a ski-photo business and doubled as a crime-scene photographer when they needed one.

Lee snapped on a pair of surgical rubber gloves and gently patted the body down. Under the parka, in the breast pocket, she could feel the bulge of what might be a wallet. Carefully, so as not to disturb the position of the body, she eased the parka's zipper down a few inches and reached inside to claim it. Not that any disturbance would matter too much now, she thought wryly. The body's position had been disturbed plenty when it had come rolling out of the container.

"Uh . . . Lee, maybe you shouldn't do that?" Tom suggested, uncomfortable at the thought that he was criticizing his boss.

"Probably not, Tom," Lee replied. "But it's gone and done now."

She flipped through the billfold.

"Well, whatever the motive was, it wasn't robbery," she said. "There's more than two hundred bucks in here."

Behind her, Patrolman Onorato was admiring the sight of Lee's jeans stretched across her buttocks as she crouched beside the victim. It occurred to him that for a sheriff, Lee Torrens cut a fine figure. And he wasn't the first man in Routt County to think it.

Born and raised on a ranch out beyond Hayden, Lee had grown up ranching and punching cattle from the time she was eleven. By seventeen, she could ride, rope and shoot as well as any man.

She stood five feet, nine inches in her socks. Her hand-tooled leather boots added another inch and a half. She was long legged, with the muscles smooth and sculpted from a lifetime of riding, hiking and skiing, slim-waisted and with breasts that were shapely and large enough to put a just noticeable strain on the buttons of her green uniform shirt.

No one would ever call Lee Torrens pretty. Her features were too strong for that. But she was a decidedly handsome woman, with high cheekbones, a firm jaw and deep-set gray eyes that had a slight tilt to them—maybe the result of an Arapaho ancestor sometime in the past. Her hair was sandy blond and now, in her thirty-ninth year, it had a few streaks of gray in it. Not that Lee was the sort of woman to give much of a damn about that.

She was the sort of woman you could describe as statuesque. The people of Routt County would describe her, and they often did, as a fine type of woman. And a damn good sheriff into the bargain.

She picked carefully through the billfold now, easing a Minnesota driver's license out of one of the card slots.

"Name's Howell. Alexander Howell," she said. She peered into the section where notes were kept, pushing the mixed twenties, ones and fives to one side to reveal a credit card receipt. "And there's a receipt here from the Overlook Lodge. Better get on to them and see if he has anyone down there looking for him."

Tom turned away, heading for the phone in the gondola office. Carruthers caught Lee's eye and tilted his head in a question.

"Need us any further, Sheriff?" he asked, adding a little apologetically, "We're a little shorthanded this weekend."

Lee shook her head, smiled wearily.

"Aren't we all?" she said, rising from her position beside Alexander Howell's body. "No. You can leave it to us, boys. Just drop in your write-up in the morning if you will."

"Can do," said Carruthers.

Lee turned to the small group of lift attendants staring at the dead body.

"Nobody here seen this guy before?" she asked. They all shook their heads, looking at the chalk-white face on the floor as if, by looking again, they might suddenly remember that he was known to them.

"Hundreds of people through here in a day," said Hostetler, unnecessarily. Lee nodded agreement.

"Yeah, I know, John. It was just a long shot that someone might have noticed him earlier." She looked at the body critically. "Not that there's anything about him you might remember," she added.

Nor was there. Alexander Howell, in life, looked to have been a most unremarkable person. Average height. Thinning brown hair. Average clothing—Levis, a plaid shirt and a now blood-soaked parka. He wore steel-rimmed glasses and Nike sneakers. You could see thousands of Alexander Howells in a day and not remember one of them.

Not until he turned up dead, of course. That gave him a certain individuality. A celebrity that he'd never known in life.

She crouched once more and resumed her study of Alexander Howell. The sightless, surprised eyes still told her nothing.

She'd heard once that if you looked hard enough into the eyes of a murdered man, you'd see the image of the murderer reflected there forever. Not once in the four times she'd inspected a body had she found it to be true.

Gently she turned the head to one side, allowing the light to fall on the wound under the chin. Hostetler stooped beside her.

"Knife maybe, Sheriff?" he ventured. Lee shook her head uncertainly.

"Mighty narrow blade if it was. More like an ice pick. Something like that," she replied. Hostetler frowned as if, somehow, the idea of being killed by an ice pick was more unsavory than if the deed were done with a knife.

"Ice pick, you say?" he said, shaking his head.

Her deputy, Tom Legros, sauntered back from the phone in the office. "They've got him booked in there at the Overlook sure enough, Sheriff," he reported.

Lee turned the face again, looking for signs of any other injuries. There were none that she could see.

"Anyone with him?" she asked, without looking up.

Tom shook his head, then realized she hadn't seen the negative answer and said, "Nope. He's on his own. Booked in for the next four days, they said. They're booked out down there," he added irrelevantly.

"Well, they've got themselves a vacancy now," said Sheriff Torrens, and the three men all nodded. Alexander Howell, naturally enough, didn't respond.

TWO

Jesse Parker hunched on his stool in the Tugboat Saloon and shoveled another handful of cheese and nachos into his mouth.

"Hear about the ruckus last night up on the Silver Bullet?" Todd said to him as he passed two margaritas to a pair of bottle blondes farther down the bar.

Jesse never failed to be fascinated how the barman could keep up a conversation while he served three other people. Never missed a beat either. He nodded. "Guy found dead, as I understand."

"Stabbed," Todd amended. "Knifed once and that was it."

"They know why he was killed?" Jesse asked.

Todd shrugged, moving down the bar to pull two draught Buds in response to a call from a couple of Australian tourists.

"Those guys sure like their beer," he commented as he returned, then, in answer to Jesse's earlier question, "Why not ask the sheriff? There she is now."

He nodded his head toward the door. Jesse turned in his seat and saw Lee Torrens entering from the cold night outside. The tall sheriff swiped a few errant snowflakes away from her jacket, then took it off and hung it over the back of a chair as she sat at a table. A few people around greeted her. She nodded in response. Then, looking around the smoky room, she caught sight of Jesse watching her. She raised her eyebrows in greeting and nodded at the empty chair beside her. The meaning was clear.

Jesse picked up his half-empty Moosehead and slid down from the tall barstool.

"Catch up with you later, Todd," he said. The barman nodded and grunted. Carrying his beer, Jesse picked his way through the crowded room to Lee's table. She was studying the menu and didn't look up when he dropped into the chair she'd indicated.

"You should know that by heart," he ventured. She grinned crookedly, admitting he was right.

"Guess I keep hoping they'll surprise me one day," she said. Without even looking, she handed the menu back over her shoulder to a waitress. One thing you could always depend on in the Tugboat, there was always a waitress standing behind you to take the menu, take your order or take your money. They liked to move you in, get you fed and move you out fast.

"Give me a half-dozen wings," she said. "And a Coors Light."

The waitress slid the menu under her arm and wrote rapidly on her order pad.

"Got it," she said.

"And bring me a bunch of paper towels," she added. She smiled up at the girl.

"Got it," the waitress replied again. There was no answering smile. There was no time for that in the Tugboat. You wanted smiles, go someplace else. She hurried away.

"So how's the case going?"

He didn't need to say what case he was talking about. With a dead body found in the trash container on the gondola, it was unlikely that he'd be talking about any other case. Lee shook her head doubtfully.

"Damned if I know, Jess. All we got is a body and a name. No reason. No motive. No suspects. No murder weapon." She slumped back in the wooden chair, stretching her long legs out under the table.

"Don't even know for sure what the murder weapon was," she concluded. Jesse frowned.

"Way I heard, it's a stabbing. You're looking for a knife, aren't you?"

Lee shrugged. "Strange kind of knife. Long, long blade. Very narrow. Went in up under the chin, through the tongue and the roof of the mouth, then into the brain. Could be an ice pick, although I've never seen one quite long enough to do the job this one did. Some kind of sharp, heavy duty spike, maybe."

Jesse looked at her curiously. "Up under the chin, you say?"

She nodded, demonstrating with the forefinger of her right hand, pressing it into the soft flesh on the underside of her chin.

"Right about here," she said. "Went straight in here and continued right up into the brain. Doc says death would have been almost instantaneous." Jesse was nodding to himself, looking thoughtful. She continued. "Painful as all hell, but just about instantaneous." She shook her head, baffled. "That's another thing, Jess. Would have taken some considerable force to get that spike up through all that tissue and into the brain."

"That's true enough," Jesse agreed.

"So how does someone make sure they can swing up under the chin hard enough and fast enough and be that accurate? Tell me that."

"I don't follow you," Jesse replied. Lee made a small gesture with her hands palm up.

"Well, think about it: you want to ram a spike up under someone's chin, right through their mouth and into their brain, you've got to take quite a swing to do it, haven't you?"

She was interrupted as the waitress leaned between them to set down the plate of wings and Lee's beer. Absently, Jesse took one of the wings and began gnawing on it. The subject matter of the discussion didn't seem to affect his appetite. But he'd spent eight years as a homicide detective in Denver and he'd heard and seen plenty worse things in his life. Lee turned to the waitress before she could make her high speed escape.

"Paper towels?" she asked. The waitress slapped her thigh in annoyance.

"Forgot 'em. Be right back, Sheriff." She darted away into the crowd and the smoke haze that filled the Tugboat. Jesse finished his wing, reached for the single paper napkin that had come with Lee's cutlery. Her look forestalled him.

"That one's mine," she said. He shrugged and licked the extra sauce and juice from the ends of his fingers. Lee picked up a wing and went to work on it herself.

"You were saying?" Jesse prompted her.

"Oh, yeah. Well, as I say, it'd take some force to do that, but the killer got it right first time. There was just one wound. One puncture. That's it. Now you'd expect, with a violent movement like that, it could take two or maybe three attempts to get it right on the spot, and on line. I mean, this guy must have been really swinging that spike, you know?"

Jesse nodded again. "Could be first time lucky?" he suggested. Lee gave him a pained look and he continued, "Or it could be something else entirely."

Her expression changed quickly to one of interest. "You got an idea on this at all?" she asked.

Jesse nodded. "Could be. Any chance I can get a look at the body?"

"Got it down at the Public Safety Building," she said. "In the morgue there." She started to push her seat back but Jesse laid a restraining hand on her arm.

"Finish your wings first," he said. "He isn't going anywhere."

THREE

The Public Safety Building was on the corner of Eighth and Yampa, almost opposite the Steamboat Yacht Club. On the drive in, in Lee's Renegade, Jesse remained silent. She glanced across at him once or twice, seeing the line of his jaw highlighted in the passing lights of other cars. She still wondered about Jesse. He hadn't been the same since he'd come back from Denver two years ago. When you caught him in an unguarded moment, like now, there was still a residue of pain in his eyes, like you'd find in the eyes of an animal caught in a trap.

There was some considerable history between Jesse and Lee. They'd grown up together, mostly on her father's spread west of Hayden. It had been in the Torrens family for four generations and it was one of the best ranches in the county.

By contrast, Jesse's pa had a small spread on poor hardscrabble land twenty miles away. He ran a few head of cattle and his wife tried to grow crops for sale. But the land could barely support George Parker and his wife, let alone their three boys. As a result, Jesse had taken a job on the Torrens spread when he was twelve, spending his time before and after school riding, herding, cleaning out barns, mending tack, fencing and branding. He and Lee, an only child, became inseparable.

Inevitably, as they grew older, their relationship turned into something more than friendship. They were both attractive, healthy young people, constantly in each other's company, and it happened without either of them even realizing that it had.

When he was eighteen and she was seventeen, there had been a brief and intense physical relationship between them, clandestine and highly satisfying to both parties. Then Jesse, appalled that he had, in his own eyes, betrayed Martin Torrens's trust, ended it. He mumbled apologies to Lee and resigned, unable to meet her father's gaze. Martin, of course, was no fool and had a pretty shrewd idea what was going on. In fact, he would have been delighted to welcome Jesse into his family. But the boy was young and Torrens felt he should see something of the world before he settled down. Above all, he didn't want Jesse to feel he was trapped into a permanent relationship with Lee. Gravely, he wished him well and let him leave and Jesse headed for Denver, where he joined the Denver PD.

Lee was devastated. The following year, in an unthinking counterpoint to Jesse's move, she became a deputy with the Routt County Sheriff's Department. Reece Colson, the county's long serving sheriff, soon began referring to her as "the best man I've got." Lee could ride, ski, shoot and track better than any of the men on the force. She was an ideal choice as a law enforcement officer in the vast open spaces and wild mountains of Routt County.

When Reece hung up his star and gunbelt in 1991, Lee was long established as his principal deputy, with an impressive record of arrests. She was a natural successor to the slow talking, heavily built sheriff. She won the election without any competition, and had continued to do so ever since.

As sheriff, she had learned the details of the tragic shooting in Wheat Ridge. She'd watched unhappily as Jesse returned to Steamboat Springs and settled into his current, directionless life. By winter he worked on the local ski patrol, refusing to take any position of responsibility or any organizational role. In the summers, he worked on construction projects or as a casual ranch hand around Yampa Valley. She and Jesse were still friends, of course. But there was a guarded reserve about him now in all his relationships. Nobody was allowed to get too close. Time after time, Lee yearned to take him in her arms and tell him everything was all right and help him get back on track. She could see a fine man drifting aimlessly through his life. She knew he'd been one of Denver PD's brightest homicide detectives. Now he was barely one rung up from a ski bum, hiding from the world. Worse, she thought, he was hiding from himself.

Jesse sat silently. But his brain was racing. The wound that Lee had described had rung a bell with him. He'd seen wounds like that before. Still, he'd wait till he'd had a good sight of the corpse before he committed himself. Maybe he was wrong.

He sensed the occasional glances Lee shot his way as they drove. He smiled ruefully to himself.

They'd stayed in touch in the years he'd spent in Denver. She went down for his wedding to Abby, then, later, spent hours on the phone letting him talk out the details of the divorce. They'd see each other on weekends when he drove up to Steamboat to ski. They'd swap stories of cases and investigations the way cops do everywhere.

And never, not once, in all those years, did either of them mention the time when they had been lovers.

So in light of that, it bothered Jesse somewhat these days that the images of that time kept recurring to him at the most unlikely and inconvenient times.

And it was happening more and more frequently.

FOUR

Alexander Howell's body was covered by a sheet. Jesse reached up and lifted the covering away from the dead man's face.

The skin was a light shade of blue by now and the body was already stiff. He looked critically at the evidence of internal bleeding around the chin and neck, then, with thumb and forefinger, tilted the dead man's chin up so he could see the entry wound. He nodded once when he saw it. It was as he had suspected when Lee had first described the injury. He flipped the sheet back over the victim's face and rolled the drawer back in again. He stripped off the surgical gloves and dropped them in a bin.

"Seen enough?" Lee was watching him expectantly.

"It looks like what I thought it might be," he replied and she cocked her head interrogatively, motioning for him to continue.

"Looks like a jigger," he explained.

Lee frowned. "A jigger? What in all hell is a jigger?" she asked. He wiped his hands absentmindedly on his jeans. In spite of the gloves, his fingers still felt slightly clammy and cold from their contact with the corpse. They always did. He knew it was his imagination, but he kept on wiping them anyway.

"Very popular with the white street gangs down in Aurora a few years back," he explained. "Full name was a 'Nigger Jigger.'"

He saw the instant look of distaste cross Lee's face and hurriedly disclaimed, "I didn't make the name up, Lee. Just telling you what they called it."

She leaned her rump on the edge of the autopsy table behind her.

"Okay, so what exactly is a jigger?" she asked.

"Basically, it's a spring-loaded spike concealed in a handle—usually about ten inches long. You cock the spike down into the handle, place it under the chin of your victim and release the trigger."

Lee was nodding her understanding. "And the spring does the rest." she said. "That explains how such a powerful blow can be delivered with such accuracy."

He nodded. "Exactly. And, the handle itself can be disguised as something totally innocuous. Then you just have to poke it at your victim, hit the trigger and—bing!" He gestured to show how easy it could be.

Lee began to pace around the room, talking as she went, more to herself than him.

"So . . . we're looking for someone who used to be in one of those white street gangs down in Aurora . . ." she said.

Jesse shrugged. "Maybe. Or maybe someone who just knows how to make himself a jigger."

She stopped and looked at him. "Do you enjoy making things hard for an honest cop?" she asked, with a slight smile.

He spread his hands in a helpless gesture. "It's the only way honest cops like it," he said.

She gave him that same exasperated look. "You want a coffee?" she asked and he nodded his acceptance. She led the way out of the cold room, switching off the light behind them and continued up to her office on the next floor. Tom Legros was on duty and she sent him to get them both a cup of coffee from the kitchen they shared with the fire brigade. She unbuckled her gunbelt and dropped it, clattering, on the desktop. Then she dropped into her seat and swung her boots up onto the scarred wood beside the gun.

Jesse eyed the single action .44 Magnum in the holster with amused tolerance.

"Still using that old Ruger, I see?" he asked her.

"Never saw a reason to change," she replied.

Jesse pursed his lips slightly as he considered her answer. "You should try one of those new Berettas they're issuing these days," he suggested.

Lee shook her head slowly. "Not fond of autos," she replied. "One round jams and that's all she wrote. At least with a revolver, you can just roll right on to the next chamber."

"So . . . look after your ammunition and make sure you don't have a round jamming. With one of those Berettas, you can crank off thirteen nine-millimeter rounds before the bad guy has a chance to move."

Lee nodded, allowing the point. Then added, with devastating logic, "Never usually need more than one round myself."

Jesse grinned at her. "I'll bet you don't at that," he admitted. "You must be the world's most parsimonious woman with your ammunition. Anyone'd think the county made you buy your own."

"They do," she replied morosely, leaning forward to slide open the top left-hand drawer on her desk. She took out a heavy pistol in a regulation belt holster and tossed it across the desk to him. "They only supply me with rounds for this useless damn Beretta."

Jesse shook his head slowly, examining the big, blue-black automatic that she'd passed him. "You're still stubborn as ever then," he said. It was a statement, not a question.

Lee shrugged. "I get used to a gun, I like to keep it," she said simply. "What about you? You telling me you used one of those teeny short barrel .38s they issue to detectives when you were down in Denver?"

"Not exactly," Jesse grinned, conceding the point.

"I thought not," said Lee. "My guess is you hung on to that old 1911 Colt auto of yours. Right?"

"That's right enough. As you say, you get used to a gun, you want to keep it."

"And those old Colts, they certainly had some stopping power," Lee mused, and instantly regretted it. She saw the quick flash of pain that crossed Jesse's face. Then it was buried under his usual inscrutable mask.

"They certainly did," he said. There was an awkward silence for a few seconds. Lee knew she'd put her high-heeled foot right in it there, but couldn't find a way to get out of the predicament. Fortunately, the silence was broken as Tom Legros pushed open the unlatched door with his hip, and entered with two mugs of coffee.

"Here you go, Sheriff, Jesse," he said cheerfully, setting the mugs down. He glanced curiously at the Beretta on the desk between them. Reminded of its presence, Lee leaned forward and scooped it into the drawer again.

Tom leaned against the nearest of the two filing cabinets that graced Lee's office, arms folded.

"So, Jess, any ideas on our victim in there?" he asked. Jesse shrugged noncommittally. Lee answered her deputy.

"Jess thinks the murder weapon was a gizmo called a 'jigger,'" she said. "A spring-loaded spike that you push up against the victim, then trigger off."

Tom shook his head, wondering. "Never did hear of anything like that," he said.

He thought about it for a second or two, then pushed himself away from the filing cabinet and headed for the door.

"Meant to tell you, Sheriff, some of the local kids have been causing a ruckus out at Payne's Crossing on their snowmobiles. Thought I'd better get down there and take a look around."

"Couldn't the town police look after that, Tom?" Lee asked him. "We're going to have our hands full around here."

Tom Legros rubbed his jaw. "They're saying it's not their jurisdiction. Payne's Crossing is way past the town limits."

Lee sighed. Everyone had manpower problems. "Take care of it then, Tom," she said. After a pause, she added, "Don't be too hard on them. They're just kids, after all."

Tom touched a finger to the brim of his Stetson. "I'll attend to it," he said, and went out, hitching up his gunbelt as he went. Jesse was interested to see that he also wore a non-regulation, single action peacemaker. He wondered if it was Lee's influence, decided it probably was.

"He's a good man," he said. Lee nodded her agreement.

"Not the most imaginative person I've ever met," she said. "But he's painstaking and he's stubborn. He doesn't give up once he's started on something."

"Good qualities to have in a cop," Jesse replied, and yawned. "Guess I'd better be getting home."

Lee started to rise from behind her desk.

"I'll drive you back to the Tugboat," she said, but he waved her back down again, checking his watch.

"Shuttle bus'll be picking up outside the Harbor in a few minutes," he said. "You've got work to do."

She sighed and sank back. "That's true." Adding, a moment later, "I hate this kind of case, Jess. Don't know how you stood it down in Denver."

He looked at her, a little puzzled. "This kind of case, Lee? What other kind is there?"

"Oh . . . you know," she gestured vaguely. "A guy holds up a convenience store and takes off for the high country. That sort of case. I know what I'm doing, where I'm going, who I'm after. I just head out after whoever it is, catch him and bring him back."

"Just like that," Jesse interrupted, smiling slightly.

But Lee didn't pick up on the irony. "That's right. It's black and white. You've got a reason, a crime and a motive. It's straightforward. Not like this." She gestured with her thumb in the vague direction of the morgue and Alexander Howell's body.

"There's always a reason, Lee," Jesse said gently. "You've just got to find it, that's all."

FIVE

The first killing had been almost too easy.

He wondered how long it would take the local cops to catch on to the hint he'd left. Wondered if they would be bright enough to realize that the body's hand simply couldn't have jammed in the hatch accidentally. It was all part of the game he'd begun to play with them. All part of focusing their attention. Well, the next one should do just that, he thought. Because the next one would be different. The next one would be a total puzzle.

That is, if tonight's experiment proved successful.

He'd had to wait ten minutes for an opportunity to board the gondola without anyone else being around. But he was prepared to be patient. Patience, in fact, was going to be essential to his task as the next few weeks unfolded. He was going to have to wait for the right conditions every time. And he was prepared to do so.

As the cabin slid quickly down the mountain from Thunderhead, he noticed with some satisfaction that the inside light, combined with the misting of the windows and the darkness outside, made the other cabins nothing but vague blurs. So far so good. Working quickly but with no undue haste, he slipped off the rucksack and began to unpack his equipment. The seventy-foot coil of rope came first. He knotted it securely to the chest harness that he was already wearing under the long-line parka.

Next, he took the lever jack that he'd built himself in his workshop back home. He fitted the two ends into the rubber seal of the gondola doors and wrenched the lever suddenly. With the mechanical advantage of the lever system, the doors were thrust open about two feet—sufficient to give him egress.

There was a length of two-by-two pine in the rucksack. He found it and jammed it between the doors to keep them open. The lever jack, released, went back in his rucksack. Then, standing in the open doorway, he reached up to the roof of the car, passing the free end of the rope through the rail that ran around the top edge. He formed the rope into a loop over itself, inserted it into the abseiling loop on his harness and dropped it clear into the night below. He glanced at his watch. Just under two minutes. Plenty of time. He shouldered the rucksack again, then retrieved his skis from the racks on the outside of the door. They were fastened together and a looped strap went quickly over his shoulder, where he could discard it in a matter of seconds. He slipped an abseiling glove onto his right hand and, holding the rail above the doorway, stepped out to hang outside the cabin, his feet resting on a small ledge at the base of the gondola. He took up the tension on the rope, jamming his right hand into his side to lock it for a few seconds, then released his left-handed grip on the railing. He balanced there, supported by the rope, his feet braced against the cabin. He raised his right foot and kicked one end of the pine-door holder. The piece of timber spun clear, dropping away into the night, and the doors sighed shut in front of him.

He checked his watch again. Three minutes. Just about perfect, he thought. Then, unjamming his right hand from his side, he allowed the abseil rope to run smoothly through the ring and drop away into the darkness beneath the gondola.

He began spinning slowly as he descended, and he was annoyed that he hadn't thought of that possibility. Still, he reasoned, it was no big deal. He'd simply have to time his release over the last few feet to a moment when he was facing downhill. He flicked on the flashlight attached to the side of his rucksack. Pointing vertically down, it had a red lens designed to throw a visible light on the snow below him, to give him a reference point and help him judge height. He looked down between his legs now and saw it—a small red dot sliding over the snow, a little faster than a man could run.

He slid farther down the rope until he judged that the red dot of light was no more than twelve feet below him. Then he shrugged off the strap retaining the skis and let them drop to the snow.

As they hit, he released another eight feet of rope in a rush and slid down to where he was skimming just above the surface of the Heavenly Daze run. He'd timed the release of the skis perfectly. As he hit his final point and checked for a moment, he was facing almost directly downhill. He let the last four feet of rope slide through his hands, felt his feet brushing the surface of the snow, bent his knees and let the rope go entirely.

He hit, absorbing the shock with his flexed knees, and rolled.

There was little impact from the height he'd dropped. The main effect was from the speed he was traveling. But he'd landed on almost friction-free snow and he simply allowed himself to roll.

It was easier than a parachute landing, he thought.

Above him, the gondola cable creaked and hummed as it carried the cabin away down the hill. The released end of the rope snaked up farther and farther until it eventually passed over the rail again and fell in an almost straight line down the hill below him. He began pulling it in, coiling it between his elbow and his wrist as he retrieved it, then finally stowed it back in his rucksack.

He took a moment to dust the snow off his clothing, then looked up again at the dim shapes of the gondola cars passing overhead. He allowed himself a small grin of satisfaction.

"This is going to work just fine," he said.

And turning, he began to trudge up the hill to find his skis.

Jesse Parker awoke in an instant and sat up straight in bed.

"Damn!" he said. "He wanted us to find it!"

It was chilly in the large room that served as both sitting room and bedroom in his small cabin. The wood-burning stove in the corner was damped right down. There was only a faint glow from the thick, heatproof window in the door. He shivered and reached for a sweater tossed on the chair beside the bed.

It was after three o'clock in the morning. A half moon had risen over Rabbit Ear Pass and its pale light, amplified by the snow all around, was pouring through the uncurtained windows of the cabin. Jesse made a mental note that the lack of curtains also contributed to the lack of heat in the room. Reluctantly, he peeled back the warm blankets and swung his bare legs out of the bed.

The boards of the floor were cold underfoot as he hurried to the stove and opened the bottom vent. There was a slight hesitation, then the dull red glow inside turned to a brighter orange flame. Quickly, he flicked open the door of the stove and tossed a couple of short pine logs in, then slammed it shut again. The flames picked up even more and he began to notice an increase in the heat radiating from the old potbelly.

He struggled into a pair of worn sweatpants and shoved his cold feet into some moccasins. Finally, he felt a little better.

He paced around the room, thinking through the idea. The more he thought about it, the more he knew he was right. He flicked on the lights and reached for the old black phone on the deal table that was the centerpiece of the room. He began dialing the sheriff's office, then stopped, realizing that it was quarter after three. Lee would have gone home hours ago to her small cottage on Fish Creek Falls Road. He set the phone down again, picked up a battered, leather bound notebook that lay beside it and leafed through it for Lee's home number. Finding it, he began to dial. He'd dialed three numbers when he paused again. After all, it was a hell of a time to be calling someone. Then he shrugged and continued. Lee was a cop. If you wore the badge, you had to put up with phone calls at inconvenient times. Besides, Jesse wanted to discuss his theory. Wanted to see if she could shoot holes in it. He finished dialing the number.

He listened to the low, insistent burr that told him the phone was ringing at the other end. It rang eight times, then Lee's foggy, muffled voice came through the earpiece.

"She'ff Torrens," she slurred. "And this had better, by God, be very important."

"Lee," he said impatiently. "It's me. Wake up."

" 'Me'?" came the sleepy voice, but now with the faintest thread of venom in it. " 'Me'? Who exactly is 'me'?"

"C'mon Lee, it's Jess. Now wake up and get your brain in gear. I've had an idea."

There was a long pause. An ominous pause, while Lee considered and discarded various unpleasant and painful things she might like to do to Jesse next time she saw him. Finally, she croaked at him, "Christ, Jess! It's three fifteen!"

"Three seventeen," he said, unmoved. "Now wake up."

"I'll kill you for this," she threatened, but he heard a rustling of movement at the other end of the line that told him she was sitting up in bed. Then she said, "Hang on a minute. It's freezing here. Let me get a sweater or something."

More movement. More rustling of cloth. Then Lee, sounding more awake but no less displeased, was back on the line.

"All right, what is it?"

"Tell me, Lee, why do you think our killer dumped the dentist in the trash container?"

Lee's temper finally took over. "Jesus suffering Christ on a bicycle, Jesse! Because he didn't have a coffin handy, I suppose!"

Jesse refused to rise to her anger. "Come on. Think now."

Her voice was heavy with sarcasm when she replied, "Well, let's see: those trash containers are picked up and taken out to the county dump beyond Hayden, then the contents are dumped and bulldozed over. I guess that he was trying to hide the body, don't you?"

"That's certainly what it looks like," Jesse agreed. Another flood of sarcasm rushed down the line.

"Well, I'm glad we agree on that! Now could I please go back—"

He interrupted her. "I said that's what it looks like. And, of course, all the pickups and the dumping are done automatically, aren't they? Chances are, no one would spot the body during that process, right?"

She breathed heavily, then said with great control, "Right."

"So . . ." he said, continuing very deliberately. "That's why the killer left our dentist's hand hanging out through the hatch. He did it on purpose. He wanted you to find the body!"

"What? Are you crazy? Why would anyone want the body found if they'd just pulled off a murder?" The anger and the sarcasm were gone now. She was wide awake and listening, although she couldn't see how he'd reached his theory.

"Think about it, Lee," he said eagerly. "You kill a man and dump his body in a trash container, right?" He paused for an answer.

"Right," she said. "Go on."

"Now, that body was pretty much on the floor of the container, correct? The trash was on top of him."

"Pretty much," she agreed. "There was some trash already in it when he was put in there, but not a lot."

"Right. So, except for maybe a few inches of trash under him, he's on the floor of the container? So how does his arm manage to stand up at a forty-five degree angle so that his hand can be caught halfway up the hatch?"

There was a pause. It hung there on the line between them. Finally, Lee began to answer, slowly, "Well . . . he maybe got it caught on something when he . . ." She stopped.

"On what, Lee? Remember, he would have put him in through the hatch. The hatch was open. So there was nothing there to stop the arm just flopping down beside the body. Now maybe if that hand had been caught down near floor level, that might have been accidental. But think on it! Where did those cops say the hand was?"

"It was halfway up the hatch. You're right, Jess. I can't see any way that it would have stuck up there waiting for the killer to close the hatch on it."

"Unless he held it there and jammed it in the gap when he closed the hatch."

Again, another silence that stretched on and on. Finally, Lee had to ask the question. The obvious question.

"But . . . why?"

And Jesse had the obvious answer. "Because he wanted the body found."

It was obvious. It just didn't make any sort of sense at all.

"Damn," said Lee, with considerable feeling. "I think you might be right."

"That's sure as hell what it looks like, isn't it?" said Jesse, with a strange sense of relief that Lee hadn't found some obvious, unnoticed flaw in his line of reasoning. Jesse hated being wrong when it came to an investigation. Hated it with a passion. That was one of the qualities about him that had made him such a good cop. On those few occasions when he had been proven wrong, he went out of his way to find the correct answer next time around.

He picked up the base of the old phone now and carried it back to the bed. He sank down on the lumpy old mattress and pulled the covers over his legs again.

Finally, Lee replied, "I'm damned if I can see any other way his hand could have been caught way up there. The sonofabitch wanted us to find that body."

"He wanted us to know someone had been killed," Jesse amended slightly. Lee took that on board, then nodded. He couldn't see her but somehow, he knew at the other end of the line, she was nodding slowly to herself.

And she was. "Okay, Jess," she said. "So where do we take it from here?"

Jesse thought for a moment, then shrugged. "Nothing much we can do about it at the moment," he admitted. "You've put a request in to the Minnesota State Police and the FBI to see if Howell had any sort of record, or if they had any sort of idea why someone might want to kill him, haven't you?"

"Yes," Lee replied. "Did that first thing this morning. Expect them to get back to me sometime tomorrow. Forensic boys from Denver are flying up to take a look at the crime scene too."

"Maybe they'll turn something up," said Jesse without a great deal of conviction. "Anyways, not much you can do now until the morning."

He yawned and stretched. He was feeling tired now. The sudden surge of energy and adrenaline had gone. The blankets felt very welcoming.

Lee said, in a measured, ominous tone, "Nothing more I can do until morning, you say?"

"That's right," Jesse yawned again. This time, Lee heard him. "Might as well go on back to sleep, Lee," he said.

"Well that might be a little hard right now, Jess. Tell me. The forensic boys aren't coming till tomorrow. The FBI and the Minnesota Police won't be getting back to me till tomorrow. Is there any goddamn reason why you couldn't have waited till then?"

Jesse heard the venom in her voice now. He held the phone away from his ear, looking at it curiously.

Finally, he put it back again and said in an injured tone. "Well hell, Lee, I thought you'd want to know about it right away."

The only answer he received was the sound of Lee's phone as it was slammed back into its cradle. That simple message spoke volumes to him. He thought it might be a good idea to avoid the sheriff the following day—at least until the afternoon.

SIX

The Minnesota Police had no idea why anyone might have wanted to murder Alexander Howell. Lee spoke to the police chief from the small town where Howell had lived for the past seventeen years. Chief Morrison was almost apologetic that he couldn't offer some skeleton from the past for Lee to hang the case on.

"Just a very ordinary man, Sheriff," he said after they'd exchanged greetings and Lee could finally ask if he had any information at all on Alexander Howell.

"Aged forty-four. Had a small dental practice here in town. From all I hear, he made a reasonably good go of it. Nothing special. Nothing outstanding, mind you."

"Were you one of his patients?" Lee asked, hoping that maybe she'd get a personal angle on Howell. The answer dashed those slim hopes.

"Not me. There're three other dentists in town and Howell's surgery was way the other side from me."

"Any professional jealousy? Maybe he'd argued with one of the others over patients? Anything like that?"

"Can't help you there either. They all seemed to get on just fine. Seems like there was plenty of work for all of them. They even used to get together for a night out once every couple of months."

Lee frowned. She was grasping at straws but that was all that was being presented.

"Is that usual?" she asked. There was a slight hesitation from the other end and she knew that Chief Morrison felt she was grasping at straws too.

"Well, I don't know how it's usual or not," he said, "but it's pretty understandable, I would have thought. Dentists are a little like cops, aren't they?"

"How's that?" she asked, not following his line of reasoning.

"We-ell, they know their patients dislike 'em, stands to reason they'd get together socially once in a while to tell each other their troubles."

He paused, then added in explanation, "Same way we cops do, without civilians around."

"I guess so." Lee sighed. "Anything else? He married? Got a girlfriend? Anything like that?"

"Divorced," said Chief Morrison. "Six years ago come February." He added quickly, before Lee could ask, "But there's nothing there either. All the neighbors have said he and the ex-wife were good friends. They agreed on a settlement and he never welshed on paying. Not in six years."

"Maybe he'd started to," Lee essayed but Chief Morrison contradicted her firmly.

"Already checked that. Thought you'd ask. As of the first of this month, he hadn't missed one support payment."

Lee thought for a long moment, then sighed heavily. "Well, thanks for your cooperation, Chief Morrison. I really appreciate it."

"Sorry I can't give you any help with it," he replied, "but my boys haven't turned up any reason why anyone would have wanted to kill him." He paused. "You got forensics on the case?"

"They're coming in from Denver today. I don't hold out too much hope that they'll come up with anything."

"They rarely do," Chief Morrison agreed comfortably. After all, it wasn't his problem. "Well, Sheriff, let me know if there's anything further my boys can do."

"Thanks, Chief," said Lee, and broke the connection.

She swung her boots up onto the desktop and fiddled for a few moments with a pencil, tapping it idly on her teeth, thinking through the conversation she'd just had. She was beginning to harbor the fear that she would never get to the bottom of this crime. Whoever it was who had murdered Howell, and why ever he'd done it, the perpetrator was probably hundreds of miles away by now, back in his hometown in Florida or the Carolinas or somewhere else to hell and gone out of Lee's jurisdiction.

There was a tap at her door. "Come," she called and the door slid open a crack to admit Tom Legros's face.

"Those scientific fellers from Denver ought to be arriving soon, Sheriff," he reminded her. "You want I should go out and pick them up from the airport?"

Lee swung her feet down from the desk and reached for her gun-belt where she'd hooked it over the back of one of her two wooden visitors' chairs. She swung it around her hips with the simple ease of long practice.

"No. I'll go get 'em, Tom," she replied. She finished buckling the belt and reached for a typed form that had been in her in tray when she'd arrived that morning. "You go take a look at this, if you will."

Legros glanced quickly at the sheet she'd given him. There'd been a break-in at a small convenience store located fifteen miles out of town. Cigarettes and liquor stolen and a small amount of cash.

"Sounds like much the same thing as happened out at the Springs City Diner last week," he mused.

Lee nodded. Someone had broken into the diner in the small hours of the morning. The MO looked similar and the burglars had taken the same mix of product and available cash.

They both exited her office and headed for the parking lot. "Take a look at it and let me know what you think."

He touched the brim of his Stetson in salute. They came out into the parking lot and Lee stopped as the icy wind hit her.

"Damn, but it's cold!" she said, pausing to zip up her windproof uniform bomber jacket. Tom looked critically at the driving mass of gray clouds that rode overhead.

"Could be in for more snow if that wind drops a little," he ventured. Lee pulled on her gloves and headed for her Renegade.

"Just what we need," she said grumpily, and yawned. Damn Jesse for waking her in the middle of the night. Things were bad enough without being short on sleep.

SEVEN

She collected the forensic team, then returned to her office. They didn't need her kibitzing while they went about their tasks and she had work of her own to do.

As ever, the paperwork on her desk seemed to have mysteriously multiplied itself tenfold since she'd been gone. It seemed to double if she simply stepped down the hall for a cup of coffee.

On top of the pile was Tom's report on the break-in at the convenience store. She rose and moved to the filing cabinet by the wall and rummaged through it until she found the file on the break-in at the diner. She compared the two. There seemed little difference between them. Probably the same perp. The MOs were identical. Door locks had been jimmied and the intruders had smashed open the cash registers in both cases, taking the cash that was in there after the day's takings. Then, in both instances, they'd helped themselves to cigarettes and a few cases of beer—the only kind of liquor that both establishments had on hand.

She shrugged. They both looked the same. But then, break and enter wasn't such a sophisticated crime that you'd find a great variation in method. A door's locked so you break it. The logical tool is a crowbar. You go in, you steal cash and any booze that's available. She guessed that one break and enter would look pretty much like another. Most of the ones she'd seen in the past had. Still, having two happen within a week was a definite pointer to one person or group being at work. Sooner or later, she guessed, they'd make a mistake and she'd nail them.

She put both files in the filing cabinet and returned to her desk. There was a memorandum from the mayor, querying her about overtime payments incurred by members of the sheriff's department during the previous month. She sighed. If only she could get criminals to operate on a reasonable timetable—say, nine to five—she'd have that problem licked. She reached for a writing pad and a pencil to draft a reply to the mayor.

The pile of paperwork had diminished by more than half when

there was a tap at her door. The leader of the forensic team put his head around the doorframe.

"All finished?" she asked and he nodded, holding up his collection of sample cases.

"I've taken scrapings from under his nails, hair samples, samples from his clothing and all the rest," he replied. "You can inform the police in Minnesota that the family can have the body for burial any-time now." Lee nodded her thanks.

"I'll drive you back to the airport," she said, starting to rise. He waved her back into the chair.

"Cab's good enough, Sheriff. You've got plenty on your plate."

She smiled gratefully. "So, when can we expect your report?"

He screwed up his face thoughtfully. "Give me a couple of days, Sheriff," he said. "It's a pretty simple case, I know, but we're snowed under down in Denver at the moment."

"It's a simple case for you," Lee said, with some feeling. "I wish it was the same for us."

He nodded. "You don't have a lot to go on, do you?" he asked.

"We sure as hell don't."

"Well, look on the bright side. Three out of five violent crimes in this state go unsolved anyway."

Lee raised an eyebrow at him. "Go ahead," she said. "Make my day."

EIGHT

*H*e'd been keeping track of the media coverage of what had become known as The Silver Bullet Murder. He smiled now, shaking his head at the fanciful term. How journalists loved to dramatize events.

But this time, the notoriety suited his purpose. In the past, he'd taken revenge on the people who had crossed him and then quietly faded away. But that no longer gave him the same feeling of satisfaction. It wasn't quite enough. He wanted something bigger, something more noticeable. Sure he had a specific target in mind, but this time, that killing was going to be the culmination of a whole series of events. He wanted more than revenge on just one person and he wanted the world to know about it. He was tired of remaining anonymous. It was time to move on to a new phase. So this time, he was going to punish the entire organization. He wanted something big. Something newsworthy. Something that attracted attention from a much wider base than just the town he happened to be in. And for that to happen, he needed the media attention that a whole series of seemingly unrelated killings would generate.

So in that sense, a phrase like "The Silver Bullet Murder" was just what he needed. It was a handle for other journalists and news services to latch on to and, in the days immediately following the discovery of the body, the Murder—he always thought of it capitalized like that—had made it onto the Channel 6 local news in Denver, and then been picked up by the CBS Network coverage as well.

He smiled cynically as he made his way into Mrs. McLaren's cozy breakfast room. Coffee was standing ready on a warming plate and the baskets of fresh rolls and doughnuts were laid out ready, as ever. He poured himself a cup of coffee and took one of the doughnuts, putting it onto a plate with a paper napkin, then moved to the two-seater, overstuffed sofa, where a copy of the Denver Post was waiting.

As he'd expected, the media reveled in a major crime being committed in a travel resort. There was something doubly pleasing to people who were slaving away at their jobs in the dead of winter to read about bad luck happening to someone who was off having a good time.

He'd been mildly interested to see that his victim had been a dentist. He'd *never liked dentists. Never understood how anyone could willingly take on such a job. Serves him right, he thought, smiling again.*

He quickly scanned the front page of the Post, a small frown forming. US troops in the Middle East were still fighting a losing battle. NASA was bleating for funds to mount a manned expedition to Mars and in Washington, the president had met with a delegation from a group of African countries asking for foreign aid.

Nothing about The Silver Bullet Murder. Apparently, the media was about to drop the entire matter now that the first sensation was over and no new developments had occurred.

It was time to give them something more to work on.

"Morning, Mr. Murphy."

It was Mrs. McLaren, the friendly, motherly widow who ran the small boardinghouse on Laurel Street. She bustled over to the sideboard to make sure the coffee was still full and there were plenty of rolls and doughnuts left for her other guests.

"Morning Mrs. Mac," he said cheerfully, letting her have the full benefit of his beaming smile. He knew she liked him. He knew he could make just about any woman, any age, like him when he turned on the charm.

"My land but you're up early," she said. "Those others won't be stirring for half an hour yet."

"Can't get things done lying in bed, Mrs. Mac." He grinned easily, and she nodded her agreement, setting another pot of water on the warming plate and changing the filter draw in the coffeemaker. It was a sentiment she approved of.

She nodded at the Post, lying open in his lap.

"What's in the news today?" she asked. He looked down at the paper, as if seeing it for the first time, then smiled back at her.

"Oh, hardly anything. Hardly anything at all," he said.

"Well," she said, "I suppose no news is good news, as they say."

She turned to head back to her kitchen. He nodded once or twice, then, after she'd gone, he said to himself, "Not for someone, it isn't."

He wondered who he'd be killing next. Then he shrugged. Not that it really mattered.

Jesse had pulled a ten-hour shift on ski patrol after two volunteer members had failed to show up for duty. He was relaxing in the

Tugboat, working his way through a burger, when Lee's call came through.

The phone behind the bar shrilled, just managing to cut through the blare of conversation and laughter that filled the place. Todd, serving up a brimming glass of chardonnay with one hand, scooped the phone out of its cradle.

"Tugboat Saloon," he said, then, "Sorry, didn't catch that."

His serving hand now free, he covered his right ear with the palm so he could hear the voice on the other end of the phone more clearly.

"Yeah, Sheriff, he's here somewhere, I'm sure," he said. "Just hang tight for a moment." He set the phone down and leaned forward on the bar, searching through the crowd for Jesse, spotting him finally at a table by the coatrack. Fortuitously, Jesse chose that moment to look toward the bar and saw Todd making unmistakable gestures toward the phone. Leaving the remains of his burger, he made his way through the crush and took the phone from Todd's outstretched hand.

"It's Lee," the barman told him.

Like Todd, Jesse clapped his free hand over his other ear to hear more clearly.

"This is Jess," he said. "Something happening?"

"I'd appreciate it if you could get down to Gondola Square." There was something about her voice, a deliberate lack of emotion, that raised the hairs on the back of his neck.

"What is it?" he asked.

"Well, don't go making a lot of noise about it up in the Tugboat, Jess," Lee said, "but we've got us another dead body on the Silver Bullet."

NINE

Once again, it was John Hostetler who had found the body. It shook him up pretty bad and Lee had Tom Legros take him to the gondola office and pour coffee into the elderly man.

John was a kindly soul. He'd lived in Routt County all his life, had raised a family here and seen them all go on to other towns, other cities to marry and bring up their own children. He had eleven grandchildren who loved to see their grandpop whenever they came to visit. His wife, Evie, had passed away three summers back and John, although well past retirement age, had taken the job at the gondola to help ease the loneliness. He was a friendly, cheerful man. A man people instinctively liked. He was the sort of man who would never willingly do harm to anyone.

A man like that shouldn't be subjected to the shock of finding a dead body hunched in the corner of a gondola cabin, eyes staring, hands instinctively clasped to the puncture wound under the chin.

He was still visibly shaken when Jesse arrived at the gondola station.

"I thought he was just drunk," he was saying for the tenth time. "I just thought he was drunk when the doors opened and he didn't move to get out. So I reached in to shake him just a little . . ."

Lee reached out and laid a comforting hand on his shoulder. There were tears forming in the old man's gentle, blue eyes.

"We know that, John. You didn't do anything wrong here. We know," she said in a soothing voice.

Tom, feeling for the old guy, patted his back awkwardly as well.

"Just tell us what happened, John," he urged. Hostetler turned his gaze to the deputy.

"I just thought he was drunk, Tom. People do that up there on Thunderhead when they go to the restaurants. They drink too much and we have to call the Tipsy Taxi for them. You know that."

The Tipsy Taxi was a community service, subscribed to by most of the bars and restaurants in town and on the mountain. When a patron got too far over the odds with his drinking, you could call Alpine Taxis and give them a chit to charge the ride against. A central fund reimbursed the taxi driver for his lost fare.

"I know that, John," said Tom. "Just tell us what happened here and I'll get you home."

The old man shook his head, as if trying to rid himself of the picture that had imprinted itself onto his brain.

"He looked drunk," he muttered. "The doors opened—they do that automatically—and nobody got out. So I just reached in to see was he all right and when I touched him . . . he just fell."

He shook his head again. "Why would someone do that? Why would someone do a thing like that?"

Lee heard the door to the office open, felt a brief swirl of cold air from outside. She turned to see Jesse looking inquiringly at her. She gestured for him to wait a moment, then spoke softly to Tom.

"Get him back to his place, Tom," she said and the deputy nodded, his concerned gaze on the emotional older man.

"Maybe I should stay with him a piece?" he suggested. "Make sure he settles down all right?"

Lee nodded. "Good idea." Then, as a further thought struck her, "Give Doc Jorgensen a call. We're going to need him to examine the body anyway. He might as well stop at John's place on the way and make sure he's okay."

Tom nodded and put his arm under Hostetler's elbow to help him from his chair. The elderly man went along with him.

"Come on, John. I'll get you home and get you settled into bed."

Hostetler hesitated a moment, looking at Lee. "You sure you don't need me here, Sheriff?" he asked. Lee touched his arm gently.

"We'll manage fine for tonight, John," she said. "I'll talk to you tomorrow but for tonight, you get a good night's sleep."

Still Hostetler was reluctant to leave. "But the gondola," he protested, "someone's got to be in charge . . ."

"We'll look after that," Lee promised him. "I've got one of the town cops here to do that. And besides, nothing much can happen till we've disconnected that cabin from the cable."

Hostetler looked around the office, confused by the rapid turn of events. "Well, I'd better call maintenance for that—" he began.

Lee made a small movement with her head toward the door. Tom

Legros saw it and began ushering the gondola attendant out, reassuring him as he did so.

"We've done all that, John," he said. "It's all taken care of. Now you come with me."

Finally Hostetler allowed the deputy to lead him from the office. Lee watched him go with a sad look on her face.

"Poor old guy," she muttered as the door closed behind him.

Jesse was about to speak when the phone on the desk shrilled suddenly. It wasn't the outside line, but a direct line to the gondola station at the top of Thunderhead. Lee motioned for Jesse to wait and picked up the receiver.

"This is Sheriff Torrens," she said. Then, after a pause, "No, we've just sent John home. He's not feeling too good." Another pause, then, "That's right. We've had a little problem down here and we've had to shut the gondola down for a while. We're waiting on your maintenance staff now." She listened for a few seconds as the voice in her ear complained. "Well, we'll get it back online as soon as we can. For the meantime, I suggest you take your customers back into the restaurants up there, out of the cold, and buy them a drink."

She waited, then finally, losing it, she snapped, "Then sell them a goddamn drink! Just don't hassle me with it!"

She slammed the receiver back into its cradle and glared at the phone for a few seconds.

Jesse grinned. "I take it they're getting restless up on Thunderhead?" he asked mildly.

Lee shook her head in exasperation. "They've got a backlog of people waiting to come down—plus God knows how many who are stuck halfway down already."

"Another body in the trash?" Jesse ventured. She shook her head.

"Sitting up in one of the cars itself this time," she said. Jesse looked up quickly.

"He put a body in one of the cars? How did he manage that?"

Lee shrugged. "Maybe he didn't put it there. Maybe he killed him in there. Either way, we've got to get that car disconnected before we can start the gondola running again."

The door flew open. More wind blew in and two men entered with it.

"Where's John?" asked the first one through the door. "Heard you need maintenance here?"

"At last," Lee said with some feeling. "We need a car taken off the cable. Can you take care of that?"

The man who'd spoken pursed his lips thoughtfully. "Can," he agreed, at length. "But ain't gonna without authorization from the lift manager and that's John Hostetler."

Lee took a deep breath, and said in a very reasonable tone, "Well, as you can see Hostetler isn't here. But I am. And as sheriff of this county, I am requesting that you remove one of those cars from the cable. How's that?"

"Like I said, we need authorization. And the way I—" the maintenance man stopped mid-thought. He'd noticed the steely look in Lee's eyes and the way she had turned to face him full on. "Which I guess you can give us," he completed hurriedly. His partner saw the look too. Around Steamboat, Lee had a reputation for not suffering fools gladly.

"Just tell us which car you want taken off, Sheriff," he said.

Lee smiled at him. It was a smile that never quite reached those gray, uptilted eyes.

"You might start with the one that's got the dead body sitting in it."

TEN

The body wasn't sitting in the cabin. It had fallen off the bench seat when John Hostetler had gone to shake it by the shoulder. It sprawled now on the floor of the cabin, head and shoulders out of the open doors.

The maintenance men looked at it nervously as they worked to detach the cabin from the drive cable. This done, Jesse and Lee helped them manhandle it to one side. Then, and only then, were they able to hit the restart button and let the gondola begin to run again.

With Tom Legros taking care of old Hostetler, Lee had requested the town police send a cop to look after crowd control. It was as well she had. Frozen, angry passengers began to disembark from the cabins as they slid in out of the cold night. Lee couldn't blame them for their anger. There was no way of communicating with the cabins. Once the gondolas stopped moving, there was no way for the passengers already on board to know if it was a short delay or an extended one. In some cases, nervous passengers had begun to fear that the gondola had shut down for the night and that they might be trapped until morning.

Once those passengers had dispersed, there was a new wave of rubberneckers. This time it was the group who'd been left at the top of Thunderhead. They knew something was going on. They didn't know what, exactly, but they planned to find out.

The patrolman had his hands full. Lee and Jesse decided to delay their examination of the detached cabin and the body until the crowd had dispersed. They draped an old tarpaulin over the cabin, concealing the corpse from view. One after another the gondola cabins whooshed in from the darkness, rocking back and forth as they hit the slower circular cable that allowed passengers to disembark easily. The doors would thud open automatically in a constant rhythm.

Eventually the doors opened on more and more empty cabins as the backlog of people thinned out. When they'd counted a dozen without any passengers, Lee decided they could safely go to work.

First of all, she lifted the direct line phone to the upper station and pressed the call button.

There was a slight delay, then the lift attendant at the top platform answered the call.

"This is the sheriff," said Lee. "You got any more customers up there waiting to come down?"

"No more customers, Sheriff Torrens. Just the staff up here. They'll be through cleaning up in half an hour or so and then they'll be downloading."

"How long you been on duty up there?" Lee wanted to know. The answer came promptly.

"Came on duty at eight. We'll be going off when the last of the people up here ride down." It was standard practice to have two attendants on duty at the top end of the gondola, to help customers board.

"Is there anyone up there can fill in for you two for a while?" Lee asked. "I need you to take a look at something down here."

There was a pause as the two attendants discussed her request. Lee knew they couldn't leave the loading bay unattended. She just hoped someone else might be qualified to keep an eye on things while the two attendants came down. Finally, the voice at the other end agreed to her request.

"Grover, the restaurant manager, can keep an eye on things for a few minutes. You need us any longer than that, Sheriff?" he said.

"Shouldn't think so," Lee replied. Then the attendant asked, with some concern in his voice, "Sheriff? Nothing's happened to John Hostetler, has it? Is he okay down there?"

"He's had a bit of a shake-up but he'll be fine. Now you boys get aboard the next cabin and get yourselves down here if you will."

"Right, Sheriff. We're on our way. What's going on? We haven't got us another dead body down there, have we?" The last was added as a morbid joke. Lee took a deep breath, decided it would be better to tell them face-to-face and avoided the question.

"Just get on down here, fellers. Bye." She hung up, looked at Jesse. "Right. Let's take a look at the scene of the crime."

Their footsteps rang in the metal and concrete interior of the building as they crossed to the cabin. Jesse pulled on a pair of rubber gloves and gently moved the dead man's head to one side and inspected the wound under the chin. There wasn't a lot of external bleeding. Once death stopped the heart pumping, the flow of blood slowed.

"Well," he said softly. "We've got us another jigger killing."

Lee knelt on her haunches beside him to look at the dead man's face. "Why aren't I surprised to hear that?" she said. As carefully as she could, she zipped open the waist-length leather jacket the dead man was wearing and felt around the inside pockets for a wallet. Finally, she found it in his shirt breast pocket. She took it out and examined the contents.

"What have we got?" Jesse asked, running his fingers up the inside edge of the double doors to the cabin and peering closely at the metal.

"Once again, we don't have a robbery. There's a hundred and thirty . . . thirty-eight dollars in here, and three credit cards."

"Any of them got a name on them?" Jesse asked. He dropped onto his back and hauled himself under the raised edge of the cabin. It was supported by a middle rail that accepted a wheeled carriage when it was taken out of service, as it was now. "Got a flashlight?" he asked, before she could answer.

Lee handed him her Maglite, then found a driver's license among the cards. She turned it to catch the light.

"Arizona driving license," she told him.

Jesse grunted. "Long way from home."

"Name of Andrew Barret," she said, reading the license. "From Flagstaff, Arizona."

"Nice town," said Jesse. He reached under the cabin to retrieve something that had shown up in the beam of the flashlight. Lee saw the movement and dropped to her knees again to watch.

"Got something?" she asked.

Jesse grunted again as he crawled out from under the cabin. "Could be." He held out his hand and shone the flashlight beam on his finger and thumb. There were a few fibers held between them. Lee leaned closer to examine them.

"What do you think they are?" she asked.

"Dunno. Could be nothing. Got a plastic envelope there?"

She nodded and fished a plastic evidence envelope out of her shirt pocket. Jesse carefully deposited the fibers in it and closed the press seal top. He handed the small bag back to her.

"We'll see what your friends from Denver have to say about it," he said.

Dusting himself off, he straightened and walked around the cabin, shaking his head. He turned back to face her.

"So tell me, Lee, how does a body get itself into the gondola without anyone noticing at the top?" He raised his hands helplessly, then let them fall back again to his sides. "I mean, the trash container I can understand. The killer had all day to plant the body in there. I'm not saying it was simple, but it was possible. But this?" he laughed humorlessly.

Lee had taken her Maglite back from him. She shone it around the interior of the cabin, leaning past the body to do so, being careful not to disturb it any further. Doc Jorgensen got touchy about things like that when he had to give a coroner's report.

"Maybe he was alive when he got in the cabin?" she suggested. "Leastways, that's the theory I'm working on."

Jesse shook his head dismissively. "And the killer got in with him, stuck him with the jigger and then flew away, right? Doesn't make sense, Lee."

She shrugged. "Makes more sense than having the killer lug a dead body into the gondola past two attendants and God knows how many other passengers waiting there and have nobody notice."

"No stoppages on the gondola just before John found the body, were there?" he asked.

Lee shook her head. "I checked the log. The last stoppage was forty minutes before. The run down from the top takes twelve and a half minutes, give or take maybe a minute, depending on wind conditions, so that couldn't have had anything to do with it."

Jesse was pacing again. "The doors shut automatically. The gondola doesn't stop. Yet somehow, someone gets in here, kills our friend from Flagstaff, opens the closed doors, steps out into thin air—remembering to close the doors behind him . . ." He paused suddenly, turned to her quickly. "The doors were closed when the cabin came in, weren't they?"

She nodded confirmation. "Yeah. John said he heard them open, then saw the body in there, only he didn't know it was a body at the time," she added.

"Right . . . so somehow, he leaves a dead body behind in a locked cabin."

"You could force these doors, of course," she suggested. As she said it, a thought struck him and he moved quickly to the cabin again.

"Have you got that flashlight again?" he asked, peering at the door-jamb and holding a hand out for the Maglite. When she handed it to him, he twisted the switch on and focused it on the edge of one of the automatic doors.

"Maybe you're right, Lee," he said carefully. "Look here. I noticed these before but I didn't think too much of them."

She looked at the beam playing on the doorjamb. There were small scratches in the painted metal. She ran a finger down the edge of the door, feeling the roughness where something had cut into it.

"And here," Jesse said, switching the beam to the other door. Again, she saw the same small patches of bare metal gouged into the paint, at roughly the same height as on the other door.

"Some kind of ram maybe. Or a jack of some kind to force the doors open," said Jesse slowly.

Lee glanced at him. His face was alive with concentration. The dark eyes were burning with an eagerness she hadn't seen there for a long time.

"So that's how he got the doors open," she agreed. "How did he get out?"

Jesse shrugged, his mind still working. "Could have abseiled down from the cabin. It's possible," he said to himself. "Those fibers . . . could be from a rope."

They were interrupted by the arrival of the two lift attendants from the top station. The men looked around curiously, saw Lee and headed toward her.

"What's happening, Sheriff?" asked one of them.

"I need you guys to look at a body," Lee told them. That got their attention, Jesse thought. Nothing like the mention of a dead body to focus a man's mind.

"Body?" said the lift attendant, his voice cracking as he hit a higher register of surprise. "You mean it's happened again?" He turned to his companion. "What did I tell you, Frank? I said, 'It's happened again,' didn't I?"

"I said it, Norm," Frank replied, a little aggrieved, and the first man waved his hands as if dismissing such unimportant details.

"So you said it. I agreed with you, so that's as good as saying it, just about." He turned to Lee again. "Who's the stiff, Sheriff?"

"The victim," said Lee, laying stress on the word, "is from Arizona. Like you to take a look at him. See if you can remember him boarding the gondola earlier tonight."

She motioned them toward the cabin. A little gingerly, the two men approached it, stopping in their tracks as they caught sight of the dead man, sprawled half in, half out of the doorway.

"Jesus," Norm said softly, taking in the staring eyes and the look of shock and pain. He swallowed heavily. "He doesn't look so good, does he?" he asked of no one in particular.

"Often happens that way when you're dead," Jesse agreed. Norm looked quickly at him to see if he was joking. Jesse's poker face was perfect. He urged the lift attendant back to the problem at hand.

"You remember seeing him board at all?"

Norm screwed up his face in concentration. He twisted around to look at the face from a more natural angle. Barret's body was, after all, lying head down out of the gondola. He began to shake his head, drew in breath to speak. They could see the word "no" forming on his lips when his buddy, Frank, got in first.

"Yep," he said simply. He was standing back from the gondola, hands in his pockets, staring fixedly at the dead man. Lee turned to him quickly.

"You sure of that?" she asked him and he nodded slowly. He took one hand out of his jacket pocket to point as he continued.

"Remember that leather jacket. Remember thinking as how I'd like one just like it," he said. He looked at his companion now.

"You remember him, Norm?" he asked. Norm, obviously not wanting to be left out of all this, screwed up his face in concentration again. They could see he was about to switch from his earlier position. Jesse glanced at Lee and turned one corner of his mouth down. Don't take

too much notice of his evidence, the look said. Lee gave a barely per‐
ceptible nod.

"We-ell . . . maybe I do at that . . ." Norm was saying uncertainly.

Frank snorted impatiently. "Course you do! Remember? That other
feller came barging out just as this one was loading."

ELEVEN

Lee and Jesse exchanged a quick glance. Lee interrupted the argument before it could begin.

"What other feller?" she asked urgently. Frank turned away from his buddy and answered her.

"This guy here had loaded aboard. The cabin was moving out when this other feller came barging out, rushing to get in the cabin before the doors closed." Again he glanced at Norm. "You must remember! You nearly missed loading his skis in the rack."

The attendants took care of passengers' skis when they boarded the gondola, loading them into racks on the outside of the automatic doors. Norm looked up now, memory flooding into his face.

"By God but you're right, Frank!" he said abruptly. "That cross-country skier feller got in as well."

This time, Jesse asked the question. "A cross-country skier, you say?"

Norm nodded several times now as he remembered more detail. "That's right," he said. "I remember because he gave me the skis. You know, those thin, free-heelers that the cross-country fellers wear."

"You remember what he looked like?" Lee asked casually. Norm cocked his head to one side, trying to remember. Reluctantly, he had to admit that he couldn't.

"He was kinda rugged up, Sheriff," he said apologetically, looking to Frank for support. The other lift attendant nodded his agreement. "You know how those cross-country fellers get themselves all rugged up. Had a beard too."

"Tall? Short? Average height?" Jesse prompted them.

The two men exchanged doubtful looks again. "Can't say for sure, Jesse." Frank spoke for the two of them. "Hard to gauge a feller's height when he's doubled over climbing into the gondola."

"You didn't notice him waiting around at the top station?" Lee asked.

"Can't say we did," said Norm, and Frank nodded confirmation. "Funny, now you mention it. He was just there, all of a sudden."

"Maybe came in from outside," offered Frank, and Norm seemed to think this was possible.

"Could have done. Might have been out by the stairs having a smoke."

Jesse looked up sharply. "You say he was a smoker?"

There was a long pause, then Norm replied, "Can't say I actually saw him smoking. Just said maybe he was outside having a smoke."

Jesse nodded his understanding, rubbing his jaw with his hand. The two attendants looked from Lee to Jesse apologetically.

"Sorry we can't be more help, Sheriff," said Norm finally.

Lee made a dismissing gesture with one hand. "Don't worry about it, boys. Hard to remember details of a person you only see for a few seconds."

"He had a knapsack," Frank put in suddenly. "A green knapsack like those cross-country skiers carry." He thought more on it. "A big one."

"Not one of those little ones the day skiers use to keep their goggles and spare gloves and so on in?" Jess asked.

Frank was shaking his head definitely now. "No, sir. It was a big one. You remember it, Norm?" Norm, thinking, nodded in his turn and confirmed Frank's statement.

"A big one right enough. Seemed to have plenty in it too."

There was a pause as both men tried to remember further details. Lee and Jesse let them go for a few moments. They both knew that unprompted memory is usually a whole heap more reliable than statements made in answer to suggestions from the questioner. Once you got to that point, there was a possibility of the witness unconsciously coming up with the sort of answer that he thought the interrogator wanted.

The silence stretched on. Finally, Jesse realized this was all they were going to get. "What about his clothes, guys? Remember what he was wearing?"

Norm looked at him, a little annoyed that he hadn't thought of this himself. "Why, ski clothes, of course. He would have been wearing a parka, wouldn't he?" Once again, Frank nodded and murmured assent.

"Long-line parka? Short-line? Any idea of color?" prompted Lee.

"Well, it would have been long-line, wouldn't it? Those cross-

country skiers always wear long-line parkas. Yeah. Long-line," said
Frank, finally convincing himself.

Jesse noticed the conditional nature of the answers now. The two
men were trying to remember, and filling in gaps with details that they
thought had to be correct. He caught Lee's eye and made a small
negative gesture. They'd be better to leave the two men now and question them further in the morning.

Lee caught the gesture and nodded. Then remembered one obvious
question they'd left out.

"One other thing, guys. Was he white? Black? Asian?"

"Maybe Hispanic?" added Jesse.

Norm frowned a little at the last word. "Say what, Jess?" he asked.

Frank nudged him in the ribs with an elbow. "He means Mexican,"
he explained. "Was he a Mexican?"

Norm shrugged. "Couldn't say as to that one," he admitted. "He
wasn't no black or no Asian though. I'd swear to that."

"Don't think he was no Mexican either," Frank added. "Sure he
wasn't, in fact."

"Is that all, Sheriff?" Norm asked. He glanced at his wristwatch.
"We ought to be getting back up to relieve Grover. He's got some
work of his own to do closing up the restaurant."

Lee patted him on the shoulder. "That's all for now, boys," she said.
"Thanks for your help."

The two men headed toward one of the gondola cabins. Frank was
shaking his head sadly. "Don't see as how we was too much help,
Sheriff," he said. "Seems a man ought to be able to remember a feller
once he set eyes on him."

"It's not as easy as it sounds," Lee told him.

Both men shook their heads. They felt that somehow they'd failed
a test. Lee tried to make them feel a little better about it.

"You've been more help than you realize," she said. "Just sleep on
it. Maybe you'll remember more details in the morning."

"Well, we'll sure enough call you if we do," Norm promised.

He stepped toward one of the slow-moving cabins when a call from
Jesse stopped him.

"Norm! One other thing: these cabin doors. Could one man force
them open once they're closed?"

The two attendants looked at the automatic doors on the gondola cabin sliding past them. They both nodded.

"Not with his bare hands, maybe," said Norm. "But you can sure enough lever them apart. Have to be able to do that so we can evacuate the gondola if we have a power failure."

Jesse was walking toward them now. He continued, "And once they're opened, do they stay open?"

Frank shook his head. "Not while the cabin's moving," he said. "Once it enters the loading zone here, it hits a safety trip that keeps 'em open. But while it's moving down the hill, you'd have to prop them open or the emergency switch would shut them again."

"Thanks, guys," Jesse concluded. "Like the sheriff says, you've been more help than you know."

The two men looked a little more satisfied at that. They weren't sure what they'd said that had been helpful but they were content to think that it must have been something.

"You finished with us now, Jess?" asked Norm and Jesse pointed them toward the gondola again.

"That's all I need from you," he said, and the two men waved, then bent and climbed aboard the cabin. The doors sighed shut and it moved out into the night, gathering speed as it hit the high-speed section of the cable.

"So," Lee said at length. "We've got us a bearded killer with a knapsack."

Jesse snorted derisively. "Don't be too sure about the beard. My guess is it's long gone, dumped in a trash can somewhere."

"Disguise?" Lee raised her eyebrows in a question.

Jesse nodded emphatically. "Can't think of a better way of obscuring a man's face. Can you?"

He took her arm and led her toward one of the cabins. "Come on," he said. "We're going for a gondola ride."

She held back a moment. "What for?" she asked. He took her arm again and moved her more forcibly toward the loading point.

"We're going to survey the ground. Our killer got on board. We know that. He killed our victim here, and somewhere on the way down, he forced the doors open and got out. Probably on a rope."

"I guess so," said Lee. "You figure he had it in his knapsack?"

"That would be my guess," Jesse replied patiently. "So let's take a look at the ground under the gondola and see if there's a likely spot to get out at."

Lee nodded her understanding. There was one more detail to take care of, however. She stopped and called to the cop on duty. "Keep an eye on things here for half an hour, would you?"

Her gesture included the gondola station, the detached cabin and the body of Andy Barret. The cop, a little thrown out of his stride, gestured to the body.

"What do you want me to do with him?" he asked.

Jesse cut in before Lee could answer. "If he moves, read him his rights," he said, and shoved the sheriff into the cabin moving past them.

TWELVE

There was the customary lurch as the cabin accelerated out into the blackness above the brightly lit gondola station. Lee and Jesse sat side by side on the forward facing bench of the gondola. Jesse sprawled his long legs out, resting his feet on the opposite bench.

Lee shivered. "Goddamn it's cold!" she complained. "Couldn't you have given me a few minutes to grab my sheepskin out of the car?"

Jesse gave no sign that he'd heard her complaint. As the car rose swiftly above the first slope, he sat up and began to pay more attention to the landscape passing by below them. Lee sighed and patted her arms to keep warm.

"We looking for anything in particular?" she asked.

Jesse shrugged. "I'm not sure. Probably for a spot where the cabin isn't too far from the ground, where there's plenty of ground cover—like trees—and deep snow."

"Why deep snow?"

"If it were me, I'd want deep snow, just in case something went wrong with my ropes," he replied. "You still got that flashlight?"

He held out one hand, his face glued now to the window, staring out into the blackness. Lee took the Maglite from its small pouch and handed it to him. He shone it out the window, was defeated by the reflection, and swore softly to himself. He reached up and unlatched the ventilator, yanking it down and shining the torch through the gap onto the snow below. The bitter wind howled through the open window. Lee moved forward onto the opposite bench, peering through the front windows of the cabin, shielding her gaze with her hands to stop reflections spoiling her sight.

"There's a grove of aspens up ahead," she said, "just after the gondola crosses Valley View. That could be the sort of thing you're looking for."

Jesse angled the little flashlight to point ahead and down. The effect of the small beam was almost negligible. There was so much ambient light reflected from the snow, he hardly needed the torch. He studied the spot Lee had pointed out as they hummed over it.

"How far would you say we're off the ground right now?" he asked her.

Lee looked down, considering. "Twenty, maybe twenty-five feet," she ventured. "I don't think it gets much lower than this."

"Uh-huh," grunted Jesse. He peered down, trying to reach the most acute angle possible. But the bottom half of the gondola blocked his downward view. "Can't see if there's any disturbances in the snow."

"Like ski tracks?" Lee asked him and he nodded.

"Ski tracks. Footprints. Signs that someone landed in the snow."

"Damn!" he said finally. "We'll have to check it on the ground." He sat back, thinking.

"They keep any snowmobiles up at Thunderhead?" Lee asked.

"Bound to," Jesse replied. "We'll get hold of one and come back down for a proper look around."

"Anywhere else?" Lee asked.

"There are three or four places that are possibilities. That's the best of the lot so far."

The gondola had started to rise higher and higher from the slope of the mountain now and it was passing over the open, groomed areas of the Heavenly Daze ski run.

"I doubt he'd try to get out here," said Jesse. "Too high for one thing. And it's a bit out in the open."

Lee shook her head. "I'm surprised that nobody saw him doing it, anyway. I mean, surely someone in one of the other cabins must have noticed a man hanging by a rope underneath the gondola?"

Jesse shook his head. "Not necessarily. Take a look around yourself." He indicated the view around them. The internal light shining on the perspex windows of the cabin created reflections that defeated their vision. The most they could see of the downward moving cabins was an occasional dark blur sliding past.

The cabins above and below them were hardly more visible.

"Remember," he pointed out, "the doors are on the far side, so even if you did look at one of the cabins, chances are you'd see nothing. Besides, most people, if they're looking out, will look at the lights down in the valley."

He indicated the brilliant spread of light that was now far below them.

"I guess so," she agreed.

"Remember too," he added, "he knew there was nobody ready to get in the cabin directly behind him. And he'd probably seen there was nobody in front either. He could wait and pick his time until he got the right conditions."

Lee nodded slowly, thinking it through. It sounded logical. It sounded so damn logical.

"I guess his biggest risk would be being spotted by people on the ground itself," she said.

"Not too many of them around at night," he said. "Just the groomers and the occasional patrol from the . . . oh, Jesus!" He stood up suddenly, his head crashing into the low ceiling of the gondola, lined with carpet to prevent condensation forming inside. He dropped back onto the bench, setting the cabin rocking wildly, then craned around to stare back down the mountain.

"Jesse, what is it?" Lee moved to his side, staring out the window behind them. She could see the headlights and the yellow strobe lights from one of the slope groomers moving down the mountain below them. Huge, tracked vehicles, with a bulldozer blade in front and dragging a heavy rubber mat behind, they were out every night, regrooming the slopes for the following day's skiing. Smoothing over the ruts and bumps and tracks that had been left behind and restoring the face of the mountain to an immaculate, smooth finish. Lee now knew what had set Jesse off.

"Oh, Christ, no," she said.

The groomer was heading straight for the area they planned to search. In five minutes' time, there'd be no sign of ski tracks. No footprints. No nothing. Just an immaculate, pristine, groomed slope. She looked at her wristwatch. They had another six or seven minutes before they reached the top. As she'd noted earlier that night, there was no way they could communicate with the top station and get them to radio through and stop the groomer.

"I don't suppose," Jesse said slowly, "you happened to bring your cell phone with you?"

She looked at him helplessly. The cell phone was in her car, safely nestled in the pocket of her sheepskin jacket.

"Sonofabitch!" she said angrily.

Jesse shrugged and sat back on the bench, his long legs splayed out in front of him again. "I thought you wouldn't," he said.

The following morning, they examined the site by daylight. As they'd expected, there was little enough to see, once the groomer had gone over the area. Close to the grove of aspens that Lee had pointed out, there were traces of ski tracks in the deep snow that had been left untouched. However, as evidence, they were hardly positive proof that this was where the murderer had left the cabin.

"I guess," said Lee heavily, "you've got to expect to find ski tracks in a ski resort."

Jesse was down on one knee in the snow, getting a closer look at the twin grooves cut in the white surface.

"Could be cross-country skis," he said without total conviction. "The tracks look narrow enough."

Lee considered them skeptically. "Hard to tell," she replied. "They may or may not be. They could just as easily be alpine skis."

Jesse rose to his feet, absentmindedly dusting the dry snow from the knees of his Levis. "What you're saying," he said, "is that we're no wiser this morning than we were last night."

"That's about it." Lee craned back to look up at the gondola cabins humming overhead. "But I still think this is the most likely spot for him to have got out."

Jesse followed her gaze. "Not that it does us much good, unless we know he's planning on doing it again."

"And unless we know *when* he's planning on doing it again," she added heavily.

"Well," said Jesse after a while. "I guess the next thing to do is see if there's any link we can find between the two victims."

"I've got Tom checking on that already." Lee took a final look around the site. The first of the morning's skiers were beginning to make their way down the mountain, their skis virtually silent in the fresh fallen snow. Jesse walked to the snowmobile they'd ridden up the mountain. He flicked the kill button up to the on position, then tugged on the starter cable. The two-stroke engine purred easily to life and Jesse swung his leg over the saddle.

"Nothing much to gain by standing around here," he said, gesturing for Lee to climb on the pillion. She moved toward the snowmobile, then stopped, leaned forward and pushed the kill button in. The noise of the engine died. Jesse twisted in the saddle to look at her.

"Something on your mind?" he asked her.

She nodded. "Jess, I appreciate your help on this. You know a hell of a lot more about this sort of homicide case than me," she began.

He shrugged. "Maybe so. Maybe not. Regardless, I'm pleased to help out."

"I was thinking," said Lee, choosing her words carefully, "that it might be time to make your position a little more . . . official. I guess you could take a few weeks' leave from the Patrol, couldn't you?"

Jesse considered the suggestion. His poker face told her nothing about what he was thinking. Finally, he replied. "I guess. You trying to give me a badge here, Lee?"

She nodded. "That's about the size of it, Jess. Of course, you don't need an actual badge but it might speed things up if you were a deputy—on a temporary basis, say."

Jesse rubbed the side of his jaw with the palm of his hand. "Don't see that it would make much difference, Lee. I'm happy to help out. Don't need to be no temporary deputy to do it."

She frowned at him. "You're not concerned about working for a woman, are you, Jess?" she asked. "Or maybe it's because it's me?" she added as an afterthought.

Jesse grinned widely at her. "Well, I'm working for you anyway, Lee, so I can't see that I'm concerned about it either way. I just don't see any reason to make things any more official than they are."

Lee sighed. She'd known that he was going to react this way. It was probably linked back to what had happened in Denver. Jesse watched her patiently, waiting for her to speak again. He wasn't helping any, she thought. Finally, she said, "Look, I assume that you'd like to look around Barret's room in the Harbor?" She made it a question and he nodded slowly.

"Could be I'd turn something up. I was going to suggest we do it."

"Well, that's the point, see, Jess?" she said, seizing her opportunity. "We'd both have to do it. If you want to nose around a crime scene, I have to be along to make things official, don't I?"

He hadn't thought of that point and he nodded again, considering. "I guess that's true enough."

Lee developed the thought further. "And let's just say that you turn up a piece of evidence. Let's say you find something that points us right to the murderer—"

Jesse stopped her, holding up one hand and grinning at her. "Slow down, Lee. I may be good. But I'm not that good. Don't go expecting me to walk into Barret's room and solve this case straight up now."

She shook her head in exasperation. "That's not what I'm saying, Jess. But if you're involved in this investigation and you've got no official capacity to be involved, that could corrupt any evidence you find, couldn't it?"

His grin faded and he frowned. "I'm not sure," he said slowly. "I hadn't really thought about that."

She didn't give him time to allay the doubt that had arisen. "Well, think about it now," she said. "Say we arrest a suspect and some smart defense lawyer works out that the investigation has been handled by a civilian with no official authority to be asking questions or handling evidence . . ." She let that last thought hang in the air for a few seconds. "It's just possible that a technicality like that might destroy any case we try to make, isn't it?"

There was a silence between them. Jesse rubbed his jaw with the palm of his hand. She knew he was thinking. She knew he was thinking that she had a point.

"Might be best," he ventured finally, "if I just got out of the way altogether."

"No, Jess!" she said vehemently. "I need you on this case! Damn it, you were one of the best homicide detectives they had in Denver!"

He looked at her quizzically, his head tilted to one side. "Is that right?" he asked her. "And who might have told you that?"

She flushed suddenly. She hadn't ever intended to let him know that she'd spoken to his bosses in Denver about his resignation. She hesitated, then said, "Your old boss, Chief Douglas, if you have to know."

His eyebrows raised sardonically. She kicked angrily at a small pile of snow in front of her, scattering it into wind driven powder.

"Chief of Detectives William Harris Douglas himself?" he mused. "And what occasioned you to be chatting with him?"

She felt the color mounting to her cheeks, faced him squarely and met his gaze.

"We were talking about you," she said bluntly. "I wanted to know if you were all right so I asked Chief Douglas what had happened. Damn it," she added. "You weren't going to tell anyone, I could see that."

"But he did," Jesse said softly. It was a statement, not a question.

Lee nodded. "Yes," she replied, keeping her voice even. "He did. He felt I ought to know, as the local sheriff and as a friend."

Jesse let out a long pent-up breath and dropped his gaze away from hers. He looked out over the Yampa Valley spread out below them, shook his head once or twice. After a while he said, "Then, as a friend, you'll understand why I'm in no hurry to put on a badge of any kind again. Lee, when I came back here, I told myself I was finished with that kind of thing."

"But you're not, Jess. You're not now and you never will be. God-damn it, I've watched you these last few days. It's like you're alive again. You've been wandering around town in some kind of fog for the past two years, Jess, and now you're almost back to the way you were."

He laughed bitterly, turned to look at her again. "There's a matter for concern, Sheriff. I come alive only when other people are suddenly made dead. I'm not sure if that's something about myself that I like."

She was angry now and she let him know it. "Damn you, Jesse! That's not the way of it and you know that! You're alive again because you can see a chance to do what you do best. You're a cop and a good one. That means you can't just sit idly by while people are being killed and throw your hands in the air and say, 'Oh my, how terrible.' Now don't pretend it's anything else."

Again, his gaze dropped away from hers. When he spoke, she could barely hear the words. "Yeah . . . maybe you're right at that, Lee."

She dropped a hand on his shoulder. He still wouldn't face her so she shook his shoulder gently until he did. "Jesse, I need you working on this case. I told you already, I'm out of my depth. If it would help you decide, the people of this town and this county need you working on it. No, damn it, they deserve to have you working on it because you're the best homicide investigator we've got."

She paused, watching his eyes carefully. She could see the acceptance growing there. "But I need you on this case officially. As a sworn-in deputy. That leaves me free to get on with running my department and you free to investigate anywhere and anytime you like." She shook him again, gently. "C'mon Jess. You know it makes sense."

He let go another deep breath. "Well, hell," he said. "If it means so damn much to you, let's make me a deputy."

THIRTEEN

The fire chief also acted as a notary public. They went back to the Public Safety Building on Yampa Street and he witnessed Lee swearing Jesse in as a deputy. At the end of the brief ritual, he nodded to them both and took his leave, returning to his office, downstairs from the sheriff's department.

Lee rummaged in the top left-hand drawer for a few moments, then tossed something on the desktop.

"There you go, Jess. Now you're official."

Jesse picked it up and studied it. It was a deputy sheriff's star. He looked at her quizzically. "Thought you said I didn't have to wear any badge?" he asked her.

"You don't have to wear it. I just have to issue you with it. Hell, keep it in your pocket if you want to. It might just make things a little easier if you want to question someone, is all." She hesitated, her hand hovering over the still open drawer.

"I'm supposed to issue you with a gun as well. I've got this Beretta here if you want it."

Jesse shook his head. "Got my own if I need one. Doubt that I will in any event."

Lee nodded and closed the drawer firmly.

"Figured that might be the case," she said. She was going to say more, but the phone on her desk shrilled and she turned to pick it up.

"Sheriff Torrens," she said. From where he stood, across the room, Jesse could recognize the high-pitched tones from the other end of the line. Ned Puckett, the Mayor of Steamboat Springs, was obviously pretty damn excited about something. Lee listened to the torrent of words, caught Jesse's gaze and rolled her eyes to heaven. Finally, there was a break in the torrent, presumably as Ned paused for breath. Lee managed to get a few words in.

"Well, of course I'm doing something about it, Ned. I've just been up on the mountain right now, inspecting the scene."

She paused as Ned opened up again, then had to admit, a little reluctantly, "Well, no. We didn't find too much of anything, as a matter of fact . . . No. No clues so far, Ned . . . No. No suspects either. I mean, let's face it, Ned, if we had us a suspect, chances are, we'd have us a few clues, don't you think?"

She breathed heavily, obviously holding her temper in check. "No. I don't think it's the slightest bit amusing, Ned. I get damned well un-amused when someone starts murdering people in my jurisdiction . . . Well, hell! I know they're tourists, Ned! That doesn't make it worse, does it?"

Apparently it did. Ned seemed to go ballistic over the phone. Lee let him run, drumming her fingers impatiently on the desktop as she did. She met Jesse's gaze once and shook her head in exasperation. He shrugged his sympathy. Officialdom didn't vary much from place to place. He'd listened to similar conversations in Chief Douglas's office in Denver. Politicians took heat from the electorate about crime, so they passed the heat onto cops. Jesse shrugged. That was just part and parcel of being a cop. He knew it. So did Lee. Finally, however, she decided that Ned had said enough. She cut across his tirade.

"Ned . . . Ned! All right! I get the picture. You're concerned—" There was a brief chatter of words from the phone before she could cut him off again. "All right, deeply concerned. We all are. Tell you what, you're in your office?" Again, a brief answer, which Lee didn't allow to become more lengthy. Jesse grinned. Ned Puckett could turn the word "yes" into a ten-minute election speech.

"Fine. Well how about I come over there now and fill you in on what we know so far and what we plan to do about things? Okay?"

Obviously it was. Ned's voice had dropped a few octaves now. Even from across the room, Jesse thought he sounded as if he were some-what placated.

"Okay, that's fine, Ned," Lee continued. "I'll be right over. Tell you what, I'm still waiting on those forensic boys from Denver to send in their report. How about I call them? Maybe they've turned some-thing up."

She looked up, met Jesse's gaze and shrugged. Part of being sheriff was placating the other town officials when something went wrong.

"Fine," she repeated. "I'll see you in a quarter hour."

She hung the phone up and let go a long sigh.

"You want to come with me?" she asked, without too much hope.

Jesse grinned and shook his head. "I think I'll head over to the Harbor Hotel and look over the victim's room. Maybe I'll find something."

"You think?" Lee asked and he shook his head.

"Not really. But you never know. Have fun with Ned."

FOURTEEN

The desk clerk at the Harbor Hotel rummaged around in a drawer and handed over a key to Barret's room.

"Heard you were helping out on this one, Jesse," he said, then added with a slightly anxious tone, "Think you'll get her cleared up soon?"

Jesse took the proffered key and shrugged. "Just as soon as we can, Linc," he told him. Obviously, murders weren't good for trade. Linc, shaking his head, confirmed his suspicions.

"Terrible, terrible affair, Jesse," he said portentously. Jesse nodded as the other man continued. "Had a group from LA cancel their bookings only this morning. Six rooms," he added heavily, "three of them doubles at that."

The new deputy looked at the desk clerk quizzically, not sure if his verdict of a terrible, terrible affair related to the murders themselves or the canceled bookings. He decided, on balance, it was the latter.

"Not the first time you've had people change their minds, I'll be bound," he offered, and Linc nodded immediately.

"Oh, that's true enough, Jess. Matter of fact, we re-rented those rooms right away. Got a waiting list long as your arm at this time of year."

"Not a problem, then," Jesse stated and Linc agreed but only conditionally.

"Not yet, at any rate. But I sure hope you and Lee catch whoever's doing this before it gets to be a problem."

Jesse stood inside Andrew Barret's room at the Harbor Hotel as the door sighed shut on its pneumatic closer.

A queen-sized bed dominated the available space. There was a dark wood dressing table, antique in style, with a hinged mirror angled slightly above it. Jesse's image stared patiently back at him with steady, brown eyes.

A leather armchair was in one corner—comfortable looking and recently restored. The leather was deep red and quilted, the sort of furniture you expect to find in gentlemen's clubs and attorney's offices. The Harbor furnished its rooms with restored antiques. The rich tone of the leather was spoiled somewhat by the carelessly flung denim shirt hooked over one side of the back and the crumpled jeans that had been dropped on the seat cushion.

Jesse edged round the bed—rooms in the Harbor weren't known for their size—and checked the bedside table. Apparently Barret was a person who preferred to sleep on the left-hand side of the bed. There was a paperback edition of a John Grisham novel lying facedown on the table, and a handful of small change that had been carelessly dropped there as well. An inhaler, the sort used by asthma sufferers, was also standing on the table, along with the remote control for the television that was hanging on a bracket from the wall opposite the bed.

Barret's suitcase was open on one of those folding metal and webbing stands that you find in hotels and nowhere else. Taking a pen from his shirt pocket, Jesse turned over a few of the items in the suitcase. There was nothing there to excite interest. He pulled on a pair of thin leather gloves and carefully closed the suitcase, zipping it shut. He'd examine the case and its contents in greater detail when he took it back to the sheriff's department offices.

The dressing table was next. It had the usual drawers for clothes and underclothes and socks, as well as a series of smaller jewelry drawers. Jesse pulled them open, not expecting to see much in them. He wasn't disappointed. One held a double-A flashlight battery, presumably used, and that was it. On an impulse, Jesse ran his fingers underneath the surfaces of the smaller drawers and was rewarded by the feeling of something taped there.

He removed the drawer and turned it upside down. It was nothing but a Visa card, made out to A. Barret. Obviously the victim liked to keep a spare handy—and didn't seem to trust hotel safe-deposit boxes. Jesse carefully peeled the tape away and put the card down on the polished wood surface of the dressing table. As a matter of routine, he'd check the Visa account number to see if any out of the ordinary transactions had been made in recent days. Odds were, however, Barret merely had it stashed away in case he lost the wallet containing his other cards. Jesse remembered seeing a Mastercard and an Amex Gold among the documents Lee had found on the body.

The rest of the drawers contained nothing out of the ordinary, just underclothes, socks, sweaters and shirts.

The closet held more of Barret's clothes. Jesse noted the two Nevica ski suits. Either Barret was a good skier or he liked to impress people with the standard of his equipment. He wondered for a moment at the absence of boots and skis, then remembered that the Harbor asked patrons to leave them on the ground floor, in the equipment rooms. There was a denim jacket hanging in the closet and a couple of shirts. A pair of Topsider loafers stood toe to toe with a pair of moccasins on the floor of the closet. Jesse grinned wryly at the yachtsman's shoes. Not a lot of sailing done in Arizona, he thought. Maybe Barret really thought the Harbor Hotel was built on a harbor.

The quiet humor of place names in Steamboat Springs had always amused Jesse. The early trappers and mountain men, hearing the chugging sounds made by the sulphur hot springs that dotted the area, had been convinced that the valley was haunted by some phantom steamboat. Hence the name. In keeping with the nautical theme, the Harbor Hotel had sprung up, then other establishments like the Tugboat and even the Steamboat Yacht Club had followed.

The Yacht Club, at least, could boast a river frontage, being built right on the edge of the Yampa River where it ran through the town. The fact that the river was, at that point, no more than twenty or thirty feet wide meant any yachts trying to dock there would suffer a pretty damn tight squeeze.

Jesse sat on the edge of the bed, surrounded by the dead man's simple belongings. The small clutter that seems to surround every skier was evident in the room: goggles hooked over the coathanger behind the door, ski gloves on the small table that held the ice bucket and tray. A pair of discarded ski socks that had been peeled off and kicked under the armchair. He'd hoped that there might be something, anything, that might give him a lead on Andrew Barret.

He always had that same hope when he went through a victim's room. He seldom found anything.

He rose and went into the small ensuite bathroom. Usually, if he found anything, this was where it was. That's why he'd left the bathroom until last.

There was no external window. He flicked the light switch up and was greeted by the subdued clatter of an exhaust fan coming on simultaneously with the light. He frowned slightly. The Harbor wasn't burning up any power bills with its bathroom lights.

"You could cut your throat shaving in here," he muttered, opening the small, mirror-doored cabinet set above the washbasin.

No drugs. No syringes. No empty glassine bags. Just toothpaste—Colgate—a toothbrush and a bottle of plain saline. He looked at the small shelf beside the basin. There was a contact lens container there, alongside a plug-in sterilizer.

The plastic shower curtain was closed. He pulled it back. Nothing there but a bottle of anti-dandruff shampoo on the soap dish. He opened it and sniffed it. It smelled pretty much the way he'd expect anti-dandruff shampoo to smell. He shrugged, put it back.

He looked under the fresh face cleaner and hand towel that the maid service had left the morning before. Nothing there.

Stepping to the toilet, he lifted the heavy porcelain lid of the cistern and looked inside. No suspicious articles left there in one of the most common of all hotel room hiding places. Nothing but water and the flushing mechanism of the cistern.

"Nothing nowhere," he said softly, going out and turning off the light and the fan behind him. "Nothing everywhere."

He sat down again, looking around the room. Looking at the forlorn evidence of occupation. Andy Barret had gone out, expecting to come back and pick up those ski socks under the chair, so he could put them in the plastic laundry bag that Jesse had seen in the suitcase.

He'd planned to finish that paperback as well, and maybe watch a little HBO before he fell asleep. And if he had something of an asthma attack, maybe brought on by the altitude here in Colorado, why he'd planned for that too. There was his inhaler, all ready for him to use it.

Only somehow, for some reason, his plans didn't work out. Someone got right in the way of them, with a savage, razor sharp, ten-inch spike in a spring-loaded handle. Someone had fired that spike up into Andy's brain and killed him deader than all hell.

Jesse squeezed his jaw between his gloved finger and thumb, rubbing thoughtfully at the slight stubble there.

"The question is, Andy, why did someone want to go and do that to you?" he asked the room at large.

But the room at large wasn't talking.

FIFTEEN

*S*itting back in the chair, he laughed quietly, the sound of his laughter masked by the constant hum of the high-speed cable driving above him. The Storm Peak Express was whipping him up the mountain at high speed. On a day like today, with the wind blowing around thirty miles an hour and snow whipping in to all but white out the top of the mountain, he'd known there'd be no lines for the lifts.

He glanced at the chair ahead of him. There was one occupant, difficult to see with the perspex hood of the chair lowered. He or she was nothing more than a vague shape huddled in the shelter of the plastic bubble against the cold. With the snow and the condensation on the bubble, it was even difficult to make out the color of the person's clothing.

He checked quickly over his shoulder, setting the chair swinging as he turned. The chair directly behind was empty. He'd assumed it would be, as there'd been nobody close behind him in the lift line. Two chairs back, he could make out two shapes but the blowing snow concealed any details. They'd be too far away to see what was going on, he thought.

The chair clattered as the drive cable ran over one of the pylons. The brief vibration stirred the huddled figure beside him, leaning into the far corner of the chair. Amusing, he thought as they sat together, how people strived to maintain their personal space. He shifted his skis on the footrest and sighed contentedly. Below him, the snow-drifted path that had been cut through the trees was virtually deserted. Only the occasional skier was coming down.

The chair was passing the Four Points Hut now, coming into the last section of its run. He leaned forward expectantly, looking through the mist and snow of the whiteout conditions. He scanned the upper expanse of Storm Peak, looking for the most likely path to take down.

As he'd thought, it would be a left turn at the top of the chair, then into the trees of the Triangle 3 run. Triangle 3 was a black diamond run, steep-pitched and heavily studded with moguls—the regular bumps in the snow, sometimes three or four feet in height, caused by the constant passage of skiers down a slope. As they turned, following the fall line, they cut a path in the snow. The *twisting, turning action threw piles of snow up on either side, creating the bumps. The more skiers came down the same path, the larger the bumps grew.*

He knew that only a good skier—a very good skier—would follow him into the trees on Triangle 3. Only an excellent skier would have any chance of catching him—even if he could see him in these conditions. He grinned to himself inside the turtleneck collar that was pulled up to his goggles, then turned to the figure beside him.

"Okay if we put up the footrest?" he asked politely. There was no answer, so he removed his skis from the rest and swiveled the metal frame up, taking the plastic bubble with it. The wind swirled in on the now unprotected chair.

It was normal to ask, even though the other man wasn't using the footrest. His legs hung down below the chair, the yellow Volkel carving skis swinging lightly in the wind and with the motion of the chair itself. They were the latest models, he noticed, almost six feet in length. They were a tough ski for a mediocre skier to handle, he knew. His companion on the chair had obviously been very good.

Until he'd died, just three minutes ago.

It had all been so easy. The other man—Harry, his name had been—was waiting at the gate to ski forward and load onto the chairlift as Murphy arrived, skiing quickly forward at the last minute to join him, and making sure nobody else was around to make up a threesome on the chairlift.

They'd nodded hello, as people on chairlifts do, then Harry had slumped into a corner of the chair. As the bubble and the footrest had come down, Murphy had pretended to be caught under the support and, at the last moment, slid to the right to be one space away from his companion on the four seater chairlift.

"Name's Ed," he'd said cheerfully, pulling down the turtleneck to speak more clearly and let his companion see his friendly, disarming grin. "Ed Montrose," he'd added.

There was no sense in using the name he was actually passing under, just in case things didn't go so well with Harry here. Just in case he somehow survived.

Harry had nodded, not too interested in conversation. "Harry Powell," he'd said briefly, then looked away to discourage further chat.

"Not too many out today," Murphy had continued cheerfully. Harry had merely grunted assent. He'd looked across at Murphy for a moment. Murphy was fussing around the zipper of his gray parka, his heavy ski gloves making it difficult to find the tag. He'd looked up at Harry Powell, grinned again and held out his ski poles to him.

"*Mind hanging onto these for a moment?*" *he'd asked with the certain knowledge that Harry wouldn't refuse. Powell had sighed, almost inaudibly. Murphy knew how annoying it could be when complete strangers on a chairlift couldn't manage their own equipment and asked for help. Hold this. Hold that. Could you hand me that for a moment? Good skiers could manage their own odds and ends. While very few people ever refused such a request, he knew it made the requester look inefficient, unorganized.*

And unthreatening.

Powell's gloved hand had closed over the two stocks. Murphy had now managed to wrestle open the zipper on his parka. His left hand had closed over the hard cylinder inside, tucked into his belt. He'd felt with one thumb to make sure the cocking handle wasn't back. The last thing he wanted was to snag the trigger in his clothing and fire a ten-inch spike into his own groin. Satisfied, he had withdrawn the black metal cylinder from his parka. Holding it in his left hand, he'd reached with his right for the ski poles.

"*Thanks,*" *he'd said.* "*I'll take those now.*" *He'd made sure he had a firm grip on the poles, then, with a deftness that was a little out of character with his former apparent confusion, had tucked them quickly under one thigh and out of the way.*

Powell had stared with mild curiosity at the jigger. "*What you got there?*" *he'd asked.*

"*Safety flare,*" *Murphy had said easily.* "*Always carry one in these conditions.*"

He'd racked the cocking handle back with a heavy double click, then held the cylinder toward Powell, as if offering it to him.

"*Take a look,*" *he'd said.*

Powell had recoiled a little into the corner of the chair. The mouth of the so-called flare was pointing directly at him and, it appeared to him, the other man had just loaded it.

"*Don't point that damn thing at me!*" *he'd said a little angrily.* "*Didn't you just prime it or something?*"

Murphy had laughed easily. "*Hell, no!*" *he'd said.* "*That was just the safety. I was making sure it was on! See?*"

Again, he'd thrust the cylinder toward Powell. Still a little wary, but not so angry now, Powell had leaned toward him to inspect it. As he made the movement, Murphy had suddenly thrust forward at him, ramming the end of the cylinder under his left arm and into the left side of his upper body.

There had been a ringing metallic crack as he'd released the trigger and the razor sharp spike had shot out of the tip of the jigger. It had slashed easily through the thick clothing Powell wore, then savaged the flesh itself, sliding upward between the ribs, as Murphy had angled it, piercing the heart itself, rupturing the papillary muscle, tearing through the left ventricle and all but destroying the right atrium and aortic valve on the way out.

Powell's jaw had dropped open. He'd tried to scream but could only make a choked, whimpering sound as he'd felt the searing pain in his chest just before he died.

Murphy had dragged the spike clear, hurriedly slamming the cocking handle back in a move that he'd practiced hundreds of times, in case Powell wasn't dead.

The shocked, rapidly glazing eyes had told him there was no need for a second strike. Casually, he'd pressed the trigger again, allowing the bloodstained spike to slam out from inside the handle. He'd leaned across and wiped the blood on the sleeve of Powell's parka, then, making sure the firing spring was in the detached setting, he'd brought back the cocking lever again, withdrawing the spike into the handle of the jigger.

He'd checked that there was no blood on the outside of the jigger. Powell's outer clothing had effectively protected it from any sudden discharge. Then he'd tucked the weapon away inside his own parka once more, and closed the zipper.

The chair shook as it clattered past a pylon and Powell sank a little deeper into the corner. Murphy winked at him, then pulled the turtleneck up again.

"Cheer up," he said, "you'll be famous tomorrow."

Clive Wallace was warm and comfortable inside the hut at the top of the Storm Peak chair. He'd glanced out at the unloading ramp a few minutes ago. There was a little soft snow building up there. He guessed that in another five minutes or so, he'd have to go out and shovel some of it clear, packing down the rest with blows from the flat of the shovel. For now, however, he was content to huddle over the electric radiant heater, peering through the large windows in front of him at the nonstop sequence of chairs passing him by and heading round the bullwheel and back down the mountain again.

"Oh, shit!"

He said it aloud. There was no one in the hut to hear him but he said it aloud anyway. Just when his feet were finally warming up, some dumb bunny tourist had missed the unload point. He had a vague impression of one skier in a gray jacket skiing off the chair while the other passenger remained firmly and determinedly unmoving.

As the chair started around the bullwheel, Clive's hand shot to the big red kill button beside him. He hit it, sounding the alarm bell briefly and bringing the chairlift sighing to a halt.

The figure in the chair was now eight feet or so from the ground. There was no way he could unload from there, Clive realized. He'd have to back the chair up, bringing the delinquent rider back to the unload ramp.

"Shit!" he said again, reaching for the door handle. As he cracked the door open, the wind shrilled in around him and the telephone linking him to the down mountain loading station rang once. He scooped the receiver up. Before Louis at the base station could ask the obvious question, Clive let him know what was going on.

"Got a skier tried to ride the chair around," he said, raising his voice against the intrusive wind. "We'll have to back her up a few yards."

Louis answered him. "Let me know when you're doing it."

Clive nodded, even though the other man couldn't see him. "Be as quick as I can," he answered, then hung the phone on its hook and stepped out into the wind and the snow.

He glanced around idly to see if the skier's companion was waiting for him. There were a couple of skiers nearby, their attention drawn by the alarm bell. But on a day like this people didn't stand around at the top of the chair. They skied or they went into one of the bars. He checked but none of them was wearing a gray parka. Dumb choice of color anyway, thought Clive. In this weather, a gray parka would blend into the background and the whiteout conditions to make its owner all but invisible.

In Clive's mind, the more visible you were on the mountain, the less chance you had of some hotshot running into you.

He slipped and slid through the snow to stand directly under the chair.

"Hey, buddy," he called. "You cannot ride the chair down!"

He spoke precisely, sounding every syllable. The guy was rugged up and the wind was blowing. It didn't make for perfect conversational conditions.

"You hear me?" he tried again. But there was no movement from the man in the chair. Clive peered more closely at him. He was slumped over in one corner. His head lolled to one side.

"Hey, buddy. You okay?" he yelled, but there was no response and suddenly Clive knew that no, he definitely wasn't okay. He turned and started to run back to the cabin, slipping and falling to his knees in the snow.

He scrambled into the cabin, grabbed the phone and punched zero. Immediately, a woman's voice answered. "Ski patrol."

"This is the top of Storm Peak Express!" Clive babbled urgently. "Get a paramedic team over here right away. We've got a guy who has had a heart attack on the chair."

The woman's voice, by contrast to Clive's, was calm and matter-of-fact.

"Heart attack, top of Storm Peak," she repeated, punching the details into the computer in front of her. "You want we should alert the Medevac chopper as well?"

There was a slight pause as Clive peered out through the windows at the unmoving figure on the chair. "I think you better," he said. "This guy doesn't look good."

SIXTEEN

'd say we've got a dyed-in-the-wool serial killer on our hands," said Jesse quietly.

Lee was back in Ned Puckett's office for the second time in as many days. This time Jesse was with her. He was standing, leaning against a filing cabinet while Lee, Ned himself and Felix Obermeyer, Chief of the Town Police, were seated around Ned's desk.

"Now then, Jesse," said Ned. "Let's not go jumping to conclusions here. Those aren't the sort of words we want bandied around where the press can hear them."

"The press have already said them," replied Felix gloomily. He was a thin, short man. What remained of his dark hair was slicked back over the crown of his head and hung long over his collar. The uniform issue gunbelt and handcuff pouch seemed overlarge on his small frame. He reminded Lee of a cross between a dyspeptic squirrel and Josef Goebbels. She wasn't overfond of him but admitted that he was a good administrator.

And he was right. The press was already using those two words to describe events in Steamboat Springs.

Jesse pushed himself upright from his leaning position at the rear of the room, against one of Ned's filing cabinets. He ran a hand through the curly brown hair that always made him seem five or ten years younger than he was.

"Not saying it won't make it go away, Ned," he said simply.

Puckett raised his hands helplessly to indicate that he appreciated the point. Yet he was reluctant to admit it. "I know that, Jess," he said. "It's just that stuff like that coming from us is liable to panic people."

"How do you suggest we describe it then, Ned?" Lee asked.

Before he could answer, Jesse had spoken again. "I mean, one killing is unfortunate. Two can look downright careless. But once you get to three, there's nothing for it but to suppose we've got a serial killer."

Ned nodded, his eyes on the unmarked blotter in front of him, accepting the inevitable. He took a couple of deep breaths.

"Lee, are you sure you guys can handle this? Maybe we should be looking for some outside help," he said.

Lee shrugged. "We've already requested it."

Ned looked at her sharply as she said it, a question in his look. Jesse stepped in and answered it for her.

"FBI," he said succinctly. Ned switched his gaze to the tall deputy. "Is there a federal angle in this?" he asked.

Jesse pursed his lips and shook his head in the negative. "Not so far," he replied. "But the FBI are always available for cases like this."

"I didn't know that," said Ned. "I thought you couldn't call in the Feebies until someone had crossed a state line, something like that."

"They'll advise," Jesse reiterated. "They keep files on serial killers and they've got a lot more computer power than we have. We'll send them details and they'll trawl through their records to see if anything matches. We'll keep doing the groundwork here."

Felix frowned. "So they're not actually sending anyone down?"

Lee shook her head. "Not at this stage. It's not their jurisdiction, after all. As Jesse says, for now, they'll keep a watching brief and see if they can give us any leads from former cases. Of course, if we find a link, they'll send in a task force if we want it."

Ned scowled. "Won't have any trouble finding somewhere to put them up." Just about every hotel in town is having cancellations—and in the busiest part of the season too. Managers are screaming. This is the worst season we've had since the gas main blew, back in '94."

The gas main in Yampa Street had exploded in 1994. The explosion hadn't harmed anyone directly, but it knocked out heating to more than half the town. Skiers canceled in large numbers while hotels and guesthouses desperately tried to find alternative accommodations. There was a flow-on effect to restaurants, bars, ski rental outlets and the mountain itself. Businesses in Steamboat went broke right and left.

"Tell them we're doing our damnedest to get this thing wrapped up," Lee replied.

"Have you got anything new? Any ideas at all?" Ned asked them. He was almost pleading, Lee thought. She tried to make a negative answer sound better than it was. "Jesse's going through the background of all three victims, looking for some common link," she began. "Don't know if something's going to show up or not yet, Ned."

The mayor looked from one to the other. He'd hoped for more concrete news, Jesse knew. City officials always did.

"Meantime, we're putting in some new rules on the mountain, Ned," he told him. "Should make folks feel more secure." He looked at Felix. "Though we might ask for some manpower from you to help out, Felix."

Lee hid a smile. There was no way Felix could object to the request now that it had been made in front of the mayor. It occurred to her that Jesse could be an astute operator when it came to small town politics.

"Sure thing, Jesse," Felix said.

If he was a trifle thin lipped about it, Jesse didn't seem to notice.

"What have you got in mind?" Ned asked.

"We're going to put a ski patroller at the top of each lift to keep an eye on things," he said.

"Thought that was the lift attendants' job," Ned said.

Jesse shook his head. "Lift attendant is there to keep an eye on the lift. That's what went wrong with the last killing. The attendant was so busy watching the guy he thought was a go-round, he missed the killer skiing off."

"So," Felix said slowly. "The patrolmen will watch the passengers— who gets off, where they're headed and such?"

"That's right," Jesse said and he saw the police chief purse his lips.

"Can't say I like the idea, Jesse," he said. "The patrollers are civilians. Last thing we want is one of them trying to tackle a killer."

Jesse nodded. "I agree," he said. "That's where your men come in, Felix. We want to station half a dozen of them on the mountain at the main choke points. Give them Ski-Doos and put them on the ski patrol radio net. That way if our guys see someone, they can trail him and call in your cops to make the collar."

The police chief nodded. The idea made sense.

"It might also make people feel a little more secure on the lifts," Jesse added. Ned Puckett looked up quickly.

"You're going publicize this?" he said. "That might scare the killer off, mightn't it?"

"If we scare him off," Lee put in, "he might stop killing people."
Ned nodded hastily. "You're right," he said. "I didn't think of that."

"And in the meantime, we'll keep plugging away, waiting for something to break," Jesse said.

"Jesus," said Ned Puckett heavily, his shoulders slumped. "Can't we be a little more . . . proactive than that?" Proactive was a favorite expression of his.

"We're working it all we can, Ned," Lee said, trying to sound optimistic. Ned looked up at her, his blue eyes, red-rimmed from too much worry and not enough sleep, met her steady gray ones.

"Work it harder, Lee," he said wearily. "Work it harder."

Jesse had appropriated a small conference room in the Public Safety Building to use as an office. His main reason wasn't the extra space provided, but the two walls covered in whiteboards on either side of the conference table.

His scrawled writing covered one of the two boards now. He leaned back in a chair, tipped back on its hind legs, his worn old boots planted firmly on the tabletop. Idly, he tapped the end of a black marker pen on his front teeth as he reviewed what he had so far.

He'd listed all the known facts about the three murder victims on the board, circling each individual fact and, where there seemed to be some possible correlation, linking them with a different colored line.

Names, credit cards and hometowns were all listed. Marital status was next. Alexander Howell and Andrew Barret were both divorced. Powell broke the pattern, however. He had never been married.

According to the local police in his hometown, he was a loner. Didn't seem to have any regular girlfriends. Didn't seem to have any girlfriends at all, as a matter of fact. Jesse had scribbled "gay?" on the board, and looped a long, green connecting line to Harry Powell's name.

Maybe he was. Maybe he wasn't. It didn't seem like much of a reason for him to be murdered on the Storm Peak Express.

The first two victims had come from Minnesota and Arizona, respectively. Powell's hometown was in North Carolina. There seemed no connection there. Jesse had checked on the three men's college backgrounds. Again, the three were widely scattered. Powell had remained in North Carolina during his college years. Barret had completed three years in a California college before flunking out. Howell had been educated in Michigan.

Nothing about the three men seemed to match. Howell was a dentist. Barret a car salesman. Powell's occupation was listed as "marketing consultant," which could mean he was an advertising whiz or that he sold Amway door-to-door. Their ages were spread as well. The dentist was in his mid-forties. The car salesman was thirty-three and the consultant thirty-eight.

About the only thing they seemed to have in common was the fact that they were all male.

"Maybe he's a man hater," Jesse murmured to himself.

The conference door swung open and Lee stepped in.

"Working late?" she asked. Jesse glanced down at his wristwatch. He was surprised to see that it was after nine.

"I guess time flies when you're having fun, just the way they say," he replied with a wry grin. The conference room was set in the middle of the building with no exterior walls and, consequently, no windows. Jesse gestured at the whiteboard-covered walls around him.

"Hard to keep track of the time when you can't see the light outside," he said. Lee nodded, hooked a chair toward her and straddled it backward, gazing at his scribblings on the whiteboard. "Is that how they handle an investigation like this in Denver?" she asked.

"It's how I do it," Jesse replied. "Lets me look at all the facts of a case at once, see if there's any relationship, any connection between the victims. Sometimes even the simplest fact can be a link," he explained.

"And?" Lee asked.

Jesse shrugged. "So far, the only thing I can see is that they're all male. That could be too simple a link." He let go a long breath. "Maybe our killer is an anti-divorce activist who also hates gays," he said. "But I get the feeling that our facts to back that up are a little thin. Other than those few facts, there seems to be nothing that these men have in common."

"Except that they were all murdered here," Lee observed.

She felt Jesse's gaze switch quickly to her. She looked at him defensively.

"What?" she asked.

He was tapping his teeth with the marker pen again. "I was just thinking," he said, "I missed that rather obvious link."

He swung his long legs down from the table, allowing his chair to thud back into an upright position, and moved to the whiteboard. In large script, he wrote: *died Stmboat,* circled the note and drew green link lines to the three names.

"That's pretty obvious," Lee said mildly. "After all, it's why we're here."

"True," Jesse admitted, staring thoughtfully at his recent addition to the board. "Just occurs to me I've been looking so hard at where and how they lived to find some connection, I've been neglecting to think about where and how they died. That could be all the connection we need."

Lee shook her head doubtfully. "I don't get it."

Jesse turned and grinned at her suddenly, the thoughtful frown disappearing from his face like morning mist when the sun breaks through. "Neither do I, yet," he said. "That's the fun of it all."

Lee gestured one thumb at the door behind her. "Well, no matter, it's time to pack it in for now."

Jesse yawned, stretched and carefully put the marker pen in the narrow tray under the whiteboard. "Man, am I hungry!"

Lee smiled, glanced around the room. There was plenty of evidence that a whole bunch of coffee drinking had gone on in here. None at all of any eating. She knew that Jesse hadn't set foot outside the room since they'd returned from the meeting in Ned's office that morning.

"You remember to have lunch?" she asked dryly.

Jesse thought about it for a few seconds, then, with that slow smile breaking out over his face again, he replied, "No. As a matter of fact, I don't believe I did. Could be that explains these strange gnawing pains in my inner self."

Lee shook her head in mock sorrow. "Planning on having any supper?" she asked.

"Guess I'll catch something at the Old Town," Jesse said. "Then head out back to my place."

The Old Town was the Old Town Saloon on Lincoln Avenue. Lee had a pretty good idea what sort of meal Jesse was planning on catching.

"Jess," she said gently, "you can't spend your life eating nothing but burgers and fries, you know."

Her deputy smiled faintly at her concern. "Well now, that's not all I eat, Lee," he said. "Just the other night I had myself a chili dog and a whole plate of nachos."

"Why don't you come back to my place while I fix you a proper meal? We could talk over old times a little as well. Haven't done that in a long time." Lee saw the hesitation. It had been like this since Jesse had come back. He was friendly but somehow distant. He never allowed situations where someone might get too close anymore. She could see the polite refusal forming on his lips.

Then, unexpectedly, he said, "Why thanks, Lee. I think I'd like that."

He grinned at her again and, this time, she laughed out loud. "Well, damn me if you don't keep a woman guessing, Jess Parker," she said. "I was sure as hell you were going to say no."

His grin faded to a quizzical shadow of its former self. He nodded. "Funny thing, right up until I said yes, I thought so too."

They left the conference room with its scribbled-on whiteboards. A note pinned to the door warned the cleaning staff not to touch anything inside. Lee snapped off the lights as they exited, the door locking automatically behind them.

Outside it was snowing heavily. The big, fat flakes tumbled down through the area lighting of the parking lot. There was a good six inches of fresh snow underfoot on the tarmac surface. Jesse stopped, leaned back and let the flakes drop on his upturned face.

"Looks like we're in for a big one," he said quietly.

Lee, looking at the sky as well, nodded her head in agreement.

"Forecast says so," she said. "That should put a smile on Tad Kaminski's face."

They both grinned. The mountain manager went through three kinds of hell every season dealing with the vagaries of winter weather. A ski resort needs snow. And a resort like Steamboat Springs needs lots of it. Lots of fresh snow. Lots of fresh powder. It goes with the reputation.

"Let's hope it keeps our killer indoors for a few days." Jesse shivered briefly as a few flakes penetrated his collar, melting instantly into freezing water, and turned away to his battered Subaru wagon, parked behind Lee's Renegade.

SEVENTEEN

"Y ou hear much from Abby these days?" Lee said.

They'd finished eating and were still working on the bottle of red wine Jesse had picked up on the way to Lee's small house.

"Not a whole lot," he said. His own tone was measured, unemotional. He wasn't giving anything away, she thought. "Occasionally she'll drop me a line—you know, birthdays and such. But no, I can't say we're regular correspondents."

Lee glanced up at him. "You ever write to her?" she asked.

Jesse took a sip of his wine before he answered.

"Can't say I do." Jesse noticed that Lee's glass was empty and leaned over to refill it.

"Thanks," she said. Then, deciding she might as well go for broke now she'd brought the subject up, added, "You miss her at all?"

Jesse raised an eyebrow. "What's this, Lee? Do you check up on the personal life of all your deputies? Is that part of a sheriff's job?"

She flushed slightly. "No, goddamit!" she snapped at him. "I'm asking the question as a friend. That's what we are, Jesse. Friends. Remember?"

There was an awkward silence as Jesse realized he'd overreacted. In a much milder tone, he said, "Sorry, Lee. I guess I'm just not used to talking about my personal life a whole lot."

"You're telling me," she said, with a wan smile. "Jess, since you came back here, you've been so damn closemouthed about yourself you make a rock look talkative. You can't keep things bottled up like that."

Jesse shrugged moodily. "Don't see how talking about things is going to make them much better."

She laid a hand gently on one of his. "That's not how you used to feel," she said. "Time was, we used to talk all the time about our troubles."

"Our troubles?" he corrected her with the faintest hint of a smile. "Seems to me all we ever talked about were my troubles."

Lee shrugged, trying to lighten the moment a little. "Well hell, I knew if I'd had any troubles, you would have been just happy as a clam to talk about them too." His smile widened a little. Just a little. Encouraged, she persisted. "Come on, Jess. You know it can help to talk things through."

"Talking doesn't change anything," he said evenly. She considered this for a moment, then nodded agreement.

"True. But it can make things more bearable. Least of all, that's what I thought when we used to talk. I thought I was maybe helping you a little."

His steady brown eyes locked on hers for a long moment.

"You helped, Lee," he said quietly. "You helped a whole lot."

"Well, then?" she said. He was silent, watching her but she sensed he was on the brink of talking, and didn't know whether to prompt him further or let him decide for himself.

Finally, the pause was just too long for her.

"Jesse, we've known each other all our lives, and I'm here to tell you that the Jesse Parker who's been skulking around this town for the past two years is not the Jesse Parker I'd got used to."

Again, the faint hint of a smile touched the corners of his mouth. She thought how much it gave him a lost little boy look.

"That what I've been doing?" he asked. "Skulking?"

She shrugged, smiling in her turn. "Something pretty close to it," she replied. He let go a long pent-up breath.

"Could be you're right at that," he said thoughtfully.

"So?" she prompted and he shifted in his seat, crossing his long legs to make himself more comfortable. For a moment, he hesitated, not sure where to start. Then he shrugged.

"Hell, Lee, you know most of it. I was a cop. Abby was a reporter with Channel 10 down in Denver. We met through the job—on the Park Hill case."

"That was a high profile case," Lee put in, and he nodded.

"Lots of media attention, and Abby was part of it. I was the lead investigator and I guess it gave her the wrong perspective on a cop's lifestyle. She realized her mistake when that case was over and I was back to working gang murders and pulling unidentified bodies out of alleys and spending late nights chasing down leads that usually went nowhere."

He shook his head sadly.

"That's how a cop's life goes," Lee said softly.

"Maybe. It's not how a TV celebrity's life goes. Abby had moved from the news to the morning show by then. She had a social life that she claimed was part of her job. Unfortunately my job didn't fit into it. We should have realized from the start that our jobs just weren't compatible."

He paused, swirling the dark red merlot around in his glass, looking down into it. "Neither were we," he added softly.

They sat in silence for several minutes. Lee remembered the period well—the agonized phone calls when Jesse would pour out his soul to her, wondering what had gone wrong with his marriage. She'd known then, as she knew now, that nothing had ever been too right with his marriage. But then, like now, all she could do was listen.

Jesse looked around the kitchen where they'd eaten. Strangely, he felt a little better for having talked about his marriage. The room felt warm and friendly. Kind of easy to be in, he thought.

"Were you planning on making coffee?" he asked, smiling.

Lee pushed her chair back from the table and stretched her long legs in front of her. She met his gaze and smiled, shook her head.

"Nope. I made the dinner," she said. "Pot's right there on the cook-top. Coffee's in the pantry. I take mine black with three sugars."

EIGHTEEN

They moved into the parlor for coffee. Then Jesse went outside and brought in more logs for the fire while Lee dug up another bottle of red.

They sat in silence, staring into the flames. It was a companionable, thoughtful silence. Not unpleasant. Lee was glad they'd finally talked about Abby. She considered whether or not to bring up the case that had led to Jesse's resignation from the Denver PD. Her instincts warned her not to.

When they did talk, it was about the obvious case: the one that had them both working full-time.

"You think we'll get him, Jess?" she asked. Jesse stared into the red-hot heart of the fire for a few seconds and nodded, almost imperceptibly.

"Yep," he said. "We'll get him."

Lee shook her head doubtfully. "We seem no closer now than we were a week ago. Three people dead and not one worthwhile clue. Not one lead. I wish I could feel as confident as you do."

"We'll get him, Lee," he said. "I don't know why I feel that way but I've just got a feeling about it. I've never had that feeling about a case I couldn't solve. I've always solved a case when I've had the feeling." He shrugged. "I'm psychic. Go figure."

Again they sat in silence. Then to her surprise, he said softly, "I never had this feeling about the Wheat Ridge case, that's for sure."

She looked at him quickly. The Wheat Ridge case was the last one Jesse had worked on in Denver. The one that had gone so horrifically wrong for him. It was the first time in two years that he had ever made mention of it. She didn't know how to reply, settled for silence. In a few seconds, he continued.

"You know about it, don't you, Lee?"

She shrugged. "I know some," she admitted. "The bare facts only. Chief Douglas told me some of it over the phone. It was a long while back," she added.

"Seeing how you've hired me, maybe it's time you knew a little more," he said.

NINETEEN

There was a long silence in the small kitchen when Jesse finished. Outside, Lee heard the slithering rush of snow finally overloading the roof and sliding off past the window. Jesse remained unmoving, staring, as he had done throughout the entire telling of the events in Wheat Ridge, into the heart of the fire. Maybe he saw something there that gave him comfort.

At length, Lee said softly, "But you can't be sure you killed him. What did the postmortem show? There must have been a ballistics report that—" She stopped mid-sentence. He was shaking his head. He finally took his eyes from the fire and met her gaze.

"He'd been hit by two 9 mm slugs from the Ingram in the upper torso. They were given as the cause of death," he said simply.

She stared at him in disbelief. "But what about your slug?" she said finally. "If they only mentioned the Ingram slugs, you must have missed him. So you—"

Jesse shook his head. "I hit him. I saw it."

"Then what happened to the slug from your .45?"

"Apparently," Jesse told her, "it was lost somewhere along the way. There was no mention of it."

Lee raised an eyebrow. "Lost?" she repeated, her voice expressionless. "How does evidence like that get lost?"

"Someone tells someone else to lose it. That's what Chief Douglas did. They covered it up. They didn't want an investigation—especially not if it would prove that one of their officers panicked and got himself shot by his partner. Tony's family had suffered enough. He was a good cop and he deserved to be remembered that way. He'd had three commendations for bravery but if this had come out, he'd be remembered as the guy who lost his nerve." He paused and shook his head. "It was cleaner and simpler to say that Tony lost his life in the line of duty, shot by a drug dealer. That's how they put it to me. And I went along with it."

Lee shifted awkwardly in her chair. "I guess you couldn't do any-thing else."

"I guess. Problem is, I can't ever be sure that I went along with it to save Tony's reputation or my own."

"Jesse, you were under fire. Some bastard was shooting at you with a goddamn machine gun, for Christ's sake!"

He smiled at her. A small, sad smile that stopped her mid-sentence.

"Lee, I'm not trying to punish myself with this. I'm stating something that I know in my heart. I killed him. Then I went along with a cover-up."

She went to speak and he stopped her with a raised hand. "It was an accident. He shouldn't have moved. He panicked. I know all this. But I also know I killed him. And when Chief Douglas, for all the best reasons in the world, made sure that my bullet disappeared, he left me with that knowledge, all on my own."

They looked at each other for a long, long moment.

She moved toward him, coming out of her chair, kneeling beside his and taking his hand in hers.

"You know you can't blame yourself for this, Jess," she said simply.

"I know it," he replied. "I've been saying it to myself for about two years. It's kind of nice to hear someone else say it to me." He paused, then added, "Someone I trust."

She nodded. She guessed he'd needed this. Needed to purge himself of the two years of guilt that he felt from concealing what he believed to be the truth.

"This is why you left the Denver PD?" she asked.

"Couldn't go on there, Lee, knowing what I knew, with the guys in the squad room all determined to believe otherwise. Nobody would talk about it. Nobody wanted to know the truth. They didn't blame me. In a way I would have preferred it if they had."

She stood and moved to the window. The snow was still falling heavily outside. Her Renegade was parked under the lean-to at the front of her yard. His Subaru was an indistinct shape under a mound of thick, fresh whiteness.

"Hell, Lee," he said, moving to stand beside her and stare out the window. "I've been wanting to tell someone about that night for the past two years!"

The glass windowpanes were old and uneven. She could see his reflection, wavy and slightly distorted by the irregularities in the glass. Lee said, "I've been here."

He let go a long, deep breath. In effect, he'd been holding that breath for over two years, she thought. Then he said, "I'm glad you were, Lee. I'm glad it was you."

She turned to face him. "That old Subaru of yours is near buried out there, Jess," she hesitated, then concluded, "Stay the night."

He looked into those gray eyes, eyes he'd known all his life. Suddenly, he was remembering her that one time—beside his pickup, outside the school dance, with one breast bared to the cool night. If he stayed, it wasn't going to be because his car was snowed in and she had to know that. He took another deep breath.

"Lee . . ." he began, then stopped. The steady, gray eyes held his.

He felt strangely short of breath. She was waiting for him to say whatever it was he'd begun to say. He paused, said again, "Lee—"

The phone rang.

He saw the momentary flicker of annoyance in her eyes, then she turned away to the phone with a gesture of apology, grabbed it out of its cradle.

"Sheriff Torrens," she said briefly. Jesse heard the thin crackle of the voice at the other end of the line. Then Lee asked briefly, "Where?" She pulled a memo block close to her and gestured for him to pass her a cheap ballpoint pen from the kitchen bench. He did so and she wrote quickly on the top sheet, tearing it off and shoving it into her shirt pocket. "Any other damage?" she asked. Again, the tinny voice babbled at her for a few seconds. She nodded. "I'll be out there directly." She put the phone down, looked up and saw him watching her, a question in his eyes.

"Another break-in," she said briefly, "out at the 7-Eleven by the US 40 turnoff."

She'd been sitting in her socks as they'd talked. Now she was pulling her boots on again.

"I thought Tom was investigating those break-ins?" Jesse said.

"He is. But he's gone the other way, out past Sky Valley Lodge. There's been some trouble with vandals out there lately and Tom's camping out in their warming hut to keep an eye on things for the night."

She had her boots on. She stamped them down once or twice. Her gunbelt was on its peg just inside the back door. She swung it on in that one economical movement she'd perfected years ago, took her jacket as Jesse handed it to her, slid her arms into the sleeves and zipped up the front. She slapped her pockets, just to make sure she had her keys, then stopped and looked at him.

"You be here when I get back?" she asked.

He hesitated for a second. The moment was gone. "Maybe I should head for home," he said. "That old clunker of mine should make it if the snow doesn't get too much deeper."

He unhooked his old green service-issue anorak from inside the back door and shrugged into it, cramming the Cubs cap down over his eyes. They stepped out into the snowy night. Lee pulled the door closed behind them, maybe just a little harder than she really needed to. Jesse hesitated, hands crammed in his jacket pockets. He looked up, met her gaze for a few seconds, then said in a low voice, "Thanks, Lee. I'm glad it was you."

Abruptly, as if he were afraid to say more, he turned and trudged through the calf-deep snow to the Subaru. She stood by her Renegade, in the shelter of the lean-to, and watched as he knocked a shower of snow off the windshield with one forearm, unlocked the little wagon and climbed in.

The starter ground slowly a couple of times. Then the worn old engine fired and clattered to life. He swung the little four-wheel drive wagon around in her front yard, then bumped down over the curb and onto the road. The wheels spun as he fed in too much power for a second, but he backed off the gas and they gained traction, biting through the soft snow and finding the tar surface underneath. She watched the mismatched red taillights as they receded.

The grinding sound of the Subaru's engine was lost in the blanket of falling snow.

Lee wrenched open the door of the Renegade and got in, angry as all hell.

"I catch whoever's doing these break-ins," she promised herself. "I'm going to shoot the motherfucker."

TWENTY

*H*e sat at one of the window tables in the book and coffee shop between Lincoln and Yampa, the pages of the Steamboat Whistle open in front of him. The skies had cleared temporarily, and Steamboat Springs was enjoying a few unseasonal hours of sunshine. It would be short-lived, as another storm front was heading in from the coast and was due to hit the Rockies the following day.

Of course, the wind still blew eddies of snow from the sidewalk with it and kept the temperature down around freezing. But here, with the sun streaming in the windows and a cup of good, hot espresso close to hand, you could luxuriate in the warmth and well-being that the sun brought with it.

He frowned slightly as he read the article that had caught his eye. INCREASED SECURITY ON MOUNTAIN, the headline read.

Underneath it, and leading into the article detailing the new security arrangements put in place for chairlifts and gondolas, was a photograph of a dark-haired man in casual civilian clothes. The caption identified him. "Deputy Jesse Parker, former homicide detective in Denver, now assisting the local sheriff's office."

Parker had plenty to say—most of it with the obvious aim of calming the fears of visitors to Steamboat Springs. New security arrangements on the mountain, the story continued, would prevent a repeat of the previous killings. From now on, no two people would be allowed to travel together on the chairlifts or in gondolas, unless they already knew each other. But for strangers, the permissible numbers would be three, four or one.

He smiled grimly. Be just your luck, deputy, if I had an accomplice. That'd spoil your game, wouldn't it?

A further subheading caught his attention: FBI BRINGS SIGHTS TO BEAR ON INVESTIGATION. Parker went on to explain how the resources of the FBI were at the beck and call of the Routt County Sheriff's Department. The FBI, he said, had enormous experience in serial killings like these. Reading the text, there was precious little else that the FBI had brought to the investigation. Still, he reasoned, it was keeping The Silver Bullet Murders in the media, and that was all to the good.

He scanned quickly through the article, making sure there was no concrete progress being reported. Then he set the paper aside and reached for the Denver Post, to see if the same article had been taken up by the city newspaper.

It had. He found it on page four, with a smaller, more closely cropped photo of Parker at the head of the article. The headline this time read: SHERIFF'S OFFICE ON TRACK OF SERIAL KILLER, which seemed to indicate that some clue might have been turned up. He read the article hastily but, in essence, it was the same as the local version.

He was interested to read Parker's thoughts on serial killers. He went back over them now: A pattern was always there, he had told the journalist. There was always some form of continuity to link the crimes, a distinguishing mark or signature about murders like these. It was usually caused by a deep-rooted lack of identity in the killer. A need to be seen and recognized—if not personally, then at least in terms of what he had done.

In this case, the link seemed almost certainly to be the bizarre choice of murder instrument. The jigger, Parker had said, was the trademark of the Silver Bullet killer. A little known weapon, virtually unheard of outside of the gang wars in Denver and Aurora several years back, it gave the series of crimes the outlandish or recognizable feature that serial killers seemed to crave.

There were several more paragraphs that dealt with the personal inadequacies and mental shortcomings of serial killers in general. Implicit in the words was a sense of weakness about the killers.

Murphy frowned angrily as he studied the photo of the thin-faced deputy sheriff.

"I'm the expert," it seemed to be saying. "I know what you do and why and how you do it. And I'm going to catch you."

Well, thought Murphy, that's as may be. But perhaps that smug expression might change if things didn't seem quite so cut and dried.

Perhaps it was time to change things up a little.

The forecasted storm front had unexpectedly veered away, swinging south to Nevada and Arizona. Jesse stood by the open window of his small hut and looked across the brilliant expanse of sunlit, snow-covered country below him.

He'd lain awake till one o'clock the previous night, struggling with his thoughts, trying to find a common link somewhere between the three murdered men. Striving for that one minor detail that could open the case up like a flower greeting the sun. It was there some-where. He knew it was. Knew it had to be. And he knew, because of his failure to find it, that he was looking in the wrong places, for the wrong thing.

Finally, just after one, he'd dropped off to sleep. And promptly dreamed that he'd solved the whole thing. Gloomily he remembered the rush of exultation he'd felt when he'd suddenly realized that the three men were all former comrades in the Special Forces in Vietnam and they'd been involved in a heroin-smuggling operation from that country into Steamboat Springs. It all fell neatly into place and he remembered Ned's words of congratulation—and the specially warm feeling that had come over him as Lee had walked up to him, kissed him gently on the lips and said, for him alone to hear, "I always knew that it'd be you."

He frowned at the words she'd used. They didn't fit entirely into the picture that had formed. He wondered why he'd thought about Lee like that. Wondered why he'd felt so damn good about it when he had.

Around about five, he woke, still feeling good about Lee. Then he remembered in a rush that he'd cracked the case.

He actually sat up and was reaching for the phone before he realized that he'd dreamed a variation on the plot of a Mel Gibson movie.

Depressed, he made coffee and sat by the window, waiting for the sun to rise. He didn't trust himself to sleep again, in case this time he dreamed that the three murdered men had conspired to steal a Maltese Falcon and Humphrey Bogart had come back from the dead to kill them.

There was a thought drifting around the back of his mind, just out of reach, tantalizing him. Something Ned had said the previous day had triggered it. He searched back into his memory. It was something about gas mains. The gas main had exploded in '94 and people had lost money.

Gas mains. Gas. Explosions. What was the link? He cudgeled his brain but nothing came.

Main.

Main Street, USA.

Main chance.

Maine. A state in the northeastern United States.

Mainlining. What junkies did when they shot up straight into a vein. Vein rhymes with main. Rhymes with pain.

The rain in Maine stays mainly on the plain. Except there aren't any plains in Maine.

Maine!

That was it. The memory was stirring now. Lee had said they were all killed in Steamboat. There was something about Maine that fit to that thought. Damn! What was it?

Jesse didn't have a computer and now he cursed the fact. There was a case he vaguely remembered. A case in Maine, some years before. He remembered because the Denver PD had been contacted to see if they had any information on a suspect in that case.

He didn't have a computer but there was one in the conference room he'd been using and it was permanently linked to the internet. He reached for the phone, realized there'd be nobody on duty in the office. He could call Lee again but he remembered her frosty reaction last time he'd woken her.

No. To hell with it. He'd drive to town, let himself into the offices and do a Google search. He might as well. He'd never get back to sleep now anyway.

Hurriedly, he began dragging his clothes on.

TWENTY-ONE

Lee woke late. She was bleary-eyed and bad-tempered. It had been after two in the morning before she got away from the scene of the 7-Eleven break-in. That would have made it a late night in anyone's language. But for some reason, she hadn't gone straight home.

She'd meant to, sure enough. She'd climbed into the Renegade, turned the heater up full and headed it back into town. But as she drove, she could see Jesse, standing in the falling snow beside that ridiculous little beat-up car of his, that tired grin creasing his face, shoulders hunched against the cold. He looked so damn . . . vulnerable, like a little boy.

And somewhere along the way she realized she'd driven right through the town and found herself climbing the series of hairpin bends up Rabbit Ear Pass, the tail of the Jeep sliding and mushing around as she went. And, eventually, there she was, pulled over to the side of the road outside Jesse's cabin, wondering should she go on in?

There'd been a slight curl of wood smoke blowing away from the pipe chimney from his wood-burning stove, but no lights showing. Hell, that was no surprise. It was after two-thirty in the morning. She wondered now if she would have gone in had she seen a light on. Wondered what she would have said if she had. Wondered what she would have done.

And then, damn it, she wondered what the hell she was doing, wondering about all these things. Jesse was a friend, for crying out loud. A good friend. An old friend. And that was all there had ever been to it.

Except that once. But they never talked about it and she sure as hell wasn't going to be the one who did it first.

She skipped breakfast. She'd send out for coffee and a doughnut from the Book Store Coffee Shop. The shower cleared her head a little, if not her thinking, and she dressed in a hurry and drove to the Public Safety Building. Jesse's battered little Subaru was in his parking spot when she arrived. In fact every parking spot was filled except her own.

"Good thing it's not an election year," she muttered to herself.

When she reached her office, she was a little surprised to find Jesse waiting for her, a thin sheaf of papers in his hand. There was a bird-dog eagerness about him.

"About time," he said cheerfully. "Where the hell you been?"

She eyed him balefully. "Don't start with me," she warned and he backed off, holding his hands up defensively.

"Okay! Okay!" he said. "Just I thought you'd like to know before I told Ned, is all."

Suddenly he had her full attention. She wondered had she missed something? God knows her brain was still on half-charge after the late night she'd put in.

"Told Ned what?" she asked, and he grinned at her.

"It's Steamboat," he said with devastating simplicity. So devastating that it totally evaded her.

"It's Steamboat?" she repeated, her voice dripping sarcasm. "What, precisely, is Steamboat?"

He was grinning still, obviously enjoying her puzzled reaction. She thought somebody should warn him that grinning was not a good idea with a woman who had been awake until close to five and who was armed.

"The victim," he said. "Steamboat is the victim."

Mayor Ned Puckett leaned forward, elbows on his desk, and frowned in concentration.

"Let me get this straight, Jesse," he said slowly. "You're saying somebody is going around murdering people because he's got some kind of a grudge against Steamboat Springs?"

"I'm saying it's a strong possibility, Ned," Jesse replied. "And the only one we've got so far."

Ned shook his head doubtfully. "It just doesn't make sense," he said.

"It makes sense all right," Lee put in. "It isn't rational and it isn't sane. But it does make sense."

Puckett looked at the two of them. He started to say something, realized he had nothing worthwhile to say and changed his mind.

"Look at it this way, Ned," Jesse began in a reasoning tone. "When you can't see a possible motive or definite link in a case like this, one way to treat it is to look at the results."

"The results, you say?" Ned said thoughtfully. He was still far from convinced on this line of reasoning.

"That's right," Jesse said patiently. "If you can't see what caused the actions, you look at what result they've had—and what possible benefit that could be to anyone."

"Well there's no goddamn benefit to anyone here!" Ned erupted angrily. "People all over town are losing money faster than snow melts on a hot spring day!"

"Exactly!" Lee cut in on him. "Don't you see? That's the result of all this. People in Steamboat Springs are losing money. Now ask who that's going to benefit."

"Well, it's already benefiting the people in Vail and Breckenridge for starters!" Ned replied with some heat. "They're booked to capacity with all the people who've canceled here. But I don't hardly see as how we can blame them for all this."

"Got to admit, though, Ned, it's a great way to take revenge against this town—if you had hold of a grudge."

Again the mayor looked from one to another. He spread his hands helplessly. "A grudge? What kind of a grudge could you have against a town?" he asked angrily.

Jesse shrugged. "Might be our man is a former employee. Someone who was sacked and felt he got a raw deal."

"But . . . to go around . . . killing people because of it? Nobody's that crazy, are they? It just ain't important enough to kill folks over."

Ned was obviously upset, Lee thought. He'd trained himself years ago to eradicate words like "ain't" from his politician's vocabulary.

"On the contrary," Jesse said. "A fellow up in Maine did exactly that five summers back. Been nagging at me since yesterday that there was some kind of connection I was missing."

"You telling me some fellow in Maine went around spiking people with one of these here . . . stabbers or whatever you call them?"

Jesse shook his head. "Not the same MO," he replied, "but similar circumstances. He was fired from one of the marinas. Sort of guy who'll never admit he was in the wrong.

"Two years later he comes back and sets in to burning down vacation houses all over—with their residents still inside."

"Jesus," Ned breathed, horrified at the thought of it. "He must have been crazy."

"Now you're getting the picture, Ned." Lee put in dryly. "Let's figure a guy feels he's got a bad call here. Hates all of us. So he decides to hit us where it hurts."

"Isn't hard to figure where that would be," Jesse said. "That gas main explosion in '94 got plenty of coverage—and so did the fact that folks around here were hurting with the loss of business."

Ned shook his head, beginning to believe that what he was hearing might just be true.

"That's for damn sure," he said. He looked at Jesse thoughtfully. "So, Jess, you think this idea of yours might just make some sense?"

"It's happened before, Ned," Jesse told him. "It's a good bet it could be happening again."

"You don't mean the same feller?" Ned began but Lee cut him off.

"Not the same guy. They caught him. He's still in an asylum. But the idea makes sense the more you look at it. And the more you see how much of a problem it's causing the town."

Ned nodded thoughtfully, pushing the idea around, looking at it from different angles. Lee and Jesse were right. It did make sense. It made as much sense as anything else, he thought. In fact, he amended, there wasn't anything else on the table to consider.

"So," he said, "where do we take it from here?"

Jesse crossed one booted foot over the other, leaned back in the hard chair.

"Hard work time," he replied. "We start going through employment records. See if there's anyone who's been fired in the past few seasons who has any history of violent crime."

Ned rolled his eyes at the thought of the task. "Jesus! That could be hundreds of people! There's sixty, seventy restaurants and bars in this town alone!"

Lee shook her head. "Murders have all been on the mountain," she pointed out. "Maybe that's significant. We'll start with records from mountain staff, ski patrol, ski school. People involved with the mountain itself."

"Expert skiers," Jesse put in. "I figure if this guy is going to take the chance of killing someone on a chairlift and escaping on skis, he must be confident of his own ability. So we'll check them first."

"Then what?" Puckett wanted to know.

"Then," replied Jesse slowly, "we hope we get lucky."

TWENTY-TWO

*S*ince he was twelve years old, he had hated people having authority over him—hated the humiliation in being subservient to someone else's wishes.

Authority was a sham, a lie and a con. It was a sick and evil joke perpetrated by people who had power but had no intention of using that power to help those under them. Authority was supposed to be partnered with responsibility. There was supposed to be a duty of care, an obligation to protect those under your care.

But it never happened that way. He had learned early that those in authority would slide away from the responsibility side of the equation, covering their betrayal with a selection of nice sounding, glib phrases that were no more than excuses for their treachery.

His father was the first of many to betray him.

He was a wealthy man, but his wealth wasn't due to any effort or ability on his part. His own father had left him a successful chain of clothing stores that spread across four states. As time passed, this inherited success became an affront to his own ability and worth—possibly because he failed to grow the chain any further. The repeated attempts he made were failures and he dealt with failure in his own way. He punished his son for it.

Aged twelve, Matthew, as he was then called, became the target for a series of brutal, sadistic beatings. The fact that they coincided with his father's increasingly frequent business setbacks was lost on him. All he knew was that the man he trusted and looked up to had turned on him, seemingly overnight. The attacks were unpredictable but they came more often as the years passed. His father, failing to find satisfaction in his business career, found it instead in the physical domination and punishment of his son. And the small boy, who had once loved and respected him, grew to fear and hate him instead.

In some ways, his mother's betrayal was even worse. She did nothing to protect him from the attacks. It wasn't that she feared her husband. She feared the loss of her comfortable lifestyle if she opposed him—because she knew that if she intervened, her husband would cast her aside.

She resolved the situation in what was, to Matthew, a typically cowardly

*way. She arranged to have the boy packed off to an expensive boarding school.
The problem wasn't recognized or resolved. It was simply swept aside.*

*"We gave him the best education money could buy," she would claim in
later years.*

*But in truth, she gave nothing. She bought. Money gave her authority and
she used it to palm him off on other people, placing him in the care of strangers
who didn't care. Who didn't know him, didn't love him. In effect, she passed
her responsibility and authority on to strangers.*

*And they, in turn, abused the trust given to them, betraying him with false
words and promises they would later recall from and deny.*

*He was one of the youngest boys in the school. He was a year younger than
the stated minimum age but his parents' wealth made up the difference. And
he was a small boy—although you'd never guess that now to look at him.
Small, weak and immature compared to those around him. The combination
made him an obvious target for bullies, and there were plenty of those available.
For a while, he suffered in silence. Then, lonely, confused and able to stand it
no longer, he had taken his troubles to a teacher—one of the few who had
shown him any attention and whom he trusted.*

That trust was misplaced.

*The teacher had taken him aside and told him that the solution to his
problem lay in his own hands.*

*"If I were to punish them, Matthew, the problem won't be solved. They'll
simply come after you again. You have to understand that bullies are cowards.
If you stand up to them and fight back, they'll leave you alone."*

*He wondered briefly why, if bullies were cowards, they wouldn't fear punish-
ment from a teacher. Surely his punishment would be more painful than any
that Matthew—small, weak, friendless Matthew—could inflict. But he trusted
the teacher and next time the bullies confronted him, he defied them.*

*The result was the worst beating he had received from them. The teacher,
seeing the bruises, smiled encouragement at him.*

*"They'll leave you alone now," he assured him. "They know you won't
take it anymore."*

*But they didn't. The pain, the beatings, the mental torture doubled and re-
doubled. And what made it worse was the fact that now he knew the teacher
didn't care. Knew he wouldn't do anything to stop it.*

He realized he was on his own. And the only way to stop the bullying was to be worse than the bullies themselves, to assume power over them. That's how it worked. That's the way it would work for him.

In wood shop he selected a two-foot piece of solid hardwood timber, using the lathe to taper it so that at one end it was a comfortable fit for his hand, while at the other, the main weight was concentrated. He could have simply stolen a baseball bat from the gym but there was something satisfying in constructing his weapon of revenge with his own hands. He hollowed out the thicker end, drilling a half-inch hole to a depth of about eight inches, then filled the gap with lead shot, topped up with rubber glue to form into a solid mass and hold it in place. The club felt good in his hands. There was a satisfying heft to it with the natural weight augmented by the lead shot. But it still needed something extra. He solved the problem simply by driving several bullet-headed nails into the wood, leaving them protruding half their length, so that, at the thick end, they stood out like small spikes.

Then he waited to catch the leader of the bullies alone.

The older boy never saw him coming. And after the attack, he saw less than he had before, as one of the protruding nails had slashed across his left eye, destroying it. In addition, he'd suffered a badly fractured skull and a broken wrist and forearm, where he had tried to defend himself. Two ribs were cracked and his body was bruised and torn from shoulder to thigh, where repeated blows from the club had smashed and ripped into him as Matthew continued to hit him long after he had ceased moving. He was found bleeding, half-blinded and unconscious, with fluid leaking from his ear, in the stairwell where Matthew had surprised him.

He remained in intensive care for a week, hovering between life and death. When, after ten days, he opened his remaining eye and spoke for the first time, he named his attacker.

Matthew was brought before the school principal, who interviewed him, flanked by two police officers. He faced them calmly, convinced that he had done no wrong. He had simply reacted to a situation and solved it as he had been instructed. He told them this. The teacher was summoned and questioned. Of course, he denied any responsibility for the savagery of the attack as Matthew looked on, watching first with disbelief, then with growing contempt. The pattern that would dog him through his life was repeated yet again.

"You told me to do it," he said. His voice was calm and the statement was one of simple fact, not the sort of hysterical denial that might have been expected.

But, of course, the teacher denied it and Matthew was expelled, charged with attempted murder, a charge that his parents' money and influence reduced to aggravated battery, and he was sent to a reform school. Even their intervention in having the charges reduced didn't carry any weight with him. If they could have them reduced, he reasoned, they could have them dropped altogether. But that would have taken more money, which they obviously weren't prepared to spend.

His reputation preceded him at his new school. He was regarded as unstable, unpredictable and someone to be avoided. That suited him fine. He wanted to be left alone. He began to fill out and grow—long, relentless sessions in the gym working with weights left him powerful and muscular.

He was obliged to spend three hours a week talking with a psychiatrist, in an attempt to bring some control to the violence that could well up in him so quickly. There had been several instances with other boys in the reformatory, all of them resulting in his victims left battered and bleeding. He went into these fights with an intensity and savagery that was disturbing. The doctor tried unsuccessfully to help him see the cause of the terrible anger that could seize him in these moments. It was all the more frightening because it was cold and calculating rather than hot-blooded and instinctive in its nature. The doctor began to sense his hatred of authority but never got a chance to reach the core of the problem.

They found Rawlings's case notes afterward. The last addition stated:

Matthew is a deeply disturbed young man with a frightening tendency to extreme violence. He displays a hatred of authority and a total refusal to respond to discipline or instruction. Any attempt to direct his behavior is likely to result in violent and unpredictable episodes. When these occur, Matthew demonstrates a total abrogation of responsibility, choosing instead to level blame at those in a position of authority over him.

In the light of these notes, Rawlings should have sensed the danger. He was a small man, in his late fifties with a heart condition. Matthew by now was tall and muscular—belying his fifteen years. They found the doctor in a pool of blood, his throat slashed open by the jagged remains of a drinking glass on his desk. The ground floor office window, one of those few in the school that were without bars, was open. Matthew was gone.

Over the ensuing years, the pattern continued to repeat itself. But of course, when it did, nobody associated it with a small, disturbed boy named Matthew. He had long since disappeared, fading easily into the anonymous background provided by the constantly shifting tide of transients moving back and forth across the face of the country.

TWENTY-THREE

Lee looked at the mass of computer printout paper that covered the table and flowed off the end onto the floor like a printed waterfall.

"I guess you haven't got lucky yet," she said dryly. Jesse looked up at her and shook his head wearily.

"You wouldn't believe how many people got fired from this place in the last five years," he said. "It doesn't speak too well for our employment record."

Lee flipped up the page nearest the end of the table and glanced at it curiously. "I guess we get a lot of transient workers in winter coming through here," she said. "Ski bums and the like who want a nice easy job while they spend their time on the mountain."

"Sure as hell looks like it," Jesse agreed.

"So, does the resort keep a special computer file of people who've been fired?" she asked, scanning the names on the paper, hoping that one might, somehow, stand out from the others and say, "Here I am! Come and get me!" None did. Somehow, she wasn't surprised by the fact.

"There isn't a file that big," Jesse replied heavily. "Denise came up with the idea of checking through all the employment files, searching for the phrase 'pay in lieu of notice.' This is what the computers turned up." He waved a hand along the sheets of paper.

Lee frowned. "So we may not even have a complete list of people here?" she asked.

Jesse's shoulders slumped at the thought of it. "Jesus, I hope so! There must be at least two hundred names on this list. Don't wish any more on me."

He was crossing names off as they spoke, running a thick black felt-tip pen through them. Lee watched as he'd cross out a name. Read, skip a few, then cross out another.

"You just eliminating them on the grounds of gut feel?" she asked. He looked up again.

"Women," he explained succinctly. "At least we're pretty sure our perp is a man. So I can thin this down a little to start."

"Couldn't the computer have done that?" she asked. "I thought those damn things could do everything."

"Apparently not," her deputy replied, scoring through another two names in quick succession. "Seems the records weren't allowed to discriminate by sex." He grinned at her tiredly. "And you can blame modern society for that, I guess. And they haven't taught a computer yet to distinguish between a Cindy-Lou and a Billy-Bob."

Lee allowed the ghost of a grin to touch the corners of her mouth. "Times I find that a little hard myself, the way the world's going these days," she said. Jesse gave a small snort of laughter, went back to his task again.

"You want to pass me half of those? I'll lend a hand." Jesse, without looking up, shook his head.

"Nah. I'm nearly done here. Thanks all the same."

Whit, whit, whit, went the black felt tip across the paper as he slashed names away. He paused momentarily, frowning.

"Billy. Now surely that's a man's name?"

"I would have thought so," she replied. "What makes you think otherwise?"

"The employer. Seems that 'Billy' worked for the Snow White Beauty Parlor and Nail Clinic." He chewed the end of the pen thoughtfully. Again, Lee allowed herself the ghost of a grin.

"Put her down as a probable," she suggested. "Cross her out with a dotted line. If you don't come up with a perp, you can always come back to good ol' Billy."

"Ah, the hell with it," he said and slashed the pen through the name. "Why can't people give their kids names that are definitely male or female—like John or Judy?"

"Or Lee or Jesse?" she suggested and her deputy made a mock angry gesture with the pen.

"Hell, we don't count!" he said. "We aren't suspects in this one." He paused, then added thoughtfully, "Leastways, I know I'm not. I'm not sure about you."

"I guess it helps to be the suspector," she reasoned. He looked down to hide his grin.

"It does that." He slashed another name, then leaned back with a sigh of relief. "Well, that's the women out of the way," he said. "That leaves me barely"—he looked at the pages of names, estimating the number remaining—"oh, say a hundred and ten to go through further."

"Hundred and ten out of a hundred and fifty?" she remarked, raising her eyebrows. "Don't speak too well of the male reliability factor, does it? That's nearly a three to one ratio of men fired to women."

"Affirmative action," Jesse said firmly. "Easier to fire men these days. Probably find half these boys were fired out of sheer frustration because their employers couldn't fire the female they really wanted to."

He began to reel in the sheets of paper, tearing them across the perforated joins as he did, and stacking the pages together.

"Once I've got these names collated and sorted, I'll send them through to Quantico. The FBI can run them through their computer," Jesse said. "That way, we'll see if any of these guys have any previous record of violence."

"And if they have?" she asked.

"Then we'll start with those ones." He grinned ruefully. "Mind you, we'll probably find it's one of the others if we do. That's the way it usually goes."

TWENTY-FOUR

Ben Fuller, head of the Mount Werner Ski School, looked up from the schedule he was preparing when he heard a light tap on the door. He grinned a welcome to Jesse as the tall deputy hovered, half in and half out of his small office.

"Jess! Come on in!" He gestured to the enamel coffeepot that sat on the top of a potbelly stove in a corner of the room. "Help yourself to a cup."

Jesse poured the thick, strong brew into a plain white mug and carried it over to the desk.

"Not interrupting anything, am I?" he asked.

Fuller spread his arms wide to encompass the office, the desk and, particularly, the paperwork laid out before him.

"Shoot, of course you are! And I'm damn glad for the interruption."

Jesse hooked a straight-backed wooden chair closer and sank into it. He took a sip of coffee and his hair promptly stood on end.

"Good God, Ben, how you ever get to sleep nights, drinking this witch's brew?"

Ben Fuller grinned. He was used to disparaging comments about his coffee. "Who has time to sleep, Jess? That's a luxury reserved only for public servants like yourself. So, what can I do for you? I take it you aren't planning on booking in for a week of ski lessons?"

"Not at this time, Ben," Jesse replied gravely. "Wondered if you'd take a look at this list of names." He passed a sheet of paper across the desk. Fuller took it, studied it briefly then looked back at Jesse, eyebrows raised.

"Couple look familiar. What's it all about?" His smile faded as he answered his own question. "It's that case you're working on, isn't it? That serial killer?"

Jesse nodded slowly. "That's right. We're working on a theory that it could be someone with a grudge against the town . . ." he began.

"A grudge against the town?" Fuller frowned. "How can someone hate a town?"

Jesse sipped his coffee again. He was suddenly very tired. He'd had this conversation around a dozen times already today. With restaurant owners, bar managers, hotel operators. The computer had spat out its list of people who'd been fired in the past five years. Now the hard grind began. The checking and rechecking. The questioning: Do you remember this guy? What kind of guy was he? Do you think he'd be capable of violence? Do you remember why you fired him?

So far, the answers were blanks. Now Jesse thought he might short-cut proceedings a little. He'd mentally kicked himself for not thinking of it earlier. The man in question was known to be an expert skier. It made sense to check first on any employees from the ski school or the ski patrol who'd been fired. There were several candidates from each.

He took a deep breath and, for the thirteenth time, answered the question.

"Well, one reason might be someone who was fired, and who felt they didn't deserve to be fired. Let that happen to a guy who wasn't completely stable and it might just take him off the rails."

Ben Fuller shook his head over the sheet of paper. "You really think someone could get so steamed up?" he asked incredulously.

"Been known to happen," Jesse answered. "I'd appreciate it if you'd cast an eye over that list and see if you remember any of those names."

Ben looked at the names again, a frown of concentration rumpling his forehead. He eased his thickset frame into the old wooden swivel chair that he used, settled his rump more comfortably.

"This guy." He tapped the second name from the top. "Got rid of him late last year, as I recall. Had something of a drinking problem."

"Violent sort of guy maybe?" Jesse suggested, but Fuller shook his head emphatically.

"Hell, no! More likely he'd fall asleep than throw punches. Even when I fired him, he just grinned and said he wondered what took me so long to get around to it. Seemed to expect it, I guess."

"How about the others?" Jesse prompted, gesturing toward the other names on the list in Fuller's hand. He studied it for a moment before he replied.

"Yeah, some of these are familiar. Let's see . . ."

He looked up from the paper, pursed his lips thoughtfully. Then looked back down at the list. His forefinger hovered uncertainly over another of the names.

"Him," he said decisively. "I remember him. Mike Miller. He was back in '01. Had to fire him and he was damned angry about it."

Jesse leaned forward slowly, set the coffee mug down on the desk. "Angry?"

Memory came back in a flood now, and Fuller nodded several times. "Mad as a hornet. Thought he was going to take a swing at me. Wish the bastard had. I'd have loved a reason to lay one on him. He caused me a whole peck of trouble."

"What kind of trouble would that have been?" Jesse asked.

"I had him assigned to private classes—just one on ones. He decided to take the idea of one on one literally. He and a client skied down Valley View, went off to the left there into an empty condo and screwed themselves up a storm. Damn near brought the mountain down."

Jesse shrugged. "I guess it wasn't exactly the lesson the client had in mind," he said. "But was that a reason to fire him?"

Fuller shook his head emphatically. "No, no, no! Frankly, I didn't give a damn. The client's husband got a little tetchy about it though. Walked in on them while Miller was busy showing his wife a whole new reason for keeping her knees bent."

"Oh, shit," Jesse said, understanding.

"Exactly. Problem was, the husband took a swing at Miller and Miller damn near killed him. Turned out he was one of these experts in kung fu or karate or whatever they call it these days. He really went to town."

"Had a violent side to him then?" Jesse asked.

"You'd better believe it. That's why I got rid of him. Hell, I might have done it over the other business. I mean we all know it goes on, and we all know the trick is not to get caught. Chances are, though, he might have got away with it. But he sent that other feller to the hospital and there was just no way I could keep him on after that. No way in the world."

"You said he turned ugly when you fired him?" Jesse reminded the ski school director.

"Oh, yeah. Ugly is the word. He stormed up and down this room. He said he'd fix me good. He'd fix the whole place . . ." Fuller's voice trailed off as he realized what he was saying. His gaze locked with Jesse's. There was a cold light in the deputy's eyes. The light that shines in the eyes of a hunting animal when the prey is suddenly revealed.

"Sweet Jesus . . ." Fuller said quietly. "It could be him, couldn't it?"

Jesse nodded agreement. "Could be, Ben. Or it could have been just talk. It's certainly something I'd want to check up on. You have any record of where he might have gone? Where he came from? Do people normally leave a forwarding address?"

Fuller shrugged. His eyes were still reflecting the sudden realization that the former instructor could be the man who'd already murdered three times. Later, the realization would dawn that he himself could conceivably be a target. That realization would cause Ben Fuller more than a few hours' lost sleep in the days to come.

"Some do. Some don't," he replied. "I'll have the office check their records and see for you, Jess."

The deputy stood up. "I'd appreciate that, Ben. Also, cast your mind over those other names, see if you can remember how come they were fired as well. See if any of the others remember."

Fuller stood to usher Jesse to the door. "I'll do that, Jess. You think it's worth checking the others though? Seems to me Miller's got to be the man you're after."

"Maybe, Ben. But we'll check 'em all. Just in case." Jesse tugged on his Cubs cap and lifted his battered leather jacket from a hook inside the outer office door. "Be in touch," he said briefly, then went out into the cold.

He went looking for Opie Dulles, the ski patrol commander. He'd hoped to find his erstwhile boss in the ski patrol office at Ski Time Square. Jenny, the dispatcher, looked up as he entered, welcoming him with a broad smile.

"Hi there, stranger," she said. "Looking for your old job back?"

He answered Jenny's question with a grin. "Not right now, girl. Got other business to take care of. Opie around?"

She shook her head. "Went up the mountain a half hour back." She reached for the two-way handset on the desk beside her, thumbed the talk button and spoke into the mike.

"Time Square base to Zero one. Do you read?"

Zero one was Opie's call sign. The patrol heads at the various huts around the mountain were One one, Two one, Three one and so on. Jenny released the talk button and Opie's distorted voice was heard through a crackle of atmospherics.

"Zero one."

"Opie? Jesse Parker's here. Wants to see you." She raised her eyebrows interrogatively at Jesse, making sure she was right in that assumption. He nodded confirmation and she continued. "You heading back this way at all?"

"Ah . . . not right now, Jenny. I'm on the Storm Peak chair heading up for the weather station. What's Jesse want?"

Again, Jenny looked a question at Jesse. He hesitated, wondering whether to go ahead with any detail, then decided against it.

"Just want to talk with him is all," he said. Jenny relayed the message to the commander.

"Well, tell Jess . . . Hold on, can he hear me?"

"That's an affirmative," Jenny said. Jesse raised an eyebrow. Jenny must have spent the summer in semi rigs. She was picking up on CB talk. Opie continued, talking directly now for Jesse to hear.

"Jess? Got to check the snow in the OB area behind the weather station. Park Rangers feel we could be heading for avalanche conditions up there if we get any more snow. I'll be looking there then heading into the station in about a half hour or so."

Jesse hesitated. He fingered the list of names that he wanted Opie to study. For a moment, he considered leaving them here with a message for Opie to look through them. Then, reluctantly, he discarded the idea. He knew from long experience that a direct approach was treated with more urgency than a relayed message.

"Tell him I'll meet him at the weather station in thirty minutes," he said. Jenny thumbed the talk button again.

"Opie? Jess says he'll meet you in the station at"—she checked her watch, then continued—"twenty after."

"That'll be fine, Jess. See you there. Zero one out."

"Base out. Keep warm, Opie." She grinned at Jesse as she added the last few words. Up the mountain the wind was cutting like a knife, dropping the temperature to well below freezing. Jesse thought ruefully of the long trek up the exposed slope to the weather station. Maybe he should have suggested that Opie meet him at the Four Points Hut farther down. Then he shrugged. He must be getting soft. Time was when a little walk uphill in the cold wouldn't have phased him any, he thought.

"Thanks, Jenny," he said, heading toward the locker room behind her where he kept his skis, boots and ski-patrol uniform.

"We're here to serve, Jess," she said lightly, picking up the paperback novel she'd been reading when he came in.

In the locker room, he changed his jeans for the windproof GORE-TEX ski pants that were part of the uniform issue. Then he pulled the blue and yellow parka on over his plaid shirt. Not that he needed to go up in uniform, but it was proper cold weather gear and there was no point in freezing his ass off in jeans and a bomber jacket.

He forced his feet into the hard, unyielding Lange boots. He hadn't worn them in over a week and they felt stiff and unfamiliar. He stamped them once or twice to settle his feet in, wiggled his toes experimentally and wondered how the hell he could ever believe ski boots were comfortable, then clumped into the ski room to collect his Rossis and stocks.

There was a one-way door from the ski room, letting out onto a metal grill staircase that led down to the gondola level. He clanged down it, clumsy in the forward canting boots, and headed for the gondola.

The mountain at Steamboat Springs was separated into two parts. The Silver Bullet, as the gondola was known, served the lower half of the mountain. From the top of the gondola, at Thunderhead, Jesse skied down a short way to pick up the fast quad chair that ran up the second half of the mountain to Storm Peak.

His patrol uniform let him skip to the front of the lines at the gondola and the chair. Not, he noticed sourly, that the lines were anything much to speak of. Normally, in a season like this, with excellent snowfalls and superb fresh powder conditions out on the mountain, he'd expect a lift line that took at least five minutes to move through. Today the lifts were barely populated.

He took a four-seat chair to himself, noticing that other solo skiers were making sure they did the same. Nobody wanted to share with a stranger these days. Not since Harry Powell had got on the Storm Peak Express alive and come up stone cold dead at the other end.

The chair clanked past a pylon and Jesse surveyed the tree runs below him. The killer had gone somewhere down there, he thought. The wind was blowing half a gale up here at the top half of the mountain and he pulled the hood of his parka up, tugging the draw cords tight. Tiny, frozen daggers of snow stung his face. He pulled the collar up farther, closing the gap between it and his goggles and shrank down into it, away from the wind.

He skied off the top of the chair and turned left, poling to get as much momentum as he could, to get as far up the slope to the weather station as possible before his speed died and he was reduced to walking. Morosely, he thought that he should have borrowed a pair of cross-country skis from the patrol office. Their bases weren't slick like downhill skis. They were designed for walking up slopes like this. Downhill skis were designed for just what the man said: downhill. He ran off the last of his speed and set into a dogged herringbone walk, splaying the skis out in a wide V-shape and setting the edges to get purchase against the slope. He glanced up into the driving wind. The weather station building huddled in the snow, a good quarter mile away. He sighed and kept on herringboning.

It was a long, cold walk for not very much.

Opie checked over the list of names. There were fewer on this list than the one Jesse had left with Ben Fuller. He shrugged. He could remember one or two of the people, but only vaguely.

"I'll have to check with the office, Jess," he admitted. "I can't really remember too much about some of these. They go back three or four years. Offhand, I don't know why they were fired."

Jesse leaned near the woodstove that was kept burning in the weather station.

"I'd appreciate your thinking about it, Opie," he said. "Anything you come up with could be useful."

The patrol commander folded the sheet of paper and put it carefully into an inside pocket in his parka.

"Of course, you could be barking up the wrong tree, checking ski patrol and ski schools for expert skiers," he said.

Jesse sensed a slight feeling of resentment. Opie didn't like the idea that anyone who'd worked for ski patrol, even though he might have eventually been fired, could end up killing people in cold blood.

"Thing is," Opie continued, "most people who get a job for the season end up pretty damn good. Every second shift waiter on this mountain is probably an expert."

Jesse nodded agreement. "True enough, Opie," he said. "But I guess I've got to start somewhere. And it gives me a sense of purpose to eliminate suspects in groups like this. Doing them all in one hit would just be too daunting."

"I guess," said Opie, sounding unconvinced. Then he zipped the front of his parka closed and headed for the door. "I was going to head over to the East Face and check the snow there. Tad thinks it might be building up for an avalanche too. Care to come along?"

Jesse hesitated, glanced at his watch. The afternoon was mostly gone. There'd be no one else for him to question until the morning and suddenly the thought of the stuffy, windowless office at the Public Safety Building was decidedly unattractive. He tugged on his gloves.

"Why not?" he said.

TWENTY-FIVE

*H*e leaned on the wooden railing of the terrace outside Hazie's restaurant, watching as the late afternoon sun dipped lower and lower over the Yampa Valley. In a few more minutes, it would be dark enough.

From his position, he could see the endless stream of gondolas surging out of the upper station, swaying their way down the mountain. None of them were full. He could tell by the skis mounted in the racks outside the double doors. Some had three skiers, some four. A reasonable proportion had one skier only. That was what he was looking for, of course. He hadn't ridden the gondola since he'd murdered Andrew Barret. He thought it might be pushing his luck— just in case he came up against the same lift attendants who'd been on duty that evening. Of course, he'd been heavily disguised, but you never knew what a person might remember. You never knew that you might not have developed some noticeable little piece of body language that could stick in a person's mind. So he'd avoided the Silver Bullet. Until tonight. Because tonight he wanted to confuse that overconfident, cocksure deputy.

They develop a pattern, the man had said, that becomes their signature. And then they don't deviate from it. Well, tonight, he was going to deviate. Not so much that they might think there was another killer out here. But enough to make them stop and wonder if they were heading down the right track.

He smiled to himself. He was sure that whichever way they were heading, it wasn't the right one. He'd watched that long-legged deputy tramping all over town a few days back, trying to establish some link between the three men who'd died. Some reason why they had been selected, over the hundreds of other possible candidates.

The smile broadened and he actually laughed softly to himself. The truth was, there was no link. There was no reason. They were available and that was all there was to it. There were in the wrong place at the right time to serve his need. So they died. He glanced westward again. The sun was balanced on the rim of the valley, dropping faster and faster. The shadows were deepening on the mountain below him. He turned and went back into the restaurant, passing through and down the stairs on the far side.

Here, outside the building, the light was almost gone. He collected his skis *from the rack by the double doors and waited, watching the last of the skiers coming down the short run that connected from the top of the Elkhead chair. Most of them peeled off to the right and headed for the higher reaches of Valley View run. But a few were heading into the gondola station, planning to download rather than ski down the second half of the mountain in the gathering dusk.*

The small numbers suited him just fine. That would mean no line waiting to load at the gondola station. So he could pick someone traveling by themselves, wait a few seconds for them to go into the station, then hurry in after them and board the same cabin at the last moment. And for them, it would pretty much be the last moment. He watched and waited and finally saw his chance. A girl in her early twenties. Not a very good skier judging by the uncoordinated way she was struggling up the slight slope to the gondola station stairs. She stopped a few yards short, breathless, and with evident relief, shoved her pole down into the release lever on the back of one binding, then another. Stepping clear of her skis, she bent and picked them up. For a moment, she juggled skis and poles, then got things organized and clumped up the steel mesh stairs, stamping her boots to clear them of excess snow as she came.

She sensed his eyes upon her, glanced across and gave him a tired grin, blowing a wisp of hair back from her forehead.

"Why do we do it to ourselves?" she said wearily. He smiled, nodded and said nothing. She hitched her skis over one shoulder and walked, with the awkward rolling gait of a beginner in ski boots, into the gondola hut.

He came to a decision rapidly. That would be the change he wanted. Three men killed, and now, a total change of pace. A young, attractive girl. That should stop any half-formed theories about some kind of homophobic campaign being waged. It should confuse the issue nicely, he thought, give the FBI and that damn deputy something new to think about.

He waited a few seconds, then swung his backpack over one shoulder. He grabbed his skis and poles and followed her into the loading bay.

He'd changed his outfit this time. He was no longer dressed and equipped as a cross-country skier. His skis were last year's model Atomic carving skis—an intermediate level ski. People tended to notice experts and their equipment and today he wanted to be just an average Joe—anonymous. Similarly, he'd abandoned his cross-country parka and ski pants for a more stylish one-piece suit. Not too new and expensive. And so, not too noticeable. Just another average skier in an average outfit, with a small backpack slung over one shoulder.

His abseiling rope was coiled in the pack, along with the mechanical ram he'd devised to force the gondola doors apart. Ironically, he thought, it was basically a scaled down version of the Jaws of Life instrument used to free trapped drivers from crushed cars.

The jigger was in a pouch he'd sewn to the inside of his ski suit. He moved his elbow slightly to feel the reassuring hardness just under his left armpit. Now he was inside the gondola station, and he could see the girl, stumbling slightly as she climbed into one of the slowly moving cars. The lift attendant had taken her skis and was settling them into the rack. He'd timed it just about perfectly. The gondola cabin had another twenty feet to go before the doors closed and it swung onto the main cable.

He'd make it just in time, and in the hurry to get his skis in the rack, the attendant would have barely no time at all to get a good look at him. His boots echoed inside the concrete and steel room, their sound dwarfed by the muted roar of the drive engine, the clunking and crashing of cabins coming off the main cable. They slowed onto the low speed detached circle, slamming into each other as their momentum, suddenly checked, caused them to swing wildly, their rubber collision strips saving them from any damage. He was alongside the cabin now, with barely ten feet to go. He raised his skis to shoulder height, aiming the butts at the squared off ski holder on the outside of the door, and started to drive them forward. He noticed the girl's face in the gloom of the cabin, a pale blur turned toward him. Then a hand caught his shoulder and twisted him off balance. The skis missed their target and clattered awkwardly against the concrete floor and he stumbled, trying to recover in time to get them into the rack.

It was too late. The doors had started closing. The cabin was accelerating. The pale blur of the girl's face was barely visible now. He swung around angrily on the lift attendant, whose hand was still twisted in the fabric at the shoulder of his ski suit.

"Hey, buddy!" he said, cold with fury. "Just what the fuck do you think you're doing?"

"Sorry, pal." The attendant's voice was controlled and even. But his eyes were anything but apologetic. He released his grip now and stepped back a pace. He was big and athletic looking and he was ready for trouble, waiting to see which way the angry skier in front of him was about to jump. His right hand curled unconsciously into a fist. He pointed with his left to a chalkboard sign propped up near the head of the loading race. The words "No two people to a cabin" were chalked in rough capitals on the board.

"*Couldn't send you down with just two of you in the cabin,*" *he explained.* "*Rule is one person, or three or more. No twos unless they know each other.*"

"*What? What the fuck is that all about? Since when are we doing things this way?*" *He was furious now. The more he thought about it, the more he liked the idea of doing it differently this time. The more he liked the idea of leaving them a young, attractive, female body to find and puzzle over. The attendant shook his head, disclaiming responsibility for the sign.*

"*Order of the sheriff's office,*" *he said, with the air of a man who has repeated the same mantra over and over throughout the day.* "*Deputy Parker was up here earlier, making sure we keep to it. It's for safety, okay?*"

He gave the angry skier a meaningful look. All staff had been cautioned about talking too much about the killings in front of customers. Specifically they'd been told not to excuse the new loading rules by pointing out that there was a serial killer loose on the mountain. He hoped the man would take the hint.

"*Parker?*" *said the would-be passenger.* "*He's that tall guy from the sheriff's office, was in the paper the other day?*"

The attendant nodded. "*That's right. If you want to complain to someone, go see him.*" *He grinned slightly, sensing that the situation was calming down a little.* "*Sorry I grabbed you like I did but it was the only way I could stop you. The doors were about to close. You came out of nowhere. I didn't even know you were here until you were trying to get your skis in the rack.*"

"*Yeah. Fine. No trouble,*" *the skier replied. He realized he was spending too much time here, giving the lift attendant time and opportunity to get a good look at him.* "*Just I'm in a bit of a rush, is all.*"

He turned away, looking for another cabin. There were plenty to choose from. Most of the skiers coming in now had opted for a few drinks in the Thunderhead bars before heading down the mountain. Cabin after cabin was swinging out into the gathering night, empty.

The attendant took his skis from him and led the way to the nearest cabin. Deftly, he speared them into the rack and stood aside as the skier boarded the cabin, stooping as he went through the low sill of the doorway.

The cabin passed the automatic trip set above the cable. The doors sighed shut on their pneumatic pistons and he swung out into the dark. Two hundred yards below him, Julia Dietrich was humming an old Eagles song to herself. One day, thirty years in the future, she'd hum that same song to her twin granddaughters. And neither she, nor they, would have the slightest idea that the song was being performed courtesy of a big, athletic-looking lift attendant in Steamboat Springs, Colorado.

Jesse tilted the straight-back chair onto its back legs. The papers spread out on the table before him were blurring into one inchoate mass. He pressed the heels of both hands into his eyes and rubbed. He groaned softly to himself. This was the part of a case that he hated. It was boring, unrewarding and soul destroying. It made digging ditches seem fascinating by comparison.

He'd tramped the length and breadth of the mountain, stopping in at the ski school, ski patrol and the seemingly hundreds of bars, ski shops, restaurants, hire shops and ski tuning establishments with his list of names. Asking the same questions over and over again, trying to piece together some picture of the men who'd been fired from the resort over the past few years. Looking for that one, casually mentioned piece of information that might just make one name stand out from the others. "Oh sure, Deputy, I remember him. He used to say that one day he'd come back here and stick a sharpened steel spike into people. That's the guy, for certain." He shook his head to clear it a little, reached for the cup of coffee he'd poured a few minutes ago, took a sip and pursed his lips in displeasure. The coffee was stone, motherless cold. Those few minutes, he realized now, were closer to half an hour.

He picked up the sheaf of notes he'd been compiling and began to check them again. There was pitifully little to go on. The former ski instructor fired by Ben Fuller was a standout so far. But instinctively, Jesse distrusted the lead. It had come too easily. It was the first name thrown up. He glanced at the name again.

"Michael Miller, Michael Miller," he muttered softly to himself. "Where are you tonight, Michael?"

"You gonna start talking to yourself, it's time you went home," said a soft voice behind him. He turned, wincing slightly as his stiff shoulders protested against the move. Lee was standing inside the door of the conference room, leaning on the jamb and regarding him with a small frown.

"Working late?" she asked unnecessarily. He glanced at his old Seiko and noticed, with mild surprise, that it was after eleven.

"Just going through these names, sorting the possibles from the unlikelys," he replied.

Lee shoved herself off the doorframe and moved closer to the table, looking over his shoulder at the notes he'd been scrawling on pages from a yellow legal pad.

"Possibles and unlikelys?" she repeated. "That means there are no probables as yet?"

He gave her a tired grin. "There never are," he said, yawning involuntarily.

"Go on home, Jesse," said Lee, in a softer tone. "I don't want you falling asleep at the wheel halfway up Rabbit Ear Pass."

He gathered his papers together and stood, moving stiffly as he headed for the door.

"Never been known to happen," he said. She followed him out, hitting the light switch as she went and leaving the conference room in darkness.

The building was on minimum lighting at this late hour, with maybe one light in five lit. There was an eerie, forlorn quality to the dim light and the deep patches of shadow that alternated along the corridor as they headed for the stairs.

It was snowing again as they came out into the parking lot. The black tarmac was almost hidden by a fresh, thick carpet of snow. Jesse took a deep breath of the cold night air.

"Great ski season," he said softly, almost to himself.

"Except for one little problem," Lee replied, and he nodded seriously.

"Yeah," he agreed. "Apart from that."

Lee dropped a hand onto his shoulder and he looked at her, a little surprised at the contact.

"Take care driving, Jess," she said, and turned quickly away to her Renegade.

He thought that maybe her voice sounded a little thick, a little husky. He wondered why that might be.

TWENTY-SIX

There was a noise on the porch. A noise that had no place in the normal spectrum of night sounds outside Jesse's cabin. It was that fact that brought him instantly awake from the deep sleep that claimed him almost as soon as his head had hit the pillow.

He lay there now, trying to re-create the noise in his mind. He'd heard it in his sleep. Now, fully awake, it was like trying to reach back into another dimension.

He tossed back the covers, shivering in the night cold, and pulled on a pair of jeans and a flannel shirt. He cocked his head to one side and listened, waiting to see if the noise would come again. It didn't. Something far more prosaic came instead—a gentle tapping on the wooden panels of the door. He reached for the lamp beside his bed and flicked the switch. Soft, yellow light flooded the interior of the cabin.

He padded to the door and threw back the solid iron bolt that secured it from the inside. Jesse was no nervous sleeper. But all cops gather enemies in the course of the job and only a fool would sleep behind an unsecured door. For the same reason, the door itself was thick, solid timber. He laid his hand on the door handle, then caution made him pause.

"Who's out there?" he asked, glancing back to the Colt where it lay on the bedside table.

"It's me, Jess," said Lee. "Open up. It's damn cold out here with no shoes on."

He frowned at the thought of it, wondering why she was in bare feet at . . . he paused, realizing that the one thing he hadn't done so far was check to see what time it was. He did so now. He always slept wearing his watch.

"Jesus, Lee," he said, opening the door. "It's after one o'clock. What are you doing out here at this hour?"

He hesitated as the door came fully open and the spill of light from inside the room illuminated the porch. The sheriff of Routt County was standing, her hair lightly dusted with snow, and her handmade high heel boots in her hand. He noticed idly that she was wearing thick white socks. She shuffled her feet awkwardly.

"You going to let me in?" she asked, with just a tad of asperity in her voice. Jesse stood back and gestured to the interior of the cabin. Lee brushed past him, shivering slightly, and dropped the boots on the bare, board floor. That was when Jesse identified the noise that had first woken him. It had been the sound of a boot being dropped onto the boards of the porch outside his front door. He looked at Lee curiously. There was a spot of color in each of her cheeks that he didn't think was due to the cold. He shut the front door, leaned on it and regarded her wordlessly for a few seconds.

"Well?" she said, finally breaking the silence. There was a note of challenge in her voice, daring him to comment on her arrival out here, boots in hand, in the middle of the night. In addition to everything else, Jesse was a cautious man.

He shrugged again. "Fine." The color flared in Lee's cheeks again.

"Fine?" she mimicked him, on a rising note. "Fine? I arrive out here near two in the morning—"

"Closer to one," Jesse put in mildly. She brushed the interjection away, irritably.

"Be nearly two before you get around to saying anything sensible," she told him. He couldn't think of anything to say to that, but figured "fine" might not be the best thing to repeat. He settled for another shrug. Lee continued, a little breathlessly.

"So do you normally have ladies arrive here at this time of night and drop their boot on your front porch? This is just another night like Wednesday for you, is it?"

This time another shrug wasn't going to do it. He just knew that. Carefully, he replied, "No. I guess it's not."

"Well, that's a relief," she said, standing feet apart, a bare two yards from him. He had the distinct impression that every inch of her body was as taut as a fiddle string. He thought if he touched her, if anything touched her, she'd twang an E above high C.

"I wouldn't like to think that women just came out here any time at all, dropping their boots on your porch like they felt they had a right to," she said.

He frowned now. The dropping of the boot seemed to have some kind of significance for her. He was damned if he could figure what it might be. He thought about not asking her, decided, on balance, that might be even more risky than asking.

"So, Lee," he said carefully. "How come you dropped that boot, anyway?" She nodded several times before she answered him. Finally, he thought, he'd got something right. He'd asked the right question. The one she wanted asked.

Then she replied. "Well now, Jess, seems I dropped that boot 'cause I sort of let go of it when I lost my balance taking it off."

He thought he'd been too hasty with his self-congratulation. Maybe that wasn't the question she wanted after all. She looked at him now, head cocked slightly to one side, still nodding a little, her eyes wide and maybe just a little crazy, he thought. He tried again, feeling his way. There seemed to be a pattern developing here and it seemed to have something to do with the boots. He thought he'd stay with that subject.

"Um . . . Lee? Why . . . were you taking your boots off in the first place?" he asked her. And finally, she heaved a great sigh of relief and he knew he'd got it right.

"Well now, Jess, do you have any idea—" she stopped, held a finger in the air. The phrasing wasn't emphatic enough for her yet. She tried another way, seemed satisfied with it and went on, "Do you have the slightest idea how foolish a girl can look trying to get her jeans off over a pair of boots like these?"

He shook his head, repeated one word. "Jeans?" he said and then realized that she'd tossed her sheriff's department parka to the floor and her hands were flying over the buttons of her uniform shirt, ripping them open as she continued talking, with that strange, slightly crazy note in her voice.

"That's right, Jesse," she said. "A girl can look downright ridiculous hopping around a room like this with her jeans snagged on her boot heels. Nothing like that to ruin the moment."

He knew he was gaping, could do nothing to stop himself. She flung the shirt back and off her shoulders, letting it drop to the floor behind her. She wore nothing underneath it and he felt the breath catch in his throat at the sight of her magnificent bare breasts, swinging slightly with the violent movements she was making as she undid the waistband of her Levis, unzipped the front, then shucked them down to knee level, finally stepping clear of them and leaving them discarded on the floor with the shirt. She wore nothing underneath the jeans, either. She stood before him now, statuesque, long-legged, lean-hipped. A seemingly remote part of his brain registered the fact that her breasts looked softer and fuller than he remembered, but still firm and very inviting, with the nipples aroused and flaring. Jesse felt himself hardening inside the hastily donned jeans. This definitely wasn't the sort of situation he'd had a lot of experience with. It wasn't a situation he'd had any experience with, come to think of it.

"Jesus, Lee?" he said, more as a question than a statement. His voice cracked slightly as he spoke and he realized he sounded vaguely absurd.

Lee made a gesture that mixed equal parts annoyance and resignation. "Hell, Jesse," she said. "I've tried to be subtle. I've tried to hint at it. I've asked you to stay the night. I guess I'm just no damn good at any of those things. So here I am."

She hesitated, then added, with an overtone of uncertainty and even a slight edge of fear, "Just, for Christ's sake, don't tell me to get dressed and go."

"Go?" he said, feeling strangely short of breath. "Why the hell would I want you to go?"

She smiled at that, a smile that was nine parts relief. She glanced down at the bulge in his jeans, now well and truly prominent.

"Well, at least you seem glad to see me," she said, nodding her head toward his bedside table, where the Colt lay beside the lamp. "'Cause I can see you've got nothing in your pocket."

He moved toward her then, laying his hands on her bare shoulders, stroking them lightly, marveling at the silky feeling of her skin. She closed her eyes, breathing deeply at his touch, and he ran one hand down to circle lightly under her left breast, then up again to cup it, feeling its weight and its softness, playing with the hard core of her nipple. She shuddered lightly and he repeated the process with the other hand.

Her own hands were busy now with the waistband of his jeans. She unsnapped the fastener, worked the zipper down. His cock, released from the constraining pressure of the tight denim, virtually sprang out into her hand. Her other arm went behind his neck and she moved into him, mouth open to his, her hand working rapidly back and forth on him. He marveled at her for a second before he let her draw him close. She was magnificent. He slid a hand down to her backside, lightly teasing the cleft between her buttocks, then ran his hand over the roundness there, feeling the softness of her skin contrasted with the firm muscle tone just below the surface. Steel wrapped in satin, he thought.

She groaned softly, and her tongue shot into his mouth, exploring, seeking, exciting. Her hands were working his jeans down over his hips now. She bent away from him for a second to get rid of the denim pants. He went with her, groaning in his own turn as her nails raked lightly over the taut stretched skin of his sac. Then the jeans were gone and they hobbled in a crazy, off-balance dance for a few seconds as he kicked clear of them.

He'd never fastened the flannel shirt and it took only a few seconds for her to shrug that off him. Then they stood, naked, aroused, straining together and he felt her, forefinger and thumb around him, guiding him into her, felt the wetness of her, felt the delicious warmth of her and suddenly he wanted nothing more than to be inside her, and then he was, and her long, long, muscular legs were wrapping around his waist and he thrust into her and felt her respond.

Again.

And again.

Their backs arced and they strained further, trying to work him deeper and deeper inside her, farther than was humanly possible but still they tried. She came and half a second later so did he, helplessly exploding away all those years of not realizing what they meant to each other, what they could be to each other.

She kissed him, wet and fierce, her legs still wrapped around him, her hips still pumping at him, still drawing him into her.

He took a few short steps and they collapsed across his bed. It skidded under them a few feet across the bare boards. And then, and only then, did she release him and smile up at him through the tangle of her wild blond hair.

"Well, Jesus, Jesse," she said. "You sure took your time coming back for more."

TWENTY-SEVEN

Jesse woke to the sight of a bare breast a few inches from his eyes. Lee was sitting up in his bed, still naked, leafing through his notes on the investigation. Without moving his head, he swiveled his gaze up to her face. She was frowning slightly in concentration as she read. The angle and intensity of the light spilling through the uncurtained windows told him that it must be around seven o'clock and another clear morning.

He looked back to her breast, watching it rise and fall slightly with her breath.

"Well," he said at length. "There's a sight for sore eyes."

She looked down at him. A smile widened her lips, reached deep into her tilted gray eyes as she looked at him.

"You never told me you snored," she said. He shrugged, or as near to it as a man could manage lying prone.

"Never seemed any call to mention it in conversation so far," he said. "I guess I would have got around to it eventually."

She smiled again, then the slight frown returned as she tapped the papers in front of her. "So you figure four possibles here?"

He nodded, then stretched and yawned before he answered. "Far as I can figure," then added, "course, odds are that the real killer will be one of the unlikelys—or someone who's not even on the list. But a man's got to start somewhere."

He slid up in the bed and sat beside her, glancing at his watch. His guess had been close to the mark. It was five before seven.

They'd made love again the previous night, after that first, desperate, headlong rush of passion. The second time had been slower, more deliberate, and just as satisfying in its own different way. He laid a gentle hand on her cheek now, marveling at the depths of desire that he had always felt for this woman, yet only realized the night before. She kissed his hand idly, then looked back to the notes.

"So what makes these four special?" she asked. He reached for the notes, brushed his forearm accidentally against her breast, stopped and looked at her apologetically.

"If we're talking business, I wonder could we do it with some clothes on?" he asked.

She grinned at him, delighted. "This upsets you?" she said, glancing down at her own bare upper body.

"Hell, no!" he answered quickly, then, being strictly honest, he amended, "Well, yes. In a way. Upsets is maybe the wrong word. It sure as hell distracts me."

She laughed, a low-pitched sound that reached right into his heart, and slid out of the bed, gathering her clothes together from where they'd fallen on the floor the night before. He watched with some regret as she dressed. There was something indescribably enjoyable about the sight of her naked in his cabin.

Or anywhere else, for that matter, he thought.

She started to pull on her jeans, stopped as she was refastening the waistband and looked at him quizzically.

"This going to be a problem for you, do you think, Jess?" she asked, serious all of a sudden. He didn't answer immediately, not sure what she meant, so she went on. "I mean, our working together and"—she grinned salaciously—"doing other things together as well. I don't exactly see this as a one-night stand, you know."

"Neither do I, Lee," he assured her, and thought he saw a trace of relief in her shoulders as she bent to buckle her belt. "And no, I don't see it as any kind of a problem at all."

He'd thought about it the night before, just before sleep had claimed him. Normally, he guessed, a situation like this could be awkward. But not this time. This felt so right, so natural, so normal. He didn't see it interfering in any way with their work together.

"Good," Lee said shortly, buttoning her shirt. "Now, if you think I'm going to stand here fully dressed discussing a case with you while you're prancing around buck naked, it must be a frosty Friday in July. Get some clothes on and show a little respect."

And grinning, she'd hooked his jeans off the floor with her foot and kick-tossed them to him. He dressed while she lit a burner under a pot of water to make coffee, then picked up the notes again.

"So what makes you pick these four as likely suspects?" she asked.

He pulled a sweater over his head, spooned coffee into his old enamel pot and moved to glance over her shoulder. She was sitting now in one of the hard chairs by the plain pine table in the kitchen area of the cabin. There wasn't much in the way of interior rooms. Aside from a separate bathroom and toilet, it was just one open-plan design, the areas defined by the furniture and fittings in each. He had a bedroom area, a living room area and a kitchen/eating area. If he owned a desk and a stereo, he could have a den area as well. He laid his forefinger on the name at the top of the list.

"This guy," he said. "Mike Miller. Sounds like a real prospect. He was fired from the ski school for banging one of his clients."

Lee raised an eyebrow at him. "They're firing ski instructors for that now?" she asked incredulously. "It's a marvel that we've got any left."

Jesse grinned. "This was a little different. Her husband caught him and our friend here beat him up pretty bad."

She frowned thoughtfully. "So he's got some history of violence, okay. But that's a long way from murder."

"I agree," said Jesse. "Except when this guy was fired, he threatened to get even. Went close to ballistic, according to Ben Fuller."

She pursed her lips, looking from him to the name on the page before her. "That's pretty thin," she said, at length.

"Tell me about it. I said there were no probables."

"I thought you were just being conservative," she said, then fingered the second name.

"What about this guy here—Anton Mikkelitz?"

He looked at the name, turned up one of the pages below the one she was looking at and checked the details he'd noted there.

"Some previous history," he said. "Not a lot, but some. He was a paramedic with the Denver Fire Department, then a smoke jumper in Oregon. Came up here for the season three years back and joined the ski patrol. Opie got rid of him because he was always turning up late for work. Sometimes he didn't turn up at all."

Her eyebrow rose again. "Tardy is hardly a reason to suspect a man," she said. He shook his head.

"It was his reaction to being fired that got him on the list. Seems Opie got mad when he ran into him on the mountain one day. The guy had called in sick and there he was bright-eyed and bushy-tailed with a group of friends. Opie kind of lost it. Reamed him out at the entrance to the Storm Peak chair, in front of maybe a hundred people. Mikkelitz didn't like it. Told Opie he had no right to do it that way—to humiliate him like that."

Lee shrugged. "Funny how people can be in the wrong and they'll blame everyone else for it."

"Too true," Jesse replied. "Anyway, Mikkelitz and Opie were yelling at each other and finally Opie had had enough. He said something along the lines of 'Try this for humiliation: you're fired.'"

"And?" Lee asked.

"And the strange thing is, Mikkelitz went real quiet. He went pale, then turned around and stormed off, shoving people out of the way. Opie never saw him after that. He left town."

Lee chewed her lip thoughtfully.

"You said he had some previous history?" she prompted.

"I checked back with Denver PD. He'd had a few priors. Nothing serious," he added, before she could ask. "Just seemed he had a habit of getting into brawls in bars. One of his victims pressed charges, then dropped them after a week or two."

"Jesus," she sighed, beginning to sound discouraged. "That's even thinner than the first guy."

"Well," he said, a little defensively, "it shows a possibility of unstable behavior—and a tendency toward violence."

Lee let go a long breath. "Yeah, I guess it does," she said. She didn't sound anything like convinced. Before she could ask about the third and fourth names, Jesse gave her the details.

"Number three was with the mountain grooming staff. Oliver Prescott by name. Fired for theft from the locker room. Nothing big. Also has a prior for grand theft auto, going back six years in Boulder. Did time in the state pen."

She went to voice the obvious and he forestalled her.

"I know. I know. There's no history of violence there. But . . . he'd been in the slammer for two years. Maybe he learned something there.

Could have picked up on jiggers in there. Some of the gang members who used them would have been doing time around then."

The water was boiling on the stove. He paused to pour it over the ground coffee in the pot, wincing slightly as the cloud of steam scalded his hand lightly.

"And don't say it. I know it's thin. They're all thin. Number four's no better. Ned Tellman. He was a chef in Hazie's. They canned him because it turned out he wasn't qualified."

"And I guess on top of that, he had a long list of unpaid parking tickets?" Lee asked sardonically. Jesse couldn't argue with her. He grinned a little wearily.

"Actually, he had a conviction for armed robbery up in Wyoming," he told her. She sat up a little straighter at that.

"Armed robbery?" she said, showing more interest than she had over the previous three candidates. "What was the weapon?"

"A knife," he replied. Then, as he saw her draw breath to say something, he held up a hand to stop her. "I know, Lee. That's the closest to the current MO we've got. But it was thirteen years ago. He was fifteen at the time and he's had a clear record ever since."

She wasn't convinced. "Except for lying about being a chef," she said. He conceded that with an inclination of his head.

"Hardly a felony," he said dryly. She had to agree.

"I guess I'm grasping at straws," she said. He poured coffee into two cups, took the sheaf of notes from her and laid them gently aside.

"Aren't we all?" he told her. "Look, Lee, it's always been a long shot that something concrete would turn up. All we can do is check out the names of these people and hope we can find some sort of link to our killer here. At the moment I'm concentrating on any of them with any sort of criminal record. If that doesn't pan out, I guess I'll have to look for something else."

"Like what?" she asked. She blew lightly on her coffee to cool it before taking a sip. Jesse shrugged at the question.

"I'll let you know when I think of it." In an attempt to cheer her up, he added, "Mind you, I'm still waiting on answers from interstate PDs on some of these names. And I'm still looking for addresses on at least a quarter of them. Maybe something more concrete will turn up."

"Maybe," said Lee, without a lot of hope in her voice. "In the meantime, I guess your best lead is this"—she hesitated, pulled the notes toward her again and read the name of the first suspect they'd discussed—"Michael Miller guy."

"The ski instructor?" Jesse said. He wrinkled his nose in a negative expression.

"Face it, Jess," she said. "He's proved he's capable of violence, and he threatened he'd get even, right?"

"Yeah," he said, sounding totally unconvinced. "I just don't think he's the one."

"Any concrete reason?" she asked and he shook his head, laughing softly at his own stubborn attitude.

"Not really," he said. "Just that he was the first name to come up when I was asking around. He's got a temper. He loses control and he's got a grudge. I just don't trust anything that comes to me too easily."

There was a long silence. Then a slow smile spread across her face.

"I hope you don't include me in that category," she said.

He grinned at her. "You call waiting eighteen years easy?" he asked her. "I'd damn near given up hope that you might walk through that door one night and have your way with me."

He managed to duck the teaspoon that she threw, just in time.

TWENTY-EIGHT

Denise, the overworked clerical assistant in the Routt County Sheriff's Department, dropped a two-page fax onto the conference room table, close to Jesse's boot heels.

"What we got there, honey?" the deputy asked. He was leaning back in the chair, eyes seemingly closed. He'd heard her and felt her presence rather than saw her.

"Fax from Quantico," she said briefly, and was rewarded by the sight of Jesse snapping upright, swinging his legs off the table and grabbing for the fax in one fluid movement.

"Nothing in it," she added, just a little too late to save Jesse the effort. He nodded, the sudden burst of energy dying as he scanned the negative report.

"Seems there never is," he said tiredly.

"You ever thought of doing this by email, Jess?" she asked. "Might be quicker and less cumbersome."

He tapped the sheets of paper in his hand. "Never been comfortable with emailing, Denise," he said with a half smile. "Too easy for people to ignore. There's something about an actual piece of paper arriving on your desk that gives you a sense of urgency and imperative. It's there. You can see it. It's not so easy to ignore."

"Some folks manage it," she said as she turned toward the door.

Jesse gave her a tired smile.

"You'll get a break soon, Jess," she said. She liked the tall, quiet deputy. She'd sensed there was something special between him and Sheriff Torrens, which only served to increase her approval rating for Jesse. Lee Torrens was a good boss, a good cop and a woman, all of which Denise found to be sterling qualities.

Anyone Lee Torrens liked was okay by Denise.

"Jeez, I hope so," Jesse said fervently.

He'd spent the last two days phoning police departments in four neighboring states, trying to trace names on the list, checking to see if any of them had criminal records. So far, his efforts had met with a total lack of results—if you didn't count the blinding headache that was pounding behind his right eye at the moment.

"Like a coffee, Jess?" That, if nothing else, was a measure of her regard for Jesse. Denise was not one of those clerical assistants who saw it as part of her job description to fetch coffee for deputies—unless she approved of them.

"I'd kill for one, honey." Jesse smiled at her, just as the phone on the table beside him erupted in a shrill burr. He hooked it to him, leaning back and swinging his feet up onto the table again.

"'Lo," he answered. "Yeah, Tenille, I'm expecting a call from the Ketchum Police. Put them through." There was a slight pause, then he spoke again. "Hello? Yes, Chief Ferris, this is Deputy Parker. I appreciate your calling back . . . uh-huh."

Denise had paused on her way out as the phone rang. She didn't know why. Maybe she'd thought that someone might be looking for her. Maybe she'd just been curious. But now, she saw Jesse's whole body become alert, and the legs swing down off the table again as he reached for a pencil and a yellow legal pad among the piles of papers there. He looked up, saw her still watching and mouthed the words "Get Lee."

She nodded and, infected by the sense of urgency in him, hurried from the conference room and headed for the sheriff's office at the end of the corridor.

Lee was consoling Tom Legros over another fruitless night spent in the warming hut—actually a tent—at the snowmobile rental ground.

"Damn it, Lee," the somewhat overweight deputy was saying. "Those little bastards know I'm out there, so they spend their time hoorahing up and down the streets in town."

Lee nodded in sympathy. "Can't be helped, Tom," she said, trying to suppress a smile. Tom's battle with the local kids racing around on snowmobiles was becoming an obsession. The boys weren't doing any real harm but they'd challenged Tom's authority. Now honor wouldn't be restored until he'd caught them red-handed. She thought it was worth trying to distract him from the case.

"You want to take a break from that and look into these 7-Eleven break-ins again, Tom?" she asked.

"Nope," he said stubbornly. Then, with an air of appeal, "Hell's fire, Lee, they're making a joke out of this and I have to do something about it. People are starting to laugh."

She understood. In a small community like this, a lot of a cop's authority hung on his reputation and the way people thought about him. Tom felt he'd been made a fool of and his authority might suffer accordingly if he did nothing about it.

On the other hand, there was a time to cut your losses. If he became obsessive about the kids and their snowmobiles, he might quickly become a figure of ridicule. It was something of a gamble.

"Okay, Tom," she said. "Hang in there, but don't get yourself painted into a corner, okay?"

He nodded unhappily. He knew the risks as well as she did. But he also knew he had to stay with this one a little longer. How much longer was going to be the tricky part.

There was a brief rap at the door, then it opened enough for Denise to put her head around. She saw Tom in the far corner of the office, acknowledged his presence with a nod.

"Pardon me, Tom," she said, then to Lee, "Sheriff, Jesse said can you come down to the conference room? Looks urgent."

Lee was out from behind her desk in one smooth movement, heading for the door. Denise stood aside to let her pass, following behind her, having to half run to keep up with the sheriff's long-legged strides.

"It's a call from Ketchum PD, Sheriff," she explained, a little breathlessly. "That's over in Idaho, isn't it?" she added.

Lee nodded. "Close by Sun Valley," she said. She knew that, in addition to the FBI, Jesse had contacted police departments or sheriffs' offices in all the major ski resorts in Colorado and nearby states, circulating his list of names to see if any of them rang a bell with local police departments. It was a worthwhile route to follow, since most itinerant workers in ski towns tended to work the circuit, going from one resort to another over a series of years.

Now, possibly, the idea had paid off. Possibly, she repeated to herself.

She went through the conference room door without bothering to knock. Jesse was just hanging up the phone, a scrawl of notes on the pad in front of him. He looked up at her as she entered and grinned.

"I think we might have something," he said. There was a note of deep satisfaction is his voice. Satisfaction tinged just a little with relief.

She dropped into a chair across the table from him. Idly, she noticed that Denise was hovering in the doorway, watching both of them. She contemplated sending her away, then decided against it. Denise could be trusted and she'd be seeing the details on Jesse's pad soon enough anyway, when he had her type them up.

"So," she prompted. "Let's have it."

"Name of Wilson Purdue," he said, glancing briefly at his notes to verify the facts. "Fired from his job as a barman at the Dos Amigos last year. Mad as a hornet when it happened, his former boss told me. It seemed someone had been skimming from the register there for weeks. Couldn't prove it was Purdue, but it sure as hell couldn't have been anyone else."

"Where's the connection with Ketchum PD?" Lee asked.

"Well, it seems the very same thing was happening there, at a place called the Western Saloon," he told her. "Mr. Purdue was also the barman in residence, was also fired from there. Again, nothing could actually be proved but there was a lot of circumstantial evidence pointing right to him."

"And this makes him our serial killer?" Lee prompted. But Jesse was taking his time, building up all the facts for her into a neat little logical sequence.

"Not exactly," he admitted. "But it seems that Wilson Purdue was extremely angry about this. He told the owner he'd settle with him somehow. A month later, the owner had his brakes fail totally driving out to the Sun Valley Inn. Luckily managed to stop the car by nosing her into a snowdrift. Shaken up but not hurt too badly." He paused.

She knew there was more to come.

"Seems that the car's brake lines had been cut through with a pair of metal shears or something similar. When the local cops checked, the guy's wife's car had been given the same treatment, and so had his son's and the car belonging to the bar manager who'd first brought the complaint against Purdue."

"What happened to him?" Lee asked.

"State Police caught him, halfway to Boise. Evidence tying him to the cars was pretty sketchy. They wanted to charge him with attempted murder but the local DA didn't think he could make it stick. In the end, they plea-bargained and he did eighteen months for attempted assault. He got out of the pen in"—he hesitated, looked again at his notes—"'98."

"Where is he now?"

"That's the problem," he admitted, with a wry look. "Last we know, he was here last year. Ketchum didn't have any other possible address for him. He wasn't an Idaho local in the first place. Point is, Lee," he said earnestly, "he's shown he has a tendency toward revenge. He's shown that he's not exactly one hundred cents in the dollar and if his little plan in Idaho had worked, he could have become a serial killer in one hit."

She nodded several times, running over his summary of facts about the unknown Wilson Purdue.

"You think he could be our boy?" she asked, at length.

Jesse hesitated, then nodded. "I think he's the best damn lead we've had so far," he said. "Ketchum PD is faxing us his mug shots in the next hour or so."

Lee stood. "In the meantime, maybe you should see if the Feds have anything further on Mr. Purdue," she suggested.

"That was the next thing I was going to do." He caught sight of Denise, still hovering, and waved the legal pad at her. "Denise, you want to type up this scrawl and fax it through for me?"

She moved into the room, took the notes, glanced quickly at them to make sure there was nothing she couldn't read—she'd seen Jesse's handwriting before—and nodded briskly.

"On my way," she said, and hurried out of the room for the fax machine at the end of the corridor.

Jesse met Lee's gaze as the girl left the room.

"This could be it, Lee," he said. "I've got a feeling about this one."

★   ★   ★

Thirty minutes later, and hundreds of miles to the east, Agent Annie Dillon hurried into the FBI comms room.

Agent Dillon was waiting on a list of specifications and serial numbers from the Boeing plant in Seattle. She was investigating a scam that had already spread across eight or nine states, involving counterfeit airplane spares and components. She needed the serial numbers of a sample of legitimate parts.

There were half a dozen cut sheets lying in the in-tray of the fax machine. Hurriedly, she glanced at the top three or four, saw they were lists of serial numbers, and grabbed the bundle, heading back to her office. She glanced at her watch. It was close to five o'clock and her husband was picking her up outside the Federal Building at five after. Both low-handicap golfers, they had planned a weekend at a country club some fifty miles south.

She made it back to her office, shoved the fax sheets into her top drawer. They could wait now till Monday, she thought. She checked her desktop, glanced once at her computer screen to check for email. The screen was clear, except for the programmed message she'd placed there to run every Friday, "Have a good weekend, Babe."

There was nothing secret about the serial numbers but, out of force of habit, she twisted the key in the drawer to lock it, then put the key in her purse. She left the lights on for the cleaners as she hurried for the elevator.

It would be Monday before she discovered the seventh sheet of fax paper that she'd inadvertently picked up. It was a query from a small sheriff's department in Routt County, Colorado, concerning the possible criminal record of one Wilson Purdue.

TWENTY-NINE

*T*here were rumors going around and he didn't like them. He also had decided
that he didn't like Deputy Jesse Parker either.

He'd heard the rumor that the damned deputy was looking for someone who
wanted revenge on the resort. That made him mad. More than mad. It made
him thoroughly pissed. Revenge, after all, was his specialty.

Dr. Rawlings had learned that. So had Sonny Voigtlander, lead hand of the
construction crew he worked with in Utah one summer. Sonny had taken an
instant dislike to him and delighted in bossing him around. He reserved the
worst and dirtiest jobs for him. If he complained, he knew he'd be kicked off
the crew, and he needed the job. It was the old story. Sonny had the authority.
The foreman would take his word over that of a wandering laborer.

There was a girl he was interested in and he knew she was interested in him
too. But Sonny stepped in and she betrayed him. He had his revenge on the
pair of them. It had been easy. Just a few loose nuts on the front wheel of
Sonny's motorcycle had done the trick. He and that two-timing bitch had spent
three months in the hospital after the front wheel came adrift at sixty miles an
hour on the interstate.

That had been his pattern since the long-ago events at his boarding school.
If somebody trod on him, they got stung. If they offended or slighted him, they
suffered. And, up until now, the cops had never seen any connection in a series
of deaths and violent "accidents" stretching from the Rockies to the Eastern
seaboard and back again. Nobody had ever connected them. Nobody had ever
realized that it was simply one man claiming his revenge.

Nobody, that is, until this hick deputy in a sleepy northwest ski resort. It
was dumb luck, of course, nothing more. It would be typical of someone like
him to luck out and chance upon the answer, without ever knowing the full
facts behind the matter.

The deputy was definitely becoming a pain in the ass. Him and his fucking
rules! People had been shoving rules in his face all his life simply because they
felt like it. Do this. Don't do that. Keep your nose clean. Watch where you
tread. Do as we tell you.

Now this damned deputy was the latest. Parker had made it impossible for him to kill that girl in the Silver Bullet. It was at his insistence that the "No two people to a gondola" rule had been enforced. Now the same rule was being applied to the chairlifts as well. One person alone, or three or four to a chair. No doubles unless they knew each other.

He'd discovered that fact the day after he'd missed out on the gondola. Reluctantly, he decided that he'd have to abandon the gondola from now on and that really irritated him. He loved the sense of mystery involved in leaving a dead body in a seemingly locked cabin, with no sign of another person having been on board. He loved the thought of the frustration it must cause the cops investigating the murder as they tried to piece together their theories as to how it had been done.

He loved the thought that, even if they guessed right, the knowledge did them no good at all.

The killing on the chair had been fun, he had to admit. But somehow, it lacked the drama and the mystery of the gondola.

Now he couldn't use the gondola and he was really, really pissed with this Jesse Parker and his fucking rules!

Well, rules were made to be broken and he was just the person to break them. He was uphill from the base of the Storm Peak chair once more, resting idly on his stocks, watching the lift line moving through as the attendants enforced the rule. He'd decided that today he'd kill again. On the chair again. Just to show Jesse fucking Parker that he could come and go and kill as he pleased. All he needed was the right situation—a few empty chairs, then a pair of skiers going up together, with a lull in the crowd behind them. He'd ridden the chair four times already without getting the right conditions. Now, as he watched, the lines had thinned out as skiers went in to eat lunch. Now would be the time when his opportunity came.

Two skiers hissed past him, heading for the roped-off races at the base of the chairlift. They stopped fifty yards below, exchanged a few words, then took off again.

This was it.

The lift race was empty now. A few singles were loading, going up by themselves, in solitary splendor on the high-speed, four-seat chair. But the pair who'd just passed him, a man and a woman, would be the only people boarding the lift for the next few minutes.

Unless he joined them.

He pushed off, skiing fast and effortlessly down the hard-packed slope above *the lift. His turns were fast, short checks, barely costing any speed as he went straight down the fall line. He was gaining on the pair already.*

They skied into the lift line, slowing down and poling up the gentle slope to keep themselves going. He slowed a little, not wanting to get too close too soon. Then he accelerated again.

They were at the right turn onto the final section of the lift line as he entered the back of the race, still moving at high speed. He didn't need to pole, letting the speed wash off as he coasted up to the right end of the race, then skidded to the right, now only a few yards behind them.

They paused at the automatic gates as an empty chair swung up and away, then the flimsy gates flicked open as the next chair detached onto the slow-speed bullwheel and tripped a circuit to open them. The couple poled forward, moving into position to wait for the chair.

He followed them, using the last of his momentum to glide through the open gates and slide to a halt on the left-hand side.

The man was now on his right. He looked up, a little startled by the sudden appearance of another skier alongside him. Then his attention was taken by the chair approaching behind them and the three of them sank back, legs swinging as the chair moved away from the loading point.

The other two let out small sighs of relief as they took the weight off their legs. The man nodded a greeting to him as he reached up to lower the safety bar, bringing the footrests with it.

"Thank God for footrests," he said, with obvious relish, hoisting his feet, awkward with the weight and length of the skis under them, onto the rest. The woman did likewise.

His legs weren't feeling any strain at all. He ignored the footrests, letting them dangle above the snow that was now whipping past below them as they sped up Storm Peak. They entered a cutting between the pines and the wind, cold and sharp on his face, dropped away as the chair stayed below the top of the trees.

As ever, his features were largely obscured by goggles and the hood of his parka. He also had a scarf wound around the lower part of his face. He huddled now, not speaking to his companions on the chair. He smiled to himself. He'd figured how to use the jigger again, in spite of Deputy Parker's security measures. In spite of the watchers at the top of the chair. He moved his right arm and felt the reassuring hardness of the wooden handle under his parka. All he needed was a few minutes of confusion at the top and he'd be away clear again.

Then let Deputy Parker explain how his precautions had proved to be useless!

They were halfway up the mountain now.

He unzipped his parka a few inches, let his left hand steal inside and close around the butt of the jigger. The couple beside him were talking in those low tones people use when they know a stranger can overhear every word. Apparently they were moving on to Jackson Hole, Wyoming, the following day. He grinned a little wider. You'd like Jackson, he told them silently. I killed a man there once. Pity you'll never get to see it.

As they talked, the man had turned slightly away from him, which suited his purpose perfectly. He couldn't see what was happening behind him, and his body obscured the woman's view as well.

Perfect.

He eased the jigger out, keeping it half-concealed in the folds of his parka. He was carrying the 7.63 mm Walther automatic as well, just in case he needed extra backup.

He glanced ahead. The lift attendant was in the wooden hut beside the bullwheel. There was a ski patroller leaning idly against a stanchion at the top of the lift as well. He'd been watching their schedule and knew the man had been on duty for almost three hours. He was due to be relieved in ten minutes. That was part of the plan too.

After three hours of standing in the cold and the snow, stamping his feet and buffing his arms to keep warm, a man tended to lose his edge of alertness. When nothing has happened for three hours, you assume that nothing will happen in the next ten minutes.

Forty yards to go. Just about right . . . now!

Left-handed, holding the jigger close to his body, he reached it across to a spot just inches from the exposed underarm of the man beside him and hit the trigger.

Just half a second too late.

With forty yards to go, the man had decided it was time to prepare to dismount. Just before the razor-sharp blade slashed out of the jigger, he turned back in his seat, sitting back as he lowered his feet from the footrest. The blade, instead of piercing up into his unprotected ribs, hit the solid muscle and tendon in his left arm biceps instead. And hit it at a moment when the man was still turning.

With a shrill scream of pain, the man doubled forward, the blade of the jig-

ger locked in the muscle as he involuntarily spasmed and doubled his arm over, tensing the muscle. The sudden movement tore the handle from the killer's grasp and all hell broke loose.

The man looked down at his arm, his eyes glazing in pain, saw the wooden handle dangling from his biceps, turned back toward him.

"You bastard!" he gasped. At the same moment, the woman had reacted to his scream of pain.

"Randall?" the woman said shrilly. "What is it?" Then, seeing the weapon embedded in her husband's upper arm, she started screaming to the patrolman, now only fifteen yards away.

"Help! Help us!" she screamed. "He's killing my husband!"

He realized what was going to happen just in time, as she screamed the first two words, he joined in, drowning out her cries with his own shouting.

"Heart attack! Heart attack!" he yelled at the top of his lungs. And kept shouting it, over and over again.

He snatched at the handle of the jigger, ripping it loose from the man's arm. But he didn't have a secure grip and the sudden, agonizing flash of pain made his victim jerk upward. His arm hit the jigger, knocking it free from the killer's grasp. It tumbled end over end before disappearing into the deep, ungroomed snow beneath the chair.

The woman was screaming for help still, but his own cries were blocking her out. Then the killer threw the safety bar up, got a hand behind the wounded man beside him and shoved him forward, out of the chair.

"Heart attack!" he yelled. "Help us, for God's sake! Get medics! Help us!"

He and the woman were both screaming at the same time, both screaming for help. To those who could hear them, it sounded as if they were together, trying to get care for the injured man. There was a flurry of activity at the top of the chairlift as the lift attendant and the patrolman hesitated, not sure what to do. Several skiers nearby stopped to watch, attracted by the shouts.

The wounded man fell six feet to the snow below the chair and doubled over, groaning. Then the chair was swinging into the unload point and the two people on it were still screaming, drowning each other out.

The patrolman had started down toward the fallen body, then he hesitated, turning back to the top of the chairlift.

The woman came off the chair at the same time the killer did. Realizing that no one had made any sense of her cries, she grabbed at him now to try to stop him before he could get away. Setting his skis, he shouldered her away violently, sending her sprawling, adding to the confusion of the moment. As she fell, her fingers grasped the goggles and the scarf wound around the lower part of his face, dragging them down.

He could see the patrolman skating back up the slight slope, only a few yards away. But the woman was sprawling on the snow between them and he knew he had a good head start for the trees down the Triangle 3 run. He set his poles and skated at the same time, picking up speed almost immediately. He turned to see the patrolman, tangled with the woman's skis as she rolled over, trying to rise to her feet again. His eyes met the patrolman's and he saw the puzzled look of recognition there.

"Mike?" said the ski patroller. "Is that you?"

Cursing, he turned away again and accelerated into the first steep drop among the trees.

He ran straight down the fall line in the deep, ungroomed snow. There were moguls—ungroomed bumps—under the fresh cover and he let his legs go loose to absorb them automatically. He checked once, turned right to miss a pine, ducked low under the outstretched branches that it flung at his face, then threw in three quick turns, still keeping in the fall line.

The goggles dangled uselessly around his neck. Eyes slitted against the wind and the glare, he could sense the other skier somewhere behind him. Not too close, but not far, either.

An access trail cut through the trees before him. He let his knees come up under him, then straightened his legs like pistons, sailing high over the trail, landing in an explosion of powder snow some five yards on the other side, his knees almost up to his chin to absorb the shock of landing.

He came upright again, maintaining his balance and speed. Check, check, check. He set his edges with lightning speed, one side to the other, his knees pumping as the bumps hammered up at him. His breath whipped away in steamy wisps in the cold air. He let his skis go where they wanted, concentrating on continuous movement and staying in the fall line, as far as the undisciplined stands of pines allowed him.

He came off another bank, soared briefly, exploded into the snow again, nearly lost it, recovered, regained speed. He heard a cry behind him, risked a quick glance and saw the patroller tumbling in a welter of arms, legs and skis as he missed his landing.

It allowed him to increase his lead even further. But, as far as he could see, the other man hadn't lost his skis in the fall and he'd be up and skiing in *pursuit within seconds. An expert skier could often simply roll out of the fall and come back upright almost instantly.*

And he knew Walt was an expert skier.

And there was the real problem of the day. He'd recognized the patrolman. Walt Davies. And he'd been recognized himself. Walt had called him by name. So, even though he could outdistance Walt down the mountain and lose himself in the tangle of trees and different runs on the lower slope, that simply wouldn't solve the problem anymore.

There was a stand of pines ahead. Thick and close together, with widespread branches reaching almost down to ground level. There was no way through them, so he slewed to the right to go around them.

He skirted the grove of trees until they thinned, then threw in a high-speed check turn to the left, reversing direction and heading into the shadows they cast.

Then he threw his skis sideways, ramming the edges hard into the snow, fountaining the soft powder up in a huge drifting cloud as he hockey-stopped in a few yards.

He jump-turned to face back the way he'd been coming. Letting his stocks dangle, he unzipped the parka, reached inside for the Walther and slammed back the action, pumping a round into the chamber. He breathed deeply to steady his hand. He could hear Walt coming, throwing in that same high-speed left turn to come around the grove of pines. He'd have no trouble seeing the way to come. The snow was carved deep with the marks of his own turn.

He saw a flash of blue and yellow between the trees, then Walt sped out into the clear, hunched low, knees pumping.

And saw him standing, waiting.

It was inevitable that Walt would come to a stop. Possibly he thought that his quarry had decided to surrender. Maybe he thought he was injured. But it was instinctive for him to stop as soon as he could. He skidded a little farther down the mountain, finishing four or five yards away.

The Walther wasn't a big gun. The slugs were not much more than a .32 caliber. But four of them were enough to kill anyone.

Walt toppled slowly, his expression one of deep disbelief. He simply knew that this couldn't be happening to him. He was still disbelieving it when he died.

THIRTY

Lee was out on Highway 129 toward Hahn's Peak when word came through about the shooting.

There'd been another break-in—this time at a gas station a few miles south of the Peak. And this time, in broad daylight.

The gas station had seemed deserted. With the recent falls of snow, the owner had expected little traffic to be coming through to the Peak and had closed down around three o'clock. To the passerby, the station would have appeared locked and deserted. But there was a storage room at the rear, where the owner had kept his pickup parked under cover, to save the tray from filling up with snow. And there was also a small, cramped office where he did his accounts and correspondence.

The side door of the gas station had been forced with a crowbar, just like the previous break-ins. And the register had been rifled, although in this case, there was little money in it. The owner had emptied the register when he'd closed up. The cash was with him in a locked steel strongbox in the rear of the building, where he'd been catching up on some paperwork before going home for the evening.

Obviously the burglar didn't realize there was still someone on the premises. Alerted by the splintering sound of the crowbar on the doorframe, the owner had come around the side of the building to investigate.

And he'd brought with him a single barrel Winchester 12-gauge.

Lee was studying him now. He was an elderly man, balding, with a few strands of hair still combed over the crown of his head, as if inviting the missing locks to return, and marking a place where they'd be welcome.

"I called, Sheriff," he was saying now, in an excited, slightly high-pitched voice. "I called and said, 'Who's there? who's in there?' But he never said nothing back. Not a word!"

Lee nodded, encouraging the man to go on with his story. There was still a good deal of adrenaline flowing, she realized, evidenced

by the way the man was rattling his words out like a machine gun, and
the higher than normal pitch of his voice.

"Then, all of a sudden, there he was in the doorway! A big feller,
comin' right at me before I had a chance to think!"

"Big, you say?" Lee interrupted gently. "How tall would you guess?"

The elderly man stopped, considered for a second. "Huge," he insisted, after thinking about it.

Lee tried again for a little more specific information.

"Huge, tall? Or huge, heavy build?" she asked. Again, he thought
about it. She noticed that the whites of his eyes were very round and she
could see them clearly, all the way around the iris. She wondered if this
might be the effect of delayed shock, thought that it probably was.

"Both," the elderly man decided, at length. "He was a mountain of
a feller, coming right at me. I didn't even get a chance to draw the
hammer on the old 12-bore here." He gestured to the shotgun that
Tom Legros had gently taken from his hands when they arrived, and
leaned against the display window of the gas station office.

"Knocked me clean over, Sheriff. Knocked me clean over on my
ass." He hesitated, bobbing his head in deference to the fact that Lee
was a woman. "Begging your pardon for that, Sheriff," he added, a
trifle embarrassed.

Lee gestured that there was no offense.

"But you did get a shot off?" she asked, and the bald-headed man
nodded several times, emphatically.

"Hell, yes!" he said. "I was rolling here in the snow while he high-
tailed it to his car, so I snapped a cap at him right enough. Would have
hit him too if it weren't for that goddamned pump."

The metal body of one of the gas pumps was scarred and scoured
by the blast of small lead pellets. The perspex window that covered the
gauge had several small holes in it as well.

"Only bird shot, mind you, Sheriff," he added. "I never keep a
heavy load in the gun. Just bird shot to frighten them away, you
understand."

"I understand, Mr. Cooley," Lee said, in her best understanding
voice. "So, did you get a good look at this guy when he came out?"

Cooley screwed up his eyes, concentrating. "Other than to see he was huge . . . not really. Apart from that he was kind of "—he searched for a word, finally found it—"average."

Lee and Tom exchanged a gloomy look. Mr. Cooley, they both knew, was not going to be what the law described as a reliable witness.

"So," drawled Lee, "huge in an average sort of way, I guess?"

And Cooley nodded. "That pretty well sums it up."

"Hair color?" Lee prompted. Ned Cooley unconsciously ran a hand over his own inadequate cover.

"Sort of . . . I don't know, brownish, I guess?" he said uncertainly. Then, convincing himself, "Maybe he had a hat on. Fact is, I'm sure he did."

Lee resisted the temptation to catch Tom's eye again.

"What kind of hat would that have been?" she asked, going through the motions.

"Unh . . . well, maybe it was one of those there Navy watch caps," Cooley said uncertainly. "Yeah, that'd be it, I guess. And he had on . . . dark clothes . . ."

Lee tried again. "Jeans maybe, or overalls?"

Cooley looked at her unhappily, went to answer, stopped and said in a dejected tone, "Truth is, Sheriff, I just don't know. I'm not even sure about that goddamn hat either."

Lee nodded. "Sometimes these things happen too fast," she offered, and he seized on the explanation.

"That's it! I mean it all just happened at once! One minute I'm standing here saying 'Who's there?'—and you know, I didn't really expect there was anyone going to be there—then I'm flat on my ass in the snow." He shrugged an apology again and she waved it away. "And that damn gun went off and blew all hell out of my gas pump. I never even meant to fire it at all. It just went off when I went over." He looked at the two of them, miserably. "I'm sorry about this, Sheriff. I never noticed too much. I'm not even sure how big the guy was. Chances were, he was just normal size."

He paused, thinking back, and said softly. "He sure seemed huge at the time though."

"That's the way of it," Tom said soothingly and Cooley looked at him gratefully.

"I'd surely like to be more help to you, but—" he shrugged, defeated and admitting defeat. Lee closed her notebook, slid it back into the back pocket of her jeans.

"Well, Mr. Cooley, if you can't remember details, it's best if you tell us rather than try to make them up. Saves us going off on wild-goose chases."

"I guess," the bald man replied. He still looked deflated. The adrenaline was dispersing now, Lee thought, and she turned as the radio in her Renegade crackled to life. She heard her name called.

"Excuse me," she said to the gas station proprietor, and made it to the Jeep in three long-legged strides. She reached in through the open door and unhooked the mike, depressing the send switch.

"This is Sheriff Torrens," she said, then released the switch so that the base station could reply. She recognized the voice as Denise's. Sometimes she filled in on the radio net when the normal operator was having a break.

"Sheriff? There's been another killing up on Storm Peak?" Somehow, Denise contrived to turn the statement into a question, as if she couldn't believe the bad luck herself.

Lee swore softly under her breath, then pressed the button again.

"Is this our boy again?" she asked. It was unlikely that someone else might have started murdering people up on the mountain, but she guessed it was always a possibility.

"That's right, Sheriff," said Denise. "Tried to kill one man with that stabber thing he's been using, then shot a ski patroller who tried to catch him—Walt Davies."

Lee let the microphone drop to her side, leaned against the cold metal of the Jeep. She knew Walt—and his wife and their twin baby daughters.

"Jesus," she said softly. She noticed that Tom Legros and Ned Cooley had moved closer to the Jeep, listening in to the conversation. Tom looked stricken at the news about the ski patroller.

"Sheriff? You there?" said the radio and she thumbed the switch again, said tiredly, "Yeah. I'm here, Denise. What's the situation?"

"They're bringing Walt down here, Sheriff. They're on their way now. The other guy, he's a tourist. They've taken him to the hospital. He was cut in the arm but Opie says he's in no danger."

"Okay," Lee replied. "We'll head on back from here. Have you contacted Jesse yet?" she asked.

"He's out of radio range, Sheriff. He went over to Breckenridge this morning, remember?"

Lee nodded now. Jesse was chasing up another lead. One of the names on his list had rung a bell with the mountain management people in Breckenridge. Jesse had gone to talk to the Police Chief there. Lee glanced at her watch. Chances were he was still there.

"Phone him, Denise," she said. "He'll be with the Breckenridge PD. Tell him what's happened and tell him to get back here." She paused. That last order was unnecessary. "Just tell him what's happened," she said. Once Jesse heard the news, he'd waste no time at all getting back. She made a mental note that she'd have to issue Jesse a cell phone. He was one of the few people she knew who never carried one.

"Okay, Sheriff. Anything else?"

"No, Denise. That's about all she wrote. We're heading back."

She re-hooked the microphone, turned to meet the two sets of eyes fixed on her. She shook her head sadly at the thought of Walt Davies.

"Jesus Christ," she said bitterly, "we've got to stop this sonofabitch."

THIRTY-ONE

Lee left Tom Legros at the gas station to finish taking Cooley's statement, then she barreled the Renegade back along Highway 129 to the Steamboat Hospital.

She was in no mood to take her time, so as she came into the outskirts of the town, she hit the siren and kept her foot hard down on the gas. She wailed up Lincoln, traffic scattering hurriedly in front of her, slammed the Jeep into a sliding left-hander at 7th Street and accelerated again, heading for Park Avenue.

She brought the Renegade skidding to a locked-wheel halt in the grounds of the small hospital. The siren wound down as she killed the ignition and swung down out of the car, slamming the door behind her and half running to the double glass doors that led inside.

Randall Hollings, the man who'd been stabbed, was in a private room on the first floor. This information was volunteered by the receptionist as Lee shouldered through the doors. She nodded an acknowledgment and, without breaking stride, headed for the broad staircase leading to the next level.

She saw one of Felix Obermeyer's town cops outside a door and figured, correctly, that was the room she was looking for. Inside, the small, one-bed room was a little crowded. There was a doctor, two nurses, Felix Obermeyer, Opie Dulles from the ski patrol and the Hollingses—Mr. and Mrs.

His upper arm was heavily bandaged and he lay back against the pillows on the bed, his face ashen with shock and loss of blood. Idly, Lee noticed the bloodstained parka that had been cut away from the wound and discarded on the floor. So far, nobody had thought to clear it up. She guessed Randall Hollings to be around forty. He was thickset, with a powerful build, and he looked as if he worked out regularly. His arms, left bare by the hospital gown that he was wearing, were well muscled.

Mrs. Hollings looked five years or so younger than her husband. She was blond, pretty and had the sort of figure that comes from a lot of time and money spent in a gym. She'd discarded her parka and was wearing stretch ski pants and a pullover. Her eyes were wild and her hair was disheveled. Lee recognized the nervous, jerky movements and the wide-eyed stare as the first signs of incipient shock.

Jeff Hardy, the young intern who'd been on duty when the Hollingses were brought in, looked up as Lee pushed the door open and entered the room.

"Sheriff," he said, and stood back from the bed to allow Lee to approach.

Felix nodded a greeting as well. She returned it and stepped forward to the bed, studying the injured man critically.

"So, put me in the picture," she said briefly.

Dr. Hardy glanced briefly at the chart in his hand and summarized. "Puncture wound to the left upper arm . . . extensive laceration and internal tearing. Could be some nerve damage. There's definite muscle damage there. Lost a lot of blood but he'll mend okay."

Mrs. Hollings stepped forward now, grabbing at Lee's arm. "Are you the sheriff?" she demanded. Then, before Lee could answer, she continued. "You've got to do something about that man! He could have killed my husband! He tried to, sure as hell! Somebody here has got to do something about him!" Her voice was rising to a hysterical edge and the grip on Lee's arm tightened. She turned to face the overwrought woman, considered prizing her hand loose, then decided against it.

"Mrs. Hollings," she said, in a calm voice. "Your husband is going to be just fine, all right?"

The blue eyes, already wide, widened even farther.

"Just fine? That maniac tried to kill him, don't you understand? And someone has got to do something about it! For all anybody seems to care, my husband could be dead!"

The grip was really tight now. Lee gripped the woman's arm at the wrist, squeezed it firmly.

"Ma'am," she said, "as I understand it, one of our people did try to do something about it, and he is dead."

The woman stopped mid-sentence. She tried to say something further, failed. Tried again, failed again. Her eyes swam with tears. Finally, when she spoke again, her voice was barely more than a whisper.

"Oh, I know! That poor, poor man! I'm so sorry ... I just didn't ..."

Her hand released Lee's arm now. Lee maintained her own grip on the other woman's wrist and moved her to one of the visitors' chairs in the room.

"Why don't you just sit down here, ma'am. I just have to ask you a few questions."

Jeff Hardy stepped closer to the two of them now.

"She's in shock, Sheriff," he said softly. "I wanted to sedate her but Chief Obermeyer here thought it would be better to wait till you'd spoken with her."

"Thanks, Felix," she said, looking briefly at the chief of the town police. Felix was a stuffy, difficult man at times, but beneath it all he was a good cop. He nodded. She looked back to the young doctor again.

"I just need to ask her a few questions," she said. "Then you can give her a shot. I guess you've already sedated the husband?"

Hardy nodded. "Had a bit of stitching to do in that arm wound," he said. "Had to knock him out for that. Lucky for him he's in good shape. The blade of that damn thing got caught up in the muscle of his arm. It saved his life, I'd say."

Lee nodded absently, then turned back to Mrs. Hollings, who was now sobbing softly. She bent at the knees to bring her face down to the same level as the other woman, took both her hands gently in her own and brought them down, away from her face.

"I'm sorry to do this, Mrs. Hollings," she said softly, her deep voice having a calming effect on the woman. "But I have to ask you a few questions."

Mrs. Hollings nodded, took a deep, shuddering breath in to stop the sobbing and managed to compose herself.

"I'm sorry," she said. "I'm okay now. I'll be fine."

"That's great. Now tell me Mrs. Hollings, do you remember anything about the man who attacked your husband?"

The woman frowned in concentration. She shook her head. "He came up from behind us," she said, thinking back to the sequence of events. "My husband was between us. I didn't get a clear look at him until we were off the chairlift."

"Tall? Short? Slim? Well built?" Lee prompted.

"Tall . . . ish. I'd say around six feet . . . it's hard to tell in ski boots," she added apologetically. "And well built but not bulky . . . you know?"

"Did you get a look at his face?" Lee asked. "They told me on the radio that you pulled his scarf off."

Mrs. Hollings shook her head. "I did, but I didn't get a chance to see anything. He'd knocked me off my feet at that stage and I was falling. The other man though, he knew him."

Lee dropped her hands as if they were red-hot. She looked quickly at Felix Obermeyer and Opie. They were both staring at the woman too.

"He knew him?" she repeated. "What other man?"

"You know . . . the one who was—the one who—the man who tried to help us."

The tears were flowing again and she buried her face in her hands again as she thought of Walt Davies's death. Lee exchanged another glance with Felix, then tugged the woman's hands away again, gently, but firmly.

"Mrs. Hollings, I'm sorry, but this is very important. You say Walt"—she corrected herself. Mrs. Hollings wouldn't know the name of the ski patroller who had died. "The ski patrolman who tried to help—you say he knew the man?"

Mrs. Hollings nodded several times. "He recognized him. I was on the ground. I'd grabbed at his scarf because I wanted to get a look at his face. Then he shoved me and I fell, holding the scarf. And then the other man, the patrolman, he said his name. He said—" She hesitated, trying to remember the name.

"His name?" Lee said, with a good deal more urgency than she intended. "He knew his name?"

Again, the woman nodded, her forehead furrowed with the effort of trying to remember that one elusive little detail. That one vital little detail.

"He said, 'Is that you . . . Mac?' " she said doubtfully, trying out the last word, not sure how it sounded.

"Mac," Lee repeated. "He called him Mac? You're sure of that?"

The woman's eyes were troubled. She knew there was something wrong with what she'd said. Something didn't sound right. Then all doubt disappeared from them. It was like the sun coming out and dispelling a light morning fog. She actually smiled as she remembered.

"Not Mac, Mike. He called him Mike. 'Is that you, Mike,' he said." She met Lee's gaze now, one hundred percent confident. "Mike. That was what he said. I'm sure of it."

Lee released her hands again and very slowly straightened up.

"You're sure?" she said, but she'd seen the certainty in the woman's eyes. She was sure, all right.

"Absolutely," Mrs. Hollings replied.

Lee let go a long breath herself. She felt a hand on her arm. "If you've got no more questions, Sheriff, I really ought to give her something," Dr. Hardy said.

Lee made an affirmative gesture. "You go right ahead, Doc," she told him. Then, to the woman, "Mrs. Hollings, thank you. You have been a great help."

The medical staff moved forward to take charge. Lee caught Felix's eye and nodded to the door. Opie followed the two of them into the corridor outside. The cop on duty stepped aside as the three of them came out.

"The name Mike mean something to you, Lee?" Felix asked.

She nodded. All of a sudden, Wilson Purdue from Ketchum, Idaho, had been relegated to second place—by a long way. Now her prime suspect was the one Jesse had felt was too obvious, too easy because it was the first one that had come to light. Mike Miller, ex–ski instructor, fired for beating up a client's husband.

Miller had threatened to get even when they fired him, according to Jesse's notes. He was violent and unstable. And now, by God, they finally had a make on him.

"A guy named Mike Miller," she said, "is one of our suspects. Right now, he's gone to the head of the list."

Felix whistled softly between his teeth. "Looks like you might have just got one hell of a break on this, Lee," he said.

"I hope so, Felix. At least now we know who we're looking for. All I've got to do now is find him."

The young cop who had been on duty outside the door stepped forward apologetically. He didn't like interrupting his own boss and the county sheriff. But he thought that what he had to say might be important.

"Sheriff?" he said uncertainly. "You talking about the Mike Miller who was on the ski school one or two years back?"

She turned to him quickly. There was something in his voice.

"That's the one," she said. "You know him?"

"Well, sure," said the cop. "We used to drink some together. I did a bit of instructing myself a few years back. Didn't get too friendly with him though. He had one hell of a temper to him when he had a mind. I wondered what he was doing back in town," he added, and Lee couldn't help herself. She grabbed his arm in a grip that made a vice seem gentle.

"You've seen him?" she said urgently, and the cop nodded confirmation.

"Ran into him in the Minute Mart across from the Harbor day before yesterday. Said hey and what was he up to. He said he was staying out past Beaver Creek Road on Highway 129. Got an old hunter's shack there."

"Damn!" said Lee. "I must have just driven past the place on my way in here. Can't remember seeing any shack."

Felix rubbed his chin thoughtfully. "Could be the cabin that Lou Pickens owns out that way. He lets it out from time to time. You can't see it from the road. There's a lightning blasted pine marks the turnoff from 129."

Lee nodded. "I know it."

"The cabin's maybe two hundred yards in from there," Felix told her. "There's a dirt track leads in."

"Well, that's just fine," said Lee slowly. A smile spread across her face but there was no humor in it at all. She turned abruptly and headed for the stairway. Felix hurried after her.

"You going out there now, Lee?" he asked her. She paused at the top of the stairs. Her gray eyes were the color of steel.

"Can you think of a better idea, Felix?" she asked him softly.

"No. No. You want I should come with you?"

"Not your jurisdiction, Felix. Thanks anyway."

Opie stepped forward, looking at her doubtfully. "Maybe you should take some help, Lee," he said.

"I don't think so, Opie," she replied. Without her realizing it, her right hand dropped to the curved butt of her Blackhawk Magnum.

THIRTY-TWO

On Mount Werner, the last ski lifts had closed down for the day. The shuttle buses had brought people back in from the mountain and now the sidewalks on Lincoln Avenue were crowded with people—strolling, shopping, looking for a drink before finding a place to eat or simply rubbernecking in the windows of the shops and restaurants that lined the main street of Steamboat Springs.

Without fail, they all turned to gape at the sight of Lee's navy blue Renegade with the blue dome light strobing and the siren letting out a banshee wail as it fishtailed around the right-angle turn from 7th onto the main street.

Once she had the 4x4 aiming in vaguely the right direction, Lee mashed the gas pedal to the floor and the big six-cylinder engine roared as she left a rooster tail of ice and melting snow in the air behind her.

Fortunately, traffic had yet to build up. What cars and pickups were on the road pulled over quickly to make a path for the careering sheriff's car.

Candy Oresto and Liddy Yale left their counter in the F.M. Light Clothing Emporium and hurried out onto the sidewalk to watch the Jeep hurtle past them. Lee's car was well-known to the locals.

"Sheriff Torrens is in one big hurry," Candy observed. Her friend shifted a slab of bubblegum from one cheek to the other and nodded agreement. She didn't say anything. Candy seemed to have covered the subject pretty thoroughly, she thought.

Behind the wheel, Lee steered left-handed while she unhitched the radio mike with her right. She thumbed the talk button.

"This is Sheriff Torrens, come in," she said crisply.

The speaker hissed and Denise's voice was back on the air. Lee made a mental note that the controller was taking one hell of a long coffee break. She'd have to look into that.

"Come in, Sheriff," Denise said. Lee raised the mike to her lips again, sawing violently at the wheel as the tail of the Renegade tried to swap ends with the hood.

"Denise, you raise Jesse yet?" she asked.

"No luck, Sheriff," Denise told her. "He'd left Breckenridge when I rang, and he's on the road back here. Still out of radio range when I tried ten minutes ago."

"Try him again now," said Lee. "Tell him I'm on my way out to collect Mike Miller. Looks like he's the man we've been looking for."

She could hear the excitement in Denise's voice as the other woman came back on the air. "You serious, Sheriff? You've really broken it?" she said.

"Looks like it, Denise. Tell Jess that this guy has a shack out on 129, past Beaver Creek Road. There's a turnoff marked by a lightning blasted pine." She hesitated. "You getting this all, Denise?"

There was a moment's silence, then Denise's voice came back, slightly deliberate now. Lee could almost see her writing the details as she repeated them over the radio link.

"Lightning . . . blasted pine . . . yeah, got it, Sheriff."

"Okay, there's a shack about two hundred yards in from the turnoff. That's where Miller is and that's where I'm headed. If Jess wants any further details, tell him to talk to Felix Obermeyer."

"Okay, Sheriff." There was another pause. "Sheriff Torrens?"

"Yeah, Denise, what is it?" Lee winced as a minibus from one of the resort hotels shoved its nose out of a side street in front of her, then registered the siren and the strobe light and locked its wheels, skidding in the slush and gravel to a stop. She jerked the wheel a little to the right to veer around the eight-seater, then straightened up again. In the process, she missed Denise's message. She thumbed the mike again.

"Sorry, Denise. Say what?"

"I said," Denise repeated, enunciating very clearly, "are you sure you'll be all right on your own?"

"Yeah, Denise, I'm a big girl now. I'll be just fine," Lee said, then mentally added, As long as I get there without rear-ending an eighteen-wheeler. The silence over the radio seemed to accuse her of being foolhardy. Maybe she was, she thought, but the hell with it. She thumbed the button again, said briefly, "Sheriff Torrens, out," and replaced the mike in its bracket.

Both hands back on the wheel, she took note of her own mental reservation. There was no real need to go careering out there at top speed. Miller was either there or he wasn't. There was no reason why he might expect her to be on her way to collect him. In fact, the siren might well alert him to her approach.

She killed the siren and the strobe. Leaning out the driver's side window, she retrieved the magnetic dome light from its position on the hood of the Renegade. At the same time, she let the pedal up a little and the speed dropped to a more reasonable fifty-five miles an hour.

With the same thinking in mind, when she reached the blackened, shattered pine tree, she didn't turn off into the side track there but allowed the Renegade to roll past some fifty yards, easing up on the gas until the car crunched to a stop in the loose gravel on the shoulder of the highway.

She stepped down from the Jeep, stopped to listen.

A long way off, she could hear the moan of a train horn as a mile-long freight ground its way through Steamboat, heading for Denver. There was a gentle susurration from the pines around her as the light breeze muttered quietly in the tops. Apart from that, and the occasional cracking sound of hot metal cooling in the Jeep's engine, there was an uneasy stillness.

She shrugged to herself. Her imagination was getting out of hand. The stillness wasn't uneasy, she was. She unsnapped the restraining strap on her open holster and slid the long-barreled Blackhawk out. Flipping the loading gate open, she eased the hammer back a half inch and slowly rotated the cylinder against the light restraint of the ratchet.

The deliberate click-click-click as the cylinder turned hung in the afternoon air. She checked the big brass cartridge cases in five of the cylinders. The sixth she kept empty as a matter of course. It was only good sense to carry a single-action pistol with an empty chamber under the hammer.

She fished in the breast pocket of her shirt and retrieved the sixth slug she always carried there. She slid it into the waiting chamber and flicked the loading gate closed.

"Ready for bear," she muttered to herself, and allowed the .44 to slide back into the leather holster.

This time she left the restraining strap unclipped.

She reached into the Renegade, pulled the keys from the ignition and locked the door. Then, dropping the keys into her shirt pocket, she crunched through the gravel back toward the blasted pine.

*M*ichael Miller paced the bare, board floor of the hunter's cabin, his boots thudding a hollow rhythm as he went five paces up, five paces back.

This last one had been too close. He knew that now. He'd taken an unnecessary risk by breaking from his previous pattern. And, he admitted, he'd been careless.

Just because all the others had gone off without a hitch, he'd assumed that this one would too. He'd gotten cocky. And he'd left the unforeseeable out of the equation. He'd been so busy concentrating on how the sheriff and her slow-thinking deputy would react that he'd neglected to think that maybe one day, one of his victims might take a hand in matters as well.

That's the way it had gone today. And he'd damn near got caught.

He opened the door of the cabin, supporting it against its sagging hinges, and walked out onto the small porch. There was a cardboard case of Bud cans against the wall. He reached in for one, popped the ring pull and drank deeply. His nerves were tightly strung. He could feel it, and he understood that this was a reaction to the close shave he'd had today.

It had all happened so fast. The sound of the gun still rang in his ears. He hadn't expected it to be so loud.

He began pacing again, up and down the porch. The beer tasted sour and he tossed the half-empty can into the pine trees.

Maybe, he thought, he'd been wrong to come back here. Then he cursed violently, kicking at the small pile of firewood he'd assembled that morning, scattering the split pine logs into the snow. Steamboat owed him! His luck had been right out ever since they'd fired him. Since then, nothing had gone right for him.

Angrily, he grabbed another can. To hell with it! He had plenty. He could take one mouthful from each one if he wanted to and he'd still have plenty.

He ripped the top open, drank deeply, then hurled the can into the trees. It bounced off one of the thicker trunks, cascading white foam into the snow.

"Fuck it!" he yelled, but the sound was strangely dampened by the snow-

laden trees that surrounded him. He looked around them. They seemed to bear down on him. The clearing around the old cabin seemed to be growing smaller by the second. He knew it was his nerves playing tricks on him. Knew it was a reaction to the close call he'd had earlier. But the knowledge did nothing to ease the sudden feeling of entrapment.

The trees hid him from sight, sure. But they also concealed the fact that the woods could be full of cops right now . . . moving in on him. He shouldn't have talked to that asshole in the Minute Mart the other night. At the time it seemed unimportant. But the asshole hadn't mentioned he was a cop these days. Miller had only learned that fact when he'd seen him in uniform the following day. How much had he told him? He tried to remember. He seemed to recall that he'd mentioned this cabin.

Jesus! What could have possessed him? He'd stayed in town for the first few days. Then, as he was constantly running into people who might recognize him, he'd moved out here. So why the fuck had he blurted it out to a cop of all people! But then, he didn't know that he was a cop. And he sure as hell didn't foresee being eyeballed by one of his victims.

His mouth was dry. His heart was still pumping. He grabbed another can, ripped it open, drank deeply, then hurled it into the trees after the other two.

"Fuck it!" he yelled to nobody. "You stay out there! You stay away!"

There was no answer from the pines. He grabbed another can. This time he didn't bother opening it. He hurled the full can of Bud into the trees, then grabbed another and sent that spinning after the others. He dived both hands into the carton, scrabbling among the cans that were now rolling loosely around. Two more went sailing off into the bushes. So what? He had plenty!

He threw an eighth can, stumbling with the effort and falling in the snow in front of the porch. He pulled himself to his feet, yelling incoherently at the trees around him.

"I see you! I know you're there!" he yelled, his voice cracking into an impossibly high register and then he knew he had to get out of here, had to break out of the cordon of trees and cops that had surrounded him.

Staggering, he turned and blundered through the knee-deep snow to the rear of the cabin.

Fifty yards from the cabin, Lee heard the first of the salvo of beer cans come hurtling through the pines. Instantly, she froze. She heard a voice yelling, although it was difficult to make out exactly what it was saying, and then more cans crashed through the pine branches. One of them landed not twenty yards from where she stood, behind one of the larger trees.

She could catch glimpses of the cabin from where she stood, and an occasional flash of movement as Miller staggered and fell and hurled cans at the woods around him.

She didn't need to make out the words to know that he sounded A-1 strung out. She waited where she was for something to develop. Now that she knew Miller was there—at least, she assumed it was Miller—she was in no hurry to be seen. She didn't think he'd spotted her so far but it didn't make any sense to let him get a look at her before she was ready.

The .44 had come out of its holster almost of its own volition. She couldn't remember drawing it but now its familiar shape and comforting weight were there, ready in her right hand. Her thumb coiled around the hammer spur but, for the moment, she left the gun uncocked. In this still air, you could never be sure how far the slightest sound might carry, and the double snick of a gun being cocked was pretty well unmistakable.

More shouting. More cans crashing and spinning through the trees. Then she heard the words, "I see you! I know you're there!" from the deranged man at the cabin. She started forward, convinced for a second that, somehow, he had actually seen her. Then common sense prevailed and she froze in her tracks. There was no way he could have seen her. Maybe he suspected the presence of someone and was bluffing. Or maybe he was just plain crazy as a June bug.

Then she heard another sound, a familiar sound, from a little farther away and suddenly she was running.

THIRTY-THREE

She broke clear of the trees fringing the cabin and stopped, for a moment uncertain of her next move. There was nobody in sight. Then she heard the sound again, realized it was coming from behind the cabin.

It was the brief coughing explosion of a two-stroke motor as someone yanked on the starter cord. The cough now swelled into a continuous roar, revved three times, then settled.

It could have been a generator. Or a chain saw. But she knew it wasn't either of those things.

It was a snowmobile starting up.

Even as she thought it, the black Polaris broke from behind the cabin with a figure hunched over the handlebars, driving the little snow bike through the deep drifts and toward the far edge of the clearing.

A tail of thrown snow hung in the air behind the drive track as Miller gunned the engine. He saw her and yelled something she couldn't make out above the noise of the engine.

She threw up the Blackhawk at arm's length, her thumb snagging the hammer back to full cock, called a warning.

"Miller! Stop or I'll shoot!"

She never knew if he heard her or not, and it was that uncertainty that made her hesitate a fraction of a second too long. She wasn't absolutely positive that this was her man. The hunched figure was sitting just above the thick blade of her foresight as she sighted, both eyes open. Then, at the last moment, she raised the sight and fired above him, the heavy Magnum load kicking her arm up to an almost vertical position. Her thumb worked the hammer again on the way back down. There was an explosion of snow and wood splinters in the pines eight feet above Miller's head, then he kicked the little snowmobile into a skidding turn and disappeared from sight among the trees.

"Shit!" said Lee, cursing herself for firing a warning shot. She blundered awkwardly through the snow to the edge of the trees.

There was a trail inside the tree line, winding down to the right, following the slope of the land. She ran a few yards farther, the sound of the engine fading among the trees, then came to a clear stretch.

Below her, down a steep, uneven slope, the trail doubled back, emerging maybe two hundred yards away. She'd never run the distance in the thick snow before the Polaris made it back to the point below her. She thought of the carbine she'd left in the gun rack in the Renegade, cursed herself for not bringing it.

The buzz of the two-stroke was getting louder now and she realized that Miller had made the turn and was heading back to the point below her. Thick scrubby bushes and deep snow separated the two sections of the trail, with an occasional full-grown pine. Beyond that, she could see what was obviously the snow-covered surface of a frozen lake. The vegetation stopped where the trail emerged from the trees and the smooth, even snow stretched away for at least a mile. At the far bank, there were more trees and she knew if Miller got that far, she'd never see him again.

She caught an occasional glimpse of the black Polaris as he threaded his way back down the trail. She guessed he'd be directly below her in a few minutes.

Lee looked around, saw what she wanted in a fallen pine—a massive mound in the snow. Climbing over it, she checked she had a clear view of the trail below, and sat back, leaning her shoulders and back against the snow-covered wood. She stretched her left leg out in the snow, bent her right knee and rested her forearm on it. Now, shoulders and back supported by the tree trunk, hand supported by her bent right knee, she had a steady platform for shooting.

Once, years before, she'd hit a rabid dog at over two hundred yards from this shooting position but, she remembered grimly, the dog hadn't been moving. There was no problem with the gun reaching the distance. The .44 Magnum is a high-velocity load and her Blackhawk had the extra accuracy of a seven-and-a-half-inch barrel. The only limitation in this situation was the shooter's ability to keep a steady hand and she figured that she'd given herself the best position for that. The knee rest was steadier than a two-handed shot, and it allowed her to set the pistol a little farther away from her eye, in effect making it a longer gun and reducing the angular variation in the shot.

Now she could see the Polaris, just ten yards or so from the edge of the frozen lake. Fortunately, there was an upward incline for a few yards and it slowed the little machine down. She centered the blade foresight on a point five yards ahead of the machine and, just before the snow-mobile had reached the point, she stroked the trigger lightly.

The original specification for a Magnum load came from the High-way Patrol. The requirement was for a handgun that had the hitting power to stop a moving car. The .357 Magnum, the first load of its kind, coupled a comparatively enormous charge with a hard-jacketed, high-penetration slug. Tested by the Highway Patrol, the .357 Mag-num slug had gone clean through the trunk of an Oldsmobile, ripped through the rear seat, front seat and firewall as if they weren't there, penetrated the cast-iron block of the engine and jammed one of the pistons on its downstroke.

Effectively stopping the car.

The slug Lee fired was also hard-jacketed. It was a heavier caliber and it had an even more explosive wallop behind it. And it was hitting something a good deal lighter than an Oldsmobile.

The thin fiberglass cowling of the snowmobile barely slowed the big .44 projectile. Then it slammed into the aluminium alloy of the single-finned cylinder head and blew an enormous chunk of it into aluminium dust. The gaping hole in the side of the head released the rapidly moving piston from its tightly contained world of controlled combustion and let it blow out to one side in a sudden explosion of gas and smoke. The connecting rod shattered, shards of metal exploded in all directions and the drive train virtually destroyed itself in the space of half a second.

As the drive track seized solid, the snowmobile slammed to a halt as if it had hit a brick wall. Miller shot forward, his face slamming into the instrument binnacle, shattering his jaw and knocking him unconscious.

He rolled sideways off the wrecked snowmobile, blood from his battered face staining the snow bright scarlet.

Lee maintained her position for a few seconds. The enormous re-coil of the gun had slammed her right arm almost vertical again and it was second nature for her to re-cock the hammer for another shot on the return movement. She held the long barrel lined up on the inert figure in the snow until she was sure there was no likelihood of him moving. Then she came to her feet and, with gun still ready, began to pick her way down the steep side of the hill, through the scrub, the stunted trees and the deep snow to where he lay.

It took her over five minutes, sometimes sinking thigh deep in the thick snow. He was beginning to stir when she reached him, but was still only semiconscious. Grabbing the back of his collar, she dragged him through the snow a little closer to the wrecked snowmobile, then snapped her cuffs onto his right wrist. She looked for a suitable anchor-point on the snowmobile, found it in the support strut for the left front skid and clicked the other half of the cuffs shut on it.

"Stay here," she told the semiconscious man, and began to leg it back up the slope to where she'd left the Renegade.

She was ten yards short of her car when she became aware of a familiar buzzbox whine of a small, worn-out engine at high revs. She stopped and looked back down the road toward the town. Jesse's battered little Subaru wagon was rocketing toward her, seeming to rear itself up from the ground as he kept the pedal firmly nailed to the floor.

She waited while he veered onto the shoulder of the road just past her and came to a halt in a welter of snow, ice and gravel. The driver's side door shrieked open and he was out of the car and running toward her.

He stopped a yard away, his eyes frantic.

"Lee?" he said, staring at her arm in horror. "Are you okay?"

She glanced down, realized for the first time that she had some of Miller's blood soaked onto her sleeve. It must have happened when she dragged him toward the snowmobile, she realized. She grinned at him reassuringly.

"It's not mine," she said. "I'm just fine."

She felt the relief radiating off him. He hesitated, then grabbed her in a bear hug, holding her tight against him and she thought how damn good it felt to have someone do that. Particularly him.

"Jesus," he said quietly. "I thought I'd go crazy when Denise said you were going after Miller on your own."

She leaned back in his arms, frowned lightly at him.

"That is part of my job specification, you know," she said and he nodded hurriedly.

"I know. I know. You've done it all before. But now it's different."

And she thought about that and decided that that felt pretty damn good too. Then Jesse was looking around, a question in his eyes. Before he could ask it, she gestured toward the dirt road leading back to the cabin.

"He's in there a piece, handcuffed to a snowmobile. I was just getting the Jeep to fetch him out."

"He's alive?" Jesse asked, not caring too much if the answer was a negative.

Lee nodded. "Got a broken jaw, I'd say. Other than that, he's fine. Crazy as a bedbug, but fine," she added.

Jesse fell into step with her and they walked the remaining few yards to the Renegade. She fished in her shirt pocket for the keys and unlocked it. As she was doing this, Jesse looked at her curiously.

"You break his jaw?" he asked, finally. She shook her head.

"Snowmobile did that," she told him.

He nodded, digesting that piece of information. "What did you do?"

"I broke the snowmobile," she said simply and he nodded again.

There really wasn't any answer to that.

THIRTY-FOUR

Miller, dazed and delirious with pain, was regaining consciousness by the time they got the Renegade back to the site of the crash.

Lee frisked him, found no weapons. She unlocked the cuff holding him to the Polaris and together they half-led, half-dragged the groaning man to the Jeep.

Lee tilted the passenger seat forward, and they heaved the injured man into the rear of the Jeep. It had been specially fitted out in the event that Lee might carry a prisoner there. There were several solid steel rings welded to the rear seat frame. Jesse snapped the empty cuff onto one of these, securing Miller once more.

"You read him his rights?" he asked, climbing into the passenger seat. Lee backed and filled several times, turning the Jeep around in the narrow track, then fed in power slowly. The wheels spun a little, then the snow tires bit down through the snow, packed it hard and found purchase, and the Jeep lurched and crabbed its way back up the trail.

"No point to it yet," she said. "He's so whacked out he can't hear a word we say."

Jesse leaned down to peer up the slope to the point where Lee had fired from. He raised one eyebrow in admiration.

"You shot from way up there?" he asked.

"Didn't have time to pick a better spot," she replied evenly. He nodded several times to himself.

"That was one hell of a shot," he said.

"I guess," she replied, her attention on the snow-covered track before them.

He looked at her with respect. Lee had a disturbing habit of hitting what she aimed at. Jesse glanced back at the prisoner. Miller was lolling on the metal floor of the Jeep, his eyes half-closed, blood streaming from the shattered jaw. Normally, Jesse knew, Lee wouldn't shackle a badly injured man in the back of the Jeep like that. But this was the guy who'd killed Walt and, somehow, Jesse didn't feel any sympathy for him.

"So, what was it that put the finger on our friend back here?" he asked.

"Walt knew him," she replied. "The woman heard him say the name 'Mike.' Put that together with the facts you'd already dug up on him, then add in that one of Felix's men actually ran into him in town a few nights ago and there you have it."

"A cop recognized him?" Jesse said incredulously. "Why the hell didn't he think to tell someone?"

"No reason why he should," she replied. "We didn't circulate a list of suspects. You were just asking around employers to see if any of them could shed a little light on things."

He realized she was right.

"Then, when I got here, he was acting crazy, yelling at the trees and throwing things. Seems he got some idea that I was here and he tried to light out on the Polaris. I gave him one warning shot and he just kept going. That sort of clinched it. I figured if he wasn't our man, there was no reason for him to run."

They'd arrived back at the clearing by the cabin. She eased the Jeep to a halt and opened the driver's side door.

"I guess we won't have to look too hard to find enough evidence to tie him to the killings," she said, leading the way to the cabin.

Where she found how wrong she was.

They were looking for rope—after all, they knew the killer had abseiled out of the gondola when he killed his first victims. But there was none. Nor was there any sort of tool that he might have used to force the gondola doors open.

There was no rucksack. No cross-country skis. There was precious little but a duffel bag containing Miller's clothes and a surprisingly large number of cases of beer and cartons of cigarettes.

"Maybe he left his gear in a locker," said Lee, a horrible fear growing in the pit of her stomach.

"Maybe," Jesse agreed. But he didn't sound convinced. Lee swung on him defensively, hearing the doubt in his voice.

"Well, for Christ's sake, Jesse! If he wasn't guilty, why did he light out like that? You tell me."

He shrugged. He was frowning at the stack of cartons by the wall.

"This guy must be one hell of a heavy smoker," he said. He flipped through several cartons, reading the brands. "Winston, Pall Mall, Marlboro . . . He doesn't seem to stick to one brand, either, does he?"

"Maybe he plans to sell them, not smoke them," Lee snapped angrily, tossing the army surplus blankets off the old wooden bunk in one corner. There was nothing under them, so she dropped to her knees and peered under the bed, saw a gleam of metal and reached for it.

"Oh Christ," she said softly as she saw it. And suddenly she knew why Miller had so many different brands of cigarettes, so many cartons of beer. Suddenly she knew why he'd run when she'd appeared. Only guilty men run. She knew that. And now she knew that Mike Miller was guilty all right. He was guilty as all hell. He just wasn't guilty of murder.

Jesse heard the change in her voice and looked across the room at her, curiously. Then understanding dawned as he saw the crowbar that she'd retrieved from under the bed.

"Oh Christ," he echoed. They looked at each other, and both of them felt a racking surge of bitter disappointment.

"He's the 7-Eleven burglar," Jesse said softly.

THIRTY-FIVE

They left Miller in a secure room at the hospital with one of Felix Obermeyer's men on guard outside. The same young doctor had examined Miller. He looked harassed and overworked, and Jesse guessed that was exactly what he was. Doctors in ski towns in the middle of ski seasons often were, and this town was having a whole spate of exotic injuries in addition to the mundane run of breaks, sprains and twists from the ski fields.

Miller's jaw was badly broken in two places. The doctor had sedated him and he was unconscious now. He'd looked sidelong at Jesse and Lee when they'd brought the injured man in.

"He could have used an ambulance with these injuries," he said pointedly.

Lee ignored the implied note of criticism.

"Doctor, we were looking for a man who has killed four people. Don't ask us to treat him with kid gloves, all right?"

The doctor straightened, turned to face her again. "You may have been looking for a killer," he pointed out, "but this isn't him. This is just the guy who's been stealing beer and cigarettes."

And, of course, there was no answer to that.

"There'll be a police officer on duty outside this room," Lee said. "I'd appreciate it if you'll let me know as soon as Miller is fit for questioning."

The doctor grunted. "Be sooner if he'd been treated properly on the way here," he said, refusing to acknowledge the more placatory tone she'd used.

Lee and Jesse exchanged a glance and left the doctor to it. Outside, they hesitated beside their cars, not sure what to do next.

"I've got more steaks at my place. You planning on eating?" she asked. He nodded.

"Eventually. Planning on a good solid drink first."

"Got that at my place too," she said and he grinned at her.

"Then what are we waiting for?"

A thought struck her. "Give me a few minutes. Got a couple of things I should tidy up at the office anyway." She reached into her shirt pocket for her keys. "You can go on back to my place and wait if you like," she suggested, sorting through the bunch till she found the brass Yale key to her front door. Jesse stopped her before she could detach it from the ring. He put his hand over hers, enjoying the contact.

"No matter," he said. "I'll come back with you. Want to see if there's been anything in from Washington."

"You still waiting on more news of that Wilson Purdue character?" she asked. He nodded, feeling in the pocket of his parka for his own keys.

"He's gone back to the top of our list as a prime suspect," he said as he turned to his little Subaru.

She followed him down 7th and across Lincoln, making a mental note to tell him that his right brake light wasn't working as he stopped at the lights.

The two cars wheeled into the parking lot at the Public Safety Building, one behind the other. Lee stepped down from the Jeep, waiting by the back door of the Safety Building as Jesse crossed the parking lot to join her. She noticed a Ford station wagon with a Channel 6 logo emblazoned on the driver's side door. Jesse had to pass it to reach her and as he did, the passenger's side door opened and a slim figure got out. The area lighting in the parking lot caught her pale blond hair, making it seem almost as if the hair was a source of light in itself. Lee felt her breathing tighten a little. She'd recognize that hair anywhere. She started toward the car as the woman spoke to Jesse.

"Hello, Jess," she said. The tone was warm, friendly, intimate. It was a voice that spoke of old memories, shared times, personal moments.

Jesse stopped as if he'd walked into a glass wall. His face, to Lee, seemed unnaturally pale in the arc lights. He stood for a moment, without saying a word, staring at the beautiful blond woman a few feet from him.

"Hello, Abby," he replied at last.

THIRTY-SIX

Abby glanced around the claustrophobic little conference room that Jesse had made his headquarters. She took in the pages of legal pads strewn across the table, the scrawled notes that covered the whiteboard. Her mouth turned up in a little smile.

"I see you still like to work in an atmosphere of ordered chaos," she said.

Jesse didn't reply for a second or two. When he did, it was simply to ask, "You like a coffee or something?"

She leaned over to peer more closely at a note on the whiteboard, frowning slightly in concentration as she tried to make out his scrawl.

"Your penmanship's still terrible," she said lightly. He didn't reply and she looked from the whiteboard to him as he stood by the door, strained and uncomfortable. She knew then, instantly, that what she'd suspected a few minutes ago was the truth. He'd been sleeping with Lee. As she realized it, she felt an irrational stab of jealousy.

"Coffee?" he prompted, and she smiled again, nodding yes.

"Love a cup. Cream, no sugar, thanks."

"I know," he said, and she tilted her head to one side in mock surprise.

"So, there are still some things you remember?" she asked.

Jesse returned her look without any hint of a smile. "There are still a lot of things I remember, Abby." He turned and left the room to fetch the coffee.

In the small annex at the end of the corridor, Jesse poured a cup of coffee, added cream and started back toward the conference room. He didn't pour a cup for himself. He paused at the door to the conference room, his hand on the doorknob, looking at the closed door to Lee's office at the far end of the corridor. As if in response to his glance, the door opened and Lee emerged. She saw him, hesitated as if she might go back into her office, then decided otherwise and came toward him. She had her uniform jacket in her hand.

"I'll be heading home then," she said to him. There was a strained, unnatural look to her. She seemed to be watching him closely, as if she were looking for some message in his bearing.

"Been a hell of a day," he said, without any particular inflection, and she nodded.

"How're things with Abby?" she asked. Lee and Abby had met before, of course, and Jesse had reintroduced them a few minutes earlier in the parking lot. Pleading urgent business to attend to, Lee had left him with his former wife and headed for her office. Now she asked the question almost too casually. Jesse shrugged.

"Well, she seems fine. Up here to do a piece for Channel 6 on our killer," he added. That much he'd been able to find out from Abby in the short conversation they'd had to date. "You want to talk to her about it?" he added and Lee shook her head, not even giving the idea a moment's consideration.

"You do it, Jess. Your case."

He nodded. "Well, fine then. If you say so. Don't believe I'll mention our friend Miller. Can't say I'd like to see the media concentrating on that aspect."

Lee flushed a little and he mentally cursed himself. The statement, intended innocently, had sounded like a criticism of her handling of the day's events. He debated whether to try to correct the impression and decided it was best not to try to retrieve the mistake. Their eyes met for a moment and he saw that she knew he hadn't intended any hurt. He was glad he hadn't said anything further.

Lee made an abrupt movement, brandishing her keys.

"I'll head off then," she said. She hesitated, debating whether to say anything more. "There's still a meal going if you have time later," she said a little tentatively. Then she added, forcing a smile, "Got a fifth of Bushmills going begging too."

He shook his head. "Maybe I'll take a rain check on that for tonight, Lee." He saw the tension leave her body, as if she'd been keyed up and waiting for his answer. As if his answer were the one she had been fearing to hear.

"Yeah. Sure," she said dully. "Any time at all, Jess."

She turned away and headed for the stairwell. He watched her go, knowing he'd said the wrong thing

She paused at the door to the stairs. "Give my best to Abby," she said.

THIRTY-SEVEN

Abby was still making a pretense of reading Jesse's whiteboard notes when he returned to the conference room. She looked up as the door opened and he came in, clearing a spot on the table and setting the thick china mug down.

"There's your coffee," he said. She looked at the single cup, raised an eyebrow.

"You're not having one yourself?" she asked. He shook his head, said nothing.

"You used to be such a coffee hound, Jess, as I recall," she said lightly, taking the cup and sipping. He shrugged.

"Things change," he said. "People change. I guess I have."

She tilted her head to one side and smiled at him. It was an old mannerism of hers. He didn't know whether it was unintentional or cultivated but he remembered how that smile, that slight tilt of the head, used to make his pulse race a little faster.

"Not too much I hope, Jesse?" she said lightly. Again, he shrugged.

"What do you want, Abby?" he asked flatly. Her eyebrows went up and she looked at him with some surprise.

"That's pretty blunt, Jess," she said. "We haven't spoken for over a year and the best you can say is 'What do you want'? Whatever happened to 'How have you been?', 'How's life been treating you?', or even 'Gee but it's good to see you, Abby?'" She smiled as she said it, disclaiming any bitterness or enmity. He ignored the smile. There were too many heart-torn nights in his past to wipe everything away and make polite small talk.

"Like you say, Abby," he said doggedly, "we haven't spoken in over a year. Don't see that there's any real need to catch up on old times anymore. They're in the past."

"Well, for Christ's sake, Jesse," she said, with a hint of bitterness behind the light laugh she tossed in. "Surely we can be civilized. After all, we don't hate each other, do we?"

"I guess not," he replied. "But then, I guess we don't do much of anything anymore, do we?"

She shrugged, set the cup down and shook her head—a picture of injured grace.

"Well, no. I suppose we don't," she agreed, letting him know in the way she said it that she didn't agree. Not at all.

"So then," said Jesse, in the same flat tone he'd been using through-out the conversation. "We come back to my question: What do you want?"

"I told you," she replied. "Steamboat Springs is news with this serial killer you've got up here. The network asked us for some coverage and the news editor picked me to come and do a story."

"He picked you, or you volunteered?" Jesse asked.

She feigned surprise, her eyebrows arcing again at his question. "Why would I do that?" she asked.

Jesse looked away from her, tired of the pretense. There had been too many conversations like this during their brief marriage. He shook his head, refused to make eye contact with her. Abby had that most important talent for a television reporter: She could fake sincerity perfectly.

"Are you listening to yourself, Abby?" he asked angrily. "You said the word 'network.' The network wanted a piece on Steamboat. Now we may not have spoken, stayed in touch or exchanged Christmas cards over the past year or so, but I'm willing to bet that you haven't changed all that much. When the word 'network' crops up, I've seen you trample old ladies to get to a story."

She laughed, with a noticeable hint of derision.

"Besides," he said, "last I heard, you weren't doing news reports anymore. You were hosting a morning talk show. So what would make your news editor suddenly decide to haul your ass up here for a news report? Come on, Abby. You asked for this assignment and I think I already know why they gave it to you."

"And why would that be?" she asked innocently. She'd adopted a tone of tolerant amusement. The tone that an adult used when talking to a recalcitrant child.

"Me," he replied bluntly.

Her eyes widened even farther and she tilted her head forward to look at him—seeming to stare at him over nonexistent glasses.

"You?" she said incredulously. "What makes you so important?"

"Don't jerk me around, Abby," he said tiredly. "It used to work for you, but it won't any longer." As he said it, he felt a faint stirring of fear as he wondered if perhaps that wasn't the truth. He realized angrily that he wasn't sure. Given enough time and the right opportunities, he wasn't one hundred percent confident that Abby wouldn't be able to drag him back into her silken net.

She perched on the edge of the table. His eyes were drawn unwillingly to the short hemline of her skirt, and the trim line of her hip and thigh. Abby had great legs. Hell, he thought miserably, Abby had great everything. And she knew how to display any and all of her features to best advantage. She seemed to notice the direction of his glance and straightened from the table, pointedly smoothing the hem of her skirt down again.

"My question stands," she said evenly. "What makes you so important?"

"Okay, I'll spell it out so we can both understand it. You hear that the network wants a piece for national broadcast. It's a case happening up here and I just happen to be the investigating officer. While your editor is figuring who's best for the story, you waltz in, point out that you and I are old, old friends—'Heck, I was married to the guy! I know him! I can get him talking'—that sort of thing. The editor asks if there's no hard feelings over the divorce. You say 'Hell no, we're really civilized, you know?' And you get the assignment." He paused, locked her eyes into his. "How'm I doing so far?"

She spread her hands in a gesture of defeat, laughing in a self-deprecating way.

"Okay, Jesse, I admit it. You've got me! But, hell, is that so bad? I mean, look at the way you just saw right through me. It just goes to prove that we still know each other. We still think about each other. We still understand each other. What's so bad about that? Okay, I admit I wanted the story. I did it pretty much the way you said, except"—she raised one perfectly manicured forefinger as he went to speak and he stopped—"that the editor did actually broach the subject with me first. He knew we'd been married and he asked if there was any bitterness, or whether I thought our relationship might help."

Jesse grunted and she spread her hands ingenuously. "Well, come on, Jesse, are we bitter? I know I'm not."

"As I recall," Jesse said, "you weren't the one to have much to be bitter about."

"Well, now, that's not exactly true, Jess," she said earnestly, and he looked up quickly at her. He'd learned to be on his guard when that earnest note crept into her voice.

"Admit it, Jess," she continued. "There were problems on both sides. I wasn't the one who'd be out till four and five a.m. on stakeouts while you were home waiting for me. I wasn't the one who was getting calls in the middle of the night and rushing out and leaving you to wonder if I'd come back in one piece."

There was no answer to that. He knew she was right, on the surface of it. But he also knew that she'd known she was marrying a cop. And he knew she'd made no great effort to accept the life he had to lead. But if they started down that route again, he thought morosely, they could do a rerun of the entire marriage breakup and divorce. He didn't want that.

Besides, he knew that when it came to a guilt match, Abby could tie him in knots without even trying. She was a grandmaster of guilt. A black belt in blame.

"Come on, Jess," she said in a placating tone. "We had some good times too, didn't we? Why should we forget them? Why can't we remember what was good and accept what was bad and be . . . well, friends? Is that asking too much?"

And there it was. If he said yes, it was too much, he would be casting himself in the role of the unreasonable, unforgiving ex-husband in the drama that Abby was directing. He went to pace the room, stopped, half-turned away, then turned back again. He must look like a chained bear, he thought bitterly.

Abby was smiling at him now. A sad little smile that allowed her eyes to plead with him for reason and forgiveness and friendship. God, she was beautiful! he thought and felt a sudden, unexpected shaft of desire shoot through him. Instantly he was wary. He knew that Abby could entangle him again so easily. Knew too that for her, it would be a short-term thing. He couldn't do that anymore. Not with her. Never with her. And not now that he'd found Lee.

As if she were reading his thoughts, Abby said, "Would you rather I spoke with your friend Lee? Maybe that would be easier for you?"

He shook his head. For some reason he didn't fully understand, he didn't want Lee and Abby talking. He didn't know how or why, but he sensed that Abby would make things difficult between himself and Lee. Maybe she'd do it, he reflected, just to see if she could. Abby could be like that.

For her part, she saw the sudden wariness in his eyes as she mentioned Lee's name. She ran her eyes over Jesse's slim build. He was still in great shape, she thought, and remembered now that his body—slim, muscular and taut—had always had an effect on her. Regardless of what had been wrong with their relationship, the sex had always been right. Very right.

And looking at him now—tired, wary and kind of beaten down—she knew that, given the chance, she'd go to bed with him in a moment. As the realization came to her, she felt a surge of anger toward Lee.

"No," he said finally. "I'll talk to you. You got a crew up here yet?"

"The crew will come up tomorrow," she said. "We'll do an interview then and you can fill me in on the investigation so far." She paused. "I understand you had a break in the case today?" she said innocently. He looked at her, wary again, not sure how much she knew about Miller and the way things had gone today.

"False alarm," he said briefly. "Nothing to get excited over."

She nodded and he knew now that she knew the full story. If she hadn't she would have continued to probe. He thought he'd have to tread very carefully around Abby. She had the instincts of a good reporter. And all the lack of heart that usually went with them. If she could do a hatchet job on the Routt County Sheriff's Department, its sheriff and its newest deputy, he knew that nothing would prevent her doing so—not their former relationship, not any possible renewal of it.

Not anything.

"We'll talk tomorrow," he said. "Call me here after nine."

He motioned toward the door, indicating that he was finished for now and that she could leave. She hesitated a second or two.

"You busy tonight?" she asked, smiling hopefully. Then, before he could answer, she hurried on. "I'm at the Mountain View and I seem to remember they used to do a great steak. Maybe you could join me? We could catch up a little?"

He met her eyes deliberately and said, very evenly, hoping that she would get the message, "Not tonight, Abby. I've got things to go over, okay?"

She smiled, looking disappointed but not overly so. "Not tonight?" she asked lightly. "Does that mean 'not anytime'?"

"It means not tonight," Jesse said evenly.

She shrugged. Can't blame a girl for trying, the gesture seemed to say.

He let her out through the parking lot door and saw her to her Ford. She smiled and fluttered her fingers in a wave good-bye as she pulled out onto Yampa.

Feeling tired and confused, Jesse climbed into the Subaru. He noticed the shriek of metal from the front door and frowned, wondering how long it had been doing that. Then he cranked the engine and pulled out, turning up toward Lincoln. The lights were green at the turnoff to Lee's house and he came to a halt there, trying to decide whether he might call in on her after all.

Eventually, just before the lights changed to amber, he decided not to and accelerated away, heading for the turnoff to Rabbit Ear Pass and his own little cabin.

He wondered why he'd decided not to see Lee and was angry with himself when he couldn't find a reason.

THIRTY-EIGHT

Abby sat on the bed in her room at the Mountain View, idly swinging one leg and staring at her own reflection in the window.

Beyond that other image of herself, she could see the lights of the groomers as they moved about the mountain. Her image ebbed and faded as the stronger light sources outside passed across it.

She was virtually naked, wearing only a pair of white bikini panties. She wondered idly if anyone outside could see into her room and see her sitting there, decided that she didn't really give a damn if they could.

She studied her reflection a little more closely, as a Snowcat's headlights passed across it, dissolving it briefly into the glare, then allowing it to fade back up again. It was a good body, she thought. A damned good body. The breasts were good and still firm. Not too big, but not too small either. They were full and rounded. Her legs were good too. Long and shapely. She raised one as she watched, seeing the play of firm muscle tone under the skin as she did so.

The stomach was flat and the hips curved nicely. If she stood, she could see that her ass was in great shape. Except she couldn't be bothered to stand. She decided to take her ass on faith.

The hair, of course, was spectacular. A glowing, almost white blond that even the subdued image of the reflection couldn't dim. She knew other women hated her for her hair. Hated her even more when they found out it was natural. They hadn't made the bottle that could give a woman hair like that.

She was angry. Angry at the way Jesse had spoken to her. Angry because she knew he'd been sleeping with Lee. She wondered how long that particular arrangement had been going on. Her instincts told her that it was a fairly recent occurrence. She'd sensed the wariness in Lee when they'd spoken, briefly, at the Public Safety Building. The sheriff wasn't totally sure of her position there. She didn't radiate the sort of self-confidence that came with a long-standing arrangement.

Still and all, self-confidence or none, Lee currently enjoyed a tactical advantage and that made her angry. Most of all, Abby was angry because, on the spur of the moment, she'd asked Jesse to join her this evening and he'd refused.

A large part of it, she could write off to injured pride. But she had to admit that, when she'd seen him again, slightly stooped, looking worn down and overtired as he was, she'd felt some of the old thrill of excitement that used to light up inside her in the old days. He'd always had that feeling of vulnerability about him, she thought.

She realized, sitting here now, that she still loved Jesse. Maybe not as much as she once had. But certainly more than she'd realized. The sex had always been great between them, she thought now. Certainly a sight better than anything she'd experienced since they'd split. She'd had several affairs with men from the TV channel, but none of them had lit the fire inside that Jesse used to.

That the mere thought and sight of him now was still able to.

"Goddamn it!" she said aloud. She stood and moved to the ridiculous little refrigerator that held the room's minibar. She selected two tiny bottles of Bacardi and dumped them into a glass, tossing ice in after the rum and topping it off with a splash of tonic.

She swirled the spirit around the ice to chill it faster and moved to the window, leaning her head against the cold glass. The window was double glazed but the inner pane was still only just above freezing. She glanced down, seeing the chill from the window puckering her nipples, bringing them erect. She thought about Jesse's tongue and the way it used to roll around them and she felt a shock of warmth in her groin. Her breathing was coming faster and shallower she realized, and she took a deep pull at the drink, feeling the bite of the spirit in the back of her throat.

She glanced down to the hotel parking lot, three floors below. Two teenage boys, no more than eighteen years old by the look of them, were standing by a beat-up old Volkswagen Kombi, staring up at her window in rapt amazement.

She smiled at them, let her free hand wander down to touch herself. The sill was low enough so she knew they could see her do it.

She enjoyed the sensation of having them stare at her, having them admire her, for a few seconds. Then she stepped slowly back, out of their line of sight.

"Sorry, boys," she murmured. "Show's over for tonight."

Then, abruptly, the enjoyment faded. She didn't give a damn about two horny eighteen-year-olds. She wanted Jesse. She wanted him now.

And maybe for more than just now, she realized with a sense of surprise. She thought about their marriage breakup. If she were honest— and with nobody else around, there was no point in being otherwise— she could admit that her career was a large factor in the breakup.

Her career, she laughed bitterly. She was the second-billed anchor for a mid-morning talk show on Denver TV. She was, she thought brutally, Hicksville's Kathy Lee to Nowhere's Regis.

Jesse had been right, of course, about the motives behind her visit to Steamboat. She'd heard the word "network" and she was ready to do anything to be the face presenting the piece. It was a chance. A moment. A possibility that some network executive might see her and she might strike a chord with him and her career could move on.

Not a good chance. Not a likelihood. A vague possibility. Not even that, if she was honest with herself.

The network shot was a dream, nothing more. It simply wasn't going to happen. She was going to stay with Channel 6 in Denver, interviewing local politicians, second-string personalities and farmers with hogs that had decided to raise flocks of ducklings as their own offspring.

She shrugged. It wasn't so bad, she thought. Then she amended it. It wasn't so good either.

But maybe now, if she wasn't chasing the phantom prospect of a career in network television, she might be able to put things back together with Jesse. She considered the idea. It had just come to her but she couldn't see anything too wrong with it.

Maybe she and Jesse could make it together. She knew he wanted to. She'd seen it in his eyes that night when she'd asked him to join her. She was sure she'd seen it. He'd hesitated. Definitely. He may have said no. But he'd hesitated. And that meant that he'd meant to say "yes."

She glanced at the phone by the bedside now. She could just call Jesse and repeat her invitation. Tell him she was waiting here. Tell him she was naked, and feeling real warm about the thought of him.

She could laugh and tell him about the two drop-jawed boys in the parking lot, staring in amazement at her breasts as she stood by the window. Naturally, she'd make it sound unintentional. But she knew that sort of innocent, secondhand voyeurism could turn a man on quicker than a light switch.

Jesse would drive on down and they could go somewhere quiet and eat and share a bottle of wine and then come back to this room and lie on the big bed, with the lights off and the curtains open and the lights of Mount Werner spread out before them and she could let Jesse make love to her again and again. Like he used to.

Then she knew she wouldn't do it. Not tonight. The time wasn't right yet. She'd wait till she'd done her piece for the channel. Jesse would see how much she cared. She closed her eyes and she could see his face, and that silly, lopsided grin that could just mess up a girl's thinking so badly.

"Fuck you, Jesse," she whispered. "Where are you?"

And on Mount Werner, the lights started to disappear as the Snow-cats moved farther and farther up the mountain.

THIRTY-NINE

Lee dropped into an old leather armchair in the parlor and picked up the remote for the television.

She was beat, physically and mentally. The day had brought another heavy session in Ned Puckett's office. Miller's arrest, and the almost certain knowledge that he'd been responsible for the spate of burglaries in convenience stores, had done little to calm the anxieties of the town leaders.

If anything, it had made matters worse. She couldn't really blame Ned or the others for that. She knew where the fault lay and that was squarely on her own shoulders. She was the one who'd made such a big play of lighting out to arrest Miller. She winced as she thought of how she'd barreled her Renegade down the main street of Steamboat Springs, siren howling and strobes flashing.

News traveled fast in a town like Steamboat and by late afternoon, most of the town knew that the sheriff's department—no, she amended with a humorless smile—the sheriff herself, had screwed up in spades.

The editorial in the *Steamboat Whistle* hadn't done anything to make things better. Usually, the local paper was sided with Lee and her actions. This time, with the best will in the world, there was little they could do but criticize. She'd jumped to conclusions. She'd acted in haste. On top of that, there was a total lack of any real progress on the case.

Now, of course, there was Abby's report, due to air on the evening news out of Channel 6 in Denver.

Abby had spent the morning taping her story. She'd interviewed Jesse at some length, then visited the scenes of the murders. She'd tried to interview the surviving victim and, when that failed, his wife. She spent a brief ten minutes with Lee herself.

There'd been no hint of criticism. There'd been no tough grilling. No sensationalism. No seizing on minor facts and blowing them all out of proportion. On the face of it, Abby had been the essence of even-handed reporting.

But Lee had been around public office and the media long enough to know that the real slant on an interview only became apparent when the report was edited.

It was then that the reporter could add in their introductions and closing comments. Often, the simplest action, such as the raising of an eyebrow, could throw a huge shadow of doubt over the truthfulness of the subjects, and the wisdom or otherwise of their actions.

So now she waited for Abby's report, fearing the worst. After all, Abby owed her no favors. She'd sensed an undercurrent of hostility from the reporter. Lee knew that Abby had guessed about her relationship with Jess—and resented it.

Lee shifted in the armchair, rolling her shoulders to relieve the knotted tension in the muscles there. Jesse had been decidedly reserved since Abby had reappeared in their lives, she thought.

He seemed awkward, unsure of himself. She was certain he was doing all he could to avoid her company. Certainly he'd spent only a few minutes alone with her in the past day. And that was in marked contrast to the closeness that had grown between them since they'd spent the night together.

Damn it, she thought. It had taken her eighteen years to find him again. Now, with Abby back on the scene, she was afraid she might lose him once more. She was a little surprised to realize just how much she was afraid of that.

The news was breaking for a commercial. An impossibly well groomed golden retriever, carrying a can of mineral water to two impossibly good-looking duck hunters in a Hollywood swamp. A cheerful voice-over told her that he was "Bringing back the brighter taste of Mountjoy Mineral."

"No shit," said Lee, and rolled her shoulders again. The tension in her muscles didn't seem to have loosened any. She wondered what Jesse was doing.

Jesse was in his cabin, watching the same retriever on his battery-powered old black-and-white Sanyo. Like Lee, he waited anxiously. Like Lee, he knew how a report could be slanted and twisted after the event. He knew there was no way to guard against being quoted, or shown speaking out of context. And he knew that Abby didn't feel she owed the sheriff of Routt County any favors.

The retriever had gone, replaced by a housewife who needed a Tylenol. Tylenol, if you could believe her, could probably solve most of the problems besetting the western world.

The music introduction swelled as the Tylenol woman faded away. And the news desk of Channel 6 filled the screen again, with the 6 News at 6 symbol superimposed over the fade up. Jesse leaned forward and tweaked the volume knob. Throughout Yampa Valley, a few thousand other viewers did much the same thing.

"Welcome back," said the anchor smoothly. On-screen behind him, a still shot of the front slopes of Mount Werner faded up, overlaid with an artist's very inaccurate impression of a jigger. It looked like an ice pick gone wrong. Jesse wondered briefly if they'd ever find the jigger. Hollings had told them that the killer had dropped it during the struggle. It was lost somewhere in the deep snow under the chairlift. Below the ice pick–jigger was a caption: "Mountain Murders."

"The search continues," said the anchor, continuing himself, "for the multiple killer who has been terrorizing the popular ski resort of Steamboat Springs. Channel 6's own Abby Parker-Taft traveled to Steamboat today to file this report."

He looked off camera, to one side. He faded slowly from sight, to be replaced by a wide shot of Abby, mike in hand, facing the camera.

She'd chosen one of Steamboat's iconic sites as her backdrop: the old timber barn just outside town, with the ski trails of Mount Werner in the background. "This is a mountain of fear," Abby was saying, her voice well modulated, calm, with just the right hint of drama.

Her pale blond hair stirred attractively in the breeze. She was wearing the kind of battered leather bomber jacket that felt as soft as a glove and cost over five hundred bucks. And tight, sea-blue jeans. She had a great ass and great legs, Jesse thought irrelevantly.

"The Mountain Killer has killed four times now," Abby was saying, "and left another victim badly wounded. Local business, dependent on the tourist dollar, is suffering."

★ ★ ★

Lee reached blindly for a bottle of red wine on the kitchen bench behind her, her eyes still glued to the report. She topped off her glass as Abby detailed how local business was suffering.

Over the next minute and a half, the screen carried a montage of nearly empty ski slopes, deserted bars and restaurants and unoccupied chairlifts as Abby described how people were staying away from Steamboat.

There was a quick sound grab with Ed Spelling, owner of the Sombrero Cantina, who looked worried at the loss of business. It seemed Ed spoke for all of Steamboat's business community.

Then the scene changed to a shot of the Public Safety Building. Lee took a deep breath. Here it comes, she thought.

"I spoke with Sheriff Lee Torrens, the senior officer responsible for the investigation," Abby was saying. The screen filled with a close-up of Lee. Abby's voice, off camera, could be heard asking, "Sheriff Torrens, are there any solid leads in the Mountain Killer case?"

The image of Lee on-screen shook her head slowly. So did Lee, watching. She frowned as she noticed the lines at the corners of her eyes. Her skin looked like old leather compared to Abby's perfect complexion.

"We're pursuing certain lines of investigation," she said.

Watching, Lee muttered to herself, "Shit."

The "certain lines of investigation" statement sounded just like what it was—another way of saying "We don't know from diddly shit about what's happening or what we're going to do."

The camera cut away to Abby, nodding sympathetically.

"I guess in an investigation like this, you have to sift through mountains of facts, looking for that one elusive clue that will break the case?" she asked.

Lee frowned to herself again. She didn't remember that question. It must have been recorded separately by Abby after the interview was completed.

The shot cut back to Lee again. "We're confident of a breakthrough soon," she said.

"Like hell we are," Lee muttered heavily. But on-screen, Abby was nodding again. She looked as if she was confident too.

The scene cut now to the top of Thunderhead.

"Sheriff Lee Torrens is a popular and efficient cop," Abby said. "She's not the sort of woman to give up, no matter how tough things are looking. Already, as a by-product of this investigation, she has personally tracked down and apprehended a dangerous criminal who has been breaking into convenience stores around the area."

"Well, I'll be damned," said Jesse, sitting up straighter and leaning a little closer to the slightly fuzzy image that was all he could get up there on the mountain. He'd been sure that Abby would use the Miller case as an example of how the Routt County Sheriff's Department was falling over its own feet in this investigation. Maybe, he thought, he'd misjudged her.

"The chief investigating officer on the case is Deputy Jesse Parker."

And there he was, as the camera panned smoothly away from Abby and picked up Jesse in the background, talking to one of the lift attendants and one of Felix Obermeyer's officers, on guard duty at the top of Thunderhead.

"A former ace homicide detective with the Denver PD, he holds several commendations for bravery and efficiency. Sheriff Torrens is confident that he's the man who will crack this case. And her confidence is reassuring to the people of Steamboat Springs."

There followed a series of random shots of townspeople, all expressing trust and confidence in Lee's and Jesse's ability.

"She's a fine sheriff," said Cyril Culpepper. "Good as any man. Hell, better even, maybe."

"Jesse, he's a good boy. He knows his job." That was Andy Taylor from the Times Square Ticket Office.

"They'll get him. Sure enough, they'll get him. They's good cops," Lorna Watson, wife of the local jeweler, expressed with confidence. "I just hope they do it sooner rather than later. It's terrible what's happened here."

Lee's eyes narrowed as she sat watching the screen. Suddenly, she knew what Abby Parker-Taft was up to.

Abby Parker-Taft was, at that moment, lying back on her bed in the Mountain View Hotel, wearing nothing but bikini briefs and a short gray T-shirt that barely reached her midriff. She was watching herself on-screen with a cool, professional detachment.

Her screen self was now on the corner of 7th and Lincoln, outside the entrance to the Harbor Hotel. It was getting on toward dusk and the neons in the street glowed behind her, blobs of unfocused color. She'd made the producer hold the sun gun to one side for this shot. Normally mounted on top of the camera, it would cast a flat, glaring, unattractive frontal light on the subject.

Held to the side, as she'd directed, it gave her a better look. Side lit, features more clearly defined and with a slight halo glow about her blond hair. She nodded to herself. She looked as good as a girl could, under the circumstances, she thought.

"This is a town in fear," she was saying to the camera. "But a town that trusts its cops to do everything in their power to keep them safe. Hardworking cops, just waiting for that one break, that one simple clue that will break this case wide open."

The shot cut back to her earlier interview with Lee, a close-up of the sheriff. Watching, Abby smiled again, the direct comparison did little to flatter Lee Torrens, she thought. She heard her own voice over the shot of Lee, as the sheriff flicked through a pile of information folders and wanted posters. Abby had asked her to do this as a fill-in shot.

"Sheriff Torrens is a good cop doing a difficult job. But she knows that, sooner or later, the Mountain Killer is going to make a mistake. One slip. One little item he'll forget. When he does, they'll nail him."

The screen now froze on a close-up of Lee, then slowly dissolved through to a matching close-up of Abby. The smile returned to her face.

Lee's face was lined, tired, lit straight on. Her hair was a tangle and the gray showed clearly. By contrast, Abby was fresh, glowing, with just a stray tendril of blond hair stirring in the evening breeze as she brushed it away from her face.

"Abby Parker-Taft, from Steamboat Springs, for 6 News at 6."

Her image remained on-screen for a few seconds, in a small frame at the top left as the studio cameras found the anchorman once again. Then the small frame disappeared, to be replaced by a still shot of the Governor's Mansion in Denver.

"In Denver today, Governor Morgan Whitton received a delegation from industry and commerce to discuss the vexed question of industrial pollution in the mile high city . . ."

Lee hit the remote switch and the screen instantly imploded to black. Almost immediately, the phone rang. She dropped the remote onto the couch and grabbed for the receiver.

"Sheriff Torrens," she said.

"You see it?" It was Jesse. There was no need for him to say what he meant by "it." He sounded vaguely pleased.

"Yep," she replied evenly. "I saw it."

"Damn me," he said. "I'm not sure what I expected, but that sure as hell wasn't it. She was pretty damn fair the way she treated you, Lee. I was half expecting she'd do a hatchet job but, by God, she didn't."

She could almost picture him, grinning with relief, shaking his head in surprise. He was pleased, she knew, on her behalf.

"Maybe I should consider running for mayor," she said, with just a hint of bitterness in her voice.

He sensed it, paused awkwardly. "You mad about something, Lee?" he asked uncertainly. "I mean, she could have been a whole lot rougher on us you know. She gave you one hell of a vote of confidence at the end there."

"Yeah, I know," Lee replied, trying to lighten up a little about it. She didn't want this conversation to continue any longer.

"Jess, there's someone at the door. I'll get back to you, okay?"

"Yeah. Sure, Lee." He sounded a little relieved now, as if he thought he'd maybe been mistaken about her earlier reaction. "But it sure was nice to get some good press for a change, wasn't it?"

"It sure was, Jess," she said, forcing a smile into her voice. "I guess for once it helped to know someone in the business. Gotta go," she said hurriedly, cutting him off.

"Sure. Bye, Lee," he said.

She heard the words thin and distant as she was already setting the receiver down. She hung the phone up and looked at it, shaking her head sadly.

"Don't you see why she did it, Jess?" she asked the silent instrument. "She wants you back."

FORTY

In his cabin above Rabbit Ear Pass, Jesse stared at the phone, a puzzled expression on his face. He'd been pleased with Abby's report. Not for his own sake. After all, it didn't really matter a damn to him what the media thought of the way he was handling the case. But for Lee it was important. She was an elected official and she needed good press during a crisis like this.

He knew there was bad feeling just below the surface between Abby and Lee and he'd expected the worst of Abby's report. She was a past master at the sly innuendo, at damning a subject with faint praise. Her cool, beautiful looks could be devastating when she turned the wick up on her sarcastic sense of ridicule. And he knew she saw the report as a chance to go on to bigger things—maybe a spot on network news somewhere. Jesse might be a country boy, but he'd been around enough to know that network news producers didn't usually give out jobs to reporters who handed in good news reports.

"Good cops, tough job" was a whole lot less likely to impress the network than "Hick cops fuck up." Jesse knew it. And if he did, he was sure that Abby knew it as well.

He shrugged, stopped gazing at the phone and moved to the kitchen, where a half-full bottle of Jack Daniel's was waiting on the bench. He poured himself a slug, thought about adding ice, decided it was unnecessary, and sipped at the smooth fire of the liquor.

He wondered if Lee was all right. It was sometimes hard to tell what a person was really thinking when you were talking on the phone. Jesse liked to be able to see a person's eyes when he was talking to them. Eyes found it difficult to lie. If you could see the eyes, he felt, you could see what the person was really feeling.

The phone rang. Taking his glass with him, he crossed the room and picked up the receiver, expecting it to be Lee, calling him back after dealing with whoever it was who had called on her.

"This is Jesse," he said.

"So it is," Abby replied. "I guess I'd know that voice anywhere."

Ready to hear Lee's voice, he was taken aback.

"Oh, hi there," he said lamely. He could hear the smile in her voice as she replied.

"Hi there? I bust my buns singing the praises of the Routt County Sheriff's Department on network television and all you can say to me is 'Hi there'?"

"Sorry, Abby," he said, recovering a little. "I was sort of expecting someone else to call, I guess."

"Lee?" she asked, her tone light and seemingly unconcerned. He wondered if he'd been wrong about the possibility of jealousy between the two women—at least on Abby's part.

"Yeah, well, I was speaking to her earlier and we got cut off, you know," he said.

"So, did she see the piece?"

He knew that, at heart, reporters were just like any other performers. They all needed praise for their efforts. He guessed that was fair enough. They got their asses kicked often enough too.

"She saw it, yeah," he said carefully.

"And?" she pushed gently.

"And . . . great!" he said, forcing the enthusiasm a little, and wondering if Lee had thought it was great. He decided to get off that uncertain ground. "I thought it was great too." This time he could be sincere. "I was going to call to thank you," he added.

"You 'were going to call,'" she said, just a hint of disbelief in her voice. "How often does a girl hear that little phrase?" She laughed softly to let him know she was joking—just a little.

"I'm sure you don't hear it too often, Abby," he replied seriously. There was a second or two of silence before she continued.

"Not often. Just from people I . . . care about," she said. He said nothing to that. There was another silence, this one stretched a little longer. Then, finally, she broke it. "Would you really have called me, Jess?"

He hesitated a second, considering his answer. Then he said, truthfully, "Yes. I would have called, Abby. It was a good piece and we owe you."

"We?" she repeated, teasing slightly. "Just who is we, Jess?"

"All of us in the sheriff's department," he said evenly. But she wasn't going to let him get away with it quite as easily as all that.

"That includes you, of course?"

"Of course." He wasn't sure where she was going with this. He wished she'd drop it. But she wouldn't.

"So, in that case, you owe me, as well as all those others, right?"

"Well, I guess I do, Abby," he said, keeping his tone light, trying to make the conversation a joke. But there was an undercurrent here that he wasn't comfortable with.

"Right," she said briskly, springing her trap. "I guess if you owe me, you can settle that debt with a good dinner. How does that sound?"

"Sure," he said, still trying to keep things nonspecific. "Any time at all."

"Tonight," she said triumphantly and he tried in vain to back off.

"Tonight, Abb? Well, I'm not sure about tonight. I'm up here in the cabin and it looks like it could snow anytime soon . . ." He let the sentence hang, hoping she'd take the hint. Naturally, she didn't.

"Oh come on, Jesse!" she said, a slight edge creeping into her tone. "Surely we can see each other just once for dinner? We've hardly said two words to each other all the time I've been here!"

"We said plenty yesterday—" he began. But she wasn't letting him get away with that.

"That was work," she cut in briskly. "I mean talk. Catch up on old times. Tell me how you've been doing. Hell, Jesse, you know damn well what I mean!"

"Well, maybe tomorrow night," he stalled, but again she cut him off.

"I'm heading back to Denver tomorrow," she said. "Tonight's the only time we've got. Now come on, Jess! I won't bite you."

He hesitated again. Part of him did want to see Abby. Part of him always did. But he knew that when he did see her, he always ended up confused. She was a breathtakingly beautiful woman and she knew how to use her looks.

He knew too that she still felt a strong attraction to him. Those two facts made a dangerous combination. He knew he shouldn't really see her tonight. But he felt his breath coming a little shorter just at the thought of doing so.

Besides, he thought, he did owe her. The department owed her. And somehow, he didn't see Lee being prepared to settle the debt by buying her dinner. He shook his head angrily. It didn't do to think about Lee when he was talking to Abby.

"Okay," he said abruptly, before he could change his mind. "Why the hell not?"

A small gurgle of laughter echoed down the line.

"How could a girl possibly refuse such a gallant invitation?" she asked.

"Give me half an hour," he said, now committed to the idea. "I'll pick you up at your hotel."

"No," she said quickly. "I'm just heading out for a workout. You know where the gym is at Sundance Plaza?"

"I know it," he said. There was a gymnasium, complete with indoor running track and pool.

"Pick me up there at seven thirty," she said.

"Okay," he said. "Seven thirty it is. Where do you want to eat?"

"Surprise me," she replied, and he could hear the smile in her voice. "Somewhere reasonably expensive." She paused, then said, only half joking, "Not the Tugboat, okay?"

He laughed. "Okay. The Tugboat is out."

"Any good music in town this week?" she asked. He knew by good music she didn't mean classical. One of the few areas of agreement they shared was a love of country music.

"There's a tolerable bluegrass band on at the Barn," he suggested.

"They do a mean steak there too, as I recall?" Abby said, and he had to agree.

"The meanest," he said. "Let's hit the Barn then."

"You got it," she said. "See you at seven thirty."

He waited, listening to hear her hang up. Then he set his own phone down in the cradle thoughtfully. He picked up the receiver again and reached for the old-fashioned circular dial. He dialed the first two digits of Lee's number, then stopped. Then firmly set the receiver down again.

He felt vaguely guilty. Then, realizing he had nothing to feel guilty about, he felt angry.

Then he felt guilty again.

FORTY-ONE

*H*e sat through the report with a mounting sense of disbelief. At the beginning, he'd made sure that he didn't show any of the sense of anticipation
he was feeling. It wouldn't do to have Mrs. McLaren, or any of her other guests,
get the idea that he was in any way pleased about the way the sheriff's department, and that long-legged deputy in particular, were stumbling and fumbling
along in his wake.

He'd assumed a thoughtful expression as the elderly landlady had turned
on the big color set in her parlor. She always watched the six o'clock local news
from Denver. Sometimes she might miss the later network bulletins, but the
state news always held her attention.

Tonight, of course, even more than usual. Because tonight there was going
to be a special report on the killings that had happened right here in Steamboat
Springs. Two other guests, both elderly men, had quietly taken seats in the
parlor to watch.

"It's that Abby Parker-Taft doing the report too," she'd told him with a
certain air of confidentiality. "She's almost a local girl you know. She was married to one of the local boys here a few years back."

Mrs. McLaren was a faithful viewer of the morning talk show on which
Abby was co-anchor. She watched every morning. It made her feel that somehow Abby was an old friend.

As the report came up on-screen, he allowed himself the small celebratory
gesture of popping the top on a can of Coors. None of the other people in the
parlor noticed the gesture. Or if they did, they didn't read anything undue
into it. As Abby began her preliminary remarks, he raised the can to his lips in
a silent toast to the upcoming public ridicule of the Routt County Sheriff's
Department.

Except it never came. He watched in puzzled silence at first, as Abby re-
frained from criticizing Sheriff Torrens. He thought that maybe she was saving
the coup de grace till later in the piece, building a picture of a fair-minded, even-
handed report before she stuck the knife in. Then, as the report progressed, and
Jesse Parker appeared on-screen, with Abby's voice-over detailing his experience
and record as a cop, he realized that the report was going to be a whitewash.

He drank a little faster, gulping the beer. It didn't help to notice that Mrs. McLaren was nodding her head wisely whenever Abby referred to "hard-working cops, waiting for that one vital piece of information that would break the case open." Without realizing it, his grip had tightened on the almost empty beer can, crushing it out of shape.

He felt angry and cheated. The news was a lie. The report was a farce. He'd had the cops chasing their own tails for the past two or three weeks. They knew nothing now that they hadn't known at the beginning of the whole thing. They had gotten absolutely nowhere with their investigations. They had made no progress.

He'd laughed to himself the day before, at the news of the farcical capture of the petty criminal who'd been stealing liquor and cigarettes from convenience stores in the area. He'd been shot at, apparently beaten up—he didn't for one moment believe the story about the suspect breaking his jaw in a snowmobile crash—all because that damn fool sheriff and her cretinous deputy thought they had cornered a murderer.

Now, according to this broadcast, that arrest was presented as groundbreaking, the result of first-class police work, and not the dumb mistake that it really was.

"They were married, you know," Mrs. McLaren was saying. He didn't catch the words the first time, glanced up at her, hastily wiping the look of anger from his face.

"Say what, Mrs. McLaren?" he asked. The landlady repeated her former statement, this time amplifying it to make sure he understood clearly.

"They were married: Jesse Parker and that Abby Parker-Taft. Couple years back when he was down in Denver. Then they broke up and Jesse drifted back up here."

He nodded to himself. Maybe that explained things. Maybe that was why that blond bitch was going so easy on the local cops, trying to make them out as hardworking heroes instead of the ham-fisted fuckups that he knew them to be.

"Shame, isn't it?" Mrs. McLaren was saying. "I don't know that young folks today really try to keep their marriages together, wouldn't you say, Mr. Murphy?"

He'd learned that whenever Mrs. McLaren had that philosophical tone to her voice, it was wisest to agree to anything she said. Otherwise, the result was a long and usually exceedingly boring discussion.

"I think you're right there, Mrs. Mac," he said, forcing a tone of interest into *his voice. "My pa always said, when he was younger, divorce just wasn't an option."*

The landlady nodded agreement. "Too true, Mr. Murphy," she said. "Why, my husband and I, we had our rough patches. There were times we could have just let go and said, 'The heck with it, let's get divorced.' But folks just didn't do that in our day. There's just too much divorcing going on entirely these days."

"It's the children who suffer too," he added shrewdly, anticipating that this would be her next tack. He'd found that staying in agreement with someone like Mrs. McLaren was a good safeguard against having her ask too many questions about his background, or becoming too interested in finding out more about him. When you agreed with people, he'd found, they tended to believe they already knew enough about you.

"That's the truth, Mr. Murphy," she said. "That is the sure enough truth." Then she added, "Though Jesse and that Abby girl never had no kids that I heard of."

They lapsed into silence again, watching the screen.

The report was running to its end now. They watched as Abby promised the viewing audience that the killer would be caught. He had to restrain his lip from curling. Then the blond reporter was back to sign off.

Obviously the report on air pollution in Denver held little interest for Mrs. McLaren. She folded her hands in her lap and nodded agreement with the sentiments expressed in their report.

"They'll catch him too, mark my words. She knows what she's doing, does Sheriff Torrens."

Perhaps unwisely, and against his normal practice, he decided to risk a mild disagreement. He was angry. The report was biased, one-eyed and inaccurate. It told nothing of the truth. It cunningly disguised the fact that he was the one who was setting the pace. Parker and the sheriff were simply dancing to his tune—and getting nowhere. He had killed, repeatedly, and left no clue, no trace that the police could follow up. It was that frustration that led him to disagree with her. Even so, his instincts made it seem like a reluctant disagreement.

"Still and all," he said, "you have to wonder if they're any further along than they were last week. They sure don't seem to be."

She shook her head dismissively at this idea. "They know what they're about. They've probably got a whole pack of clues they aren't telling us."

For a second or two, he wondered if she might be right. If the police might know something and not be letting on. Then he thought of the tired, defeated look about Lee Torrens, and the lack of conviction in her eyes. It was the eyes that told you every time. No, he thought. They knew nothing. He decided to stir the pot a little.

"Well, maybe so," he said, making sure he sounded reluctant to say it. "But you have to wonder about a sheriff's department that can't catch a bunch of boys on snowmobiles. They can't do that, how they going to catch a murderer?"

She turned to look at him with new interest.

"Those boys been back again?" she asked. A few nights back, a group of teenagers on snowmobiles had careered through the snow-covered fields behind the boardinghouse, shattering the night with the roar of their engines and the shouts of the boys. Mrs. McLaren had been suitably scandalized at their behavior. He shrugged now.

"Heard them again last night," he admitted.

Mrs. McLaren frowned. "Well, I swear I didn't." She turned to one of the others. "You hear those boys last night, Carl?" she asked.

Carl, a mournful-looking, long-faced clerk at the Rabbit Ear Motel shook his head doubtfully. "Can't say I did," he said, then, after a moment's hesitation, "Maybe I did at that. Heard something late last night, that's for sure."

Murphy smiled to himself. Tell Carl that something had disturbed his sleep and it was odds on he'd agree with you. What Carl had probably heard was what he heard every night: his own thunderous snoring.

"You should have said," she told Murphy, forgetting Carl. Mrs. McLaren felt a responsibility for her guests' well-being and comfort.

"Nothing much you could do, Mrs. Mac," he said. "Job for the sheriff or the town police really."

Now she was indignant at the thought that one of her guests was being inconvenienced and the local police forces were doing nothing about it.

"You should complain," she said, nodding vehemently to confirm the thought. "You should complain to the sheriff's department. After all, it's your right to do it."

He spread his hands in a gesture that showed his unwillingness to be a burden to others.

"They've got enough on their plate. Besides, don't seem right for me to do it. I'm a visitor in your town after all."

Just as he'd hoped, she took the bait he'd dangled out there in front of her.

"Well, I'm no visitor and I'm not having my clientele"—she savored that

word. She loved referring to her "clientele"—"being woken up in their beds by a bunch of boys hoorahing around on those noisy darn machines." She stood up, full of self-importance and the dignity of a citizen. "I'll complain to Sheriff Torrens myself," she said, "next time I'm passing by the Public Safety Building."

"Oh now, Mrs. Mac, no need for you to go bothering yourself and the sheriff . . ." he began, and let the sentence hang. As he knew she would, she leapt into the breach.

"Mr. Murphy, you're my client and I have a duty to you. It's no bother to me. And if it's a bother to the sheriff, well maybe she should start looking for another job."

And so saying, she swept out of the room to begin preparing supper. Carl looked at him, long-faced, and shrugged. He mirrored the gesture. Inside, he laughed quietly. The blond bitch on TV might have let the sheriff and her deputy down lightly, he thought. But at least now Mrs. McLaren would be there to make their life miserable.

It was almost an even trade.

FORTY-TWO

Abby had chosen her ground carefully. It was no accident that she had asked Jesse to pick her up at the gym. Originally she'd considered suggesting that he call for her at her hotel room, but she knew he'd be on his guard there, ready to resist any invitation to come in for a drink.

By contrast, the fitness center seemed like neutral territory. But it gave her the opportunity to dress in the sort of clothes she knew Jesse liked: casual, but designed to show off her body to best advantage.

He saw her almost instantly as the little Subaru clattered around the last bend before the center. She was standing outside, under one of the area lights that illuminated the parking lot. The light caught her pale blond hair, turning it into a beacon. She was doing a little jig to keep warm.

He noticed her legs, clad in black tights that clung to her shape, accentuating the curves of her calves and thighs. Over the tights, she wore an expensive-looking, down-filled parka—long-line, with a waist drawstring and a fine fur collar that stirred in the slight breeze.

He tapped the horn to draw her attention, then slid the little Subaru up to the curb beside her. She picked her way through a mound of snow that the plows had thrown up curbside and climbed into the car, hefting her gym bag over into the backseat. A few drifting snowflakes clung to her hair, melting almost instantly as she entered the warmth of the car. She grinned at him.

"Cold out there," she said, then leaned across to let her lips brush lightly against his. They were cold, of course. But every bit as soft as he remembered them to be. It was something that had enthralled him with Abby during all their time together. Her lips were remarkably full and soft. The touch of them was pleasantly erotic.

She shivered theatrically, then huddled herself into the fine fur collar of the parka.

"Good workout?" Jesse asked her, easing out the clutch and guiding the Subaru back onto the main road. She nodded enthusiastically.

"Great!" she said. "They've got some good instructors in there. I did a whole class with one of them. Just what I needed."

"Uh-huh," he said noncommittally, keeping a cautious eye on a Chevy Blazer that didn't seem totally sure of which lane it wanted to be in. He tapped the horn once to let the driver know he was there. Silhouetted against the other car's windshield, he saw the driver raise his middle finger. Jesse eased up on the gas and let the Blazer get ahead of them. He was in no hurry.

"Just like LA," Abby said, grinning. He looked at her and couldn't help grinning back. She looked cute and little-girlish, sitting there, huddled up inside the fur collar of her parka.

His eyes dropped to her legs. They didn't look so little-girlish.

She put a hand lightly on his right hand, where it rested on the steering wheel.

"Jess," she said seriously, "I'm glad we can do this."

He grinned at her in his turn. "Go driving where Chevy drivers give us the bird?" he suggested, and she smiled and shook her head.

"You know what I mean," she said patiently. "I'm glad we can see each other. I'm glad we don't have to hate each other anymore."

He hesitated, then said a little awkwardly, "I never hated you, Abby."

The fingers around his right wrist tightened a fraction.

"Didn't you?" she asked earnestly. "Times there, I was sure you did. And I never wanted that, Jesse. There was too much between us that was good, wasn't there?"

He shook his head, not in response to her question, but to emphasize his earlier statement. "I never hated you, Abby. I was angry maybe. And maybe I might have said some hard things. But I never hated you. You should know that."

She smiled widely at that, took her hand away and folded it in her lap.

"I'm glad to hear that," she said. "Now let's go eat."

"Sounds good to me," He took his eyes off the road long enough to grin at her. That crooked little grin of his that could still make her breath come a little quicker. Then he looked back at the traffic and she studied his profile, backlit by the streetlights and the glare from the headlights of passing cars. She liked what she saw, she decided.

★ ★ ★

The Barn was crowded, warm and friendly. The lighting was low-key and they sat close together in a small booth toward the back of the restaurant. They had to pitch their voices up a little to cut over the background babble of conversation. She ordered a steak, rare. Jesse ordered ribs. Knowing his preferred drink was usually beer, she decided he wouldn't drink red wine, and so ordered a bottle of cold Napa Valley Chardonnay.

He hesitated over his almost automatic choice of a Moosehead, then shrugged as Abby raised an eyebrow.

"I can't drink a whole bottle of wine myself," she said. He looked at her, head tilted to one side.

"You must be slowing down," he told her. "Time was, you sure could." Then turning to the waitress, "Okay, I'll have the wine as well."

She tossed out their napkins into their laps with a practiced flick of her wrist, then hurried away to place their orders.

They looked at each other. For a moment, there was nothing to be said. Finally, Jesse broke the silence.

"So, did the network pick up your piece? Or haven't you heard yet?"

She made a small moue with her lips, shook her head.

"They passed," she said. "I heard just after I spoke to you this evening. Seems nobody wants to hear good news about cops, Jess."

"You could have made it bad news if you'd wanted to," he said.

She raised an eyebrow, questioning the statement. The waitress chose that moment to return with the bottle of chardonnay. Abby inspected the label, the year, the drops of dew that covered the bottle and nodded her approval. The girl busied herself stripping the foil from the cork, then carefully removing the cork from the bottle, easing it out the last few tenths of an inch so it didn't pop. Abby frowned slightly. She wondered why waiters did that these days. The pop was one of the more enjoyable moments in a bottle of wine, as far as she was concerned.

"Just pour it," she said. "I'm sure it's fine."

The golden-colored wine spilled into their two glasses, frosting the outsides almost immediately. Abby picked up her glass, paused with it on the way to her lips.

"So," she said lightly. "Just how could I have made the network with that piece?" Her eyes smiled at him above the rim of her glass. He took a deep drink of his own, felt the chilled wine bite against the back of his throat, felt the slowly releasing glow of the alcohol fuse through him. Then he answered.

"You could have come down heavy on us," he said. "You know it. I know it. You did everything you could to make us look good."

She nodded to concede the point, then said distinctly, "Well, fuck the network. Maybe I don't need them quite as much as I thought I did."

That stopped him, as she knew it would. Truth to tell, she admitted to herself, it had stopped her when she first thought about it. She allowed herself a wan little smile.

He said nothing. But she knew she'd set him thinking. She shrugged to herself, took a slightly larger drink of her wine than normal.

Their meals arrived and they changed the subject to less challenging matters. Jesse expressed his regret that she wouldn't have time to ski before heading back to Denver. It seemed a shame to miss out.

"Snow's pretty near perfect the past few days," he said. She shrugged again. Channel 6 had given her a leave of absence from the morning program while she did the special report. Now she'd filed, she had no real excuse for staying on. Also, she'd sensed an undercurrent of anger from the head of News and Current Affairs when he'd called earlier. The channel would have enjoyed the prestige of having one of its reports picked up for national broadcast and she thought her boss knew she'd blown the chance intentionally with her choice of angle on the story.

"I guess it's good skiing at the moment?" she asked, and he nodded.

"Knee-deep powder everywhere," he said. She thought about it. She was a good skier, although try as he might, he'd never been able to convince her to ski moguls. She could imagine the mountain in weather like this. It was exhilarating skiing Mount Werner at any time. With soft, aerated, super-light powder flying waist or chest high, it would be simply great.

"Maybe I'll try to get back later in the season," she suggested.

Jesse shook his head. "Time to ski is when the snow's good," he said. "It's good now."

She laughed lightly at him. Skiing to him went beyond a recreation. In his eyes, it was almost a religion, and not to ski when the snow was perfect was very close to blasphemy.

"Things I've got to do back in Denver, Jess," she said. She hesitated, waiting to see if he'd try to convince her to stay longer. But he said nothing.

On the small stage at the far end of the room, a five-piece bluegrass band started playing. They stopped their conversation, turning slightly in their seats to watch.

"Fiddle player's good," she said. Jesse nodded. The fiddle was sawing out the two-string stops of "Orange Blossom Special," then flying into the fast-paced notes of the solo. The girl playing the piece couldn't have been more than twenty years old. In spite of the frantic pace of the music, her face was relaxed, calm, almost detached.

The boy playing the five-string banjo beside her joined in, trading breaks with her. They blended easily, grinning at each other.

"Five-string's no slouch either," Jesse agreed. Abruptly, Abby came to her feet.

"Dance with me, Jess," she said, knowing that this had been in the back of her mind hours before, when she'd asked if there were any good bands playing in town. Jesse hesitated for a moment, not sure if he wanted to revisit that area. She caught his hand and dragged him to his feet, leading him between the tables to the dance floor.

There were a few couples already swing dancing to the fast, rippling music as they stepped onto the polished parquet tiles that made up the dance floor.

One thing that they had always done superlatively was dance together. They both loved country music and, individually, they were both excellent swing dancers. But as a pair, they had a chemistry, a special, instinctive understanding that let them blend smoothly together. He stood behind and to one side, set his left hand on her hip, took her right hand in his and they started.

And, instantly, the old magic was back. They glided across the floor, feet moving in half steps, then full slides, then heel kicking behind. It was instinctive, totally unplanned, absolutely coordinated. Then he swung her out and they faced each other and went into another of the complex routines they'd danced years before.

There wasn't another pair on the floor to match them and the other dancers, sensing their expertise, moved to the outer limits of the floor, simplifying their own movements to watch, acknowledging their superiority. The musicians noticed them, as did people at the tables close to the floor, who started clapping in time to encourage them.

They spun, kicked, stamped. He marveled at the fact that he knew, simply knew, every small move she was going to make just before she made it, and matched each one with his own.

Onstage, only a few yards away, the fiddle player and the banjo picker exchanged a quick glance and upped the tempo progressively. It was a challenge to the dancers to see if they could maintain the rhythm with them, to see if they could keep the beat with their complex steps and moves. And they could.

Until finally the band capitulated, bringing the piece to a close with a repeating eight-bar riff. As the banjo rang out the closing chord in a loud *rasgueado,* the other dancers clapped and cheered and the people at the tables stood and applauded.

Breathing hard, sweating freely, Jesse and Abby laughed into each other's eyes. The banjo player leaned down to shake hands with Jesse.

"Nice going, man," he said, grinning. "You ready for another?"

Jesse grinned back, shaking his head, still a little short of breath. "Not just yet bud," he replied. "Got to get some O_2 back in the lungs here first."

The banjo player smiled and turned back to his companions as the fiddler began the introduction to "Earl's Breakdown." Jesse looked back to Abby. He was conscious of the rise and fall of her breasts under the soft lambswool sweater she was wearing. He was aware that she was wearing no bra, or anything else, under the sweater.

She grinned at him, brushed a stray tendril of her glowing blond hair back from her eyes.

"Let's finish that wine," she said happily.

She took his hand to lead him from the floor, guiding it to slip naturally around her waist as they walked back to their table, then moving it just a fraction lower. He could feel the warm, firm flesh under her tights, and felt no ridge of a waistband or legband under them. Unobtrusively, she moved his hand with her own, allowing him to confirm the thought, letting his hand stray over her buttock and hip. She was naked under the tights and the sweater and he felt a sudden rush of warmth in his groin.

In her hotel room, she stood nude before the big windows, pulling the curtains aside to let the lights from Mount Werner in.

He watched her, fascinated by the perfection of her body, reveling in the play of light and shade on the perfect curve of her hip and thigh. She turned slightly, allowing the cold light to play on the swell of her breasts, and smiled at him.

She moved toward him and he rose to meet her, his erection throbbing almost painfully. She slid the zipper down on his jeans, laughing softly as his erection forced its way out through the gap. Then, with increasing urgency, she shoved his jeans and briefs down, kicking them free, leaving him as naked as she was.

She thrust forward against him and he moaned softly. There was a distant part of his mind telling him he shouldn't be here, shouldn't be doing this. Then his hands went under her firm, muscular buttocks and he lifted her as she let her legs twine around him. He was searching for her and he felt her hand on him, guiding him into the amazing heat and wetness of her. He moved slightly, resting her on the dressing table, letting it take some of the weight, then began thrusting urgently into her, feeling her matching his movements as her legs tightened around his waist, then he lifted her clear off the table, allowing her to slide down upon him, taking her full weight as he strained to reach farther and farther inside her and then, shatteringly, explosively, he came. And came. And came.

Legs wrapped around his waist, arms twined around his neck, she smiled down at him and kissed him, open-mouthed. Then she smiled at him.

"Let's try that one again, shall we?" she said.

FORTY-THREE

It was wet and cold in Virginia. Agent Annie Dillon hung her raincoat on the hook on the back of her office door and settled down in front of her computer. The message "Have a good weekend, Babe" scrolled endlessly across the screen. She grunted at it. The weekend hadn't been wildly successful. She'd caught a large piece of near frozen ground with a five iron and damn near wrenched her left wrist out of its socket. It hurt like hell at the time. By Sunday night, she couldn't move her left hand at all without intense, searing pain.

As a result, she'd spent most of Monday morning with doctors, X-ray technicians and physiotherapists. Now it was nearly midday and she was hours behind in her work. She brought the computer online from its standby setting, unlocked her top drawer and took out the sheets of part numbers that she'd received on Friday. She sighed as she glanced down the ranks—four columns to a page, forty-three lines to a column.

She flicked through the pages to get a quick count, and frowned. The last two pages were a different format—an address sheet from a sheriff's department in some godforsaken place called Routt County, out in Colorado.

Frowning, she read the note and reached for her phone. She could pass this on to one of the research interns but she felt a little guilty about it. It was her fault that the request had gone unanswered for almost three days. She'd do it herself.

She dialed the library and requested a copy of any information they might have on a Wilson Purdue. Telling the clerk that the job was urgent, she requested the file ASAP.

It arrived fifteen minutes later, a single sheet. She glanced quickly at it to make sure it was complete, not really taking in any details. Then, making a note of the Routt County Sheriff's Department fax number, she headed for the fax room at the end of the corridor.

★　★　★

Several hundred miles away in Denver, Carrie Tolliver was back at work after an absence of several days.

Carrie was an administrative assistant with the Denver Fire Department. She looked after paperwork, filing, interdepartmental communication and requests from other authorities for assistance or information.

But a flu epidemic was sweeping Denver and health authorities had estimated that city residents had a one in three chance of catching the bug, sooner or later.

Carrie had caught it sooner. She fought for a day against the aching head, the soaring temperatures and the dry, rasping throat.

Then, finally, she gave in. She went home, gulped down a handful of aspirin and fell into bed for four days, rousing herself at irregular intervals for soup, hot tea and more aspirin.

Now, she was back at her desk, working her way through the mountain of paperwork that had built up in the time she'd been away.

One form caught her eye as she sifted through yet another stack of departmental mail. It was a fax page, with an unfamiliar crest. She slipped it from the pile and studied it more carefully. It seemed that the Routt County Sheriff's Department had requested background information and an ID photo of a former Denver Fire Department paramedic named Anton Mikkelitz. It seemed a routine request. There was no urgency indicated on the form. However, as she glanced at the date of the fax, she realized that the request had been made nearly a week ago. It had obviously gone from desk to desk before ending up on hers. At that rate, she thought the request deserved some priority.

She took a note of the name and walked through to the personnel department.

It took her another quarter-hour to find the personnel sleeve for Anton Mikkelitz. She'd started out by looking in the current employee files, not realizing that he'd left the department several years previously. Finally, she found it, took the top sheet, with home address, age and personal details, and the five by four copy of the ID photo and returned to her own office.

She attached the photo to a larger sheet of paper, fed it and the details sheet into her fax, checked the return number on the fax sheet from Routt County and punched it in. She waited for the metallic shriek that told her the faxes were connecting, then hung up the receiver and watched the sheets of paper roll into one side of the fax and out the other. Technology, she thought, was a wonderful thing.

It might have been an even better thing if it had provided Routt County with a fax that could receive two messages at once. Because as Carrie Tolliver was sending the details of Anton Mikkelitz through, Annie Dillon was attempting to fax a file on Wilson Purdue to the same number. She sighed with frustration as the busy signal beeped back at her. She broke the connection, hit the redial button and waited.

Just as the second sheet in Denver was feeding into Carrie Tolliver's fax.

Again, Agent Dillon heard the mocking tone of the engaged signal. It was a sound that seemed to be designed specifically to annoy, she thought. She let it beep for several seconds, then broke the connection again. Her finger was reaching for the redial button once more when the fax rang. She started with surprise, then realized that the function display panel on the machine was registering "Receiving." The first of an eighteen-page report on new office communications procedures was coming in from Washington, DC. She saw the cover sheet as it rolled out, read the legend "page one of eighteen," and sighed in exasperation. She could have left the fax machine on auto redial but she didn't know that. She picked up the Purdue file and returned to her office. Routt County would just have to wait a little longer.

FORTY-FOUR

There was something wrong. Lee knew it. She could sense it, feel it and see it in every line of Jesse's body. He was ill at ease with her, and his gaze slid away from hers when they met in the parking lot outside the Safety Building.

"So, where were you last night?" she asked, trying to keep her voice easy. That was when Jesse's eyes had refused to make contact with hers. He suddenly noticed that one bootlace wasn't sufficiently tight, dropped to one knee, undid it and made a production of re-tying it, getting it just right.

"Last night?" he said, then replied with a question of his own. "Were you trying to reach me last night?"

She hated this. She'd actually begun the conversation quite innocently. She'd assumed he'd gone out for a beer or a meal at the Tugboat. All she wanted to do was to bring their relationship back to normal. She'd realized after she'd hung up on him the night before that she'd overreacted to the situation. She'd spent the next hour wondering why the thought of Abby had made her so defensive, so much on the alert. Then, around eight, she'd phoned Jesse to apologize for her attitude. To set things right between them again.

And got nothing but an unanswered ringtone.

She'd tried again around nine with the same result. After that, she'd gone to bed early and laid awake till around one, feeling like a fool. She'd made up her mind that, first thing in the morning, first chance she got, she'd set things right. Just start up a normal, unimportant conversation to let Jesse know things were fine between them. And to give him a chance to let her know the same.

And then, damn it, before she could stop herself, she'd picked the one topic that made her sound as if she were checking up on him. Where were you last night? Jesus! she thought, what a question to ask him. It smacked of accusation. And now, just to make it worse, it seemed that Jesse had been somewhere, with someone, that he didn't want to discuss. She tried to lighten the subject, made her voice very matter-of-fact, tried to make it sound unimportant.

"No. Just called you back around eight. Figured you'd gone out." She gestured to the Book Store Coffee Shop on the corner, determined to get off the subject of Jesse's evening. "Want to grab a coffee? The muffins should be just coming out of the oven right about now," she added with a slightly forced cheerfulness.

Jesse chose to ignore the invitation, and the opportunity to change the subject. He seemed to come to a decision. He rose to his feet, and this time, met her gaze. His eyes were a little angry, she thought.

"I went out," he said flatly. "I took Abby to dinner."

And there it was. Their eyes were locked. She didn't want hers to be searching for an answer, but she knew they were. And she saw the answer in Jesse's anger, his stubborn refusal to accept the sidetrack she'd offered. She shrugged, tried to look casual.

"Fine," she said. "I guess she deserved it after the good PR she gave us."

"I guess she did," he said.

The smile was locked on her face. She couldn't let it slip, couldn't let on that she knew. He'd taken Abby out. They'd had dinner. They'd fucked. She felt like a gargoyle with that ridiculous smile plastered to her face. They'd fucked? Why not think of it as "they'd made love"? Maybe it was more than just physical. Maybe there was still a spark there and the situation had fanned it back into a flame. She nodded several times, meaninglessly.

"Well . . ." she said, finally. "Coffee?"

He shrugged. "I'll take a rain check," he said. "I've got to go back to square one, start going through the list of suspects again."

"I guess so," she agreed, glad that they were finally talking business, glad she could unfasten that idiotic smile and put it away again. "I've got a few calls to make. I'll see if I can give you a hand in an hour or so, maybe review what we've got so far."

He nodded heavily. "Ain't much," he said. "I'd like to know where that Purdue fellow has got to in the last few years though. He's our best hope at the moment."

They mounted the back stairs and went inside. Lee breathed a sigh of relief to be in out of the cutting wind. She loosened the zipper of her jacket.

"Thought you were going for coffee?" he asked as they reached the door to the conference room he had claimed. She shrugged.

"Maybe later. Remembered I had a few too many things to attend to." She turned away, heading for the end of the corridor and the door to her own office. "I'll catch you later," she said back over her shoulder. He nodded, said nothing.

He stood for a few seconds, hand on the doorknob, watching her walk away. Her long-legged stride had a feline grace about it. Below the short waistline of the jacket, her behind stretched the denim of her jeans into a perfect, rounded shape. He felt a surge of desire for her, then shook his head in self-disgust.

Jesus! Can't you make up your goddamned mind? Angrily, he flung the door open and went into the conference room, shutting the door behind him a little more forcefully than he'd intended.

He slumped into the nearest chair and stared moodily at his notes on the whiteboard. The photos of suspects and victims were taped along the bottom of the board. He noticed one gap in the photos and leaned forward to peer closer. Mikkelitz, he noticed dully. The former paramedic from Denver. He was sure he'd put through a request to the fire department for a copy of his ID photo. He shrugged. Probably got lost in someone's in tray, he thought. He made a mental note to call Denver later and put in the request verbally.

He guessed that the next step would be to take all the ID photos and canvass the witnesses he had available, to see if any of them looked familiar. Mrs. Hollings would be the best chance, he thought. At least she'd seen the killer's face, if only for a few seconds. But he'd also try the lift attendants and the gondola attendants who'd seen the mysterious cross-country skier. Maybe they'd remember something. Maybe one of the photos would trigger a memory.

Maybe.

Maybe hell would freeze over one day.

Damn Abby! Why did she have to come back now, just when he and Lee had finally got themselves sorted out.

He loved Lee. At least, he thought he did. No, he was sure of it. Almost sure.

So, he asked himself, if he loved her, if he was so sure, how come he'd spent the previous night screwing Abby till the early hours of the morning? His groin hardened again at the thought of it. What did he feel for Abby? It was physical, sure. He had the evidence of that between his legs. Hard evidence, he told himself grimly.

But there was something more than just a physical attraction. Maybe it was history. He'd loved her once, he knew that. Maybe he was falling in love with her again. Maybe she really had decided to give up her ambitions for a network spot. They'd talked about that and she certainly sounded genuine.

Still, he cautioned himself, Abby sounding genuine and Abby being genuine were not necessarily the same things.

Complicating matters, he did believe that she loved him. That made it difficult to assess his own feelings for her.

All he knew was, whenever Lee's level gray eyes looked into his, he was sure that she could see images of him betraying her with Abby. He knew he'd hurt her. Badly. And he'd never wanted that.

Miserably, he put his head into his hands. He'd never wanted to hurt Lee, he'd just wanted to fuck Abby three or four times.

"Jesus," he said to himself.

There was a light tap at the door. Wearily, he raised his head, leaned back in the chair, then realized that this position made his physical arousal a little too evident and hunched forward, elbows on the table.

"Yeah?" he called, "Come on in."

For some reason he was expecting Lee, maybe because he'd just been thinking of her. He was a little relieved when Denise entered, a couple of sheets of paper in her hand.

"Fax for you, Jess," she said, dropping the sheets on the table in front of him. "From Denver Fire Department," she added.

He brought his mind back to the investigation with an effort.

"Oh, fine. Thanks, Denise," he said, rubbing his eyes with forefinger and thumb. Denise looked at him critically.

"Late night, Jess?" she asked. His eyes were red-rimmed, she noticed, and assumed it was lack of sleep. He shook his head. Last thing he wanted after telling Lee he'd taken Abby to dinner was talk around the office about him having a late night.

"Just couldn't sleep, Denise," he smiled tiredly. "Got a few things on my mind." He indicated the fax on the table, and the whiteboard full of notes, photos and fact sheets. Denise nodded sympathetically.

"I can imagine," she said. "Get you a coffee if you'd like one?" she suggested, and his smile widened a little.

"I'd probably kill for one, honey," he said and she smiled.

"No need to go that far. Just black?"

"Just black."

She nodded and slipped out, closing the door softly behind her. Idly, Jesse inspected the ID shot that Carrie Tolliver had finally sent through by fax.

Anton Mikkelitz was a reasonably good-looking guy, apparently in his mid-thirties with a thick head of blond hair. There was nothing outstanding about him. No scars. No distinguishing marks. No swastikas tattooed on his forehead. No sign around his neck reading "Serial Killer. Keep clear."

He rose, moved around the table to the whiteboard and taped the photo in position.

Now everything was in its place. Everything was complete. And he was still nowhere.

Then a thought struck him. Of course, everything wasn't complete.

He reached for the phone, checked on one of his yellow legal pads for the FBI's number and punched the buttons.

Agent Annie Dillon's mind was slowly turning to oatmeal as she tried to compare the list of real aviation spares with the false ones. The parts had serial numbers up to thirteen digits long, with sub-classifications and model categories added to that. The variations between real and counterfeit were absolutely minimal and they tended to occur anywhere through the serial number. Just keeping track of them was enough to make an agent weep, she thought. But she'd already isolated one likely distribution center in Topeka, and now she thought she was onto a second in Oregon.

The phone beside her rang and she answered it irritably. For a few moments, she wondered why a deputy sheriff from Colorado would be calling her. Then she remembered the information request that she'd tried to fax through. She hesitated guiltily.

"Oh Jesus, I'm sorry, Deputy Parker," she said. "I've been really snowed under here."

"I know how it can be." The voice on the other end of the phone was friendly and unhassled. If he'd been at all argumentative, she would have probably told him to take a flying leap and hung up on him.

"As a matter of fact, Deputy, I tried to fax that sheet through a while back and your line was engaged. I meant to get back to it but I completely forgot. I'm real sorry. I'll send it through right now."

The deputy paused a moment. "No rush," he said finally. "I'm just heading out for an hour or so and it's a long shot anyway. Send it through when you get a moment."

She glanced at the tables of figures on the screen of her computer, hazarded a guess at how much longer she'd want to work at them before she was driven screaming into the rain outside.

"Forty minutes, no longer," she promised. "I'll send it through in forty minutes or so."

"That'll do just fine," Jesse told her. He broke the connection and she hung up. She turned back to the computer, then stopped, shuffled through the papers on her desk until she found the forgotten dossier and placed it conspicuously on top of the pile.

She didn't plan to forget it again.

FORTY-FIVE

When the fax about Wilson Purdue finally came through, Jesse was out doing what cops spend most of their time doing: pounding the pavement.

He'd gathered up the photos of the suspects on his list—the possible suspects, he corrected himself morosely—and had gone to interview the small list of witnesses that he had available.

Maybe, he thought, there was something in one of the photos that might trigger a memory. A subconscious thought or idea or fact that was lying there buried, just waiting for a small, not-too-well focused ID photo to release it.

He'd also included a couple of completely unrelated photos in the small pile that he'd gathered. It was a control system that he'd used many times before, when checking on eyewitnesses in Denver. Eyewitnesses, really, were the worst witnesses of all. Most people make it a practice not to take notice of the appearance of strangers.

Sad to say, in this modern, caring world, noticing strangers is not always such a great idea. Making eye contact with strangers has led to people having their skulls parted with tomahawks, or their bodies torn apart by high-powered bullets, or ripped with knives.

As a consequence, most people go through life making sure they don't notice people around them. Until something happens—and then it's too late.

Jesse understood how witnesses could feel embarrassed by the fact. To stand and watch a mugging, or a murder, or a beating and then have to admit that it was the event that drew the attention, not the detail of the perpetrator's height, size, coloring or distinguishing marks, was none too easy, he knew. A person in that situation could feel like a damn fool.

And to compensate, all too many witnesses would try to make any available aid to recognition fit the facts. If a perpetrator had been short, fat and swarthy and an eyewitness was shown a photo of a six-foot-tall Nordic blond, more often than not, the witness would discard his vague memories of the event until he would say with absolute certainty that, yes officer, this is the man I saw.

Otherwise, reason asked, why would the officer be showing me the picture?

For that reason, Jesse always tried to have as many different photos as he could. It reduced the chances of the witnesses trying to second-guess the investigator. So, along with the photos of Wilson Purdue, Anton Mikkelitz, Ned Tellman and Oliver Prescott, he carried small snapshot photos of old friends—a ski instructor from Copper Mountain and one of the detectives from his old squad in Denver. It rounded the pile out a little.

So far, none of the photos had struck a chord. He'd called on John Hostetler first. Jesse liked Hostetler. He'd gotten to know him as a nodding acquaintance, during his time with the ski patrol. The elderly lift attendant welcomed him warmly, looked obligingly through the photos, then shook his head sadly.

Strike one, Jesse thought.

Next up to bat was the lift attendant who'd been on duty when Harry Powell, the marketing consultant from North Carolina, had been left slumped in the Storm Peak chair. That killing, Jesse thought, showed a pretty thorough understanding of the working of a ski mountain.

Any lift attendant would have to be distracted by the sight of a passenger who failed to unload. Passengers like that were the bane of attendants' lives. Go-rounds, as they were called, meant the lift had to be stopped, then backed up, then stopped again, while the unfortunate person was allowed to dismount. And chairlift stoppages meant disgruntled paying customers. What's more, each lift on the mountain was automatically monitored, so a record of stoppages was kept each day. As a consequence, lift staff watched for go-rounds like hawks, and any attendant who had two or more in a week was usually in for a torrid interview with the lifts manager.

Under those conditions, Jesse was pretty sure the lift attendant in question, Clive Wallace, would have taken no notice at all of the other rider on the chair, who'd skied off into the trees.

And he was right. Morosely, he wondered why he had to be right on that particular item. Wallace stared blankly at the six photos, then shook his head.

Strike two.

It was Randall Hollings's wife who made the first positive identification.

Her husband was still recovering in the local hospital. He checked his notes and confirmed that she was staying at the Torian Plum condos, overlooking the lower slopes of the mountain. He called the condos, found her and arranged to meet her.

Emma Hollings was eager to help. Her initial, angry reaction to Lee had been the result of shock, nothing more. As the days passed and she realized how lucky her husband had been, and how tragically Walt Davies had died, she had calmed down. Now she was willing to do anything within her power to help the Routt County Sheriff's Department in its hunt for the killer.

And she told Jesse as much over the phone.

He parked outside the elegant timber building and took the elevator to the third floor. Emma Hollings was waiting for him. She offered him coffee, which he refused, thinking that another cup would set his kidneys into overdrive. As he had with Clive and John Hostetler, he explained that he was following up on a minor chance, just letting her see photos of some possible suspects in case one might jog her memory.

He spread the photos out for her on the coffee table and she hunched forward, frowning, to look at them. After a few moments, she smiled at him apologetically.

"Excuse me, Deputy Parker," she said, rose and went into the bedroom. When she emerged, she was carrying a pair of half-frame reading glasses, which she perched on the end of her nose as she studied the photos once more. She glanced up, smiled again, a little sadly.

"We're none of us getting younger, are we?" she said.

Jesse shrugged. "Can't remember what it felt like to be that way," he admitted.

She nodded once, then went back to her perusal of the six photos. She hooked one of them toward her with a forefinger. Jesse held his breath, leaned forward a little to see which one it was. It was Anton Mikkelitz, he saw—the paramedic from Denver whose photo had come in that morning. Then she frowned again, shook her head and muttered "No" under her breath and pushed the photo back into line with the others.

Jesse leaned back, allowing his pent-up breath to escape slowly in a long, silent sigh.

Mrs. Hollings's forefinger was patrolling the line of photos again, wavering back and forward along the line, her elegantly shaped and varnished nail hovering.

Then, it stabbed down. Definite and unwavering, like a red hawk dropping onto a jack rabbit.

"Him," she said briefly. "I'm sure of it."

Jesse looked quickly at the photo skewered by her fingernail.

"You're sure?" he asked. "You only caught a brief—"

She didn't let him finish.

"I'm sure," she said definitely. "I may have only seen him for a few seconds, but it's imprinted on my mind. I can see him now. I guess when the adrenaline is running, you see things more clearly, don't you? You notice things. That's him. Definitely."

And to emphasize her point, she tapped her finger on the photo of Detective Sergeant Miles Ferris, of the Denver PD.

Strike three, thought Jesse.

He had no better luck with the lift attendant who'd been on duty the same day.

Inevitably, the lift attendant had been diverted by the crumpling figure of Randall Hollings as the killer shoved him free of the chair and the injured man fell in the path of unloading skiers. His first instinct had been to drag the fallen man clear—to avoid one of those much-hated stoppages if he could. It was only then that he'd realized that Mrs. Hollings was screaming and struggling with the other occupant of the chair.

But by then, Emma Hollings was sprawling in the snow, the killer's back was to him and he was skiing flat-out for the trees above the Triangle 3 run.

End of the innings, thought Jesse.

He sat in the little Subaru in the no parking area by Gondola Square. While he'd been interviewing the witnesses, some eager-beaver new kid from the town police had written a parking citation for the Subaru and left it under the windshield wiper. He leaned back, rolling his shoulders and neck to ease the cramp there. He was tired and dispirited and at a dead end. Some time later today, he'd have to get Denise to sort out the traffic citation with Felix Obermeyer's office. He cursed quietly. Didn't the dumb bastard of a cop notice the shiny new police department radio that was installed under the dash of the battered little wagon?

As he thought about it, the radio crackled to life.

"Jesse? You there? Come in please if you are?"

He smiled tiredly. Radio discipline in the mountains wasn't quite the way it had been in Denver. Then he'd been Tango One Four and calls to him from base had been a damn sight more formal than a simple: "Jesse? You there?"

He unhooked the mike, thumbed the talk button.

"This is Jesse, Denise. Talk to me."

"Jess, that fax you been waiting for came in an hour or so ago. Just noticed it in the tray and I thought you'd like to know, case it's urgent or something."

The carrier wave hissed briefly as Denise released her mike button. He pressed his again. "Thanks, Denise. It's not too urgent but I might as well head back and take a look at it." He paused. "Did you show it to Lee at all?" If there was anything significant in the fax, Lee would have noticed, he thought.

"Uh, no, Jess. Lee's out Emerald Meadows way. Been a fight in a bar there and she went out to sort things."

"I've got money says she will," he said quietly. Then, into the radio, "Okay, Denise, I'll head back in now. Out."

"See you, Jesse," she replied. She didn't bother with "out." She rarely did. He fished in his jacket pocket for his keys, inserted them in the ignition and cranked the starter. The engine caught on the third try and he swung in a wide circle toward the road back to town. The wind caught the parking citation on his windshield and whipped it away, fluttering in his wake. He glanced in the mirror and saw the paper blowing across the road toward the pile of dirty, discolored snow melt that had been piled on the road's edge by the snowplows.

"Best place for the goddamned thing," he muttered.

FORTY-SIX

Wilson Purdue was dead.

Jesse sat in the stuffy little conference room, surrounded by his notes and his sheets of legal pads and his scribbling on the whiteboard, staring at the sheet of fax paper in his hand.

Purdue, his strongest suspect from the list of former employees with a possible grudge against the town, had been picked up for armed robbery in California eighteen months ago. Sentenced to five to ten in the State Penitentiary, he'd died three months earlier from an AIDS-related disease.

Pneumonia, Jesse noted dully.

Well, he thought, that was often the way with AIDS cases. The lack of activity, the enforced bed rest, was an almost surefire precursor to pneumonia. And once it set in, with no immune system to fight the effects, the result was usually fatal.

"Damn," he said quietly. "Goddamn."

He looked at the ID photo of Purdue on his desk, put down the fax sheet and picked up the photo. Very carefully, he tore it into small pieces and tossed them in the general direction of the bin in the corner.

"Guess I won't be needing you anymore," he said.

Some of the pieces made it. Others fluttered to the carpet around the bin. He didn't give a damn. Someone else could pick them up. Jesus, he thought, what now? He rubbed the heel of his hand into his right eye. He could feel a headache forming back behind that eye, throbbing just below the surface, waiting to blossom into fully fledged pain a little later in the day. There was a tap at the door.

"Come," he said listlessly. He didn't remember closing the door behind him. He must have done it automatically as he walked in from the corridor, reading the mocking words on the fax for the third or fourth time.

The door opened and Lee was standing there.

She looked at his slumped shoulders, saw the look of defeat on his face and guessed the worst.

"Bad news, I take it?" she asked and he nodded.

"Purdue. Number one suspect. Dead three months."

Lee shook her head slowly, turned and paced the length of the room while she thought about the implications.

"Shit," she said finally and he nodded.

"Couldn't have put it better myself," he agreed.

There was a long silence between them. Then Lee asked, "So, where do we go from here?"

He didn't answer immediately. Didn't want to put into words the thought that was gnawing away inside him. He swung his feet onto the scuffed tabletop, rocked his straight-backed chair back into a precarious balance on its hind legs.

"I don't know, Lee. I just don't know. I'm beginning to think this theory of ours is way off base. Maybe it's time to admit we're barking up the wrong tree and head in another direction."

She half sat on the edge of the table.

"Which direction you got?" she asked, and again he shrugged. It occurred to him that it was a fine day for shrugging. There was a lot of it going on today.

"Dunno, Lee," he admitted. "I guess it's time I sat here and stared at all these damn clever notes I've made and found some other connection. I'll let you know when I think of one."

"Shit," she said again. He tilted his head to one side to look at her.

"Already said that," he told her.

"It bears repeating," she replied.

The phone rang. They both looked at it. She was marginally closer to it than he was and she looked at him interrogatively. He waved a hand to it.

"Go ahead," he said and she picked up.

"Sheriff Torrens," she said. Then he saw her stiffen slightly before she continued. "Yes. He's right here."

She held the phone across the table to him.

"For you," she said. Then added, without any expression at all, "Abby."

Their eyes met for a second or two. Then, as they had each time Abby had been mentioned between them, his slid away. He simply couldn't meet her gaze. She knew why. And he knew she knew.

He rocked the chair forward, thumping down on its front legs and reached to take the receiver.

"This is Jesse," he said, keeping his tone neutral. He was conscious of the fact that Lee was now making a point of not looking at him. She remained half perched on the table, her head turned away, for all intents and purposes studying the notes on the whiteboard.

Abby's voice was a purr. "And how are you today, lover?" she asked. He glanced quickly at Lee again, fearful that she might have somehow overheard.

"Um . . . what can I do for you, Abby?" he asked. His voice was stilted. He knew it. Couldn't do anything about it. There was a long pause at the other end of the phone. Then Abby repeated, with an incredulous edge in her voice, "What can I do for you? That's all you've got to say after last night?"

She was amused, he realized. Amused but incredulous. He fumbled for words.

"Um . . . yeah well, we're pretty busy here right now, so—"

"I won't keep you," she said, dropping the teasing tone she'd been using. "I just wanted to know, what are we doing tonight?" She paused, then added with a soft laugh, "Apart from the obvious, I mean."

He hesitated. "I thought you were heading back to Denver today?" He was trying to keep his voice neutral and matter-of-fact and he knew he wasn't doing any sort of a great job of it.

There was a note of affectionate reproach in Abby's voice as she answered him.

"Well I was, Jess, but that was before last night. I'm surely not heading back now that we're together again."

"Yeah," he said and then dried up abruptly.

Lee listened to him stumbling through the conversation and felt a sudden, deep running sadness inside her. She hitched herself off the table, looked at him and said, "Maybe I'd better give you some privacy."

He covered the mouthpiece with one hand as she headed for the door.

"I'll be right with you when I'm finished here," he said stiffly. She smiled at him—a sad, understanding smile.

"Yeah, when you're finished," she said and went out into the corridor, turning toward her own office, a lifetime away.

He heard the door click shut softly behind her. Still, he kept his voice down.

"Abby, I'm not sure I can make it tonight. I thought you were heading back . . . and . . ." The words faded away. She let the silence hang for a few moments. Then said, still with that slightly amused edge, "I get it. She's there, is she?"

"She?" he asked, knowing full well who she meant. The note of amusement in Abby's voice now mingled with a touch of hurt as well.

"Your sheriff," she said simply. "Lee. She's in the room, is she?"

"No!" he said, knowing instantly that he'd said it too quickly. "She's not here Abby. It's just I . . ." Again he ran out of words. To be truthful, he didn't know what he thought, what he wanted anymore.

"You know, Jess, I didn't see last night as some kind of one-night stand."

Jesse went to speak, then stopped. He didn't know how he saw the previous night. He wasn't sure he saw it any way at all. It had just . . . happened. That was the best he could do. His silence seemed to tell Abby everything she needed to know.

"Look, if you and Lee have got something going, just tell me. I'll understand," she said. But he knew it wasn't going to be that easy. For a start, did he and Lee have something going? He'd thought they had, before Abby had arrived back in his life. Before last night. He thought they still might have. But the situation with Abby was confusing the hell out of things.

"I know you weren't acting last night, Jess," she continued. "There's still the old spark between us, isn't there?"

"Abby," he began, then didn't know where to take it. There was definitely something still there, he had to admit it. "It's just . . . I've got a lot on my mind right now with this case . . . you know?"

He was sliding away from the issue and he knew it. But right now, he needed this sort of complication in his life like he needed a hole in his head. Come to think of it, he thought, rubbing his eye as the headache now throbbed into full life, a hole in the head might be preferable in some ways.

He could hear the hurt in Abby's voice as she spoke again. "I think maybe we'd better get together, Jess. We need to talk."

He wondered if the hurt was genuine or whether it was another of Abby's little tricks. She was, he knew, a consummate actor. Even so, he owed her at least a hearing. He needed to say to her face that there was nothing there between them.

He needed to see her again, just to make sure that it was true.

"I guess you're right, Abby," he said wearily. "You say where and when."

The answer came so promptly that he instantly found himself wondering if he'd been set up by Abby's manipulations once more.

"Tonight. Eight o'clock at Hazie's," she answered crisply.

"Hazie's?" he said, a little incredulously. "On Thunderhead?"

Hazie's was in an idyllic, romantic setting, overlooking the town and Yampa Valley from the top of the first slopes. It was hardly the place for a serious discussion. More the setting for a romantic tryst.

"Hazie's," she repeated. "I like Hazie's and I haven't had a chance to get there this trip. And, God knows, this might be my last one," she added, turning the guilt screw a little on him.

He gave in.

"Hazie's," he said. "Eight o'clock."

FORTY-SEVEN

*I*t was time to go back to the place where it had all started—the Silver Bullet Gondola. He'd lost the jigger—his trademark weapon—in his failed attempt on the chairlift and that still rankled. If he used a knife or a gun now, the tall deputy might not link his next killing with the previous attacks. So he'd go back to the gondola, just to make sure they knew who they were dealing with. He'd thought about it for days, trying to figure a way around that damn deputy's restrictions on people riding the gondola in pairs. He thought he had the solution to it now. It had come to him the previous day, waiting in a lift line to ski. The key to it was a time-honored practice in ski resorts all over the world. It was something that happened constantly in lift lines. So constantly that everyone merely accepted it and ignored it at the same time.

But there were a few items of equipment he'd need first, and he knew where to find them. Rather, he thought, with an amused nod of his head, he knew who would give them to him.

He'd followed his target home from the slopes the previous day. Once the idea had occurred to him, he'd sought out the right person, managed to engage him in conversation and ascertained that today was his day off.

That was just fortuitous. He would have waited all week if necessary. But once he had found out, he'd waited round Gondola Square until the man came off duty, then followed him home.

He lived alone, in a small apartment over a cheap restaurant at the bottom end of Lincoln, down by 12th Street. Again, this had been a stroke of good luck. But Murphy believed good luck sought him out. It was his due. As such, he accepted it gracefully. And this morning, he was ready to act on it.

His hand touched the zipped inner pocket of his parka, making sure the .38 Special was there. He felt its comforting hardness and hurried on, hunched against the cold wind that eddied up the street.

He stopped in the F.M. Light store on Lincoln to buy a long woolen scarf. He didn't rush the purchase. It had occurred to him that people might well remember a man who entered, walked straight to a display and bought the first item he laid hands on. He examined several, eyeing the colors critically, and finally selected a plain, navy blue number—although the color meant less than *diddly shit to him. But it amused him to pretend it did. It amused him to play the part of a harmless shopper. Having spent a reasonable time with the selection, and so having merged into the faceless mass of customers that would come through the store that day, he paid cash for the scarf, allowed the sales clerk to put it in an F.M. Light plastic bag for him and left, heading for the bottom end of town.*

The Ham Hockery was closed, of course. He winced at the cutesy-pie name and the cartoon illustration of a happy, smiling, impossibly fat pig, whose nether regions were reduced to slices of ham. Restaurants came and went in Steamboat Springs. Today's Ham Hockery might well be tomorrow's haute cuisine Restaurant Francais, or the day after's Trattoria Milanese.

He peered in the shopfront window, making a pretense of studying the menu taped to the inside.

The chairs were stacked on tables, bare of linen or crockery, and the lights were off. As near as he could tell, there was nobody in the kitchen area at the rear. Certainly there was no light showing from the doorless entryway that led to the back. The restaurant had that slightly tired look that most night places assume by daylight. He noted the opening hours, six p.m. to one a.m., printed on the menu and nodded to himself. It was barely ten now. He wouldn't expect the kitchen staff to arrive and begin their preparation until early afternoon.

He stepped back from the window and took a quick glance around.

Nobody seemed to be watching him. A big eighteen-wheeler rig was pulling into the Amoco gas station opposite, its air brakes huffing and hissing and squealing as the driver jockeyed into position beside the diesel pump. Half a block up, an elderly man sat in a hard-backed chair tipped back against the wall of a curio shop, a battered Stetson tilted down over his nose, dozing in the bright sunlight. Apart from him, there were a few people moving around. But, as yet, it was too early for any real pedestrian traffic in the streets. Most of that would come later, after the day's skiing was done. At this time of day, the vast majority of visitors to Steamboat Springs, depleted as their numbers might be, would be peeling off for their first runs down the groomed slopes.

Casually he stepped around the corner of the alley beside the restaurant, heading for the rear stairs that he'd observed the night before. There was a Dumpster sitting outside the kitchen door. He took the F.M. Light scarf from its bag, wadded the bag up and tossed it into the trash. The scarf he kept in his hand, folded into a neat bundle.

He eased his way up the back stairs. They were wooden and they groaned a little as he climbed up them. A light still shone above the top landing and he took that as a good sign. It meant that his quarry probably hadn't surfaced yet. Not surprising. He'd sat and watched him tie on a really late one at the Old Town Saloon the previous evening. He'd wanted to make sure that the man went home. Alone.

The landing door was unlocked and he let himself into a small vestibule— obviously the place where the apartment's tenants could remove coats and jackets out of the weather. The door to the apartment faced him. He stepped quietly forward, placed his ear against it.

Nothing. No radio. No television. No sound of voices in conversation. In the silence of the little vestibule, his own breathing sounded inordinately loud. He slipped the short-barreled Colt from his inside pocket, swung out the cylinder and checked the load. The six brass jacketed .38 Specials winked back at him in a stray ray of sunlight through the upper glass panel of the outer door. He clicked the cylinder shut, began winding the three-foot length of wool scarf loosely around the revolver and his right hand.

He'd chosen the Colt Detective Special with this in mind. The Walther, being a self-loader, might snag on the material of the scarf as the action slammed back and forth during firing. The Colt was a simpler, more dependable weapon for this purpose. He made sure that he kept the scarf clear of the hammer spur, wrapping it around the cylinder and the muzzle of the barrel. They were the two areas where gases escaped violently from a pistol. Consequently, they were the main sources of noise when a shot was fired.

He finished winding the scarf, leaving about twelve inches hanging from his hand. He experimented, snicking the hammer back to full cock, then easing it down again several times. Satisfied that there was nothing to impede its move- ment or the cylinder's rotation, he took a deep breath and rapped sharply on the door with the knuckles of his left hand.

No answer. He rapped again, louder this time, and longer. Again, he heard nothing. He was raising his hand to really hammer on the thin wooden panel of the door for the third time when he heard a hoarse voice mumbling from inside.

"Yeah, right . . . coming, okay?"

Footsteps shuffled inside the apartment. He heard the rattle of the security chain on the other side of the door as the man inside released it.

"Who is it?" called the same voice, thick with sleep and hungover.

"*Dunkin' Donuts,*" *he called brightly.* "*Got your delivery. Doughnuts and hot coffee.*"

He figured that no one waking with a hangover would refuse the offer of coffee and doughnuts. They might query the fact that they hadn't ordered them, but they wouldn't refuse outright. The lock rattled briefly, then the door swung open. A man stood before him. He scratched his head and yawned. He was wearing red boxer shorts and a gray T-shirt. His feet were bare. Obviously he'd only just gotten out of bed.

"*Didn't order no doughnuts—*" *he began, then frowned as he saw Murphy's right hand coming up, noticed the swathing of navy blue material around it.*

And Murphy shot him through the center of the forehead.

The muffled .38 made a noise like a hammer hitting a table—hard. It was louder than Murphy expected, but still not so loud that it might draw attention. Above all, it didn't sound like a gunshot.

The man was slammed backward by the impact of the bullet. His bare heels skidded on the cheap carpet of the apartment, then he lost his balance and crashed over on his back, colliding with, and splintering, a wood veneer coffee table on his way down. Then he lay silent.

Murphy stepped inside and closed the door behind him. He leaned over the prone body, ready to fire again if there was any sign of life. But the man was dead. The bullet had destroyed the major part of his brain tissue, bouncing and caroming around inside his skull cavity like some evil pinball game.

Murphy straightened and stood still for a few seconds, listening.

There was no sound outside other than the distant hum of traffic on Lincoln, no sign that anyone had heard the shot or the crash of the falling body and breaking furniture. Unwrapping the singed wool scarf from around his hand, he stuffed it inside the parka. The pistol he returned to the inner zipper pocket.

He left the dead man where he lay, eyes staring sightlessly at the peeling paint of the ceiling, and moved quickly through the apartment. There wasn't much to see. A small bathroom and toilet. A galley-style kitchen with a few days' worth of dirty dishes in the small sink, and a bedroom. That, apart from the living room he'd entered, was it. The bedroom had a window that overlooked the river running through the back of town, a few empty lots and a ski repair business. A little farther away, beyond the river, the twin tracks of the Denver and Rio Grande Western railroad ran east and west out of town.

Murphy pulled the shade fully down. The man's wallet was on the bed-side table, as he'd expected. He picked it up now and rifled through the thick wad of crumpled bills in it. There must have been close to two hundred dollars there. He stuffed the money into his pocket and dropped the wallet to the floor. He was wearing thin kid-leather gloves, so there was no problem with fingerprints.

He'd known the money was there. The dead man had been a big winner in a darts tournament at the Old Town Saloon the previous night. Murphy had watched him collect his winnings before he followed him out into the night. He smiled grimly. More good luck, he thought. It gave the cops a motive for the murder. He didn't want them linking this killing to the Silver Bullet killer. This was just a means to an end. Chances were, they might not ever realize the real motive.

That was in the cheap plywood closet, which was the major piece of furniture in the bedroom. He checked it briefly, nodding to himself as he found what he was looking for. Then, carefully closing the door of the closet, he made his way to the kitchen again.

There was a brown paper grocery bag there. He'd seen it crumpled and half folded off to one side of the work area. He opened it now, saw that it was empty. He carefully folded the item he'd taken from the closet and slipped it into the paper bag.

As an afterthought, he set the bag down on the sofa close to the front door, then went back into the bedroom. He jerked open the three drawers of the bedside unit, scattering their contents at random across the room. Then he re-opened the closet. One side was hanging space and he pushed the various items on hangers close together, to conceal the fact that one had been removed. Then he repeated his scattering with the contents of the drawers on the other side of the closet. Socks, underclothes and T-shirts were pulled out and thrown around the room. He left all the drawers half-open. One he pulled too hard and it came right out and fell on the floor. He turned it upside down with his foot, spilling out the few remaining items in it, and left it lying there.

He stepped back to admire his handiwork. The room looked as if a hurricane had hit it. Doors hung open, drawers sagged on their runners and items of clothing covered every surface.

The empty wallet still lay in plain view, upside down and spread out like a bird's wings. He considered it for a few seconds, then nudged it under the unmade bed with his foot. Let them work to find it, he thought. Then they'll feel like real cops.

He backed out of the room, picked up the paper bag from the sofa and let himself out. He paused inside the outer door, grateful for the glass panel. Peering left and right, he could see no sign of anyone paying undue attention to the back stairs. Satisfied that he was unobserved, he pulled the collar of the parka up around his ears and tugged the peak of his baseball cap down.

He continued down the side alley to the street at the rear of the apartment, walked two blocks east before he turned north and headed up to Lincoln again. Another restaurant provided another Dumpster and he dropped the wadded up scarf into it, shoving it down beneath a pile of paper napkins and cardboard cartons.

He paused at the corner of 9th and Lincoln and took a deep breath. The crystal cold air seared into his lungs and he exhaled with a contented sigh.

Now he was ready to get back to business.

FORTY-EIGHT

Lee stood in the ruined bedroom, studying the chaos of clothes and personal effects that had been hurled around.

Ned Roberts, a sergeant in the town police, edged his way through the door behind her, whistled as he caught his first sight of the room and its contents.

"I guess he was looking hard for something," he said softly. Lee nodded. She reached into her jacket pocket and took out a pair of thin Italian leather gloves, and pulled them on.

"You could say that," she replied. Then her gaze lit on something just visible under the bed. Her eyes narrowed and she dropped to one knee, reaching under the edge of the disarranged covers and brought out the wallet. She flipped it open.

"Empty," she said briefly. Roberts nodded thoughtfully.

"You think maybe this was a robbery?" he asked. He wasn't the brightest of cops. He'd made sergeant more as a result of long service than any intrinsic brilliance or ability.

"Could be," she said evenly, setting the wallet down on the bedside table. "Most folks usually have a bill or two in their wallets—unless he'd had a bad night at poker."

Roberts nodded again, frowning in concentration. "I guess that's a possibility too." Lee rolled her eyes heavenward. He didn't see the gesture and didn't notice her repressing a sigh.

She examined the drawers of the closet for any further items of interest, found none. There appeared to have been nothing in the drawers other than underclothes, socks, a few shirts obviously washed and folded by the local laundry service—and a few other small items like handkerchiefs, again folded and pressed at the laundry.

The victim didn't seem to be a man who cared to do his own washing.

She rummaged carefully through the hanging space, pushing the clothes apart to see better. A Nevica ski suit, maybe four or five years old, a tweed sports jacket and a couple of thick plaid jackets, three pairs of slacks on one hanger, a Land's End Windbreaker and, between it and the sports jacket, a spare hanger.

In other words, nothing.

She edged her way around Roberts—he was a bulky man and it wasn't the largest of rooms—and returned to the living room.

There wasn't a lot of spare space here, either. The photographer was doing a series of different views of the body, while two other uniformed officers from Felix's office searched the room. She watched them for a few seconds, then left them to it. They were both capable men. They knew their job and if there was anything worth finding, she knew they'd find it.

Doc Jorgensen was off to one side, stripping off a pair of surgical gloves. The fingers were stained with the blood from the dead body. Sitting to one side, a dazed look on his face, was the man who had discovered the body some forty minutes ago—a friend of the victim who had come by to go for a beer.

Doc Jorgensen dumped the gloves in a black plastic trash bag, sealed it and put it with the coroner's kit for safe disposal. These days, anything with blood on it had to be disposed of. He glanced up at her, inclined his head in a friendly gesture of greeting.

"So, what have you got for us, Doc?" she asked.

He hesitated a moment, gathering his thoughts before he answered.

"Cause of death, obviously, one gunshot wound to the head," he said. "No other visible marks on the body. No sign of any struggle. I'd say he opened the door and the killer just let him have it. Popped him straightaway. Hard to be exact about the time, but I'd say no more than a few hours. Maybe two. Maybe less."

She glanced at her watch. "So, sometime this morning, you'd say?"

"I reckon. He definitely hasn't been lying there too long," the doctor told her. "Be able to make a better estimate later."

"Any make on the gun at all?" she asked. Jorgensen obviously hadn't had time for a full autopsy but he was an experienced medical examiner and he'd seen a lot of gunshot wounds over the years. This was, after all, hunting country. He pursed his lips, weighing his answer.

"I don't think it's our boy, if that's what you're getting at," he said finally. She raised her eyebrows, signaling for him to go on.

"Well," he said, "the guy who's been loose on the mountain used a

Walther .32 on poor Walt Davies. This is something bigger. A .38 or a 9 mm, by the look of it."

"How can you tell that?" she asked. "You haven't got the bullet yet, have you?"

The gray-haired doctor shook his head. "No-o," he said precisely. "It's still in there somewhere. But there's extensive damage to the back of the skull—I'd say it's fractured. You can feel the damage there."

"And the bullet did this?" she asked. He nodded agreement.

"I reckon so. Must have bounced around inside there like a pea in a whistle. Hit the back of the skull from the inside and nearly made it out. Just pushed the bone outward, softened it up some. You can feel it." He gestured to the body, in case she wanted to feel for herself. She shook her head.

"I'll take your word on it," she said, and he smiled grimly.

"Yeah. Anyways, I don't see a .32 doing that sort of damage. Most of its energy would have been absorbed going in through the front of the skull. And a .45 would have come out the back and taken half his head with it. So that leaves something between the two—a 9 mm or a .38. I'm guessing a .38."

Again, she invited him to continue with a tilt of her head.

"No shell-casing found so far," he explained. "All the 9 mms I've ever seen are automatics. Would have tossed the shell-case out somewhere."

She nodded, not convinced. "Could be he picked it up," she ventured. Doc Jorgensen pushed his bottom lip out in an expression of reluctant agreement.

"Could be," he said. "But it's easier to get your hands on a .38 these days than a 9 mm. More of them around. They're cheaper too," he added.

"I guess the important thing is, you're pretty sure it's not a .32," she said and he nodded emphatically.

"Bet my ass on it," he said. "We've got us a brand-new killer for this one."

Lee shook her head wearily. "Jesus. Just what we needed," she said. "Well, I guess a change is as good as a vacation."

He smiled at her sympathetically.

"How's it coming with the big case?" he asked. "Jesse turned anything up so far?"

Lee shrugged. "No, goddammit. We just hit a blind alley. Our best suspect turned out to be dead for the last three months."

"I guess that's as good an alibi as anything," the medical examiner said. Gathering up his bag, he took his leave. "I'll be at the hospital. I'll do the full examination this afternoon," he said. "Let you know if anything new turns up."

She nodded her thanks. "Obliged to you, Doc," she said. "I'll be in my office when I've finished here."

He paused at the door. "I'm still betting it's a .38," he said.

She smiled at him. A tired smile, but a smile.

"I'll buy the beers if you're right," she said.

"Hold you to it," Jorgensen replied. He waved, then let himself out. Lee took a deep breath, looked around the busy crime scene and realized that the man who'd found the body was still sitting there, ignored by everyone else in the room as they went about their tasks.

She moved over to him, smiled sympathetically and sat down on the couch beside him.

"I guess this is all a hell of a shock to you—" She consulted her notepad. The town police had filled her in with a few details when she'd arrived. "Mr. Kramer."

He nodded several times. A nervous, jerky movement of his head. He was still reliving that moment when he'd let himself in and seen his friend lying dead on the floor, blood seeping from the neat, blue-edged hole in his forehead.

"I . . . walked in and he was just . . . lying there . . . you know?" he said. His voice was a little higher in pitch than normal.

"The door was open?" she asked and he shook his head distractedly.

"No. No. Jerry leaves a key on top of the lintel there—outside the door. I let myself in. I always do. And there he was." He shook his head as the scene replayed itself in his mind again. He looked across to where the body of his friend was still lying. One of the town cops was carefully tracing a yellow chalk outline around the body. Within a few minutes, they'd remove it and take it to the hospital where Doc Jorgensen could carry out his autopsy.

"When did you last see him?" she asked. Kramer shook his head, still dazed.

"Last night," he said. "Last night at the Town Saloon. We played in the darts tournament there. We do that every week."

"And what time did Mr. Marrowes leave? Did you see him leave?" she asked.

Again, Kramer nodded assent. "Wasn't till late. Maybe one, one thirty. Said he wasn't working today so he'd sleep in late. We arranged to go back to the Saloon for lunch today. That's what I was doing here."

Lee doodled on the notepad in front of her. So far there seemed nothing worthy of note.

"You known the victim long, Mr. Kramer?" she asked. Kramer considered the question briefly.

"Year or two, I guess. We met working together on ski patrol last season. Don't see much of each other in the summer. I usually look for work up north in summer."

"You're in the ski patrol?" she asked.

Again she got the nervous nod from the man. "Both of us"—he paused, then amplified the statement—"I'm on the professional staff. Jerry, he's—" He stopped himself. "He was a volunteer."

Lee nodded to herself. Most ski patrols were organized that way. A small cadre of professionals, supplemented during the high season by amateur volunteers. The volunteers were repaid with a season ski pass, a free uniform and a lot of time on the mountain. It was a popular job. But it didn't leave a lot of time to earn a living, which might explain the empty wallet.

"So I guess Jerry—Mr. Marrowes—was a little hard up for cash?" she suggested. It was often the case with people working in ski towns. But she was wrong.

"Hell, no. He made good money in the summer. Worked on one of them oil rigs down in the Gulf of Mexico. They make good money there. Plenty enough to see him through the winter. And this place didn't cost him much in rent," he added.

Lee looked around the small room with its worn carpet and cheap, second- or third-hand furnishings.

"I guess not," she agreed. "So you'd think it unusual that there was nothing in his wallet when we found it?" she asked. Kramer for the first time lost his dazed look. He was definitely surprised to hear that news.

"Can't be," he said emphatically. "Jerry was the big winner in the tournament last night. You know," he added, "we all throw in ten bucks a head and the winner takes it all. He must have walked out of the saloon last night with close to two hundred bucks on him."

"Well, it surely wasn't there this morning," Lee told him.

He shook his head sadly. "Two hundred bucks. You think someone killed him for just two hundred bucks, Sheriff?" he asked. Lee snorted briefly.

"Folks been killed for a lot less than that," she said. Kramer raised his eyes to her sadly.

"I guess that's true," he said.

"So . . . anyone in that darts game get mad because he won?" she asked carefully. But Kramer saw the track she was heading down and blocked it indignantly.

"No way, Sheriff! This wasn't done by any of those boys!" he said. "Hell, we're all friends. Known each other for years, most of us."

"Still," Lee said gently. "Maybe someone lost big and got mad . . ."

But Kramer was positive in his denial.

"No one lost big!" he said heatedly. "All's we put in is ten bucks apiece. Ain't none of us can't spare that much! It's just a bit of fun, Sheriff, that's all. Just fun. Nobody's going to get mad over ten lousy bucks!"

She put up a hand to calm him down. "Okay. I understand," she said. "We've just got to look at all the possibilities. How about other people in the saloon? Anyone see him walk out with that money?"

Kramer spread his hands in a helpless gesture. "Well, hell, I guess most people did. Or could have if they'd been looking. We didn't make any secret about it."

Lee sighed. "So I guess we could be looking for anyone who was in the Old Town Saloon last night," she said. Kramer agreed with her.

"I guess," he said.

"Or for anyone who might have talked to someone in the Old Town Saloon," she added. Kramer was watching her apologetically, as if he felt maybe this was his fault. She smiled at him, closed her notebook and slid it into her inside pocket.

"Sorry, Mr. Kramer," she said. "Just sounding off a little. Maybe you'd like to go with one of the officers here and let him take down a full statement?" She indicated the two town cops, who had just about finished turning the room over.

"Fine," said Kramer. "Anything I can do to help, Sheriff."

She smiled again and stood up.

"I may talk to you again later on," she said and he shrugged.

"As I say, anything I can do to help."

"Okay, Mr. Kramer. Be seeing you."

She nodded to the two cops and made her way to the door. In the vestibule, she noted the parka hanging outside the front door and an old, battered pair of Timberlands. Marrowes's, she guessed.

She made for the door, but paused. An ambulance was stopped at the bottom of the stairs, and the two paramedics were hustling the gurney out of the rear. They'd come for the body. They heaved the gurney, leaving its legs collapsed to negotiate the stairs, then hurried up to the apartment. Lee stood aside to let them through. She wondered what the rush was all about. Marrowes certainly wasn't going anywhere in a hurry.

As she made her way down the stairs, she heard the familiar rattle of a worn four-cylinder motor and turned to see Jesse's Subaru pull in behind the ambulance. She gave him a tired wave and went to meet him.

"Heard we had another one," he said. She shook her head.

"Doesn't look like it," she replied. "Take a look if you like, but it seems like a totally different MO."

He hesitated. She knew he was desperate for any new lead at all in the case.

"You sure?" he asked and she shrugged.

"Well I'm not one hundred percent sure," she said, "but it's a different gun, according to Doc Jorgensen, and there's two hundred bucks missing from the dead guy's wallet. Two hundred bucks that maybe fifty people knew he was carrying," she added. She saw Jesse's shoulders slump.

"Who's the victim?" he asked. "Another out-of-towner?"

"Not really. He worked on ski patrol." She checked her notebook. "Jerry Marrowes. You know him?"

He frowned, running the name through his memory.

"Doesn't ring a bell," he admitted. "He a pro or a volunteer?"

"Volunteer," she answered and he nodded, understanding.

"That explains it. There's a lot of new guys in this year. I don't know half of them anymore. Maybe I'll take a look anyway, now that I'm here."

"Be my guest," she said. "Can't do any harm."

He nodded and headed for the stairs. She'd parked her Renegade on Lincoln and she headed for it now. At the corner, she stopped and looked back. Jesse was just entering the door at the top of the stairs. She watched him sadly. She wondered what had gone wrong between them.

FORTY-NINE

Doc Jorgensen phoned around five o'clock, confirming that he'd extracted a .38 Special from the skull of Jerry Marrowes.

"That's a beer you owe me, Lee," he said. She could hear the grin in his voice. The ME was inordinately pleased when one of his hunches was proved right. They most often were too, she thought morosely.

"I'll get around to giving it to you, Doc," she replied.

"I'll make sure of it," said the doctor.

"You usually do."

There was a pause, then Jorgensen's voice lost its joking tone. "One other thing. I found traces of fabric in the wound."

"Fabric?" Lee asked. "What kind of fabric?"

"A wool-rayon blend. There were a few strands there—badly scorched, but recognizable. Couple that with the fact that there were no powder burns on the victim, even though I'd say he was shot at fairly close range."

He paused while she digested those facts.

"You think he had something wrapped around the gun. Is that it?"

"I'd say so, Lee. That way, he'd keep the noise down a little. Not as good as a silencer, but it'd still quieten things down a piece."

She felt a quick surge of hope. "So . . . is there anything special about this fabric? Is it traceable at all, Doc?"

She sensed the slight hesitation, felt the quickly born hope stifled. She knew what he was going to tell her.

"Shouldn't think so, Lee. Every second sweater or pair of socks or scarf is made from that sort of blend." He paused, then knowing she would be let down, added, "Sorry, Lee."

"Yeah," she said heavily. "Well, it isn't your fault, Doc. Thanks for the information."

"Only thing is, if the killer still has the sweater or whatever with him, it'll have scorch marks and powder residue from the shot. That could be handy," he suggested.

"If he still has it," she replied. "Odds are he's already gotten rid of it."

Doc said nothing for a few seconds. They both knew she was right.

"Nothing much else turned up in the examination, Lee," he told her apologetically. "I'd place the time of death as between nine thirty and ten thirty this morning. That's about all I can give you."

She sighed. This was just what she needed right now, she thought. Another murder case with little prospect of a successful conclusion.

"Let me know if anything else occurs to you, Doc," she said.

"You know it," the elderly man replied and he broke the connection.

Lee stood up and walked to the window overlooking the river and looked across to the ski-jump hill behind the town. As she watched, a jumper came hurtling down the run, took off and soared high above the snow, seeming to hang in the air for an impossibly long time, before making smooth contact once more with the hard-packed surface. He ran another fifty yards or so, then skidded the big, wide jumping skis sideways to halt in a flurry of snow.

Something was bugging her about this case. There was something in the back of her mind, nagging away in the half-light, refusing to come out and be seen and recognized.

She swore softly to herself, then turned as there was a tap at the door.

"Come in," she said briefly.

The door opened and Packer Thule entered.

"Afternoon, Sheriff," said Packer. "Opie Dulles asked could I drop this off to you on my way home."

Packer was wearing the deep blue uniform of the ski patrol, with a large yellow cross emblazoned on the back. It was a high quality, expensive outfit. It had to be, Lee thought, as the ski patrol stayed out long hours in all weather, making sure the mountain was safe. Consequently, their uniform was comprised of a wind- and waterproof longline GORE-TEX parka and ski pants—the sort of thing that would cost maybe six or seven hundred bucks if you bought it privately.

In some cases, Lee knew, it was actually quite an incentive to join the ski patrol. In addition, the uniform gave patrollers automatic priority at lift lines, a fact that had caused one hell of a dogfight the previous season, when patrollers were found wearing their uniforms and jumping lines on their off-duty days.

The practice still continued, she knew, but not quite as blatantly as before. She knew Packer well. He was a longtime member of the patrol and they'd worked together several times in the past when skiers had gone missing. He was holding out a manila folder to her now. She looked at it with idle curiosity.

"Marrowes's personnel file," Packer told her, interpreting the look. She understood suddenly, nodded her thanks and took the file.

"Yeah, thanks, Packer," she said. "My mind was a long way away there for a moment. Opie said he'd send over the file. Maybe there's something in it."

Packer shook his head sadly. "Sure is a shame about Jerry," he said. "He was a nice feller."

Lee glanced up at him. "Got on all right with everyone on patrol, did he?" she asked and Packer nodded affirmative.

"Wasn't anyone didn't get on with him," he said. "He was a popular guy."

It never failed to amuse Lee that, once a person was dead—particularly as a murder victim—he or she automatically seemed to cease having any enemies in the world. Understandably, people knew that if they mentioned any long-term enmities, they were inevitably casting a shadow of accusation.

Still, she thought to herself, maybe in this case it was true. Packer seemed to be pretty genuine, and they'd known each other for quite some time.

"Well, one thing's for sure," she said finally. "He was unpopular with whoever killed him."

Packer rubbed his jaw between his forefinger and thumb. "It's a bad time, Sheriff," he said. "First poor Walt Davies, now Jerry. People in the patrol are mighty upset, I tell you."

Lee met his gaze evenly. "I'm none too pleased about it myself, Packer," she told him. "But at least we know it's not the same guy."

"How's that?" Packer asked quickly. She realized that an undercurrent of tension must have been developing among the ski patrollers. Maybe, she thought, they'd begun to believe that someone had a vendetta against them.

"Different MO for a start," she replied. "The guy obviously followed him home and then killed him. Plus there were no previous robberies. And Marrowes's killer used a .38. Walt was killed with a .32."

Packer nodded several times as he took this in. "So," he said finally. "You don't think this is someone aiming specifically at the patrol?"

She realized her earlier assessment had been accurate. She shook her head.

"Doubt it, Packer. Looks more like coincidence here."

Some of the tension seemed to have gone out of the man.

"Well, if you say so, Sheriff. Makes me feel a little easier about being out on the mountain late in the afternoon. This uniform was starting to make me feel like a target, you know?"

"Yes," she said thoughtfully. He'd tripped something in her mind there. That thought that was hovering just out of reach seemed to move a little closer, then recede once again, mockingly. She knew the best way to have it surface was to try to forget it entirely. The harder she tried now to isolate it, the more elusive it would become. She shook her head irritably.

"Like some coffee, Packer?" she asked. "There's some fresh made."

He shook his head. "Best be going, Sheriff," he said. "Mandy's got supper waiting for me."

She glanced at her watch. It was barely five o'clock. Still, Packer would have put in a hard day's work and she guessed he'd get to bed early. She knew that ski patrollers certainly rose early enough. They had to sweep the mountain before the lifts began running.

She walked with him to the door, opened it for him.

"Thanks for dropping in the file, Packer," she said. The patroller shrugged.

"Just hope it might be helpful, Sheriff. Still and all, I can't see why anyone would want to kill poor Jerry."

"Looks like two hundred bucks is the reason," she replied. He shook his head sadly at the thought of it.

"Damn," he said. "We're getting more like New York every minute, aren't we?"

She smiled sadly. "I don't think we're quite in that league yet, Packer," she said. "Let's do our best to keep it that way."

He went out, heading for the stairs. She was about to close the door again when she caught sight of Tom Legros in the hallway. She beckoned to him.

"Tom? Got a moment?"

The burly deputy was carrying a coffee mug in his left hand. He hitched his gunbelt a little higher on his belly with his other hand and headed toward her. The belt promptly slid back down the reverse slope to its original position. Lee guessed that Tom spent a lot of time hitching his belt up. She guessed that his belt spent a lot of time riding right back down again too.

He stepped into her office, taking a sip of coffee as he did so. He sighed with pleasure. There was nothing like the first sip of a fresh cup of coffee.

"You want me, Sheriff?" he asked.

Lee waved a hand to a yellow message slip on her desk.

"You know a Mrs. McLaren at all, Tom?" she asked. The deputy frowned a moment, then answered.

"Alice McLaren?" he said. "From up Laurel Street way?"

Lee checked the message slip again. "Yeah, that sounds like the one. You know her?"

Tom planted himself on the seat in front of her desk, tipping it back on its hind legs. The hind legs creaked a gentle warning. Lee raised one eyebrow in Tom's direction. She'd mentioned this to him before—several times. With a slightly guilty look, he let the front legs of the chair drop back to the floor.

"She's a nice enough lady," he said, after considering the question. "Runs a boardinghouse on Laurel. Takes in maybe eight people each season—room and board type of thing. Is there some problem?"

Lee flipped the message slip across the desk to him.

"Seems like she's complaining about those damn kids on their snowmobiles. They've been out that way the past few nights, waking people up. Some of her customers were disturbed and she's none too happy about it."

Tom shook his head in annoyance.

"Damned old busybody!" he said. "She's always minding other folks's business for them."

In spite of the day's events, Lee couldn't stop herself from grinning.

"She sure went from 'a nice enough lady' to a 'damned old busybody' in no time," she said.

Tom shrugged and looked a little embarrassed at his sudden change of heart. "Yeah, well I'm sorry, Sheriff. It's just these kids are really starting to get to me, you know? I guess I'm a little raw on the subject."

"I can understand that, Tom. Try not to take it personally."

Legros nodded moodily. "I'm trying, Sheriff, believe me. I'm trying."

"Well, call her up anyway and tell her we're doing all we can and we expect to make arrests in the near future—you know the sort of thing."

Tom took another sip of his coffee. A great deal of the former pleasure from it seemed to have evaporated now.

"Okay, Sheriff," he said. He took the yellow message slip from the desk and tucked it into his shirt pocket. He was about to say something else when a tap at the door interrupted them.

"Come," Lee called.

The door opened and Jesse entered. He saw Tom, hesitated, then came on in.

"Any further word on that killing this morning?" he asked.

Tom Legros looked at him curiously. There was a stiffness in his manner—almost as if he seemed awkward in Lee's presence. Then, as the sheriff replied, he sensed that she felt the same.

"Doc rang a few minutes ago. Doesn't seem to be our man. It was definitely a .38."

Jesse pursed his lips, unwilling to give up so easily. "Guy could have two guns," he said.

Lee inclined her head, conceding the possibility. "I guess so. But we've got a different motive on this one, Jess. The victim was robbed. Different weapon. Different MO. I'd say it was a different person."

Jesse thought about it for a few seconds. He rocked on his heels.

"We're sure of that, are we?" he asked.

Lee showed a flash of anger. "No! We're not sure of anything, Jess.

You know that. I'm just saying that all the evidence points to this being a different perp." She paused, meeting his gaze for a few long seconds, before his eyes slid away from hers. "Okay?" she finished, moderating her tone a little.

"Yeah. Okay," he mumbled. "I guess I'm grasping at straws here. Keep seeing this guy behind everything." He tried a grin, a shadow of its normal self, and said to Legros, "I guess next I'll start trying to tie him in with those kids on snowmobiles."

Tom shifted awkwardly. He returned Jesse's grin halfheartedly. He didn't like the vibes that he was feeling between Jesse and Lee. As long as he'd known them, they'd always been easy in each other's company. Now there was a definite strain between them and he wished he wasn't here to witness it. He wondered if the investigation was to blame. Maybe Lee had been getting on Jesse's case to turn up some hard evidence or a concrete lead, he thought. That wasn't like Lee, he knew, but maybe this serial killer was getting to them all. Whatever it was, he didn't like it.

Jesse finally broke the long silence in the room.

"I guess I'll be heading off," he said. "Maybe we should talk things through tomorrow, Lee. I don't seem to be getting too far on my own."

Lee nodded. "Sure. Maybe we can come up with some kind of theory if we look at it all from a fresh angle," she said. Jesse thought about that, nodded several times.

"Worth a try," he said. Then, with a vague wave of the hand, he let himself out and closed the door behind him.

Tom Legros looked at the closed door after Jesse had gone, then looked at Lee. She appeared to be intently interested in something on her desktop. He cleared his throat nervously, not knowing whether to say anything or not. Then decided, the hell with it. He'd known them both long enough to ask.

"Uh . . . something wrong between you and Jesse, Sheriff?"

Her eyes flicked up to meet his instantly and he saw a quick flash of anger there.

"Just make that call, okay?" she said crisply and he backed off, making a defensive gesture with both hands in front of him.

"Sure, Sheriff. Whatever you say," he replied mildly.

Maybe he hadn't known them both as long as he thought.

FIFTY

It was one of those nights, unfortunately rare, when the view from Hazie's was nothing short of spectacular.

The lights of Steamboat Springs and the Yampa Valley stretched out in all directions below them as Abby and Jesse sat in a window seat. Closer to hand, the flashing yellow strobes and glaring headlights of the grading machines cast a weird, flickering light over the snow and among the bare trunks and limbs of the aspens.

It was all very beautiful and very romantic, Jesse thought. And he wished to God he was somewhere else. Anywhere else.

He toyed awkwardly with his fork, forcing himself to meet Abby's eyes across the table. He could see the hurt there. Some of it, he felt, was genuine. Maybe all. Maybe not. And that was the trouble. With Abby, he never knew. Never had known. Never would know. Abby was a consummate actress and could play on a person's emotions like a virtuoso on a violin.

"So . . ." she said at length, drawing a long, uneven breath. "The other night? What was that?"

And of course, he knew it would come to this. The other night had been spectacular. It had been amazing. And, he knew, it hadn't been one hundred percent physical. There was an emotional bond still there. He knew it and so did she. But he could never be sure with her as to just how much was there. You couldn't simply wipe out the past they'd had together, he thought morosely. Maybe if they'd split in a violent, bitter confrontation, maybe if one of them had been unfaithful, maybe then you could wipe out what had been between them.

But it hadn't been that way at all. They'd simply drifted, unaware that their life paths were slowly and inexorably diverging. They'd bickered. They'd quarreled, sure. But there had never been any one final showdown between them. It was simply a case that most of what had brought them together had evaporated like mist on a clear morning.

Most of it. Leaving some of it still there. And that was the some that was making him feel so damn guilty right now. He knew he'd never be able to put it into words. Abby could always tie him in knots when it came to words. But he tried anyway.

"The other night"—he looked for the right words, didn't find them—"shouldn't have happened. That's all."

She shook her head, the blond hair gleaming in the subdued light inside the restaurant.

"No, Jess, that's not all. That's not all by a long shot. It should have happened and that's why it did happen. It was terrific, Jess. Tell me that it wasn't."

And he couldn't, of course. It had been terrific. Hell, if they could harness what they'd had the other night, he thought, the energy problems of the world could be solved.

"It was sex, Abby, that's all. Just sex," he said quietly. But the blond head was shaking again. She laughed, but without any real amusement.

"Oh no, Jess. It wasn't 'just sex.' Tell me you've ever had better sex than that. Go ahead and tell me, honestly, and I'll walk away right now."

Once again, he couldn't speak. He hesitated, letting his eyes drop to the fork he was turning over and over in his hands, and she seized her advantage.

"Is it better than that with Lee, Jess? Tell me it is."

His eyes shot up to meet hers at that. He was angry and she knew instantly that she'd made a mistake.

"That's nothing to talk about here!" he snapped. She weighed her next move for an instant. She'd been wrong to bring Lee into it, she knew. But she sensed she'd compound the error now if she retreated. Instead, she made her voice low and intimate and sad. There was a part of her that was sitting a little to one side, watching her and judging. It approved of the way she was handling things so far.

"Isn't it, Jess?" she made a helpless little gesture, then put her hand gently over the top of his, stopping the incessant twirling of the fork. "I'm talking about our future here. I'm talking about saving what we once had. Putting it back together again. And Lee's a part of that, Jess, you have to realize."

"I don't want to talk about her," he said stubbornly, his jaw set in a rigid line. The truth was, he didn't know the truth. He was frightened that if he did get drawn into discussing his relationship with Lee, if he did examine it too closely, he might find there was nothing there other than a natural reaction to loneliness.

Damn it! He thought, and in a sudden, explosive movement, bent the fork double. None of this had been a problem up until he and Abby had spent the night together. Her voice continued now, low and calm. Full of reason.

"Jesse, you can't throw the other night away as just sex. You don't have sex like that unless there's something else behind it. We're good with each other, Jess, we always have been."

Their waitress loomed up beside the table, smile fixed to her face, pad and pen poised ready in hand. They'd ordered drinks earlier and asked her to give them a few minutes. She interrupted breezily now.

"You folks about ready to order?" she asked.

Abby's head snapped around, annoyed, the blond hair swirling momentarily over her face, then swinging clear again as she shook her head in a short reverse movement.

"No!" she snapped angrily and the girl backed away, smiling still but mentally cursing people who delayed their orders. The later the order, the later the meal. Then the dessert. Then the coffee. Then, when the waitress should have been joining her friends downtown for a drink and a game of pool, she and the others were still here cleaning up and putting things away.

Abby looked back at Jesse, the sad, wistful look back on her face. But in that one instant, she had blown it.

Sad and wistful. Angry and abrupt. Sad and wistful again—all in the space of a second or so. That was Abby as he remembered her. And he knew that, even though there were currents of real attraction between them, he could never trust her enough to really know how deeply those currents ran, how true the feeling was. Life with Abby, he knew, would be a continuing cycle of uncertainty and doubt.

And if he chose that cycle now, he would never see Lee again.

He set the mutilated fork down, his hands finally still, took a deep breath and said, "No, Abby."

She cocked her head to one side quizzically, a half smile, half frown on her face. "No what, Jess? What do you mean, 'no'?"

"I mean no, it will never work between us. No," he said finally.

The half smile vanished, her lips opened slightly and he could see the tears gathering in her eyes. She shook her head slightly, unbelieving.

"Are you going to make me beg, Jess? All right, I'll beg if you want," she said, her voice shaking slightly. He closed his eyes to block out the sight of hers, shook his head slowly in a wide, sweeping motion.

"No, Abby. Don't beg. Just accept. The answer is no."

He knew this was the only way. Knew he couldn't become entangled in a discussion of the matter. Just make it clean and definite. Just keep saying no.

"Jesse . . . surely we can talk about this . . . I love you, Jess. I realize that now. I love you," she said. He looked at her again and the tears had welled up now and were flowing down her perfect face. She ignored them. Maybe she didn't even realize they were there.

She was beautiful and vulnerable and hurt and he didn't hate her and he hated to see her this way. He wanted to soften things, to console her. But he knew if he did he would be drawn back into her silken web.

He knew the best answer was to tell her that he didn't love her, even if that wasn't totally true. He did, in a corner of his heart, still love her a little. It would be better to deny that now but he couldn't do it. He couldn't face those eyes and all that had been between the two of them and say "I don't love you, Abby." It would be too cruel. He steeled himself, said nothing.

They faced each other. He was stone-faced, holding himself together with an enormous effort. She was collapsing in front of his eyes, the tears streaming freely until she noticed them at last.

She fumbled for a handkerchief, then saw the crisp linen napkin folded next to her cutlery, grabbed it and wiped her eyes with it.

He wanted to tell her he was sorry. He actually took a breath and went to say it, then stopped, said nothing. She dabbed at her eyes, head down, hiding the tears from him and the other diners in the room. Fortunately, he thought, the restaurant wasn't too full tonight. The silence between them stretched until it seemed to have gone on forever. Finally, head still down, she pushed her chair back and rose hurriedly.

"Ladies' room," she said huskily. He stood as she picked up her purse and hurried toward the door that led to the restrooms, still holding the napkin and still with her head and shoulders down. Jesse sat down again, exhausted.

"Jesus," he said quietly, staring morosely out at the lights of Yampa Valley. Fog was beginning to roll in over the mountain and the lights to the northwest were slowly winking out behind it.

The waitress rematerialized, hefted their wine bottle out of the ice bucket and examined it. There was just under half left. She filled his glass, then Abby's, leaving barely three-quarters of an inch in the bottom of the bottle.

"You folks care to order another?" she prompted. Jesse looked up at her, registering her presence for the first time.

"I don't know," he said briefly.

He grabbed at his glass, took a deep swig of the wine, feeling the alcohol bite deep inside him. The girl shrugged and moved away again. Damn fool of a job, she thought. She only came here for the skiing. The way things were shaping up here, she could tell she wasn't going to get away early for that pool game. And damn it, she thought, tonight was the night that cute guy from the hot-air balloon company had said he was going to be there.

Murphy had been watching them from the bar, nursing the one can of Coors Light as they'd made their way through the bottle of wine. He'd recognized the tall deputy immediately, of course. He'd seen enough of him around the mountain and on television in the past few days not to.

The girl had taken a few minutes longer. She was familiar, of course, but from where?

Then he realized she was the reporter from the Channel 6 feature that he'd watched a few nights before. The one who'd told the world what a bang-up job the sheriff's department of Routt County were doing on the Mountain Murderer investigation. He'd felt a quick knot of anger in his gut as he recognized her. Then the anger was replaced by a growing resolution. He'd come up here tonight to pick a target. He'd had no one in mind but he thought it should be a woman. After all, he'd stalked a woman last time on the gondola and if it hadn't been for that fucking interfering lift attendant, he would have gotten her.

Tonight, he'd planned to leave another victim in the gondola. How wonderful, he mused, if it could be Abby Parker-Taft—the name came back to him from the superimposed title that had been on-screen below her on the TV report.

Before he could manage that, however, he'd have to get rid of the deputy.

He pondered the situation for a few minutes. He could simply wait and ride the gondola down with them when they finished dinner. That way he wouldn't even need the protective coloration he'd stolen from the apartment that morning. Once in the gondola cabin, he'd need only a few seconds for a head shot from the Walther. That would settle the deputy's hash, but getting those few seconds might be tricky. Parker didn't look like the sort of man you'd catch napping. He was a cop, and cops were suspicious sons of bitches, always watching you, always waiting for you to step out of line. Reluctantly, he decided it was too risky.

He frowned. He'd planned to leave the body of his next victim on the floor of the gondola. That was another reason for the stolen ski patroller's uniform that he was wearing.

Ski patrollers were the invisible men of the lift lines. Ski patrollers could barge in at the head of a line any time at all. Lift attendants barely noticed them doing it, other than to make room for them. He'd known that the uniform would ensure that he could board a gondola with a single passenger traveling alone.

Nobody would suspect a ski patroller of being the Mountain Murderer. He smiled to himself, amused at the capital letters in the name. You just knew when a newscaster referred to the Mountain Murderer, he was capitalizing the words in his mind. It gave him dignity and a sense of identity, he thought. He liked it. It was strange, he thought, after years of killing anonymously, he was beginning to enjoy the sense of his own celebrity—it was another twist of the tail to those people who tried to run his life for him.

So, he thought, dragging his mind back to the problem at hand. He'd planned to single out a victim, ride down with her, kill her and leave her body crumpled on the floor of the gondola. The lift attendants at the base, seeing a man in a ski patrol uniform alighting from the gondola, wouldn't bother to move closer and offer assistance. Ski patrollers knew the ropes. They didn't need help to stop them tripping over their own feet. More important and to the point, they wouldn't sue the town if they happened to. He knew he could successfully block the attendant's view of the interior long enough to let the doors close again and the cabin start on its way around the bullwheel.

Then, when it reached the top station again, the attendants there would find a dead body, stuffed down between the seats and out of sight through the windows.

He'd laughed when he'd first thought of the plan. Their immediate reaction would be to assume that the lift attendants at the base had murdered the woman.

Yes, he thought, it was definitely going to be a woman—the waitress, as he'd originally planned. He'd prefer the blond reporter but it just wasn't worth the risk.

Besides, he didn't really want to kill the deputy to get at her. Maybe later, but not now. The deputy should be left alive to puzzle over the latest killing. To realize once and for all that he was up against a brain superior to his own. He thought that maybe he was becoming a little fixated on the deputy, but that wasn't surprising. Parker was the sort of arrogant authority figure he hated so much. And he seemed to be always getting in the way of his plans. He decided that he'd definitely kill Parker eventually, but not tonight.

First, Deputy Parker had to be humiliated—humiliated on behalf of Steamboat Springs, as Steamboat Springs had once humiliated him.

He sighed, taking another sip from the still half-full can of beer. He wished he still had the jigger. It just wasn't the same shooting his victims.

Somehow, it lacked finesse.

FIFTY-ONE

Jesse finished the last half-mouthful of wine in his glass and stared moodily out the window.

The fog had rolled farther in as he'd been waiting. The lights from the bottom of the mountain had that wet, swollen look to them that told him he was viewing them through a thin curtain of suspended moisture.

He glanced at his watch. Abby was taking her time, he thought. Then he shrugged. He was in no real hurry to continue their conversation. He guessed she could take all the time she wanted.

The waitress was back. Her long-suffering look told him in no uncertain terms that she wasn't amused by all this delay.

"So, did you still want to order, or will you be leaving too?" she asked.

"What do you mean?" he asked quickly. She jerked her head toward the door. The restrooms were outside the main room of the restaurant, and just past them was the exit and the way to the gondola.

"Your friend," she said, then, as if he needed further explanation, "the lady? She's decided she's not having dinner."

He frowned. "What did she say?" he asked, then regretted it instantly. The waitress was having her revenge for being kept standing around, and for Abby's quick flash of anger before.

"She didn't say anything," she replied. "I just saw her leaving."

"Goddamn it," Jesse muttered explosively. He stood up quickly, setting his chair rocking precariously before it found balance once again, and started out around the table. The girl blocked his way.

"Just a minute," she challenged. "You haven't paid for this."

"This" was the empty wine bottle, now half-floating in the melted ice and water of the bucket. Jesse cursed under his breath, fumbled his wallet out of his back pocket and hauled out a handful of notes. He flicked through them. As was always the case, they were all ones. He finally found a ten spot and dropped it on the table. The girl didn't budge.

"Thirteen eighty, plus tax," she said firmly. Jesse met her gaze, holding his anger with great difficulty. He started counting out singles, then realized there were at least eight or nine there and dropped the lot on the table, in a creased heap.

"There. Keep it," he said and shoved past her. The girl raised one eyebrow as she watched him go, then quickly counted the notes. She'd made about five bucks on the deal, she figured. She decided there was no need to share the tip with the other waiters and the kitchen staff—tips here at Hazie's were usually pooled—and stuffed the excess notes into the pocket of her apron.

*H*e was still at the table when she'd come out of the ladies' room. Going in, she'd walked with her head down, a small handkerchief to her eyes. She was upset about something, he knew that.

He'd watched their conversation. Their table was too far from the bar to hear anything they said, but the body language was plain. This was not a happy couple. He wondered now why they were arguing. After the paeans of praise she'd heaped on him and the sheriff, he would have expected them to be more friendly.

He shifted on his barstool to watch for her reappearance. Something told him that she wouldn't be going back into the dining room. It was an instinct. A gut feeling. But his instincts had been right more times than he could count in the past.

Then the ladies' room door opened and she re-emerged.

She hesitated a moment, glancing at the double glass doors that led back into the dining room. He followed her glance. He could see the deputy still sitting at the window table, his long legs splayed out underneath it as he stared out the window. The waitress was serving appetizers to a table near the doors.

Abruptly, the blonde seemed to make up her mind. She squared her shoulders and moved to the hat rack, taking down the expensive, fur-trimmed suede parka that she'd hung there and tossing it angrily around her shoulders. Some sixth sense made her aware of his scrutiny and she glanced at him. He dropped his eyes to the bar instantly. No harm done, he thought. A woman like that was undoubtedly used to finding men looking at her.

She crossed the bar in quick steps. The deputy missed seeing her. He was still looking out the window. The waitress looked up, saw her as she opened the outer door.

There was a brief swirl of cold air in the bar as she opened the door, then it closed behind her and she was gone.

Without appearing to hurry, he straightened from the barstool and dropped the five bucks that he'd had ready for the last ten minutes onto the bar.

The barman nodded an acknowledgment of the one dollar tip as he moved away from the bar, following the blond woman to the door.

"See ya," he said briefly, and the barman grunted in reply, continuing to polish a glass with a white cloth. After the cozy warmth of the bar, the cold night air hit him like a barrier, bringing tears to his eyes. The wind swirled around the stairway that led down to the gondola loading base. He saw the lower door just easing shut on its pneumatic closer behind the woman. He took the stairs two at a time to make up ground. As he put his hand on the door handle, feeling the intense cold of the steel through his thin leather glove, he heard the whine and clunk of the gondola cable shudder to a halt.

No need to appear rushed now, he thought. He gave it a few seconds, then opened the door and walked casually through. The gondola had stopped, he saw, so that the attendants could unload a cargo of soda and beer cans sent up from below. The woman was standing at the loading point, outlined against the night mist that was now beginning to swirl around the station, her hands deep in the pockets of her parka. She wore no hat.

The two attendants worked quickly, stacking the cartons of soda and beer cans to the rear of the station. Finally, they were done and they gestured for the woman to move forward from the ready point and board the nearest car. He stepped out of the shadows as she moved, knowing they hadn't noticed him so far, and followed her.

One of the attendants glanced up as he moved forward, looked as if he was going to say something, then recognized the distinctive ski patrol uniform and stopped, waving him forward.

Just as he'd thought. Ski patrollers were the invisible men of the mountain. He stepped easily into the car, still swinging slightly from the motion of the woman boarding, and dropped with a sigh onto the thinly padded bench opposite her. She glanced up idly and he smiled politely as they made brief eye contact. Then she looked away, out the window at the surrounding mist.

He felt a surge of elation. It was working, he thought. It was working. He moved his left elbow slightly against his body, feeling the hard outline of the Walther in its shoulder holster.

He glanced back and saw one of the attendants moving toward the big green go button that would start the cable again. There was a brief whirring, then a clunk of gears. The car swung back momentarily as the cable lurched forward.

Then another clunk and crash and the car was swinging in a wild arc as the cable abruptly stopped again. He felt a quick surge of anger, wondering if the attendants were having second thoughts, in spite of the ski patrol uniform. Then, as he leaned forward to get a better view of the control station, he saw the deputy hurrying toward the gondola in long strides.

Jesse came down the stairs three at a time, pulling his leather jacket on as he went. Subconsciously, he was aware of a change in the natural rhythms around him. Something was missing. Then he realized what it was. The gondola had stopped running. The deep background hum of the drive machinery and the regular clunk and crash of doors opening and cabins disengaging from the main cable was an all-pervading constant in the Thunderhead Station. Now it had stopped. At least, he thought, Abby wouldn't have left yet.

He emerged into the cold wind and fog that swirled around the loading station, just as one of the attendants hit the start button and the machinery ground into motion once more. The cabins began their swaying, dipping dance as the cable began to move again. He could see two dim shapes in the cabin that had just passed the loading point. It hadn't yet reached the automatic trip that would close the double doors.

He hesitated, measuring the distance, wondering if he could make it in time before the doors shut. Deciding he couldn't, he swung back to the control panel a few paces behind him and crushed his fist down on the big red emergency stop button.

The whirring and clunking died again. The cabins bounced as the cable stretched and retracted, reacting to the sudden stop. He heard the angry voice of one of the attendants behind him as he started toward the cabin, felt a hand on his shoulder, pulling him back.

"Hey, mister! What the hell are you doing?"

He swung around angrily, shoving the hand away, letting the attendant see his features. His right hand was already reaching into his wallet pocket, where he kept the deputy star that Lee had given him. Then he saw the attendant was one he knew and there was no need for further identification.

"Official business, Frank," he lied crisply, seeing the man's expression relax a little as he realized the gondola had been stopped by a cop. He jerked his head toward the cabin. "Someone in that cabin I need to talk to, all right?"

He was striding toward it as they spoke. Frank, with his shorter legs, was having to half run to keep up. He looked a little aggrieved still.

"Well, okay, Jess. But next time, how's about you tell me what you're up to before you just crash in here and hit the stop?"

"It's urgent, else I would have," he replied briefly, his eyes fixed on the gondola cabin. He thought now he could make out another figure inside it. He frowned slightly. Maybe Abby wasn't in there after all. He knew the rules on no two people riding down unless they knew each other. Hell, he'd instituted them. So, if there were two people in this cabin, he didn't see how one of them could be Abby.

He glanced quickly around at the other cabins in sight. There was only one other where passengers might have already boarded. It was fractionally before the loading point, doors wide open, under the full lights of the station. It was obvious there was no one in it. He hesitated, then started back toward the first cabin. Now he could see the pale gleam of blond hair in the seat with its back to him and he knew it had to be Abby. He lengthened his stride.

"Start her up again, Frank." He tossed the comment briefly over his shoulder, sensed the other man slowing down and dropping behind him. The gondola swayed as he stepped quickly inside, then the cable engaged, the doors clamshelled shut and they were moving out into the thickening fog above Yampa Valley.

FIFTY-TWO

Abby looked up quickly as he boarded the cabin and sat opposite her. He could see the anger in her eyes still.

"Abby . . ." he began, in a conciliatory tone, but she put up a hand, as if to ward him off.

"Just leave it, Jess," she said tightly. "You've said all there is to say."

"Let's not finish like this," he said, then, conscious that there was a third party present, he looked sidelong, saw the ski patrol uniform for the first time and understood why the attendants had allowed a second person to load with Abby. He frowned slightly. There was something vaguely familiar about the man, although his face was partly obscured by the upturned collar and the wool cap pulled down low over his eyes. Sitting alongside him the way he was, it was difficult to get a clear look at his features without being too obvious. Maybe he'd seen him around the ski patrol headquarters. There were so many new faces that came and went each year on the patrol and he couldn't keep track of them all. He dismissed the man from his thoughts, turning back to Abby.

"So, Abb," he said gently. "Where to now?"

She looked around at him, the anger and the hurt still evident.

"For us, you mean? Looks like nowhere, doesn't it?"

"I meant for you," he said, deliberately not rising to the bait she'd offered. She shrugged, huddled herself deeper into the fur-trimmed parka. He'd loved her once, he realized, but even then, he'd known she had the capacity to act like a spoiled child.

"I guess I'll go back to my room at the Mountain View," she said. "Then tomorrow, I've got a taxi ordered for eleven to get me to my flight from Hayden."

"Back to Denver?" he asked. Again, her eyes accused him.

"Where else?" she replied. "At least there's something for me in Denver."

He felt the man beside him move slightly. He glanced sideways at him, with a look that apologized for involving him in a personal scene like this. Caught unawares, the other man was watching them intently. He'd moved slightly away from Jesse, leaving a small space between them. As Jesse's gaze caught him, he turned away abruptly, obviously embarrassed at being caught listening in so openly. He stared out the far side window at the fog.

"I'll drive you to the plane," he suggested, turning back to Abby. She smiled. The smile never reached her eyes.

"Taxi's fine," she said shortly. Then her eyes slid away from him to look at the man beside him. Jesse followed her gaze. The man had been fumbling with the zipper of his parka. As Jesse looked at him, his hand dropped to one side. He grinned at the deputy.

"Little warm in here," he said. Jesse cocked his head thoughtfully.

"Wouldn't say warm exactly," he replied. "Sure is a lot colder outside in that wind," he conceded. As if in answer to his statement, a gust of wind rocked the cabin, clearing the surrounding fog slightly and showing the lights of the condos on the hill as they slid down past them. The other man shrugged. He seemed a little tense, but then, Jesse thought, he'd be the same way if he had to sit in a gondola cabin listening to a relationship hit the rocks and break up.

As if he was thinking the same thing, the man turned away, peering out the window into the night. It was the nearest he could get to not being there, not witnessing their argument, Jesse thought. He glanced over his shoulder—he was sitting facing uphill—and saw the misty lights of the bottom station looming out of the fog behind him.

"Nearly there," he said, to no one in particular. The man turned back and, just for a moment, Jesse thought he saw a trace of anger cross his face. Then it was gone, if it had ever been there at all, and the next minute, they were sliding into the light and the noise of the bottom station. The doors chunked open and the gondola rocked as it came onto the slow speed detached cable. Jesse stepped down at the unload point and turned to offer a hand to Abby. She ignored it pointedly, steadying herself with one hand on the side of the gondola as she stepped down.

"I'll drive you back to the hotel," he said, falling into step beside her. She shook her blond head angrily.

"I can get a cab," she replied shortly. They came out of the gondola building now and he gestured toward the Alpine Taxi rank. It was empty.

"You'll have to call for one. Could be waiting twenty minutes or more, this time of night."

It was just on eight thirty, a time when most people were heading out for their evening of après-ski activity. Even with the reduced number of tourists in town, the half-dozen taxis that served Steamboat would be running flat-out. Abby hesitated, then shrugged, realizing the sense of what he'd said.

"All right," she said. "Drive me back to the hotel. Then get the hell out of my life."

She turned toward where they had left his dented Subaru an hour ago. He had to walk quickly to keep up. Idly, he glanced around to see where the ski patroller had gotten to. But there was no sign of him anywhere.

Lee had spent the evening wandering aimlessly around her small house. She'd made a quick, thrown together meal of hamburger, hash browns and beans, then turned the TV on. After a few minutes, she turned it off again, went through to the kitchen and sat at the kitchen bench for twenty minutes, cleaning and oiling the Blackhawk. She lined the five heavy .44 Magnum slugs up on the bench, spun the action several times, checking for dirt or grit, eased back the hammer, let it down again, spun the action again and then reloaded the five chambers.

As ever, she left the one under the hammer empty.

She thought about Jesse, wondering where he was, what he was doing. Instinctively, she knew that he was with Abby and she didn't want to think about that. She pushed the subject to the back of her mind.

Something was preying on her consciousness. Something about the downtown killing. There was something she was missing, she just knew it.

She bundled the kitchen trash into a paper bag and crunched through the crusted snow to the garbage can just inside her front gate, crushing the new load down on top of the already full contents. She jammed the lid back down again, fastened the clips that held it in place and went back into the warmth of the kitchen.

She still couldn't place it. It was nagging at her and she still didn't know what it was.

Annoyed, she flipped on the TV again. Letterman was explaining to a New York audience how they'd arranged for a man leading a tame bear to try to get entry to the Russian Tea Room. A remote camera was following the action. The studio audience shrieked. Letterman arched his eyebrows and his bandleader sidekick made a few seemingly serious protests. If you believed the studio audience, it was hilarious stuff. Lee watched it, stone-faced.

On the other channel, Jay Leno was interviewing one of the seemingly endless succession of near identical Baldwin brothers on the latest in a seemingly endless succession of near identical action movies. They showed a clip. The Baldwin brother was hanging off a train as it sped into a tunnel. There was a ball of flame as the carriage exploded— Lee wondered why a railway carriage would explode in a ball of flames. Then a stuntman leapt from the exploding/burning carriage onto a grassy slope beside the tracks, tucking into a ball and rolling. Then, in close up, the Baldwin brother—she thought it might be Alec—rose groggily to his feet, wisps of grass in his hair and dust covering one shoulder of his carefully ripped leather jacket.

She killed the TV for the second time in half an hour.

Damn! she thought. What was it? What was the small detail that was gnawing away at her subconscious? She'd tried ignoring it, tried to concentrate on other things, hoping that would allow her brain to sort it out and present a solution to her out of the blue.

Only it hadn't happened. So now she tried the other way. She dropped into her customary armchair, hooked one leg over the arm and concentrated. In her mind, she went over every detail of her time in the apartment.

The empty wallet. The clothing scattered across the floor. The dead body, staring sightlessly up at the ceiling.

No powder burns. Was that it? She shook her head. Doc had explained the absence of powder burns, with his theory of a cloth wrapped around the killer's gun.

Was it something that the victim's friend had said? She racked her mind again, going over his words. She rose, went to where her cold weather uniform jacket was hanging on the back of the kitchen door, took out her leather-bound notebook and checked through the notes she'd made.

She had an uneasy feeling that the fact had to do with some-one other than the victim and the killer. Someone she'd seen in con-nection with the crime. Unbidden, a picture of Packer Thule came to her.

Packer, in her office, in his blue and yellow patrol uniform, worried that someone might have a grudge against the ski patrol. Was that it? Was that the reason for the killings?

She shook her head irritably. The first three victims had no connec-tion at all with ski patrol.

Maybe that was the killer's plan? Kill three unconnected men to throw suspicion away from his true aim—to kill members of the ski patrol? No, damn it. It was too bizarre.

She got up abruptly, pacing the room in long, impatient strides. The wood in the slow-burning stove was almost consumed, so she fed another two logs in, moved them around with a poker so they were settled in the hottest section of the embers. That killed three minutes or so. She glanced at her watch. Twenty-seven minutes past ten.

"Shit," she said quietly. She hated it when this happened.

She moved to the bedroom, shivering a little as she left the warmth that the stove provided to the kitchen and living room. She pre-ferred to sleep in an unheated room—it was just the transition from one to the other that was a problem. Quickly, she stripped off her plaid shirt, jeans and underwear, folding the shirt and jeans carefully and laying them on her bureau, kicking the underwear into a half-full laundry hamper by the door.

Her naked skin goose-bumped in the chill air and she felt her nipples harden. She glanced down at them idly, couldn't help thinking about Jesse and felt a quick wash of sadness over her. Nude, she slid under the down-filled duvet, shivering slightly at the cold touch of the sheets. She curled up, waiting for her body heat to warm the bed around her, wished that Jesse were there, then wished that she hadn't thought of him. Her hand crept to the warmth between her thighs, hesitated a moment. Then she swore quietly, knew if she started that she'd start thinking about Jesse even more. She rolled over abruptly, shivered again as her skin made contact with a new, ice-cold part of the sheets and tried to sleep.

It was over an hour before she managed it.

FIFTY-THREE

The early morning sun streamed into Lee's bedroom, moving with deceptive speed as it traced a path closer and closer to the bed.

Finally, the first rays touched her face. She frowned, still sleeping, as she felt the warmth, then suddenly was wide awake, sitting bolt upright.

"Jesus," she said to herself. "The closet. It's the closet."

She tossed back the bedclothes and ran to the door. The remnants of the logs she'd put on the fire the night before were still glowing in the stove and the room was a good ten degrees warmer than her bedroom. She barely noticed it as she scooped the keys to the Renegade from the bench that divided living room and kitchen and jerked open the front door of the house, gasping as the intense cold hit her.

The Jeep fired on the second crank and she jerked it into drive, the wheels spinning as they cut through the crust of snow, then biting on the tarmac underneath. She hesitated at the intersection, saw there was no cross traffic, then gunned it toward the town center.

The low angle, early morning sun reflected blindingly from the snow on the sidewalks, trees and buildings. She fumbled in the glove box of the Jeep, found a pair of Ray-Bans and put them on one-handed, flinching slightly as the ice-cold metal made contact with her skin. There wasn't much traffic around at this hour of the morning. She glanced quickly at her wrist to see the time, remembered that she'd left in too much of a hurry to put on her watch. It was still on her bedside table. The dashboard clock read 6:25.

Six twenty-five on a perfect, sunny, ice-cold morning.

The lights were with her as she came to Lincoln. She turned right, barely slowing down and letting the Renegade fishtail just a little. She thought of winding up the siren and beacon, decided she didn't need them. There wasn't enough traffic around to warrant it. And besides, she'd done enough racing down Lincoln with the siren howling this week, she thought. She shifted uncomfortably as she remembered the last time—and the aftermath.

She was coming up on the Ham Hockery now. She eased up on the gas, waited for a gap in the light traffic coming in the opposite direction, and took a left into the alley beside the restaurant, parking behind the Dumpster.

She sat for a moment, studying the area. The crime scene tapes were still in place. A team of Felix's men would be back later in the day to continue sifting through every possible shred of evidence in the little apartment. She took a deep breath, opened the door and stepped down from the Renegade. A passerby stared curiously at her as she made her way to the wooden stairs. She nodded good morning but he continued to stare. She frowned slightly, then shook her head and dismissed him from her thoughts.

She went up the stairs deliberately. It was the closet. She knew that. Something in the closet. She didn't know what it was, just knew it was there. She reached the top of the stairs, reached for the door handle to the vestibule and paused, conscious of a muttering of voices below her. She glanced down into the alley. There were half a dozen people there now, along with the man she'd just passed, all staring up at her, all muttering quietly to each other. Something about her seemed to fascinate them.

She ducked under the yellow and black striped tapes, let herself into the vestibule, tried the door into the apartment.

Locked, of course.

A thought came back to her. Something the dead man's friend had told her. She reached to the lintel above the doorway, felt along it and, sure enough, there was a key. She could imagine him now, on the morning of the murder: finding the key, unlocking the door, replacing the key, entering and finding his friend dead on the living room floor. She slid the key into the lock, cracked the door a couple of inches, then replaced the key in its hiding place.

She stepped into the apartment. The body was gone, of course. In its place was the yellow chalk outline, covering the floor and overlapping onto the splintered remains of the coffee table. There was a dark stain on the carpet in the area marked by the head of the chalk outline. No need for DNA tests to prove whose blood it had been, she thought.

Apart from the missing body, everything else appeared to be just as it was when she was last in the room. She crossed quickly to the bedroom.

Bed still unmade. Socks and underclothes scattered in front of the closet. One drawer upside down on the floor in the middle of the confusion. The wallet was gone, of course, bagged and tagged and taken away as evidence: Exhibit A. Empty wallet. Proof of motive: robbery.

"Maybe," she muttered to herself. She was beginning to think that this case wasn't as cut-and-dried as it seemed. She stood for a long moment, looking at the closet. The door to the hanging space was closed. She frowned. She didn't remember leaving it that way. Maybe Felix's men had closed it after they'd inspected the contents.

She reached her hand out to the wooden handle, seized it, hesitated. She didn't know what she was looking for. She didn't even know why she was looking for it. She just knew that there was something in this closet, something out of place. Something not right. She jerked the door open.

And screamed.

Pinned to the back wall of the closet by a long, needle-sharp spike that transfixed his heart, his eyes staring widely, tongue lolling grotesquely. Dead. Dead. Dead.

Jesse.

She screamed again, the sound rising from the pit of her gut, bursting out through her throat and her mouth as she slammed the door of the closet on the horrific sight, as if closing it from sight would make it not be.

She staggered blindly from the bedroom, stumbling across the living room to the door, scattering evidence in the crime scene as she blundered into furniture, hurled it from her path. Oh God. Not Jesse. Not now. Not ever. She was sobbing, her hands across her eyes in a vain attempt to wipe the scene from her memory.

The eyes. The tongue. The dried banner of blood that trailed from his chest down the front of the old, worn denim shirt. The feet in their supple old cowboy boots, lifted neatly off the floor of the closet. Oh Jesus. No. No. No!

The door slammed open against her weight. She staggered through the vestibule to the top of the stairs, went out the second door and stopped.

Faces below her. A small crowd now, waiting for her to re-emerge. Staring up at her and Christ Jesus, Jesse was dead back there and there was no point calling for help. He was beyond help.

He was dead.

And the first man she'd seen in the alley was stepping forward and pointing at her and laughing and saying something to the man beside her. Laughing, while Jesse was dead. Pinned to the back wall of a closet. And he was laughing. Instinctively, her hand dropped to where the butt of the Blackhawk should have been, felt the bare flesh of her hip. She looked down, puzzled, confused, realizing she was standing at the top of the stairs, bare-ass naked except for a pair of Ray-Bans. Remembering now, throwing back the bedcovers and running to the Jeep without pausing to cover herself.

And woke up. This time, for real.

Soaked with sweat. The sun through the open curtains flooding the room as before. She'd tossed the covers off in her dream and she lay there now, her breasts heaving as she felt an intense flood of relief flow through her. She'd been dreaming. The drive through the early morning streets, walking naked through the alley, Jesse's body in the closet. None of it had been real.

"Jesus," she muttered, grinning weakly to herself. No wonder the guy in the alley had stared at her. No wonder the crowd had gathered, waiting for her. She sat up, wiped the sweat from her shoulders and breasts with the sheet. Outside, the temperature hovered around zero. In here, with the sun streaming through the double glazed windows and filling the room, it was positively hot. Almost tropical. She slumped back against the pillows, letting the sun wash over her. Eyes closed, she felt the warmth on her face, could see the red glare of it beyond her eyelids.

Dreams, she thought. Where was the logic in them? Why had she dreamed she'd driven nude through the town to find Jesse's body stuffed in a cheap, plywood closet? She shuddered uncomfortably at the memory of the sight, pushed it quickly away.

Unbidden, the scene returned, as her hand reached out for the closed door of the closet, grabbed it and . . .

The closet!

Her eyes slammed open. Suddenly, she knew what it was that had been haunting her. She could see the one small detail that was wrong in the overall picture. She hesitated, making sure that this time, she was really awake. Then, satisfied that this was the real world, she slipped from the bed and padded barefoot to the shower.

There was no need to revisit the crime scene. She knew what she'd seen there. Or rather, what she hadn't seen. She showered, dressed and drove to the Public Safety Building.

Grabbing a coffee and a muffin from the Book Store Coffee Shop, she went up the back stairs two at a time, checking first in the conference room to see if Jesse was in. She hadn't seen his Subaru in the parking lot, but she checked anyway.

There was no sign of him so she headed for her own office. She'd barely got the lid off the cup of steaming coffee when Tom Legros put his head around the door.

"Sheriff?" he said hesitantly. "You got much on this morning?"

She smiled to herself, thinking about running around stone-cold naked in her dream. It put a different spin on his choice of words.

"What's the problem, Tom?" she asked, realizing that he was frowning at her, wondering what she was smiling about. Hurriedly she got rid of the smile.

"Well, it's that Miz McLaren . . ." he began. She frowned slightly, not recognizing the name.

"Over on Laurel Street?" he added. "The kids on snowmobiles?"

Her memory clicked into gear and she nodded. "Right. Got her. What about her?"

Tom shifted unhappily. She knew he felt he'd failed over this snowmobile business. In fact, he had, she reflected. But it didn't really matter too much of a damn. The kids were hardly the James gang on snow. Tom shouldn't have let the matter get so important to him, she thought. He still hesitated to speak, so she prompted.

"Tom? What about Ms. McLaren?"

"Well, hell, Sheriff, seems like one of her customers was complaining to her about the noise and she feels it's her duty to make an official complaint."

Lee spread her hands in acceptance of the idea. "Fine," she said expansively. "Let her make an official complaint and take official notice of it. You listen to it just as officially as hell, Tom," she smiled.

"To you," he finished, and her smile faded quickly.

"To me?" she repeated. The overweight deputy nodded several times.

"To you in person, Sheriff. She was on the phone just ten minutes gone, saying she wanted to speak to the sheriff in person and voice an official complaint."

"You tell her you're the officer handling the case?" Lee asked and he nodded, hesitated, his face reddening.

"She said something about 'organ-grinders and monkeys,'" he replied.

Lee nodded sympathetically. "Tom, don't let this business get you down. It's just kids letting off steam you know."

Legros sighed and walked a few paces around the room. "I know that, Sheriff. Trouble was, I let it get personal. I let those boys get to me."

"Well, yeah, that is the trouble, isn't it?" she said, not unkindly. "Thing is, Tom, if those boys were robbing a bank and you called on them to stop, you could just blaze away at them and you'd be some kind of hero. It's a mite difficult to open fire on kids playing around on Ski-Doos, isn't it?"

Tom nodded mournfully. "I know it, Lee. I handled it wrong from the start. I should have treated it as a joke."

There was a silence between them. Lee smiled sympathetically.

"As I say, Tom, don't let it get you down. It ain't that important."

Tom sighed again and hitched his gunbelt once or twice. "I know that, Sheriff," he said. "Thanks for listening. And about Miz McLaren?" He let the question hang there. Lee smiled at him again.

"I'll see her when she comes in," she told him. "We'll both see her, Tom."

That satisfied him. He gave her his trademark salute with one forefinger, hitched his belt again. It slid instantly back down the reverse curve of his belly. He turned to go.

"I'll let you know when she comes in then, Sheriff," he said.

"You do that," she said. Then, as he was going through the door, she called after him. "Oh, Tom? Take a look and see if Jesse's in yet, will you? Ask him to come see me if he is."

Legros glanced down the corridor.

"He's in sure enough," he said. "Just saw him going into his room. I'll tell him you want to see him."

He started to move, but Lee held up a hand to stop him.

"No matter," she said, picking up the waxed coffee cup and holding it carefully between one finger and thumb. "I'll go see him myself."

FIFTY-FOUR

Jesse looked up at the light tap on the doorframe. Lee was standing there, a take-out cup of coffee in her hand. As he looked up, she sipped cautiously.

"Can I come in for a minute?" she asked. He nodded, waved a hand to indicate the several chairs set around the table.

"Take the weight off," he invited, removing the lid from his own cup of coffee. He did it carefully. The girls at the Book Store Coffee Shop tended to overfill the cups so that when you removed the lids, you spilled hot coffee on your hands. He managed to prize the plastic lid loose without losing a drop.

Lee hooked a chair out with one foot and slid into it. She watched him carefully. He had that haunted, almost hangdog look to him again. She sighed inwardly. He was back to the old Jesse that she'd known when he came back from Denver. Cautious, reserved, with the barriers well and truly up, excluding people from making close contact. For a few brief days there, he'd come out of that shell. He'd been alive again. They'd been alive together. Mentally, she cursed Abby for interfering, then shook herself out of the introspection. This wasn't getting the work at hand done. She realized that Jesse had finished with the coffee cup lid and was looking up, watching her watching him.

"So what can I do for you?" he asked.

"That shooting yesterday," she began. She paused and he nodded, inviting her to go ahead.

She hesitated, wondering exactly how to put it, then decided to just plunge in. It was an idea. A hunch. Not even a theory at this stage. Just a fact that seemed to have no relevance in the crime that had been committed.

"I'm not sure that there isn't more to it. I've got a feeling about it," she said. He nodded slowly. He knew her well enough to understand that when she had a feeling, it was worth paying attention to.

"Anything concrete to go on?" he asked. She nodded slowly.

"Just one thing. Not definite, maybe. But a possibility. I don't believe the motive was robbery. I think that was done to throw us off the scent. I think it was our Mountain Killer."

Jesse sat up a little straighter. The hangdog look had gone. He was all business now that there was a possible lead.

"What makes you think it?" he asked.

"There was something missing from the closet in the apartment," she told him. "I remember, I looked in there. There were a couple of casual jackets, a ski suit, things like that. And in the middle of the other clothes, there was an empty hanger."

Jesse thought about it. He pushed his bottom lip out, doubtfully.

"Doesn't prove something was taken," he said. "Maybe the guy just had an extra hanger. Been known to happen," he added mildly, looking up at her. But Lee was already shaking her head.

"The guy was a ski patroller," she said. "There was no uniform in the closet."

Jesse, already sitting up to take notice, straightened even further. He was like a bird dog who's heard the first faint rustle of quail in the grass before him.

Lee continued. "I've been trying to work out what it was that bothered me about that closet," she said. "Then I remembered that Packer Thule dropped by the office yesterday—in his uniform. The guys in the patrol don't change on the mountain, do they? They wear their uniforms to and from work."

"Most do," he replied. "A few of us have lockers, but they're only for squad leaders and above. The rest wear their uniforms to and from work like you said. They're good parkas." He smiled. "Besides, most of the volunteers like to be seen wearing them around town."

"Now think about this," she said, leaning forward and locking his gaze into hers. "A guy in a patrol uniform can go anywhere on the mountain, no questions asked. He can jump lift lines. He can barge in anywhere. He is the invisible man."

"Oh, Christ," he said softly, and the sound of his voice stopped her in mid-flight. She looked at him. He was staring into the distance, remembering, seeing nothing.

"Jess?" she said, concerned for him. "What is it?"

The color had drained from his face. Literally. He stood up and walked to the end of the table. The wooden pointer from the whiteboard lay there. He picked it up in both hands, gripping the wood until his knuckles whitened.

"Lee, I saw him. Last night. It was him."

"You saw him?" she asked, incredulous. He nodded several times, his eyes unfocused, seeing the scene in the gondola once again.

"A guy in a ski patrol uniform. He looked kind of familiar, I don't know why. But he was in the gondola, watching us. It was him, Lee, I know it was him. I feel it."

She took a pace toward him, put out a hand to touch his arm then let it drop. "Ease up, Jesse," she said slowly. "Just because you saw a guy in a uniform doesn't make him the one who stole it."

His eyes came around to her and burned into hers. "He was watching us the whole time. I kept turning around and catching him. Watching. It was him. It had to be him."

She made a placating gesture with both hands. "Could have been coincidence, Jess. Let's keep our perspective. It could have—"

There was a knock at the door. She turned, angry at the interruption.

"What is it?" she snapped and the door opened to admit Tom Legros, a few steps behind an indignant elderly lady.

"Sheriff Torrens," Mrs. McLaren began. "I pay my taxes and I vote when it's time to do so. I have a say in this community and that gives me the right to complain to you in person . . ."

Lee held her anger in check. Legros made an apologetic gesture behind the woman.

"I'm sorry, Sheriff, I tried to tell her you were busy—"

Mrs. McLaren cut him off. "Busy? Busy my foot, Sheriff! An elected official is never too busy to speak to one of the people who elected her. That's what I told this fool."

Lee moved toward the indignant woman. "That's true, Mrs. McLaren . . ." she hesitated, glanced at Tom. "I assume this is Mrs. McLaren?" she said. Tom nodded wearily and she continued. "You have every right to come see me and make your complaints. But right now, Deputy Parker and I are in the middle of—"

She stopped. The older lady wasn't listening to her. She was frowning in concentration, peering at something across the room. As Lee watched, she ferreted in her handbag and took out a pair of blue plastic-framed glasses, perching them on the end of her querulous nose to get a better look.

"Why have you got a picture of Mr. Murphy here? What has he done?"

She was pointing at the bulletin board, and the ID photo of Anton Mikkelitz that Jesse had hung there.

"Mr. Murphy?" Lee began. "You mean you know this man, Mrs. McLaren?"

There was a crash of furniture at the end of the table as Jesse kicked a chair over in his haste to get to the photo. He ripped it from the wall, looked at Lee, his eyes burning.

"This is him! The guy in the ski patrol uniform! I knew he looked familiar!"

He dropped the photo, threw both hands up to his face in despair.

"How could I have missed it?" he said to himself. Mrs. McLaren had reached across the table and picked up the photo herself. Lee repeated her question.

"Mrs. McLaren, you know this man?"

The woman frowned, turned the photo on an angle and studied it more closely. "He's not blond," she said, then, with increasing certainty. "And he's a few years older now. But it's him. Mr. Murphy. One of my guests."

"And he's been with you how long?" Lee asked slowly. The boardinghouse proprietor considered the question, looked to the sky, counting off days in her mind.

"Oh, I'd say a good three weeks now. Paid a month in advance. Why have you got his photo here?" she asked, her suspicions now aroused that she might have misjudged Mr. Murphy.

Jesse moved around the table, studying the woman carefully. "Mrs. McLaren, is this Mr."—he searched mentally for the name, found it—"Murphy at your place now, by any chance?"

She shrugged. "Well, he may just be," she said. "I didn't see him go out so far. Usually when he goes skiing, he doesn't leave till after eleven. But what has he done?" she repeated, and again, they didn't answer her. Jesse and Lee were exchanging a long, meaningful look. Tom Legros, who'd understood maybe half of what had gone on in the room, was as puzzled as Mrs. McLaren.

"Mrs. McLaren." Lee took the older woman's arm gently. "I'm going to ask if you'll accompany us to your boardinghouse, and show us which room we might find this Mr. Murphy in. Will you do that for us?"

"Why certainly, Sheriff Torrens, but I'd still like to know . . . oh my good God almighty!"

This last was torn from her as she glanced round to see that Jesse had taken his .45 Colt from the back of his waistband and was quietly checking the magazine and the round in the chamber. He lowered the hammer with his thumb, clicked on the safety and replaced the pistol.

"Now just settle down, Mrs. McLaren," Lee said soothingly. "I'm sure there'll be no trouble—"

"But your deputy . . . that gun . . . surely he thinks . . ."

Jesse tried to smile reassuringly at her. It didn't quite come off.

"I'm just being on the safe side here, Mrs. McLaren," he said. "I'm sure there'll be no need for guns."

He took her other arm and, between them, they moved her from the conference room to the corridor, and then to the stairs. Tom Legros trailed along behind, an interested and confused spectator.

"You want me to come along too, Sheriff?" he asked. Lee shook her head.

"You keep an eye on things here, Tom. Jesse and I will manage just fine on our own," she told him.

They took one of the department Oldsmobiles for the drive to Laurel Street. For a moment, Lee thought about using the siren, then reason prevailed. If Murphy-Mikkelitz was at the boardinghouse, the last thing she wanted to do was alert him to the fact that they were on their way.

Mrs. McLaren, by now totally confused and more than a little afraid, was in the rear seat.

"Sheriff," she asked hesitantly. "What on earth is going on here?"

Lee and Jesse exchanged a glance. Almost imperceptibly, Jesse nodded. There was little point in keeping the old woman in the dark any longer.

"Mrs. McLaren," Lee said gently. "You've been reading about these murders on Mount Werner, haven't you?"

"Well of course I have!" said the landlady, with some spirit. "Been a little hard not to hear all about them, what with the news being all over the papers and on television and all. Why, only the other evening, I saw the two of you interviewed on television talking about it all. I was watching it with Mr. Murphy—" She suddenly stopped in mid-flow. Then, after a long pause, she said quietly, "Oh my good God almighty."

Jesse glanced over his shoulder at her. The puzzled, confused look had gone from her face. Her color had drained totally. She was chalk white now as she realized what Lee had been about to tell her.

"You're telling me that Mr. Murphy is the one who's been doing those dreadful things? Is that what you're saying?"

Her eyes met Jesse's. For a moment, he thought she was going to be physically sick. He replied carefully.

"Now, Mrs. McLaren, we're not sure of anything here. We just know that Mr. Murphy, or, as we call him, Mikkelitz—"

"Mike!" Lee interrupted him suddenly. He looked at her, head cocked to one side. She glanced quickly away from the road.

"Mike," she repeated. "That's what Walt Davies called him, just before he was shot. He said 'Is that you, Mike.' That's what made us go after Miller, remember?"

Jesse whistled softly. "So it did. I guess it doesn't take much to shorten Mikkelitz to Mike."

"It all starts adding up all of a sudden, doesn't it?" Lee said.

Jesse was nodding, thinking further into it. "Even his background. He was a paramedic down in Denver around the time of the gang fights. Odds are that's where he picked up the jigger. He probably attended fight scenes two or three times a week." He shook his head ruefully. "I might have even seen him there and not known."

"As I said, it all starts adding up," Lee replied.

"Always does, after you know the answer," Jesse told her. "Before that, everything's just one unrelated fact after another."

"What are you planning to do, Sheriff?" Mrs. McLaren asked quietly.

"Why, we'll just quietly go in and speak to this Mr. Murphy of yours, Mrs. McLaren," said Lee. "And we'll hope that he's going to be reasonable about things."

She glanced in the rearview mirror, catching a look at the landlady. She was mildly surprised, knowing what she did of Mrs. McLaren, that there'd been no outburst along the lines of, "Why he seemed such a nice young man," no denial that the suspect could possibly be a guest at her boardinghouse. The older woman was shaking her head, and the expression on her face was a mixture of sadness and anger.

"Killed Walt Davies, you say?" She addressed the question to Jesse. He shrugged.

"We're not certain of that. But it sure looks like it," he replied.

She let go a deep sigh. "Knew Walt since he was a boy. Knew his mother, Cassie. Fine, decent woman she was. Brought young Walt up after her Roy didn't come back from that Vietnam place." She pronounced it more as "Veetnam." "He was a good boy, Walt."

There was a silence in the car.

Lee felt she had to comment on what the woman had said. "He was that, Mrs. McLaren," she agreed.

Again, the older woman shook her head. "Well, you two try to speak to him, as you say. But if he tries to run for it, you shoot that evil sonofabitch, Sheriff. You shoot him down like a dog."

FIFTY-FIVE

There were several guests in Mrs. McLaren's parlor. None of them was Mikkelitz.

Mostly older folk, they glanced up with mild interest as the landlady showed the sheriff and her deputy through, ushering them to the hallway that ran to the part of the big old frame house where the bedrooms were grouped.

She pointed to the door on the left at the end.

"That's his," she said in a whisper. Lee nodded, glanced at Jesse, received his nod in return. He had the big .45 automatic out now and she saw his thumb reach up and flick down the safety lock on the side of the receiver. Then he snicked the hammer back to full cock and nodded again.

Lee eased the Blackhawk out of its holster. Her thumb rested lightly on the hammer, not cocking it yet. Her forefinger, like Jesse's, lay along the outside of the trigger guard. Lee only put her finger near the trigger when she definitely wanted the heavy .44 Magnum to go off. She held the barrel down, pointing to the ground in front of her feet. Jesse, she noted, in a detached sort of way, held his gun up. Between them, if things went wrong, they could blow away the ceiling and the floor, she thought, irrelevantly.

She laid her left forefinger over her lips, catching Mrs. McLaren's eyes and raising her own eyebrows to emphasize the need for silence. Then she led the way along the corridor.

She went past the doorway to Mikkelitz's room, flattening herself against the wall, just past the doorjamb. Jesse stopped on the other side, holding out his left arm to stop the landlady from moving forward, keeping her back from the door.

He raised an eyebrow at Lee, mimed knocking on the door with the back of his left hand. She nodded, but indicated for him to wait. Then, pointing to Mrs. McLaren, she mouthed the words, "Call him."

The landlady frowned, hesitated, cocked her head to one side.

Lee repeated the words, mouthing with exaggerated care this time, and the older woman got the message, nodding her head in understanding.

Lee was suddenly uncomfortably aware that the wall she leaned against was nothing more than lath and plaster, covered with a floral pattern wallpaper. If Mikkelitz had the slightest notion they were outside, she thought, and he'd ever seen a movie about cops, he'd know they'd be standing to the side of the door. In that case, he was likely to empty a magazine on either side. In his place, she knew she would. Even the relatively low power .32 caliber slugs from his Walther would rip through the lath and plaster like wet paper. Then she recalled that Mikkelitz's latest victim had been killed with a .38 and her flesh cringed instinctively. She realized that Jesse was waiting on her, frowning slightly, as if wondering what the delay was about. She shook herself, raised the Blackhawk and nodded.

He rapped lightly on the door. There was no need to prompt Mrs. McLaren. She called, after a second or so, "Mr. Murphy? I've got clean sheets and towels for your room. Are you there?"

Silence. No word from the other side of the door. They all exchanged a glance. Lee nodded at the door again and Jesse knocked again, this time a little more firmly. Responding to his cue, the landlady raised her voice a little as well.

"Mr. Murphy? Clean linen. Can I come in please?"

Again, nothing. Lee could feel her heart rate accelerating as the adrenaline began flowing through her body. Her breathing was faster as well, she was aware. Jesse seemed unaffected.

Seemed. He could feel his own pulse rate racing. No matter how many times you did this, he thought, you never got used to it. And Jesse had done it plenty of times in his days with the Denver PD.

Lee was motioning at him now, pointing to the doorknob and making a gesture that indicated she wanted him to try it. He shook his head. If Mikkelitz was in there, he'd be watching for just that movement. A turning knob would give him a signal that whoever was out here was ready to come in. Better to just kick the door in and go in in a rush, fanning out to either side, ready to shoot if necessary. The town could always buy Mrs. McLaren a new door.

Buying a new sheriff and deputy was a slightly more expensive matter.

It was time now to get the landlady back out of harm's way. He touched her shoulder and, when he had her attention, pointed to the end of the corridor, making a shooing motion with his other hand that indicated she was to leave them now. She nodded, understanding and looking a little relieved to be able to get out of the way. He pointed for her to walk close to the walls, where there was less likelihood of loose floorboards squeaking. Again, she nodded, then walked away, moving carefully and quietly until she'd reached the end of the hallway. She glanced back at them, tension plain on her face. Jesse made the same brushing motion again and she reluctantly disappeared around the doorway at the end of the hall.

He hoped she'd have the good sense to get clear of the house but there wasn't time now to go after her and tell her.

He checked Lee to make sure she was ready. He wondered if he should remind her that her gun wasn't cocked, then decided there was no need. One thing Lee knew about was guns. She could cock that big single action and get off a shot in one smooth motion, he knew.

He stepped out into the doorway, bracing his back against the wall opposite. He signed to Lee that he would go in first, and move left. She would follow and go right. That way, Mikkelitz's attention and focus would be split.

At least, that was the theory. There was always the chance that he would simply concentrate on the first person through the door, in which case, Lee would have no trouble nailing him.

Which would be damn little compensation to Jesse.

He took a deep breath, leaned back against the wall behind him, then sprang up and kicked, flat-footed against the door, as close as he could to the lock. There was a splintering crash as the softwood frame gave way and the lock tore loose. The door slammed open and Jesse was already through it, crouching and moving fast to the left, the Colt held in front of him, weaving side to side as he searched for a target. Behind him, a fraction of a second later, he felt rather than heard Lee enter the room and move right.

He didn't look at her. There were still too many hidden places in the room. Places where Mikkelitz might be. Because he sure as hell wasn't in any of the obvious ones. The bed was unmade and empty. The small, tub-shaped armchair beside it was unoccupied.

The curtains were pulled halfway across the window. Plenty of room there for a man to hide, and the bed blocked his view of the bottom of the curtains, where he might—might—have seen Mikkelitz's feet. Lee was in his peripheral vision now, as she moved up level with him. She'd noticed the curtains too and took a pace toward them.

"Wait," he said. His voice seemed higher than usual, he thought. His throat and his lips were unusually dry too. He reached behind him, found a heavy vase on the bureau and tossed it, underhand but hard, into the curtains on the left side of the window. It clunked against the wall behind the fabric. He was satisfied there was nobody there, repeated the action on the other side, this time tossing an alarm clock from the bedside table. The vase, made of thick, heavy cut glass, survived the operation. The alarm clock didn't do so well. The thin glass of its face splintered as it dropped to the floor under the curtains.

"No one home," said Lee. He glanced at her in admiration. Her voice was level, unaffected. His own throat was dry and constricted with tension. He knew if he tried to get more than one word out, he'd choke and stumble. He swallowed several times, then noticed that the bed was an old-fashioned brass type. Its high legs held it well clear of the ground and the covers, unmade, had been pulled back so that they draped on the side of the bed nearest him and Lee.

The concept of a man hiding under the bed might seem like something out of a Charlie Chaplin short. But when the man was a proven killer and armed with at least two handguns, it was hard to laugh at it too much. He gestured to the bed with the muzzle of his automatic. Lee caught on, raised an eyebrow, and swung the Blackhawk to cover the bed. Now, he heard the distinct double snick as she thumbed back the hammer. The sound seemed deafening in the room.

They edged apart, guns and eyes trained on the bed. Aware that they were totally occupied with it, he jerked his gaze away for a quick glance around the room, just to make sure Mikkelitz hadn't suddenly appeared in the window, or that he wasn't emerging from the closet.

Then, without warning, he dropped prone on the floor, right arm thrust out, pointing under the bed, breaking his fall with his left hand.

No one there.

Which left the closet. Lee was nearer to it. He regained his feet, waited a second for his breathing to return to something approaching normal and gestured for her to open the door.

She did so, springing to the side as the door swung open under her grasp. Jesse held the Colt in a two-handed combat grip. He was slightly to the side and had a clear view of the closet interior.

Which held everything you might expect a closet to. But not Anton Mikkelitz.

He let go of the breath he'd been holding. There was nowhere else in the room he might be. There was no connecting bathroom here. The communal bathroom and toilet were at the end of the hallway. As he realized it, he also realized that Mikkelitz might, just might, be in there. It had happened in the past, he knew. More than one criminal had been saved from a surprise raid by a sudden desire to take a piss.

"Looks like he's a flown bird," Lee said evenly.

"Maybe," Jesse replied. "We better check the bathroom first. Outside chance that he might be in there."

He wasn't. Finally satisfied that he was nowhere in the immediate vicinity, Jesse let the hammer down on his Colt, snicked up the safety lock and slid the gun into his waistband.

"What now?" Lee asked him. He shrugged.

"Maybe he's gone skiing," he said. "Maybe he's gone to the store. I guess the only thing we can do is stake the place out and see when he comes back."

She nodded. "I'll get on the radio to Felix," she said. "Get some of his men up here. Then I guess we simply sit around and wait."

He shrugged philosophically. The tension of the last few minutes was slowly abating, the adrenaline surge gradually dissipating through his system.

"That's the way it usually goes," he agreed.

She led the way back through the boardinghouse. By now, the other occupants were more than a little alarmed at the proceedings. They'd heard the crash of the door being kicked in, the thuds of the vase and the clock hitting the walls. They wanted to know what was going on. Mrs. McLaren, with the commercial instincts of a good landlady, wasn't letting on. She had a pretty good inkling of what might happen if other guests found out they had a real honest-to-goodness murderer living under the same roof as they were.

Lee saw the anxious faces and hurried to forestall any questions.

"Just calm down, folks. There's nothing to get excited about," she said, as they surged forward to question her. "The situation's under control and there's no danger to anyone."

There were subdued mutterings as they heard her. Before they could begin to discuss the matter, Lee continued. "However, we are going to have to ask you people to spend a few hours away from this house, I'm afraid."

The muttering suddenly increased in pitch. One of the guests, an older man with a bald head, except for two white tufts of hair over the ears, stepped forward, frowning.

"A few hours? Just what do you mean by that, Sheriff."

Lee smiled at him with what she hoped was a winning smile. It was a dismal failure. The man's frown deepened and he shook his head, turning back to talk to his companions.

"Want us to move out without so much as a by-your-leave. I want reasons before I'm going anywhere. I want to know where I'm going and I want to know for how long."

The other guests, three of them now, Lee noticed, chorused their agreement. Out of deference to Mrs. McLaren, Lee was trying not to alarm the other guests. But now she could see she was going to have to give them some details. Her main consideration now was to avoid being drawn into a long debate over the matter, particularly when Mikkelitz could return at any time. She turned to Jesse and indicated the department car.

"Get on the horn to Felix and let's get a stakeout set up here. I'll soothe the locals while you're doing it."

Jesse nodded agreement. She realized that he'd probably had more experience getting stakeouts organized than she had anyway, so it was the right division of labor. As he turned away to the Oldsmobile, she had a further thought.

"Oh, and Jess—" He stopped, half turned back to her. "Get Tom

Legros to get hold of a minibus or something of the kind. We'd better provide transport for these people."

"You've got it," he said, and walked quickly to the car.

Lee took a deep breath, grateful that things were at least under way. Then, plastering the smile back on her face, she turned to face the knot of stubborn boarding house residents.

"Folks," she said quietly. "It seems like we have a situation on our hands."

FIFTY-SIX

Lee glanced at her watch, yawned, and reached into the greasy brown paper bag of doughnuts that Tom had just delivered.

"How do you contain yourself amongst all this excitement?" she said.

She was sitting in the front bedroom of the Munsings' house on Laurel. The Munsings were a middle-aged couple who ran the hardware store downtown. They were law-abiding, pleasant people. They went to church regularly. They contributed to worthwhile charities and, presumably, were kind to small animals and elderly people.

More importantly, their house was directly opposite the McLaren boardinghouse and Lee had commandeered it as a command post for the stakeout.

She'd positioned a Carver chair from the head of the dining room table close to the window. With the shades almost drawn, she was sitting, keeping watch on the street and the entrance to the boardinghouse. Jesse was across the room, out of the line of sight from the window, in one of those shell-like armchairs that people seem to place in bedrooms. His long legs sprawled out in front of him. The Cubs cap was tilted over his eyes. He didn't move it as he replied.

"Patience is a virtue," he said simply. She gave him a look of utter disdain. The effect was wasted, she realized, as he couldn't see it.

"Still and all, I'd rather be out looking for him, you know?" she said. She shifted her position in the wide, wooden chair. It was comfortable enough, but not so comfortable that she was likely to doze off. She looked at her watch again, realizing that she hadn't registered the time the last time she'd looked.

It was a quarter after ten. They'd been here for over fifty minutes. She had six men from Felix Obermeyer's town police force as backup. Four of them were in two unmarked cars, positioned around the corner at either end of Laurel Street, where they could keep an eye on the approaches to the house without being obvious. They were wearing plain clothes and they'd been told to keep down and out of sight as they waited. The other two were in a house backing onto Mrs. McLaren's. She and Jesse had taken the frontal position. The Munsings were already at work in their store and they'd been asked not to come home during the day but to check in with Tom Legros at the sheriff's office in town if they needed to for any reason.

Lee, Jesse and Felix had debated the need to evacuate the street itself, but decided against it. In a town as small as Steamboat Springs, such activity would almost certainly be noticed. People would start talking and word could reach Mikkelitz. As it was, she'd arranged to keep Mrs. McLaren and her other guests incommunicado for the day. They were sequestered in the Public Safety Building. They had a TV and a supply of movies. They had music. They had an endless supply of coffee. They had their meals supplied from the Steamboat Yacht Club and brought in by Denise.

The one thing they didn't have was the freedom to wander around town, talking about it all.

"Well, you know, Lee," said Jesse slowly, in answer to her last statement, "we could go looking for him. Problem is, we don't have the faintest idea where he might be."

"We're going to look a bunch of damn fools if he's up on the mountain and someone else gets killed today," she said shortly.

Jesse tilted back the cap and sat up a little. He thought about it for a second or two, then shook his head.

"Unlikely," he said finally. "After all, we found the ski patrol uniform in his closet. There's no reason why he should suppose we're on to him, so there's no reason why he wouldn't wear it again if he had another killing planned."

"I know that, Jess," she said, with just a touch of asperity. "I'm just saying I'd rather be out looking than just sitting here waiting."

He shrugged, tipped the cap forward again and settled back in the chair. She looked at him in exasperation. The morning had started relatively well. It had been good to work as a team. There was a lot of mutual trust and respect there, and the adrenaline rush as they'd gone into the boardinghouse had given her a sense of togetherness with him once more.

It had affected him as well, she knew. There had been no room for the cautious, guilty look to his face. There had been no time for her to wonder what was going on between him and Abby, no time for him to stew over it.

Now, there was.

They were sitting cooped up in the Munsings' bedroom, with nothing to do but wait for Mikkelitz to arrive home. Morosely, she realized that he could be out all day. She and Jesse could spend the next eight hours snapping quietly at each other's heels.

The handheld radio on the bedside table beside her crackled to life.

"Someone coming."

It was Felix Obermeyer's voice. The town police chief had decided that this was a big enough case to involve himself personally. He'd taken a position in the car at the eastern end of Laurel, accompanied by one of his officers.

Lee reached for the radio to ask for more detail. As her hand touched it, Felix's voice came again.

"False alarm. It's old Ted Horton from down the street."

Lee settled back in her chair again. Out of the corner of her eye, she saw Jesse's tense body relax.

From under the baseball cap, he spoke. "I'll take over now if you like."

There was an underlying apology in his tone. He was doing his best to set things right between them, she knew. But, perversely, she refused the tentative olive branch. It was all very well for Jesse to make magnanimous gestures, but taking over the watch a mere ten minutes before he was due to wasn't going to make up for what he'd been doing with Abby.

"We'll stick to the schedule," she said shortly and he shrugged to himself.

Which led her to ask, for the hundredth time: What had he been doing with Abby? And what right did she have to resent it?

After all, she and Jesse had slept together once. And that had hardly been his idea. She squirmed mentally with embarrassment as she recalled that night at his cabin, hopping one-legged on his porch while she tried to get rid of her boots, then stripping naked in front of him. No wonder he'd screwed her, she thought. She'd hardly given him any choice in the matter.

But he'd promised nothing. She'd thought she knew his feelings but, obviously, she'd been wrong.

Proximity, she thought. That was all it was. After all, what was a man expected to do with a nude woman in his room, all heated up for him and raring to go?

Shake hands and say, "No thanks"?

She would have killed him if he had.

The more she thought about it, the more she realized it was her own fault. Jesse wanted her as a friend. He always had. When he'd finally opened up to her about the trouble in Denver, she'd put another value on it entirely. She knew she loved him. She'd loved him for years, even though she only realized it these last few days. And because he'd sought her out as a friend, she'd let herself assume that he loved her too.

"Shit," she said to herself quietly, not even realizing that she'd spoken aloud.

"Say what?" said Jesse, sitting up in the ridiculous, feminine little chair. He stretched his arms and legs and yawned.

"Nothing," she said, feeling her face heat up just a little. "I was just thinking out loud."

She picked up the folding pair of Nikon binoculars and made a pretense of studying the front door of the boardinghouse. Behind her, she heard Jesse pacing quietly. She was glad to see that the waiting was getting to him too.

"Think I'll make some coffee," he said finally. "You want some?"

She nodded, glasses still up to her face.

"Might wash the taste of these doughnuts away," she said. She heard Jesse give a short snort of laughter as he rustled around in the bag.

"Kind of explains Tom's waistline, doesn't it?" he said mildly. They'd asked Tom to bring them something to eat, hadn't specified what. In retrospect, Lee realized that they should have expected the tubby deputy to get them a bag of doughnuts.

She grinned to herself, heard the door close behind Jesse as he went to the kitchen in the back of the house. She set down the Nikons, leaned back in the chair, shifting to a more comfortable position.

It was nearly over, she thought. Weeks of hunting, thinking, trying to find some clue to the identity of the murderer, and suddenly, one day, an old landlady walks in to complain about kids on Ski-Doos and says, "What's Mr. Murphy's picture doing on your wall," and it all falls into place.

And now it was all over except for the shouting. Or the shooting, she amended.

But at least that part she felt capable of handling. If it came down to it, she knew she could more than hold her own in an arrest of an armed man. That was her forte. She was a hunter and a tracker. If, at the end of the hunt, there was shooting required, she could accommodate the need.

Jesse, on the other hand, was more of a thinker than she'd ever be. He seemed to be able to get inside the thought processes of a criminal. To understand why he was doing what he did.

Not that Jesse was any slouch when it came to the rough end of police work, she thought. She couldn't imagine anyone she'd rather have backing her up in a firefight. He was a damn good shot. She was better, she knew without any false modesty, and so did he. But he was good.

Ruefully, she thought to herself that they could have made a hell of a great team. Between them, they covered all the skills necessary for law enforcement in a place like Routt County. They could do a great job together.

Could have done a great job together, she corrected. She knew that she couldn't face Jesse on a day-to-day basis anymore. It wasn't enough for her to be a good old friend, someone whose shoulder he could cry on. She wanted more of him.

She wanted all of him. But, deep down, she knew Abby had him.

The doorknob rattled and Jesse re-entered, backing in as he shouldered the door open, carrying two brimming coffee mugs. He set one down beside her and the hot coffee slopped onto the polished wood of the bedside table.

"Careful," she said. He muttered apologetically and she grabbed a handful of tissues from under the table and mopped up.

"May as well take a break now," he suggested. "It's near enough to time."

She checked her watch. It was ten twenty-eight and they'd agreed to change at ten thirty. Close enough, she agreed. She eased out of the wooden chair, moving between him and the bed to get out of his way.

There was a brief moment of body contact, then Jesse had settled himself in the chair. He tweaked the curtains back a touch, then sat back, with a clear view of the boardinghouse's front porch.

Lee took the ridiculous little armchair. She sipped her coffee. That was another thing she knew she'd miss about Jesse. He made good coffee. She made an attempt to normalize the atmosphere in the room. It was strange. For a few minutes, there'd be the old bond between them, the quiet comfort of being in each other's company without the need for words. Then, from one or the other of them, the awkwardness would radiate out like a light, and the tension between them would become almost palpable. It had happened just now as their bodies brushed against each other.

"You do a lot of this sort of thing when you were in Denver?" she asked.

He nodded, hesitated a second, then replied. "Too much. Tony used to say that a cop's life was sixty percent sitting in a car on a cold wet night, sixty percent writing up reports and one percent doing anything interesting."

She studied him carefully. It was the first time she could remember him making any reference to his former partner. Maybe those old ghosts were finally being laid to rest. She smiled tentatively. "That can't be right. It totals one hundred and twenty one percent."

He nodded, grinning in spite of himself. "Yeah, true," he replied. "Better cut the one percent doing anything interesting."

The cell phone on the bed suddenly chirped to life. It was closer to Jesse. He looked at her, a question in his eyes and she nodded for him to answer. He picked it up and activated it.

"This is Jesse," he said. He heard Tom Legros's voice at the other end of the line.

"Jess? Lee told me to let her know if anything was happening around town." The other deputy paused. He seemed to want some reply from Jesse.

"She certainly did, Tom. I heard her. So has something happened?"

Lee sat upright, half out of the armchair, her head tilted in a question. He held up a hand for her to wait.

"Well, I'm sorry to bother you when I know you're busy, but she did say—"

Jesse cut him off impatiently. "Tom, does this have anything to do with Mikkelitz?"

The other deputy sounded apologetic. "Well, no, Jess. That's why, as I say, I'm sorry to bother you with it . . ."

Jesse signaled for Lee to relax, shaking his head in answer to her unspoken question. She settled back in the chair, eyes still on him.

"Never mind that, Tom," Jesse told him. "Just tell me what's happened and I'll pass the details on to Lee, okay?"

"Fine, Jess. I mean, it's nothing important. Nothing I can't handle, but she did say to—"

"Yeah, Tom, I know she did say that." There was a definite edge to Jesse's voice now.

Lee tried to suppress a grin. She knew better than anyone how roundabout Tom Legros could be in his explanations.

Jesse continued. "Just tell me what's happened, okay?"

"Well, it's a mugging, Jess."

Jesse caught Lee's eye and repeated the phrase. "A mugging," he confirmed.

"That's right. Down at the taxi depot—you know the Alpine Taxi depot out on the edge of town? Well, it seems someone coldcocked Alby Maroody when he was starting out for work. The dispatcher found Alby unconscious behind the Dumpster in their parking lot. Someone had really cracked him. Doc says he may have a fractured skull. He doesn't look too good, believe me."

"You're there now, are you, Tom?" Jesse cut in.

"That's right, Jess. I know Lee told me to keep an eye on those folks from the boardinghouse, but I figured this should take priority over them, okay?"

"I'm sure that's right, Tom. Hang on while I fill Lee in on the details."

He set the phone to one side and quickly recapped the situation for Lee. She listened, nodding, as he described the situation, taking a lot less time than Tom had to get to the salient details.

Finally, she asked, "Anything stolen?"

Jesse nodded, recognizing that was the one fact that Tom hadn't passed on so far. At least, that was one fact. Knowing Tom, there could be half a dozen others. The taxi driver could have been mugged by aliens and Tom wouldn't mention it unless specifically asked.

He put the cell phone to his ear again.

"Tom?" he said. "Lee's asking was anything stolen?"

The other deputy hesitated. When he spoke, he sounded uncertain.

"You mean apart from the taxi?" he asked. Jesse held back a grin, covered the mouthpiece with his hand and looked straightfaced at Lee.

"He wants to know, apart from the taxi," he said.

Lee rolled her eyes to heaven. "Jesus," she said. "He's a tiger for mentioning minor detail, isn't he? Yes. Let's see if anything was stolen apart from the taxi, shall we?"

Jesse spoke into the phone again. He had some difficulty keeping the amusement out of his voice. "Tom," he said. "Yeah, aside from the taxi, anything else gone? You know," he added, "the safe from the taxi company, or half a ton of gold bullion, anything like that?"

"Gold bullion, Jess?" Tom was even more confused now. "What are you talking about?"

"Just my little joke, Tom," Jesse said apologetically. "Can you find out if anything else was taken?"

"Well, I guess I'll have to go see Alby again. The ambulance just took him to the hospital. I guess I could go on up there and ask him some more."

"I guess you could, Tom. Why don't you do that, then call us back with the details." He hesitated, then added, hoping that Legros would get the hint. "All of them."

"Sure, Jesse. I'll call you from the hospital. Bye now."

He heard the clunk at the other end as the phone was replaced on the hook. He shook his head wryly at the cell phone in his hand, then flipped it closed.

"Jesus," he murmured.

FIFTY-SEVEN

Jesse never knew what triggered the phone call. Some instinct deep inside—the one that made him a good cop—was at work, sorting facts and information, making possible connections between seemingly unrelated items.

All he knew was that, ten minutes later, he suddenly grabbed the cell phone again and flicked the mouthpiece open. He glanced up at Lee, who was watching him curiously from the armchair by the bed.

"The taxi company," he said. "You know the number?"

Lee thought for a second.

"Zero-zero-eight-eight," she said. He dialed the local prefix, then the number she'd given him, pressed SEND on the cell phone and waited a few seconds.

"Alpine Taxis." It was a bright female voice, one that was vaguely familiar, he thought.

"Hi," he said. "This is Deputy Jesse Parker from the Sheriff's Department." He gave it a second or so for that to sink in. Before he could say anything further, the girl on the other end replied.

"Oh, hey there, Jess. It's Elaine Dixon here."

He knew now why the voice had been familiar. Elaine was an attractive brunette he'd dated once or twice—casually. She'd been keen to make it something less casual but he hadn't been. Still, she was good company: bright, funny and with a great pair of legs.

"Oh, hi, Elaine. Look I wonder could you—"

"So, Jess, you back doing police work, are you? That's real fine, you ask me," she interrupted. Obviously, it was a slow day on the switchboard and Elaine was ready to chat. He cut short any such ideas.

"Uh, yeah, Elaine. Look, honey, this is kind of official, okay?"

He could almost see her sit up straighter in her chair. The change in her tone of voice was obvious. She wasn't looking for casual chat anymore. This could be pay dirt.

"Well, what can I do to help you, Jess?" she said.

"Elaine, you had one of your drivers mugged this morning. An Alby—" he hesitated, searching his memory for the name.

"Maroody," she said quickly.

"That's right!" he replied, remembering the name now. "Funny sort of a name," he mused.

"He's part Arab," Elaine offered. Like a good Coloradan, she pronounced it "Ay-rab."

"Uh-huh, that would explain it then. So Elaine, can you tell me, was he booked on any sort of a pickup?"

"Just a moment, Jess," she said. He heard a quick rattle of computer keys. Alpine Taxis obviously were right up to the moment with their radio call records. There was a slight pause, then he heard a clatter as she picked up the receiver again.

"Jess, you there?" she said. He grunted a reply and she went on. "Matter of fact, Alby did have a call to make. Mountain View Hotel."

Jesse felt his skin tingle. "You got a name for the passenger?" he asked slowly.

"Nope. We don't keep that on the computer, Jess. Hotel desk usually just rings us and books. Most times, there can be three or four people traveling."

"You got a number of passengers for this one?" he asked, but again she replied with a negative.

"No luck there either, Jess. Would have had it at the time, but we don't keep it as a back record. Odds are the trip was to the airport, this time of morning. Be in time for the flight to Denver."

"Right. Right." His mind was racing now. He could see that Lee, sensing something was amiss, had sat up straight in the armchair, her eyes locked on him. He felt like every hair on his head was standing on end.

"Now, one thing more, Elaine," he said deliberately. "Has the Mountain View complained because this Mahoody guy—"

"Maroody," she corrected him. He shook his head impatiently.

"Maroody. Whatever. You had any complaints coming through about him not turning up?"

"Hang on a minute, Jess. I've only just come onto the switch. Jenny's the usual girl and she's on a break. I'll see if she's written up a complaints form."

There was a dull clunk as she set the receiver down once more. He could hear her sorting through papers and her strangely detached voice as she asked someone else in the office if they had seen the complaints file for that morning. Jesse drummed his fingers impatiently on the phone as he waited.

Lee had stood now and moved over beside him, her head tilted to one side, questioning. Finally, Elaine rattled the receiver against her desk once more and said, "Jess? Doesn't seem to have been any complaint. Mind you, often if a taxi's late, the hotel will lay on a car for their guests anyway. Maybe they did that today as well."

"Yeah. Maybe," he said, not convinced. "Okay. Thanks for the help, Elaine."

Before he could break the connection, she hurried to ask a question, her curiosity piqued by their conversation. "Jess? Something going on here to do with Alby, you think?"

For a moment he was tempted to try the "just routine" line, then knew it would never wash with a girl like Elaine.

"Not sure, Elaine. Can't say anything at the moment. Just asking the question, all right?" Then, before she could speak again, he hurried on. "Thanks for your help. You take care now."

And broke the connection.

He sat back, let go a long breath. Lee was watching him intently, he knew, but he wasn't ready yet to put his suspicion into words. There was a vague superstition deep inside him that if he said it, it would become true. He flicked open the phone again and dialed the operator.

"Give me the number for the Mountain View Hotel please," he said briskly as the girl answered. There was a notepad on the bed. He reached for it. Lee saw what he was after, got to it first and passed it to him. He nodded his thanks, then wrote the number down as the operator gave it to him. Hurriedly, he hung up, dialed the number of the hotel and waited.

The phone burred four times before anyone answered it.

"Mountain View Hotel. This is Dave speaking."

Dave sounded about twenty-five.

"Uh yeah, this is Deputy Parker from the sheriff's department here. Wanted some information on a call to Alpine Taxis this morning."

"I see," Dave sounded a little cautious now. "And how exactly can I help you, Deputy?"

"You had a call in to Alpine Taxis this morning—for a ten forty-five pickup? I was wondering if you could tell me the name of the party you called that taxi for. And the destination?" he added as an afterthought.

"Well, you know, Deputy, it's not our standard policy to release guest details over the phone to just anyone, and I'm not sure—"

"Dave," said Jesse, cutting him off before he could find out what it was that he wasn't sure about, "that's real discreet of you and I'll be sure to mention it to the hotel chain. But this has to do with a murder investigation so I think you had just better find yourself a new policy."

"Well, that's all very well." Dave was decidedly unhappy about all of this now. He didn't want to get involved, Jesse knew.

"But," he continued, "I don't know that you really are a deputy, do I? You could be anyone."

Jesse closed his eyes briefly, holding his temper in check.

"Jesus," he muttered to himself. Then, into the phone, he said, "Dave, is your head porter on duty at the moment? Morg Buchanan?"

"Um . . . yes. He's just at the front door now," the clerk answered.

"Good. Just call him to the phone, will you?"

"Well . . . but why?" said the clerk, puzzled now as well as unhappy.

"Just do it," Jesse said, with an edge creeping into his voice. Dave heard it, recognized it and decided to obey it. Jesse heard him, muffled as he covered the receiver and called to Morg Buchanan.

Morgan Buchanan was an old friend of Jesse's. At one stage, he'd even worked cattle on his dad's ranch. That was when Jesse's dad could afford to pay a few salaries. Since that time, Morg had been at the Mountain View, working his way up to head porter. Jesse instantly recognized the bluff, friendly voice as Morg took the phone.

"Hullo? This is Buchanan. Can I help you?"

"Morg, this is Jesse Parker. You recognize my voice?"

"Well, hell, yes I do, Jesse. How're things with you? I see you're back with the sheriff's department these days?"

"That's right, Morg. Look, I just need you to tell Dave on the desk that I really am who I say I am. I need some information about—" He paused, realized that Morgan would probably be a better source for the information anyway. "No, forget that, Morg. Tell me, you have any guests miss a taxi for the midday Denver flight today?"

There was a slight pause. Then, "No. Nobody missed anything. Matter of fact Jess, Abby was here. She checked out this morning. Not ten minutes gone."

"But her cab didn't turn up, right?" said Jesse, hoping Morgan was going to answer in the affirmative. He felt an icy hand grip his stomach as the porter continued.

"No. Her cab was here all right, Jess. He was running a few minutes late, but he got here all right."

"Jesus," muttered Jesse quietly. "Um, Morg, was there anyone else traveling with her? Any other guests going to the airport?"

"No, Jess. Just Abby. I was going to say hi, but then I thought hell, she probably wouldn't remember me, you know? After all, she only saw me out at your father's spread one or two times."

Jesse stopped him. "Morg. The driver. Did you know him?"

"The cabdriver you mean? No, can't say I did, Jess. But you know how it is around here, new people come and go all the time."

"Okay, thanks, Morg. I'll . . . um talk to you later, okay?"

Jesse closed the phone, cutting off the last few cheerful words from the burly hotel porter. He sat, shoulder slumped and head down. Lee dropped to one knee in front of him.

"Jess?" she said anxiously. "What is it?"

He looked up slowly and she saw the despair in his eyes as he faced the fact that they'd been wasting their time waiting here for the past hour.

"Oh, Christ," he said softly. "He's got Abby. The bastard has got Abby."

FIFTY-EIGHT

The taxi was ten minutes late. As a result, Abby was waiting in the lobby when it arrived. She glanced up from the copy of the *Steamboat Whistle* that she was leafing through—not really reading, and barely taking notice of what was on the pages—as the eight-seater van pulled into the semicircular driveway outside the hotel doors.

Her experience as a reporter meant she was used to traveling light. She had her attaché case slung over one shoulder, and a single hard-shell American Tourister. She stood quickly, not waiting for the driver to come into the lobby to ask for her, grabbed the drag handle on the suitcase, and hurried out through the revolving doors.

As always, the cold hit her as she exited. The morning had started out clear. Now there were clouds blowing in from the northwest and the temperature was down around zero. She huddled a little deeper into her collar.

"Ms. Parker-Taft?" the driver said, grinning easily at her.

She nodded, not returning the smile. The taxi was running late and she had a plane to catch. She knew there was still plenty of time to make it to the airport but she didn't want to take any chance of missing the flight. She'd been in Steamboat long enough.

Idly, she noticed that the driver looked vaguely familiar as he took the suitcase from her. The passenger side door of the van was already open. She climbed in, glanced back at the lobby to make sure there was no one else traveling, and slid the door shut, settling into a seat behind the driver's.

The van rocked slightly on its suspension as he went a few rungs up the steel ladder that was welded in back and hefted her case up into the shallow cage roof rack. She heard his boots crunch on the gravel of the drive as he dropped back to the ground. Then he climbed in and slammed the door behind him.

The engine was still running. He slid the shift into drive and pulled away from the hotel. Involuntarily, Abby glanced at her watch. She wondered what Jesse was doing.

"Heading for the airport, right?" the driver tossed back over his shoulder. She'd made her point by not returning his smile earlier, she decided. She thawed a little.

"That's right," she said. "Midday flight to Denver."

The radio crackled briefly and he reached forward quickly to turn it off. She was glad he had. It was a good forty-minute drive to the airport and she could do without the constant one-way chatter of the dispatcher talking to other cars whose replies she couldn't hear. They hit the main road and he turned left, not right. He was heading away from the airport, toward Mount Werner.

Abby pursed her lips with annoyance. Obviously, the driver had another pickup to make. Leastways, she hoped there was only one more. She always preferred to be the last person to join a cab like this. It seemed like an inescapable law of nature that other people were never ready when a cab arrived for them—even one running ten to fifteen minutes late, like this one.

"Someone else traveling?" she asked. The driver nodded, glancing up at the rearview mirror to make eye contact.

"Couple up on Ski Trail Lane as well," he said easily. She saw his eyes on her in the mirror once more. "Plenty of time," he added. She glanced at her watch again.

"Not all that much," she muttered. The puddle jumpers that flew to Denver from Steamboat had to be hand-loaded. There was no sophisticated luggage handling gear, like on the larger aircraft that flew back to the East or West Coast. Consequently, they needed people to check in early. And they tended to close the flights early as well.

"We'll make it fine," the driver replied, with the confident air of someone who didn't have to get on a flight.

Shit, Abby thought to herself, and glanced morosely out the window. There was nothing she could do about it, in any case. Deep down, she realized that she would actually be on time for the flight. But she'd always been a person who liked to be early, who hated last-minute rushes, particularly in the disorganized chaos of a small-town airline feeding a popular ski resort in the middle of the season.

The wind had freshened, she could see. People on the street were leaning into it as they walked. They had that head-down look of people who were anxious to get back to the warmth and shelter of their cars or their houses. She craned to see up. Clouds were scudding fast and low across the sky. The last traces of blue were rapidly disappearing. Typical mountain weather, she thought. Bright and sunny one moment, overcast and blowing the next.

"More snow coming by the look of it," said the driver.

She said nothing, wondered why taxi drivers inevitably seemed to be possessed of the ability to state the goddamn obvious.

Jesse punched Felix Obermeyer's number into the cell phone. He drummed his fingers impatiently, waiting for the police chief to pick up. He glanced up at Lee.

"I should have realized it," he told her. "He was in the gondola with us the other night, listening to every word we said."

"That could have been coincidence."

"Maybe, but—"

The phone answered at the other end and he held up a hand in apology to her. "Felix? Jesse here. This is a bust. Can you guys get up to the Munsing house right away?"

She heard the brief crackle of Felix's voice in the earpiece, as the town police chief obviously asked a question. Jesse hesitated for a moment, then made a decision.

"No," he said. "Leave the other guys in place for the moment. Just you and Frank." Another question from Felix and she saw Jesse's shoulders drop slightly in defeat.

He flicked the phone shut and turned back to her. For the moment, he'd forgotten her last comment. She began to restate it.

"Just because he was in the gondola doesn't—" she began. But now he remembered what he'd been about to say. He stopped her again with a quick hand gesture.

"He was stalking her," he said. "He didn't get in with us. He was already in there with Abby when I boarded. We'd sort of . . . had an argument and she walked out," he added. There was an awkwardness in his voice as he mentioned the evening with Abby. Lee suddenly knew, without knowing how, that they'd been talking about her. She felt her face starting to heat up, realized how damn ridiculous that was in a grown woman. For a moment, there was a tangible shroud of embarrassment hanging between them. Then Jesse went on.

"I had to stop the gondola to catch up," he explained. "She was already in there. So was he."

"They let two people travel together?" Lee asked. "I thought we—"

"The ski patrol uniform," he explained. "That's why he stole it. Remember what we said? Nobody notices a ski patroller. They just automatically jump lift lines whenever they want. And everyone trusts them."

"So you think he'd targeted Abby as his next victim?"

He shrugged. "Maybe not specifically." He frowned, trying to re-member. Something was coming back to him as he tried to recon-struct the scene at Hazie's the night before. Then he had it.

"He was in the bar," he said slowly. "He was in the bar when we arrived. He must have been waiting for someone—anyone, maybe—to board the gondola alone."

"And Abby was his first chance?" Lee asked. Again, he nodded, reconstructing the probable chain of events in his mind.

"She left . . . must have gone straight past him in the bar, and he simply followed her out. Then all he had to do was hang back till she was about to board the gondola. The lift guys would have let him through, no problem."

"Particularly if he only made it at the last minute and they didn't have time to think it through," Lee put in.

"And then I spoiled things for him," he went on. "I came running out to catch up with her . . . I had to hit the emergency stop."

In spite of the bigger picture, Lee couldn't help herself feeling a small shaft of pain as he mentioned the fact that he'd come running out after Abby. Angrily, she pushed the thought aside. Jesse's eyes were far away now as he remembered the scene in the cabin.

"Jesus!" he said abruptly. "No wonder he kept staring at me!" He looked up at her and explained, "I kept turning around to see him looking at me—you know?" Another thought filtered back. "And he kept fiddling with the zipper on his parka. Damn me. Probably had a gun in there and couldn't quite make up his mind if he had time to use it or not."

He broke off as a car pulled up to the front of the house. They both looked out the window and recognized Felix Obermeyer's Trans Am. The police chief was on his second divorce and, as a direct result, his first sports car.

Jesse led the way out of the bedroom to the front door. Felix and one of his senior officers, Frank Latimer, came into the Munsings' small parlor, where Jesse quickly filled them in on what he and Lee had been discussing.

"So, Jess, what makes you think he's abducted Abby?" Felix asked. "It's a pretty long bow to draw, isn't it—just because somebody's hijacked a taxi?"

Jesse shook his head impatiently.

"Don't you see?" he said. "He sat there listening while Abby told me she was leaving this morning, going back to Denver. Jesus, she even told me she had a taxi booked and she was going on the midday flight!"

The others fell silent. They all shared the growing conviction that Jesse was right about this, and none of them liked the feeling. His next comment finalized things.

"And the key point is, a taxi did arrive to pick her up this morning, although Alpine Taxis didn't send a replacement."

"Jesus," said Lee quietly. "I think you're right, Jess."

He looked at her, then at the other two.

"I know I am," he said.

There was a moment's silence, then Felix gathered himself. "So, what do we do now?" he asked.

Lee was already hitting the numbers on the cell phone.

"Four ways he can go," she said briefly. "Highway 40 to Kremmling, 131 to Stagecoach and Vail, 129 to Hahn's Peak or US 40 west to the airport. Let's get roadblocks on all those routes." She looked up at Jesse. "Try calling her. She's got a cell phone, surely."

Jesse nodded. Abby had given him the number on the first night she'd arrived in town. He'd written it in his notebook. He picked up the landline phone on the parlor side table and punched in the numbers. He heard a singsong electronic tone followed by a female voice and hung up.

"Out of reach or switched off," he said angrily. Felix nodded.

"Lot of dead spots around here. The mountains tend to block the signal."

Lee had reached Denise and was instructing her to put out requests to the state police and highway patrol for the roadblocks. Jesse left her to it and led the other two men to one side a little.

"Roadblocks shouldn't have too much trouble spotting a taxi," Frank Latimer said.

"That's assuming he's left town," Jesse replied, and Latimer looked at him curiously.

"You think it'd make any sense for him to stick around here, Jess?"

"Frank," Jesse replied, "nothing this guy does has made any sense. We're dealing with a killer here. Look at last night. He was obviously planning to kill Abby in the gondola and just get out at the other end and walk away. He didn't have any abseiling gear on him—and I assume that's how he got out of the damn thing the previous time."

"Maybe," Felix said thoughtfully, "he realized he didn't need to abseil out. After all, just walking away from it all worked pretty well for him on the chairlift, didn't it?"

Jesse nodded his agreement. But there was something else in his mind. A feeling he couldn't explain that convinced him that Mikkelitz hadn't left the Steamboat Springs area.

"There's something else, Felix," he said. "This guy knows Abby was with me. And I guess he knows I've been running this case. I think this has gotten personal. I think he's doing this to mess with my head."

FIFTY-NINE

The taxi had wound its way up the steep hill beside the ski slope, past the condominiums and private homes that had been built to offer the coveted "ski-in, ski-out" facility to prospective renters.

Abby tried to contain her impatience. She had the feeling that the driver had slowed to a crawl, just to piss her off. With a great effort, she restrained herself from checking her watch again. She could sense his eyes on her in the rearview mirror.

At last, the van pulled into the driveway of one of the larger condo blocks, nearly at the top of the hill. There was a wide, aspen-lined snow trail leading from the back of the building to the ski slopes. That, she recognized, was the "ski-out" facility. Another narrower trail wound down from a point farther up the mountain. That was where residents could ski back in the evening.

The driver reversed the van into a parking spot in the building's forecourt. He cut the engine and leaned around to talk to her.

"Just be a minute, Ms. Parker-Taft," he said cheerfully. "I'll help the people here with their luggage, then we'll be going."

He opened his door and stepped out, hurrying toward the entrance to the condo block. Abby shook her head in annoyance, then huddled a little deeper into the fur collar of her parka. The sun had disappeared behind low, driving clouds now and the temperature had dropped accordingly. She let go a deep breath, trying to hold her impatience in check. Abby was always impatient. Once she made up her mind to go somewhere, she simply hated to be delayed. For the fifth time, she checked her wristwatch, frowned a little.

They still had time to make the flight, she reasoned. But it was going to be close. Particularly if there were two or three flights going out around the same time—as there usually were.

She was roused from her thoughts by a tap on the window glass next to her head. Looking up, startled, she saw the grinning face of the driver, only a few feet away. He made a motion for her to unlock the sliding door, and she reached forward and pulled up the lock button.

He nodded his thanks, heaved the door back on its track and gestured with one thumb toward the building.

"Ms. Parker-Taft," he said, and she thought how his constant use of both surnames was starting to get under her skin. Although Abby was usually identified visually as Abby Parker-Taft when she did a report, most of the time she simply signed off as "Abby Taft." Most people who watched her knew that. She sensed that the driver knew it too, somehow, and was only using the full name to annoy her. She didn't know how she sensed that. There was just something in his manner.

"What is it?" she said, doing her damnedest not to show that she was annoyed. He grinned at her again.

"There's a phone call for you inside," he said, and this time, she frowned in surprise.

"For me? You're sure?" she said, and he nodded, shrugging.

"That's what they said. They phoned the Barretts—they're the people I'm here to pick up. Must have got the number from the dispatcher at the taxi company," he added, by way of explanation.

Abby still couldn't understand it. "Why would they call me here?" she asked. "Why didn't they call my cell phone?" Like all reporters, she was never without one.

Again, the taxi driver shrugged. "This whole side of the mountain is a dead spot," he said. "They'd know that at the office."

She rummaged in her shoulder bag for the cell. When she found it, she saw he was right. The power was switched on but there was no corresponding row of bars showing network coverage.

"They sounded like it was urgent, you know?" the driver prompted, gesturing toward the building. Abby sighed with annoyance. Another damn delay was all she needed this morning, she thought. Abruptly, she swung down from the van and hurried across the parking lot to the building.

It was dim inside and her eyes took a few seconds to adjust. Even though the day was overcast now, they were close to the ski mountain and the snow-covered terrain seemed to create its own light source. She knew that wasn't possible. Knew the snow simply reflected whatever ambient light was there. But somehow, it seemed like there was an inner light on the mountain.

The driver gestured her toward a flight of wooden stairs leading down.

"This way, Ms. Parker-Taft," he said, standing aside to let her go first. She hesitated. She'd been expecting to go up to one of the condos.

"Down here?" she queried, and he nodded confirmation.

"They've got a basement apartment," he offered by way of explanation. Impatiently, Abby shrugged and started down the stairs. There was a heavy wooden door at the bottom of the flight. She pushed against it, felt it give and went in.

She found herself in a ski room. Racks of skis stood around the walls. To one side there was a workbench with an old electric iron standing on its end. The smell of wax was strong in the room. At the far end, she could see ski boots resting on long pegs set into the wall.

Wherever they were, it wasn't an apartment, she thought angrily. She started to turn to let the driver know, when she felt an arm go around her throat from behind, and the hard pressure of something cold pressing into the skin of her neck, just below the base of her skull.

She opened her mouth to scream and felt the arm tighten painfully on her throat. There was no need. The scream never came. It froze in the back of her throat, stillborn. Abby knew she was in trouble—and in a big way.

"That's a gun you can feel," the driver said softly, right next to her ear. "You scream or try to fight me and I'll blow your fucking head off, okay?"

She said nothing. Her voice seemed to be paralyzed. He shook her roughly, then jabbed the gun harder into her neck.

"I said, okay?" he repeated, and she finally found her voice. Only a whisper, but enough to say, "Okay."

The pressure around her throat relaxed a little and he shoved her across the room to a door set in one of the side walls. They paused before it.

"Open it," he said, jabbing again with the gun. She reached down, turned the knob and pulled the door open. He shoved her through.

They were in a garage. That much she could see, even though there was very little light. The shapes of cars were unmistakable.

Close to them was another shape—a snowmobile. A two-seater, she saw now. He shoved her toward it, one arm around her throat and the gun still forced into her neck. She wished to God he'd move that gun. She knew enough about guns to know that they have an unfortunate tendency to go off by accident, and stumbling and shoving someone else in front of you seemed like one hell of a way to have yourself an accident, she thought.

She gasped in relief as the arm released its grip on her throat. Before she could turn—even if she'd had a mind to—her left hand was seized in a hard grip. The gun left her neck and she heard a click of metal. The something cold was on her left wrist and there was the rapid clicking of a ratchet and she realized he'd snapped a handcuff onto her wrist. And snapped it tight. The skin was pinched and painful underneath it. She cried out in pain.

"Shut up," he said roughly, and dragged her forward and down by the handcuff. There was a metal handhold in front of the pillion seat on the snowmobile—a half circle of leather-covered chrome steel. He whipped the other handcuff around it and fastened her securely to the little vehicle.

He took a few quick steps to the wall and hit a switch. Cold fluorescent light flooded the parking bays around them. She could see him clearly now and she realized why she'd thought he was familiar. He was the ski patroller who'd traveled down with her and Jesse the night before.

And suddenly, she knew he wasn't a ski patroller. She knew who he was and she knew what he wanted. The realization hit her like a physical blow. It turned her knees weak and for one awful moment she thought her bladder was going to let go.

"Now, here's the deal," he said softly, putting his face barely a foot from hers. "We're going out of here on this snowmobile. You'll be handcuffed to that handle there so there's no way you can get away. Got it?"

He paused, looked at her angrily for some sign that she understood. She nodded dumbly. That seemed to satisfy him.

"Okay. Fine. Now, you try to call out to someone, you try to tell anyone what's going on, and you are dead one second later. You with me still?"

He held up the gun—a flat-sided automatic, she could see now. It wasn't as big as the one she'd seen Jesse carry but it still looked as if it could do the job required of it. She nodded again. He nodded in reply, apparently satisfied again that she understood the situation.

"And you make no mistake, Abby," he said, injecting her first name with unmistakable venom. "I will use this gun." He paused, looked deep into her eyes. "You know who I am, don't you?"

She met the look, determined not to flinch away from it. Then she saw the depths of anger and madness that lay behind those eyes and she had to drop her own gaze.

"Yes." Her voice was a barely audible whisper. "I know who you are."

He smiled at that, pleased with the power that had dropped her eyes from his. He would make her pay. This was the woman who had tried to tell the world that the Routt County Sheriff's Department and that dumb fuck of a deputy were doing such a bang-up job hunting him down.

"Yes," he agreed with her, whispering as well. "You know who I am."

There was a long-line parka draped over the handlebars of the snowmobile and he was shrugging himself into it now, fastening the zipper clasps at the bottom and pulling the zipper up.

"Where—" she began, but her voice betrayed her and the word was a cracked little sound. She swallowed and tried again. "Where are you taking me?"

"Up the mountain a ways," he said, leaning down to find the fuel tap on the two-stroke engine. He turned it to open and thumbed the tap once or twice to prime the carburetor.

"I left some things up there the other day. We'll go up and get them, you and me," he said, and smiled easily at her.

And right then, when he smiled, so friendly and unthreatening, was the moment Abby knew she was going to die.

SIXTY

The roadblocks were in place. One by one, the confirmations came in over the radio to the sheriff's office in the Public Safety Building. As the last exit from Yampa Valley was sealed off, Lee gave a small grunt of satisfaction.

"State Police are in position on 129 to Hahn's Peak," she said, setting the phone back in its cradle. Felix, standing by the large-scale wall map of the area, marked a final X on the acetate sheet that covered it.

"That should just about seal it off," he said, looking critically at the circle they'd drawn around Steamboat Springs. "He wouldn't have got halfway that distance by now, less that old Dodge Ram has sprouted wings."

"Unless he's switched cars," Jesse put in, eyes fixed on the map, and the network of smaller roads they'd have no chance of covering. "Or unless he's just holed up somewhere inside the circle here."

"Best we can do, Jess," Lee said simply, and he nodded, acknowledging the fact.

"I know it, Lee. It's just that knowing it and feeling happy about it are two different things. I don't believe our boy has ever planned to try to get out of the area."

Obermeyer shrugged. "You saying you want us to call in those roadblocks, Jess?" he asked. Jesse glanced at him sharply. Felix could be one damn sarcastic sonofabitch when the mood took him. He could also be supremely obtuse at times and Jesse wasn't sure which quality had prompted the remark.

"No. I'm not saying that, Felix. We've sure as hell got to go through the motions, just in case. But I reckon we're going to find Mr. Mikkelitz somewhere close to Steamboat Springs." He walked over to the map, stood in front of it, rocking slowly backward and forward on his heels.

"That's where all his activity's been concentrated so far," he said, almost to himself. "That's where he'll keep it going."

Lee joined him, looking at the map as if it could tell them

something—almost as if she expected the scene of the next crime to light up somehow of its own accord.

"You don't think he'll make a run for it, Jess?" she asked. The deputy rubbed one hand across his jaw before he answered.

"He'll make a run all right. But not the way we're expecting."

"I guess he could even have a light plane stashed out to Hayden somewhere," Felix offered. "We're covering the commercial flights but he could fly private."

Lee shook her head. "Thought of that," she said. "The tower isn't giving any clearance to private flights out unless one of your guys out there gets to eyeball the pilot and any passengers."

"You think he'll try to take Abby with him then?" Felix asked. He was way out of his league with this one. The town police usually dealt with traffic offenses, drunken tourists and domestic arguments in town limits. He asked the question of Lee, but it was Jesse, still standing, apparently engrossed in the map, who answered.

"No. He'll kill her first. Then he'll get out," he said simply. The other two cops looked at him. Both felt the same sense of horror at the matter-of-fact way he stated it. He met their gazes, looking away from the map for the first time in some minutes, and shrugged apologetically.

"Only makes sense," he said. "He's been building up to something bigger every time; first it was a body in the trash; then one in the gondola; then he killed in broad daylight on the Storm Peak Express. And then tried it again when he knew we were waiting for him and watching the chairs. He's been thumbing his nose at me"—he stopped, and amended the words, although it was obvious he still meant them in their original form—"at us, I mean, for weeks now. Then the other night he tried for Abby. I guess he knew that she and I were . . . connected."

Lee cut in then. "He's not a local, Jess. And he could have been following her before he saw you."

"Maybe," he admitted. "But there's maybe a dozen people in town could have told him. Or maybe he just saw us in Hazie's and decided then and there to go after her. Anyway, the point is, he knows now."

"That's true enough," Lee admitted.

"I said before, he's messing with my mind." He shook his head angrily. "Damn it. I should have known better than to let Abby plaster my face all over the TV. And she should have known better than to do a whitewash on us," he added.

Lee cocked her head at him curiously. "You'd rather she'd done the hatchet job we were all expecting?" she said, and Jesse spread his hands in a gesture that just reeked of futility.

"She might have been better off if she had," he explained. "Don't you see, Lee? These killings, they're a gigantic ego trip for this guy. He's flaunting them in our faces, saying, 'Come and get me if you can.' hen Abby made out that we had the whole thing pretty well under control and everyone had confidence in us, he simply had to do something about it."

He paused while Lee and the town police chief digested what he'd said. Then he added quietly, and with a chilling note of certainty, "That's why he's taken Abby. She did the report, so she's going to pay for it. And she's connected to me, so I'm paying for it too."

Nobody said anything. Jesse went back to staring at the map while Lee and Felix exchanged glances. They both believed him. Both knew he was right.

"Well," Lee said at length, "I guess we could start out by trying to find that taxi."

Felix's entire force was already deployed on that task. In addition, of course, the state police and highway patrol had blocked all major roads surrounding Routt County.

"Odds are he'll have gotten rid of it by now," Jesse told her. "It's too damn easy to spot and he'll know that."

"Maybe. But it'll give us some idea what direction he's taking," she replied evenly. Jesse was like a wound spring, she knew, and with every passing minute, that spring was winding tighter and tighter.

"I know where he is," he said abruptly. "He's on the mountain."

As he said it, he turned and headed for the door. Lee moved slightly to block him.

"Jess? What are you talking about?"

"Stands to reason, Lee. Everything he's done has been centered on the mountain. Even killing poor Jerry Marrowes."

"That happened in town," Felix put in, not understanding. Lee had seen the connection already and she answered him.

"Maybe. But the only reason he killed him was to get the ski patrol uniform. And that took him back to the mountain."

Jesse nodded impatiently. "Exactly. And that's where he's headed now. Bet on it, Lee."

He started forward again and she put one hand on his shoulder, gently restraining him. "Just a minute, Jess, think this through. There's no reason why he should take Abby there now. In fact, if he's smart, it'll be the last place he'll go."

"Oh he's smart, Lee. But he's working off his own twisted sort of logic. If this revenge theory is right—and it sure looks that way now—then the thing he hates most is the mountain. It's the center of the town. The whole reason for being.

"So his final act is going to be there as well. It just doesn't make any sense if it isn't."

"You're guessing, Jess. You're only guessing," she told him, and he met her gaze frankly and agreed.

"That's right. And that's what ninety percent of police work comes down to. I'm heading up there now, Lee. He's somewhere on that mountain and I'm going to find him."

She stood aside then to let him go. Then she asked the question none of them really wanted to face.

"And Abby?" she said quietly.

He hesitated. He knew the odds against Abby's survival grew steeper with every minute that passed. But he had to stay positive.

"With any luck, I'll find her too."

Lee nodded, then held up a hand for him to wait. She went to the drawer of her desk and took out a handheld comm unit, tossing it to him. He caught it deftly.

"We'll stay here and monitor things," she said. "You keep in touch with that. If you find him, call in and I'll haul ass up there after you."

He looked down at the compact little radio, then up to her steady gray eyes. He nodded once, acknowledging her promise of support.

"I appreciate it," he said. Then, pulling on his battered leather jacket, he half ran down the hallway to the stairs.

In the parking lot, he hesitated. His Subaru was wedged in its usual spot. But the worn out little engine and the suspect clutch didn't fit with his mood of urgency somehow. Closer to hand was a Harley belonging to the town police. He walked quickly to it, noting that the keys were in the ignition. He gave a grim little smile. Cops were notoriously the worst people in the world when it came to vehicle security. He threw a leg over the big bike, turned the ignition on and thumbed the starter. There was brief electric whine, then the 1.2-liter engine caught and thumped to life, setting the whole bike vibrating gently beneath him. He racked the twist throttle once or twice to give it a perfunctory warm-up, slotted her into gear and dropped the clutch.

The Harley's engine note rose in a deep-throated surge and he peeled out of the parking lot, heading for the mountain.

SIXTY-ONE

The garage door was on a counterweight. Abby watched from her position beside the snowmobile as Mikkelitz heaved the big double door up, getting it moving so the counterweight could take over the effort. Daylight streamed in, drowning the cold glare of the fluorescent lights in the garage.

He went a few steps outside, checking left and right to see if there was anyone watching. Apparently satisfied, he walked quickly back in, moving to the snowmobile.

"Get on," he ordered briefly.

She hesitated. All her instincts were telling her that if she went with him, she was going to die. She couldn't see any way out of the predicament. All she could do was delay things as much as possible. He looked closely at her, reading the beginnings of rebellion in her eyes.

"Get on," he repeated, calmly. Still she hesitated, unwilling to make the first move toward obeying him. Her eyes dropped from his and she never saw the blow coming.

He hit her with a closed fist, flush under the cheekbone on the left side of her face. And he hit her hard.

She screamed briefly with the shock and the instant flash of pain from her face, staggered with the force of the blow and fell across the snowmobile.

Now she looked up at him. There was no emotion in his eyes. He watched her impassively. It was that, coupled with the unnecessary force of the blow, and the fact that he'd hit her as he would have hit a man, with a closed fist, that finally cowed her.

Her eyes streamed with tears—brought on by fear as much as the pain. She raised her free hand to the spot where he'd hit her, felt the soft skin of her face swelling immediately into a bruise.

He took a deep breath, an expression of rapidly dwindling patience, and jerked his head toward the snowmobile again.

Her nose had started to drip and she wiped it with the back of her hand. He made a little movement toward her and she cried out in fear, shrinking back from him.

"Scream all you like," he said. "There's no one to hear you. The place is deserted. Seems everyone left town on account of this Mountain Murderer."

She moved to the snowmobile and threw her leg over the saddle. He nodded approval.

"Relax," he told her. "I'm not going to hurt you unless you disobey me. Or try to hold things up like you were just doing."

He seized the tab of her parka zipper and tugged it up, closing the parka. "Cold out there on the mountain," he said.

He bent down, jerked on the starter cord for the snowmobile and the big two-stroke racketed into noisy life. Donning a pair of Ray-Bans with leather windshields clipped to the sides, he swung aboard the little vehicle and clunked it into gear.

The hard rubber track made an ugly tearing sound on the concrete floor of the garage, and the front skids squealed on the hard surface as they slithered out of the garage. Then they were across the tarmac parking area and into the snow that the little bike was designed for and the noise fell away.

He gunned the snowmobile up the narrow trail that Abby had noticed before. Crouched behind his broad back, crying silently to herself, she tried to take note of their surroundings, hoping that maybe someone would notice them, someone would see her plight and somehow tell Jesse.

She tried to think of Jesse now—tall, quietly spoken and capable. She realized suddenly that it had only been his presence in the gondola that had saved her the previous night. Her skin crawled with the thought of what could have happened. Then, with a rush of terror, she realized that it was probably going to happen anyway, and soon.

The snowmobile lurched as it hit a small ridge in the trail, canted downhill and, for a sickening moment, she thought it was going to roll and go sliding down into the trees. Her heart lurched, then settled again as he powered up and steered up into the slope. The cat track beneath her gripped the soft snow, compacted it underneath the hard rubber tread and gained good traction. They fishtailed slightly and he steered out of it.

The trail wasn't so steep here and he opened the throttle. The bare aspen trunks flashed by on either side and she was deafened by the sound of the two-stroke's engine, slightly sickened by the oily smell of the exhaust. They slid and slithered in the soft snow, bouncing from one irregularity to the next. He was obviously a good rider, but she could sense that he was riding on the edge of control—testing himself, almost daring the mountain to beat him.

From time to time, she thought she heard him say something as the bike lurched and skidded. She couldn't make out the words, finally realized that there were no words—just grunts of triumph as he took on the mountain and won.

Finally, they flashed out of the dim cover of the trees onto the open spaces of the lower reaches of the mountain. Below and behind her, there were rows of condos—on-mountain accommodations, the brochures called them. From several, wisps of smoke from the chimneys betrayed the fact that the residents weren't skiing today, but taking it easy in front of the open fires and slow combustion stoves.

There was a tang of woodsmoke in the cold air. Tears welled in her eyes as she thought how she'd always loved that smell as a girl. It was the smell of winter and holidays in the ski fields of Colorado. Now it would be one of the last smells she'd ever know.

She thought of Jesse again and the tears flowed faster, then froze and hardened on her cheeks. She wiped them roughly with the back of her free hand, almost lost her grip as Mikkelitz suddenly gunned the motor again and skidded the snowmobile out onto the groomed snow of the Heavenly Daze run.

There were only a few skiers coming down the run. This was the lower half of the mountain and, at this time of day, most skiers headed to the upper reaches. Mikkelitz ignored them, racing the snowmobile across the run, heading uphill at an oblique angle. One skier had to bail out in a hurry as he realized the careering snowmobile wasn't going to give way. She saw him go down in a welter of thrown snow, heard him shouting abuse behind them.

She looked around desperately, hoping for some sign of a ski patroller, someone who might notice Mikkelitz flouting the rules of the road and stop them. Dully, she recognized that if that were to happen, the patroller would be dead within moments of their stopping.

The slope was steepening now and she felt the motor straining as Mikkelitz fed it more power. But with two on board, the snowmobile couldn't cope with a straight uphill run. He swung the head slightly downslope, looking for an access trail through the trees. They were going to have to zigzag up the mountain, she realized, using the maintained trails to get to wherever they were going.

He cut left now, following one such trail across the top of Vertigo and Concentration runs. The steep, mogulled ski trails dropped away below them, then they were in among more aspens between Thunderhead and Arrowhead chairs. She could hear the clank and rattle of the old, slow chairlifts above her. Then the snowmobile nosed unexpectedly into a steep drift and slammed to a halt. She crashed forward, her face driving into the back of Mikkelitz's parka. Able to brace himself against the wide spread of the handlebars, he'd absorbed the impact a lot easier. Now as she hit him, he drove forward as well.

"Fuck!" he said, his voice cracking with rage. Roughly, he shrugged her back off him, swung off the bike and promptly went thigh deep in the snow.

"Fuck!" he said again.

The snowmobile had missed a turn and had buried its nose into the built up snow at the uphill side of the trail. The engine had stalled and she heard the loud ticking sounds of the overheated metal as it began to cool in the frigid air.

Mikkelitz grabbed the handlebars and heaved sideways.

The little vehicle was heavy, but he had gravity on his side. He heaved twice, then the snowmobile slid sideways, clear of the snow that had buried its nose cone. As it moved, he floundered in the deep snow, sprawling full length.

He was breathing heavily from the exertion as he regained his feet. She didn't dare meet his eyes. She knew he was on the point of snapping. He grabbed the handlebars and climbed back aboard, reaching down for the starter cord.

He tugged. The engine coughed and refused to fire. Another attempt and a cloud of rich blue smoke shot from the exhaust.

"Fucking thing's flooded," he grunted to himself. He opened the throttle wide and tugged again. This time, the motor stuttered, died, picked up again, stuttered twice, then suddenly roared as the excess fuel burnt off and a new rush of power went through to the combustion chamber. A haze of two-stroke exhaust stained the air behind them. Among the aspens like this, there was virtually no breeze and the smoke seemed to hang over them like a pall, gradually moving in one undissipated mass down the mountain.

He clunked into drive and gunned the engine, tail-sliding the snowmobile around the bend that he'd just missed, using the power to let the tail arc like a pendulum through the turn, then meeting it and countering the slide with opposite steering and another burst of power.

Unprepared for the violent maneuver, Abby lost her grip on the grab handle this time. She was restrained only by the handcuff clipped to the handle and she felt the chrome steel bite painfully into the soft skin of her wrist. She hung there for a few seconds, then gradually regained her grip. Blood ran briefly on her wrist, then froze in the cold air.

As before, Mikkelitz continued to ignore her.

She could sense the general direction he was taking now and realized that he must be heading for the top of Storm Peak. She wondered vaguely what was there that was so important to him. There was nothing there but the weather station building by the boundary to the ski area—a single-story timber building that was, for the most part, unoccupied, and was used for storing weather study equipment.

Then she remembered what he'd said earlier. He had a few things to collect up on the mountain, he'd said. There was nowhere else that he might have left things. They must be heading to the weather station.

The question was, what had he stored there. And why?

And what did he mean to do with her once they got there?

She tried not to think about that. She tried to think about Jesse again. She wished to God that Jesse knew what was happening, then realized dully that there was no possible way he could.

SIXTY-TWO

There was more traffic on Lincoln than Jesse would have expected midweek. He glanced down at the panel beneath the headlight binnacle and saw a toggle switch labeled "lights and siren." He flipped it up and the siren cut in instantly, a high-pitched whoop whoop whoop that cleared the road in front of him like magic. The sidelights on the Harley flashed on and off at the same time, leaving other drivers in no doubt as to where the urgent sound was coming from.

He grunted in satisfaction as the cars before him peeled off to one side, leaving the center of the road free. He dragged the throttle open and the deep grunt of the Harley rose in pitch a little. The big bike surged forward and he slitted his eyes against the freezing wind, wishing he'd taken the time to put on sunglasses or goggles.

The speedometer hit seventy and he kept it pegged there as he pounded up the hill to the ski area. Coming closer, the road narrowed and curved and there was more traffic and pedestrians. He kept the siren whooping, but had to slow down considerably over the next few hundred yards.

In the parking lot, he flipped the toggle switch down again and killed the siren. He braked to almost walking pace, steered to the edge of the parking lot and gunned the Harley slightly to take it onto the walkway. The front suspension telescoped slightly and he stood in the saddle as he rode up the step.

The small number of skiers heading for the ticket office parted before him and he rode the big bike all the way up to the ski patrol office. He hit the kill button and the throbbing of the engine ceased mid-beat. Then, remembering his thoughts about vehicle security, he took the keys from the ignition and ran into the ski patrol office.

Bud Alton, the duty controller, looked up in surprise as the tall deputy came running in. He grinned as he recognized him.

"Hey, Jess, how's it going, man?" he began.

Jesse cut him short with a raised hand.

"Bud, is the patrol Ski-Doo still up at Thunderhead?"

The patroller nodded, mildly surprised that Jesse would even ask. There was always a patrol Ski-Doo at Thunderhead.

"Sure is, Jess. We haven't changed things any since you left," he replied. Jesse shook his head impatiently.

"I mean, is it there now?" he demanded. "I need it right away. Have any of the boys taken it on patrol or is it available?" Alton pursed his lips a little at the abrupt tone in Jesse's voice, and the note of demand.

"Well, wouldn't know for sure, Jess," he said coolly. "I guess I'd have to check."

He reached for the phone on his desk, stopped as Jesse said, "Do it."

"Now look here, Jess," Alton began angrily. "There's no—"

"Goddamn it, Bud! This is urgent! Now, for Christ's sake, pick up that phone and find the hell out!"

Finally, it occurred to the patrol commander that Jesse was here in his official capacity. He stopped arguing, picked up the phone and hit the nine button. He heard the ringing tone sound twice at the other end before a female voice answered.

"Ski patrol, Thunderhead Station."

"Noelle," he said, recognizing the voice. "Is anyone out on the Ski-Doo at the moment?"

"Hell no, Bud," came the answer. "We're all in the patrol room at the moment. It's cold out there, you know?" she answered cheerfully. Alton thought sourly that she could afford to be cheerful. She didn't have an angry deputy breathing down her neck. He looked up at Jesse, covered the mouthpiece with his hand.

"Ski-Doo's there all right, Jesse," he said.

"Good," the deputy told him. "Tell them to keep it there. I need it right away. In fact, tell them to get it warmed up and ready for me." He started toward the door leading to the gondola building as Alton passed on his instructions to the Thunderhead Station. Then he stopped, halfway out the door.

"Bud," he asked, "there been reports of any unusual activity on the mountain today?"

The commander frowned at that. "Exactly what do you mean, Jess?" he asked. Jesse made an impatient gesture. He didn't really know what he meant. He was just asking on the off-chance.

"I don't know . . . anything . . . a man and a woman fighting . . . anyone causing trouble. Anything at all," he concluded. Bud Alton scratched his chin thoughtfully. Jesse had really made him pissed, barging in here and throwing his weight around. Now he realized that something was afoot and his curiosity was piqued.

"Can't say I can think of anything. Other than the guy hoorahing on the snowmobile," he added. Jesse took a pace back into the room.

"Snowmobile? What happened?" he asked.

Alton shrugged. "Weren't nothing much. Some guy—and a girl as well, as I remember—cut across a few skiers coming down Heavenly Daze. Nearly rode one guy into the trees. They complained at the bottom but there wasn't much we could do about it."

It wasn't much to go on. But it could be them. "When did it happen?" he asked. Alton cocked his head to one side.

"Couldn't be more than ten minutes ago. The guy only just reported it at the ticket office."

"Thanks," Jesse said. He was about to leave again when he noticed a pair of 7x30 binoculars on the file cabinet. He grabbed them.

"I'll leave these at the top for you," he told Alton, then just remembered to add, "Thanks," before the door closed behind him.

"Jesse?" Alton had begun, "What's going on?" But the door had already slammed shut behind the rapidly moving deputy. The commander threw his hands up in an exaggerated shrug.

"Well, it's been my pleasure, Deputy Parker," he said, his voice thick with sarcasm. The pity of it was, he thought, Jesse wasn't there to hear it.

Jesse half ran to the gondola loading station. There were maybe fifty people lined up there, shuffling forward in a controlled line, loading in groups of eight. He vaulted the steel fence and pushed his way to the front. One of the lift attendants saw him and started forward. A few of the skiers muttered angrily.

He grabbed the deputy's star out of his shirt pocket and held it up for the attendants to see.

"Sheriff's office," he called, his voice echoing in the big concrete and steel-lined room. "Official business. Let me through here, please."

There was a cabin moving up to the load point, and a group of eight waiting to board. Jesse, still holding up the star like a talisman, shoved past them and dived into the empty car.

"Sorry folks," he called, "take the next car please."

He could see their angry faces receding as the car slid smoothly away, then gathered speed as it came off the detached cable and onto the high-speed section. The mountain slid by below him. He brought the 7x30s up to his eyes, fiddled with the focus for a few seconds to adjust them, then began sweeping the mountain below him.

They'd been traveling across Heavenly Daze, Alton had said.

Ten minutes ago. They could be anywhere on the mountain by now.

The comm unit in his jacket pocket gave an urgent buzz. He grabbed it out, thumbed the speak button.

"This is Jesse," he said.

"Jess, this is Lee." Her voice was thin and metallic through the tiny speaker. "One of Felix's men just found the taxi. It was up on Ski Trail Lane, in one of the condos. Side door was open and the keys were still in it."

He heard the carrier wave as she released her talk button to let him speak.

"I copy that, Lee, thanks," he replied.

"Jess . . . one other thing . . ." Even with the lack of definition in the tiny two-inch speaker, he could hear the hesitation in her voice. Then she continued in a rush, "Abby's suitcase, Jess. It was on the roof rack."

He took a deep breath. Then spoke again. One word only.

"Copy."

"And it may mean nothing, but there were tracks of a snowmobile heading up toward the mountain."

Involuntarily, he glanced to his right, in the direction of Ski Trail Lane. A snowmobile coming from that quarter would end up crossing the lower reaches of Heavenly Daze.

"Sounds like them, Lee," he said, working to keep his voice even.

There was a long pause. No sound but the faint hiss of the carrier wave. Then, finally, "Stay in touch, Jess."

"You know it," he said, and shoved the comm unit back into his jacket.

He trained the glasses out to the left now. Murphy was obviously heading up and across the mountain. To where? And for what? He swept the narrow viewing field of the binoculars across the mountain. But there were just too many trees, too many dips, too many hills and gullies. They could be anywhere on the mountain and the chances of him seeing them were lower than zero.

And then, miraculously, he did see them.

Just for a second. Far out to the left, almost at the top of the first section of the mountain, a snowmobile flashed into view in a gap between the trees. It was the movement that drew his eyes and he swept the glasses up instantly, trapping the little vehicle in the magnified view. And for less than a second, he saw the unmistakable flash of Abby's blond hair. Then the snowmobile was gone from sight again and he pounded his fist against the side of the cabin in a fever of impatience.

"Come on, for Christ's sake," he muttered, willing the gondola to move faster. Suddenly, it seemed to be barely crawling. He frowned to himself. He would have thought they'd be farther up the mountain by now—if that's where they were heading. Unless something had delayed them.

He shrugged, guessing that he might never know. But at least now he had an idea of their general direction. And the speed of the gondola, plus the fact that it traveled in a straight line, whereas a snowmobile heading uphill would have to zigzag along the access trails, would just about bring him level with them by the time he disembarked. The gondola clattered over the last pylon before the top station, then the cabin was swinging smoothly into the unloading bay, rocking and swaying when it came off the drive cable and slowed.

The doors were only half-open when he forced his way through and hit the concrete, running. He heard someone shout at him, presumably one of the lift attendants, and a hand went to clutch at his shoulder. He brushed it away and shouted back something unintelligible. The words "urgent" and "sheriff's office" were in there somewhere and they seemed to do the trick.

Then he was out in the cold air and running for the patrol hut.

SIXTY-THREE

Lee paced restlessly. Her office wasn't very big, so she didn't have far to go. Just four paces up and four paces back, but she did it anyway. Felix Obermeyer sprawled in the swivel chair behind her desk, watching her with idle curiosity. Felix thought of himself as a patient man. Unexcitable and clear thinking.

Others, more accurately, regarded him as dull and lacking in imagination.

Lee was consumed with uncertainty. The taxi had been found some fifteen minutes ago and she'd passed the message on to Jesse as soon as she'd heard it. It looked as if he'd been right in his guess that Mikkelitz would head for the mountain.

Then again, he could have gone in any direction after ditching the taxi. Maybe he was second-guessing them—leaving the Dodge van where it could be easily found. Where it would seem to point toward the mountain. Maybe he'd had another car stashed in the condo garage and even now was on US 97, heading for Denver and laughing fit to bust.

Her instincts were screaming at her to get up to the mountain with Jesse. But instinct wasn't enough. She knew she had to wait here, where she could monitor reports from the State Police, the Highway Patrol and Felix's men, spread out in almost a dozen different directions and locations.

If Jesse was right and he caught up with Mikkelitz, he'd let her know and she could break speed records getting up there.

The thought had barely crossed her mind when she had an idea. She cursed herself for not having thought of it sooner. She stopped pacing, reached across the desk and grabbed the phone. She jammed her finger on the zero button and waited while Denise answered from the switchboard.

"Yes, Sheriff?"

"Denise. Get hold of Ray Newton, out at Hayden, will you?"

Denise hesitated. The name wasn't familiar to her.

"Who's that again, Sheriff?" she asked uncertainly.

"Ray Newton. He runs a helicopter charter service." She thought briefly, trying to remember the company name. Then it came to her. "Snowshoe Charter," she told the switch girl, visualizing the Bell Jet Ranger with the stylized snowshoe rabbit on the fairing just under the engine. "Look it up," she added unnecessarily. She hung up before Denise could reply.

Felix was looking at her inquiringly.

"I'll get Ray to bring his Jet Ranger down here. Then if anything breaks, we can cover it in a hurry," she told him.

He nodded, acknowledging the value of the idea. "Good thinking," he said.

"Yeah. Should have done it sooner," she replied. She wasn't pleased with the way she'd handled things this morning. But at least now she felt better to be actually doing something.

The phone shrilled and she grabbed it. It was Ray.

"Good day to you, Sheriff. What can I do you for?"

She skipped the pleasantries and came straight to the point.

"Ray, I want you to get that Jet Ranger of yours fired up and bring it down here to town. Put her down on the sports field, the other side of the river, all right?"

"My chopper, Sheriff?" he said, a little slow on the uptake.

"Yes, damn it," Lee answered a little more crisply than he might have deserved. "We've got a major manhunt going on down here and we're going to need you and your chopper."

"Well . . . I've got a charter in an hour's time—" the pilot began.

"Cancel it," she ordered. "I need you on standby right here."

"In the town itself, Sheriff?" he queried and she sighed with exasperation.

"Yes, Ray. In the town. Not much use to me having you on standby out there, is it? Not if I need you here in a hurry."

"Yeah, well I understand that, Sheriff. But you know, town ordinances say I can't land my chopper in the town limits. Remember, we had those complaints about noise pollution two, three years back?"

"Ray, listen to me," Lee said quietly. "Fuck the town ordinances and fuck the noise pollution. And fuck you if I don't see that goddamn chopper on the sports field in the next ten minutes."

There was a moment's silence on the other end of the phone. Before the pilot could speak, Lee added, "I'm warning you, Ray. Get that chopper down here or I'll arrest you as an accessory to murder. And Ray," she said, "you know I'll do it."

"Well, okay, Sheriff, but you'd better square this with the mayor and the town council," he said in an aggrieved tone.

"I'll take care of them, Ray," she promised. "You just get that chopper down here fast."

"Well, all right. Long as you say it's important, I guess I'm on my way."

"Good, Ray. You just set her down there and stay right by her. Keep the engine running or whatever you do with those things. If I need you, I'm going to need you in a hurry."

"Okay, Sheriff."

She sensed he was going to say something more but she'd finished with the conversation. She set the phone back in the cradle and met Felix's gaze. The town police chief was looking a little amused.

"That Ray, it's as well he can fly one of those whirlybirds, 'cause he ain't too quick on the uptake at much else, is he?" he said.

Lee shook her head in mock weariness and rolled her eyes. "Jesus," she said. "Noise pollution?"

"Getting harder to be a cop every day, Lee," Felix told her sympathetically.

Jesse raced the Yamaha diagonally up the ski trail, sliding and bouncing as he headed for an access trail halfway up. The ski patrol vehicle handled the slope easily. It was a three-seater, built to take a driver and two pillions, and with an engine sized up accordingly. With just one person on board, it had more than enough power to head up the slopes. He figured that with Mikkelitz and Abby riding two-up on the other snowmobile, he'd make faster time up the hill—and he could take a more direct route to the top.

Assuming they were going to the top. He still couldn't fathom what

Mikkelitz had in mind. He seemed to have cornered himself here on the mountain. There was no way out other than back down.

Beyond the ski boundary, there was nothing but the wilderness of a national park—thousands of acres of trees and unmarked trails.

And then he realized that that was where Mikkelitz was heading. He'd leave the snowmobile—it could hardly cope with the deep snow of the forest—and head out on cross-country skis. Probably take a pack with him and a tent. He could survive for days, weeks, in the wilderness.

And come out anywhere it suited him. Alone. Because somewhere on the way, Jesse knew he was going to kill Abby.

He twisted the throttle full open. Even with an edge in speed, he knew they had too much of a lead for him to catch up. But he had to keep trying, even though there was a lead ball in the pit of his stomach as he realized the effort was futile.

The Yamaha's engine note rose to a howl and a rooster tail of thrown snow blossomed in its wake.

Mikkelitz saw the log a second too late. It was freshly covered and it looked for all the world like one more soft pile of mounded snow—the kind of thing that presented no obstacle to the snowmobile.

Then, at the last moment, he saw the black shape of a branch protruding from the snow and realized they were heading for a heavy tree that had fallen across the trail and been covered by falling snow. He yanked the steering to the left to try to miss it, but the snowmobile skidded sideways, tried to mount the thick trunk, and began to topple back downhill. He yanked the steering back right again, trying at the last second to ride up and over the massive hump in the snow, gunning the last ounce of power from the engine as he did so, and for a moment the snowmobile hung there in the balance.

It was Abby who made the difference. Instinctively, as she'd felt the little vehicle sway farther and farther to the left, she'd leaned her weight uphill, to the right, to try to counter the movement. Murphy was doing the same thing in front of her. He was actually off the seat and had all his weight on the uphill footboard, leaning way out as he steered to the right and gunned the engine.

Then she realized that any chance she had of rescue depended on her ability to delay him as much as possible. And this was a perfect opportunity, because he'd never know she'd done it.

She'd seen enough of him to know that if he thought she was delaying him, he'd have no hesitation in killing her right away.

So now, as the snowmobile tottered on a knife edge of balance, and actually began to surge forward over the tree, she threw her weight to the left.

That was all it took. The delicate contest of power, momentum and gravity suddenly had a winner and it was gravity. The snowmobile seemed to rear up on its hind end. The runners actually came free of the snow and the engine raced as the little vehicle toppled back and over.

As it went, Murphy screamed his fury and jumped clear, throwing himself uphill to save himself being pinned under the vehicle. Abby, handcuffed to the pillion handgrip, had no such choice.

She lost her grip on the handle, felt the flesh on her wrist tear as the handcuff ripped into it again. The snowmobile was toppling and her throat went dry as she felt she'd be pinned under it.

Somehow, she scrambled and kicked away from the snowmobile as it plunged over on its side. If it rolled, she knew, it would go right over her. If it just kept sliding on its side, and if she could just keep scrambling to stay ahead of it, she might survive relatively intact. She felt it start to roll, felt herself being drawn by the tethered wrist under the body of the machine. Desperately, she kicked at it to try to stop the motion. She didn't know if her actions had any effect, but the roll stopped and the snowmobile continued its slide. The drive train, free of the snow, thrashed wildly and the engine was revving like crazy. The spring return on the twist throttle must have jammed, she realized vaguely.

The sliding and bucking seemed to go on forever. She missed her footing, her leg going deep into a patch of soft snow, and felt the heavy machine start to slide over the top of her. Desperately she floundered, her mouth and nose full of snow, but she was being borne under and the hot metal of the exhaust was burning her leg. She could feel the weight of the snowmobile pinning her as it moved inexorably farther over her and finally she thought, fuck it, why bother? Why fight? And just gave in.

And the snowmobile stopped sliding.

SIXTY-FOUR

Jesse barreled the Yamaha up a steep incline at breakneck speed. The snowmobile left the ground, seemed to hang in the air for an eternity, then slammed back onto the hard-packed snow, landing unevenly, one runner hitting before the other and slewing the machine to the left. He tried to compensate, but the impact with the firm snow of the groomed ski slope had thrown him off balance and he felt himself toppling off the snowmobile.

He hit the snow with his left shoulder, tucked his head and rolled, coming to his feet ten yards down the slope. The Yamaha, with a dead man's throttle, had returned to idle the moment he let go of the twist grip. It slid quickly to a halt, engine burbling unevenly.

He was covered in the fine, dry snow from head to foot. He brushed himself off, wincing as his shoulder sent a shaft of pain through him, then stumbled awkwardly back up the hill and threw a leg over the saddle.

"No sense killing yourself," he muttered, and opened the throttle once more—a little more deliberately this time. The Yamaha surged away under him and he corrected the incipient skids and swings that were a fundamental part of its motion. But, he realized, he was right. Careering flat out up the hill, half out of control, wasn't the way to travel. He was a reasonably proficient rider, but nowhere in the league of the sports riders who took jumps much higher than the one he'd just attempted as a matter of course.

It wasn't going to do Abby the slightest bit of good if he lost it somewhere and broke his fool neck—or even an arm or a leg. He compromised, moving faster than was comfortable, but nowhere near as fast as he wanted to travel.

He cut through a patch of thick, ungroomed snow and found himself at the bottom of a steep, long mogul run. The old chairlift—abandoned and unused now since the Storm Peak chair had been built—stretched above him, the wind whistling around its thick cable, and in the taller branches of the pines that surrounded it. It wasn't the most comfortable of terrain for a snowmobile; riding up those endless mounds of hard-packed snow would be like windsurfing across solid waves, he thought. But it was a direct route to the top. He twisted the throttle experimentally, felt and heard the reassuring note of the engine as it revved easily beneath him, then swung the snowmobile up the hill.

It jarred and thudded over the succession of moguls in the snow, nearly burying its front skids in the downhill sides of the mounds. He realized quickly that a direct approach wasn't going to work. The moguls were too steep. He took it the way a cruising skier would negotiate the moguls downhill, threading a winding path through the small valleys carved out between the humps.

Even at that, the snowmobile was too wide for the trails he followed—carved by skis. The Yamaha continued to lurch and slam wildly into the mounds. His wrists ached from dragging it back on course as the terrain tried to shove him downhill. His shoulder, already wrenched from the heavy fall he'd just taken, was a dull pool of agony.

He skidded the tail around as he crested a mogul, letting the machine arc back through ninety degrees, tacking back and forth up the slope like a yacht on a solid frozen seascape of wild waves.

Solid frozen, he thought grimly, and tilted at a crazy forty-degree angle to the vertical.

He crested out onto one of the higher access trails. He figured he was around two-thirds of the way up the mountain. Instinctively, he was heading toward the top of the Storm Peak chair. Something inside told him that this was where Mikkelitz was heading as well. He didn't know why he knew. He just felt it somehow.

He looked at the remaining half of the mogul field under the chairlift. He was near exhaustion, his breath coming in giant gulps, his wrists, forearms and shoulders racked with the strain of wrenching the snowmobile back on course. He wasn't sure he had the stamina left to continue the same way. Reluctantly, he swung the Yamaha to the left and cracked the throttle wide open, sending it screaming along the access trail.

★　★　★

She was facedown in the thick, soft snow, in real danger of drowning in it. Vaguely, a long way away, she could hear someone cursing—repeatedly, in a mad litany of invective. A man, she thought. Slowly, her senses were returning. Something was tugging fiercely at her left wrist, and there was a sharp stab of pain there as the tug persisted.

She remembered . . . the snowmobile, sliding and bumping down the mountain above her, as she'd tried desperately to scramble and claw her way ahead of it. Then, as she gave up, she remembered seeing one of the runners rearing up beside her, felt the sharp impact against her head. She was puzzled and disoriented for a moment.

Then it all came back in sharp focus.

It was the killer's voice. The tugging at her arm was the handcuff and now, as she blinked her eyes open and raised herself painfully out of the snow, she could see his legs close beside her as he heaved and struggled with the tipped over snowmobile. And with every heave, the handcuff that still attached her to the rear pillion grip cut deeper and more painfully into the skin of her wrist.

There was a red mist about him. It was her blood, she realized, streaming down her face from the spot above her eyebrow where the skid had hit her. She shook her head to clear it, tried to ask him to stop jerking and heaving at the snowmobile.

The only sound that came was a strangled, choking grunt. She swallowed half-melted snow and saliva, choked slightly, coughed rackingly. Mikkelitz heard her and, thank God, stopped his insane straining at the snowmobile. His chest and shoulders heaved explosively and he staggered back a few paces.

"Fuck!" he shouted viciously. "Fuck, fuck and fuck this fucking whore of a snowmobile!"

She tried to stand, but her free arm went deep into the soft snow, gaining no purchase. And besides, the pillion handle to which she was handcuffed was almost at knee level. The snowmobile was tipped over almost three-quarters of the way on the downhill slope. It hadn't quite rolled upside down, thank God. Otherwise she would have been well and truly trapped beneath it and, by now, she probably would have suffocated.

Mad with rage and frustration, Mikkelitz had been trying to roll the little vehicle upright—against the slope of the mountain. The slope and the weight combined were simply too much for him.

She could smell the harsh fumes of gas and saw red fuel dripping from the air vent in the gas tank cap, spurting out through the tiny hole with the pressure of a full tank behind it.

Mikkelitz, his breathing a little more regular now, moved forward and grabbed the handlebars, straining to lift the snowmobile back upright. His feet churned in the soft snow and he was thigh deep. He could succeed in doing no more than moving the machine in small jerks—enough to lacerate her wrist again. She cried out with the pain.

"Stop it!" she said. "For Christ's sake, you're breaking my wrist!"

His face was close to hers as he forced his body lower, trying to gain purchase. The eyes were bulging and the effort was making his face scarlet.

"Heave, you bitch!" he spat at her. "Help me or I'll cut your fucking arm off!"

And she tried. But even with both of them shoving, it was no use. To all practical purposes, they were trying to lift the machine almost vertically, and turn it over at the same time. And they were trying to do it from a base that gave them no solid footing to work on.

"Stop it!" she gasped again. "It's useless! Can't you see it's useless?"

Whether he stopped because of what she said, or whether he was simply exhausted for the moment, she didn't know. She was just grateful that the heaving and jerking had stopped. She slumped beside the snowmobile, one arm pinned underneath it. He dropped across it, his breath coming in huge, ragged gasps. For a minute or so, he dropped his head onto his forearms, crossed over the side of the snowmobile's engine cover. Then he looked up at her, shaking his head in exhausted fury. She met his eyes and let her own slide away from what she saw there. He was insane with rage, almost crazy in his impotence. Her life was hanging by the slenderest of threads, she knew. In a second he would kill her, just to vent his rage and frustration. She gestured weakly at her trapped arm.

"Undo . . . me," she said haltingly. "Get . . . handcuff off . . . and"— she indicated a rolling circle downhill—"roll it right over and down."

He was uncomprehending for a second or two. Then he frowned as he saw the reason behind what she'd said. If she were out of the way, it would be a reasonably simple matter to roll the snowmobile completely over—lying on its side on the slope it was already two-thirds of the way there anyway—and let it come back upright after completing a full revolution. Instead of trying to lift it against its own dead weight, he'd have gravity to help with the task.

He fumbled in his shirt pocket and she felt a sudden flush of hope through her heart as he fished out the key to the handcuffs.

Once she was uncuffed and he was concentrating on righting the snowmobile, she'd take off like a startled deer, she decided. She'd roll, slide and tumble but she'd go.

He was coming toward her now, sinking deep with each step. Eagerly, she clawed at the snow with her free hand, clearing a space so he could get at the handcuff around her wrist. Looking at it now, she could see the snow around her hand red with the blood she was shedding.

He dropped to his knees on the snow beside her and bent forward, peering under the fallen snowmobile to the chrome grab handle. Her heart fell as she realized he wasn't undoing the cuff around her wrist. He was unshackling her from the snowmobile, unlocking the cuff around the chrome bar.

As the hardened steel cuff came loose, he grabbed it firmly and stood back, jerking her upright with him. Again pain flamed in her wrist and she gasped. He glanced around, saw what he was looking for and dragged her across the deep snow to a young aspen.

The main trunk was about six inches in diameter. But about four feet from the surface of the snow, the tree forked. The secondary branch angled out at around twenty degrees from the vertical and was about the thickness of a man's wrist. Wrenching her in a final spasm of pain, he clamped the empty cuff around the branch. As he let her go, her knees buckled and she hung by one arm, half sitting in the snow at the base of the tree. The branch extended another fifteen feet or so. There was no way she could slip the cuff off it. And it was too thick for her to break. She tried, in a dispirited way, seizing the short chain between the cuffs with her free hand and heaving at it.

It was no use. Her legs gave way under her again and she swung by the chain and slumped to the snow.

He backed away to the snowmobile, watching her feeble effort to break loose with a satisfied smile. He was beginning to feel on top of things again, she thought, and realized that had probably saved her life, at least for the moment.

Rolling the snowmobile downhill was obviously an easier task. He quickly had it upside down, then over on its other side. The next step—getting it upright—was the hardest. But even that was easier than trying to lift it back against the slope of the hill. He strained and heaved at it. His feet still sank into the snow up past his knees. But now he was standing above the snowmobile and the fact actually helped rather than hindered. It brought him down closer to the level of the snowmobile, allowing him to get a more direct thrust at it, and use the strength of his back and legs to do the pushing.

She watched him as he heaved and shoved at it, nearly having it upright, then at the last minute letting it fall back on its side. Then, with a final convulsive heave, he had it over and the snowmobile crashed over onto its runners, showering loose snow in all directions. For a moment, it looked as if it might tip all the way over again and he lunged at it, grabbing the uphill handlebar and throwing his weight back into the slope of the hill to steady it.

He looked around at her with a fierce gleam of triumph in his eyes. Triumph and something else. She realized she was dealing with someone who was totally unstable, poised right on the brink. She shivered uncontrollably and he saw the movement and smiled. Then he jerked on the starter cord.

The exhaust belched blue smoke. The motor tried to fire, then died. He kicked it savagely, splitting the fiberglass cowling of the engine in his fury, jerked the cord again.

Again, blue smoke, a coughing grunt from the motor, then silence.

She watched as he made an enormous effort and got control of himself. He reached into the engine and turned off the fuel tap so that no more would flow to the engine. Then he held the throttle wide open and tugged again.

This time, along with the cloud of blue smoke, the motor ran for half a dozen uncertain beats before dying. He tried to catch it with the throttle, just missed it and cursed again.

She was looking around, trying to find a way to leave a message.

Jesse would come looking for her, she knew that. She didn't know how she knew it. She had no reason to believe that Jesse even knew she was missing.

She just believed it. Because if she didn't, she had to believe that she was going to die. But she had to tell Jesse where Mikkelitz was taking her so he could go looking there.

She glanced furtively at him. He was head down over the snowmobile, paying no attention to her. She smoothed a section of snow beside the tree and traced the initials "APT" for Abby Parker-Taft, then, with her forefinger, a little smaller, the letters "WS" and an arrow pointing up the mountain in the general direction she thought the weather station lay.

As she was doing so, she realized, with a detached part of her brain, that she could hear another snowmobile somewhere in the distance, the rasping note of its two-stroke cutting through the cold air.

She frowned at the letters in the snow, wondering if she could do more. A quick glance at Murphy showed him with his back still to her and she decided she had time to write the words "weather station" in full. She quickly smoothed over the "WS" and began to print carefully, when a sudden explosive roar from the snowmobile made her start with fright.

The motor was running and he wound the throttle open and closed a few times to clear the plugs, sending clouds of oily blue exhaust drifting in the light breeze. Then he started toward her, reaching into his shirt pocket once more for the key. Frightened, she glanced down at the incomplete message in the snow. She had managed only the letters "WEATH—" but it might just be enough.

Except he saw the direction of her glance and saw what she'd written. The triumph in his eyes died suddenly, replaced by the cold anger she'd seen before, in the garage of the condo on Ski Trail Lane. Even though she knew he was going to hit her, she never saw the backhanded blow coming, just felt it explode off her lip and knock her spinning, hanging against the cruel bite of the handcuffs again.

"You fucking bitch," he said quietly, obliterating the letters in the snow with a quick arc of his boot. "I told you. Didn't I tell you?"

She tried to regain her feet, her free hand up to her mouth where blood was running again. Her lip felt twice its normal size. She didn't register that he was still talking to her.

"Didn't I?" he said, then, in a rising tone, "Didn't I?"

And when she didn't answer him, he hit her again, the arm swinging back in the opposite direction and knocking her from her feet yet again. She sobbed in pain and fear, managing to gasp out, "Yes! You told me! Sorry! Sorry, please . . . I'm sorry . . ."

Then he grabbed her by the hair and she felt her eyes water with the pain as he pulled her face close to his own.

"Listen, bitch," he said. "You do as you're told, okay?"

"Okay," she whimpered, cowed and beaten, hating him, despising herself. And he shoved her backward so her head slammed against the aspen and her vision blurred for a second or two.

"Please . . ." she tried to say, but her voice was barely more than a sobbing whisper. "Please, don't—" But he hit her again, open-handed this time, across the mouth, and her lips felt like swollen balloons. She forced her eyes open, seeing his hand drawing back for another blow. Then he stopped, as the motor of the snowmobile coughed once and died. He hesitated, cursed violently, then released her to slump semi-conscious in the snow as he started to move toward the snowmobile.

Just as another snowmobile skidded to a halt on the access trail above them.

And somehow, she knew, Jesse had found her.

SIXTY-FIVE

Lee was pacing again, up and back, up and back. She'd tried to sit calmly but somehow she just couldn't hack it. Felix watched her with a tolerant look on his face. At first she was going to stop for his sake, realizing how annoying her action could be. Then she'd noticed his look and thought to hell with him.

She let go of a pent-up breath and stopped by the window, staring out across the snow-scattered street and the river to where Ray Newton's Jet Ranger was sitting in the athletics field, its big single rotor slowly turning as he kept the jet turbine at idle.

She leaned her knuckles on the cracked paint of the windowsill, put her forehead against the chill glass of the inner pane. Like most business premises in the town, the windows were double glazed for insulation. Even so, the glass felt cold enough to freeze water.

A bunch of town kids on snowmobiles and mountain bikes had clustered around the chopper, wanting to come closer and get a good look. She could see Ray nervously shooing them away, casting worried glances at the rear of the chopper to make sure none of the kids were sneaking around there, trying to get close without him seeing them. Few people realized that the rear of a helicopter was the most dangerous quarter. It was instinctive for people to duck their head under the main rotor as they walked out to a chopper. Yet the big rotating blade was well clear of them. Even if they jumped way up, they'd likely not make contact. But the tail rotor, spinning so fast it was almost invisible, was the real danger. More people had been killed, Lee knew, walking into the whizzing tail rotor of a helicopter than had ever made contact with the big, high-set main rotor. It just went to show. The world was full of careless people, not Michael Jordan look-alikes.

No wonder Ray looked nervous, she thought. Then she shrugged. That was his problem. She wondered if maybe some of those kids weren't the ones that had been giving poor Tom Legros hell over the past few days. She turned over the idea of getting Tom to go help Ray keep the kids away from the chopper. It might do his punctured authority a little good. Then she realized it might be a recipe for disaster as well, if the kids chose to make it that way. Besides, Tom had his hands full with the residents of Mrs. McLaren's boardinghouse. They were still in the building. She'd decided to leave a pair of town cops out at the boardinghouse in case Mikkelitz showed up there. They were settled down in the front room of the Munsings' house. Any sign of him and they'd be in immediate radio or cell phone contact.

She pushed away from the windowsill and began pacing again. Felix let go an almost inaudible sigh and she ignored him. Finally, he said mildly, "Pacing don't get it done, Lee."

And she had to look at him. He indicated the old leather sofa against the far wall. "Take the weight off your feet," he suggested. She shook her head. But at least, he thought, she'd stopped her goddamn pacing up and down like a caged tiger.

He went back to cleaning his fingernails with an unbent paper clip. He could almost feel the tension radiating from the sheriff, like heat. He shook his head mildly. Patience was what a job like this needed, he thought. And patience was what he'd got plenty of.

Abruptly, Lee came to a decision.

"Damn it," she said. "I'm going up there."

Felix frowned at her, letting his tilted chair drop back onto all four legs and swinging his feet down from the desktop.

"Up there?" he repeated. "Up where?"

She jerked a thumb in the general direction of Mount Werner. "The mountain," she said briefly. "Jesse's right. That's where he is."

Felix shook his head at her, smiling patiently again. "You don't know that, Lee," he began, but she cut him off angrily.

"No. I don't know that. I sense it, all right? I feel it. Jesse's right. He's up there somewhere and I'm going up there too."

She'd already swung the .44 in its belt holster around her waist in one movement of wrist and hips and was buckling the gunbelt as she spoke. Finished with that, she took her green sheriff's department Windbreaker from the hook behind her office door and slipped it on. Felix tried reason.

"Lee, your place is here. This is the communications center. What if he's not up there on the mountain? What if he's heading for Denver or Vail and the state police spot him? What good will you be, chasing around on the mountain?"

She eyed him calmly. Now that she'd decided on a course of action, the tension had flooded away from her.

"Well, I'll be just five minutes away by chopper, Felix," she told the town police chief. "And I'll be in touch with you, so you can let me know the minute anything happens."

She took another comm unit from the desk drawer, similar to the one she'd given Jesse, and slid it into the zipper pocket of her Windbreaker. "Just whistle me up if there's any news, okay?"

He shook his head, annoyed at her. "Lee, you're the sheriff and we've got a manhunt in progress. Your place is here."

"That may be, Felix," she replied. "But I'm going." She opened the door to the hallway, paused before leaving. "Keep in touch," she said, and was gone.

She covered the ground to the athletics field in long, purposeful strides. Ray saw her coming and opened the left-hand side door. The kids, sensing a development, started to move in closer as Ray headed around to the pilot's side door of the Jet Ranger. Lee waved them back.

"You kids get back out of it," she called, "or we'll have your little heads chopped off and rolling in all directions."

Reluctantly, they gave ground. Teasing fat Tom Legros was one thing. The long-legged sheriff, with her shapely, tight jeans and a pair of gray eyes that could bore right into your soul, was another matter entirely. All the boys respected her authority. Most of them held her in awe, having heard wildly exaggerated stories about her proficiency with the big .44 she wore strapped to her right hip.

More than half of them had fantasized wildly erotic activities with her. In their imaginings, of course, she'd been totally compliant to their wishes, a love slave to them—the way they figured most beautiful older women would be with a fifteen-year-old pulsing with testosterone.

Lee, perhaps fortunately for her own mental well-being, was totally unaware that she was a minor sex symbol to the town's youth. She swung up into the passenger's seat of the Jet Ranger, fumbling the safety belt inside the butt of the Blackhawk and buckling up.

Beside her, the pilot was doing the same thing. Then his hands flew over the control console, hitting switches in a rapid pre-flight routine. He gestured to the headset hanging on a hook on the left dashboard and she put it on as he wound up the jet turbine and the big rotor, lazily flapping past her vision up till now, began to spin faster, beating the air with the characteristic whop-whop-whop of rotary wing aircraft everywhere.

"Where we headed, Sheriff?" his voice crackled in her headphones. She angled the boom mike down to her mouth, saw him point to a foot operated switch on the floor by her feet and depressed it to talk.

"Mount Werner," she said briefly. "Storm Peak."

He nodded, slipping a pair of Ray-Bans on. He hit another channel switch on the radio and she heard him request a takeoff clearance from Hadley Airport, letting them know his position, destination and the maximum height he expected to reach. She guessed that made sense. Along with the United Express puddle jumpers that flew in and out of Hadley, there were American Airlines MD-80s and Air West 737s.

An uninterested voice from Hadley control, some twenty miles away, told Ray that he was clear to take off for Mount Werner, cleared to three thousand feet above ground level. The voice had barely finished when she felt the Jet Ranger stir under her, rising up and sliding sideways a little as Ray fed in the collective with his left hand. The whop-whop-whop of the rotor increased in volume as the little aircraft rose higher, then the note changed as Ray flattened the blades a little and the Jet Ranger, with that peculiar nose-down attitude common to helicopters, banked toward the snow-covered mass of Mount Werner.

They were cutting across the grid of the town's streets at an angle now, gaining height rapidly. Lee always found it fascinating to look down from this elevated position—barely three hundred feet above the moving cars on the roads below. They were strangely remote, yet they were close enough to make out small details. The rotor whacked the air loudly above the townsfolks' heads, yet few of them looked up. Helicopters were no novelty in this area. It was like being in a big, noisy, invisible, buzzing bug, she thought.

She could make out the shuttle bus heading to the mountain. The ski racks along its side would normally be bristling with skis at this time of season. There appeared to be no more than half a dozen pairs. She shook her head sadly. If Mikkelitz's motive had really been revenge on the town, he'd succeeded.

The chopper rose higher and the town slid under her. Now the bulk of Mount Werner was ahead, dominating the landscape. The pure white of the ski trails carved their way through the dull gray of the winter aspens and the rich green of the pines. Her headphones were filled with the extraneous chatter of the controllers at Hadley as they directed local traffic in and out of the airport. Somewhere in the area, a hot-air balloon was asking permission to untether and rise to two thousand feet. She craned around to her left, looking to the flat fields where the balloon companies operated, and saw it—an immense, swollen, red and gold ball down at ground level. Ray saw her looking and hit the intercom switch, cutting off the external chatter and switching to the closed channel within the helicopter.

"Don't worry," he said. "We won't come anywhere near him."

She nodded. She wasn't worried but she guessed Ray was used to soothing the spiky nerves of joy-flight passengers around the valley. He kept the switch open and spoke again.

"Where you heading, Sheriff? Base of the mountain?"

That was where all the administration buildings were, of course, so it was logical for him to assume it. She shook her head and hit her talk switch.

"Right to the top," she said, pointing. "Storm Peak."

"Uh-huh," the pilot replied thoughtfully. She glanced sideways at him. The Ray-Bans hid his eyes, but she could see a slight frown creasing his forehead.

"Problem?" she asked. He chewed thoughtfully on his inner lip before answering.

"Too risky to set down there," he said. "There's no designated landing area and you've got skiers coming and going all over the place. Like as not, I'll put down there and someone will ski right into that tail rotor. Can't do it without someone on the ground to keep an area clear for me."

She nodded, understanding. Even with the comm unit, she had no way of contacting the lift attendant at the top of the chair. She guessed she could do it indirectly, by calling Denise and having her call the ski patrol and having them call the attendant's hut. Then maybe they'd have things organized by sometime next May. She came to a decision. Her choice of Storm Peak was an arbitrary one anyway. There was a simpler solution to hand.

"There's a helipad on top of the old weather building," she said. "Put me down there."

The weather station was a quarter mile up the slope from the top of the Storm Peak chair. She could leg it down from there. Or, if there happened to be a pair of skis and boots that were anywhere near fitting her, she'd borrow them. She knew the meteorologists who occasionally used the building kept their ski gear there.

"You want I should wait there with you?" Ray asked. Again, she considered before answering. She was coming here on a hunch, pure and simple. Because she expected Mikkelitz to show up here. On the other hand, there was no reason why he should be expecting her, or any other cop, to show up. If he saw a helicopter in the area, it could be enough to warn him off.

"Just drop me off and go. Stay in the general area, but don't make yourself too obvious, okay?"

The pilot nodded. "I'll orbit over the wilderness," he said, pointing to the miles and miles of thickly treed slopes beyond Mount Werner. "You need me, give me a call and I can be back in a few minutes. I guess you've got a radio?" he added, and she touched her pocket and nodded to him. He continued. "Just set it to guard frequency if you want me. I've got a second radio that monitors that all the time, okay? You know the setting all right?"

She nodded. She knew the frequency for the guard channel.

There was a faint beeping sound coming from somewhere in the cabin. She saw the pilot glancing around, puzzled. He didn't like hearing sounds that he couldn't account for and she didn't like to be in an aircraft where the pilot was puzzled about something.

She slipped her headphones off to hear more clearly, realized that the sound was the comm unit in her pocket. She grabbed at it, making an apologetic gesture to the pilot. He nodded and she could see the slight trace of relief in the way his shoulders relaxed and that frown straightened out on his forehead once more. The little radio had an earplug attached by a coiled lead. She put it in her ear now and pressed transmit.

"This is Sheriff Torrens," she said, holding the tiny unit as close to her mouth as she could. Even with the background noise of the wind and the whine of the jet engine, she instantly recognized the voice that replied.

It was Jesse.

SIXTY-SIX

Jesse saw the snowmobile first, a Polaris, he recognized. It was heavily crusted with snow, with deep pockets of it on the footboards, the seats and in the instrument binnacle between the handlebars. It had obviously been rolled to get in that condition and, instinctively, he skidded the Yamaha to a halt on the access road. There were two figures near it. One right beside the machine and another a few paces behind, slumped under the trees.

His first thought was that this was a simple accident, and he didn't have the time to stop and help. For a second, it didn't occur to him that this was the snowmobile he was looking for. He assumed that Mikkelitz had too big a lead for him to make up. Then he recognized the flash of pale blond hair under the trees and saw the other figure raise his arm and he rolled off the Yamaha, putting it between him and the man beside the snow-covered machine.

The flat crack of the Walther and the spang of the .32 slug off the Yamaha's cowling came almost together. Jesse lay flat on his belly, peering under his snowmobile, between the front skids. He could see a little—just enough to know that the other man had also dropped into cover behind the Polaris.

He scrabbled behind his back for the Colt in his waistband, got it free and thumbed down the safety lock on the slide. For the moment, he left the hammer down. There was already a round in the chamber. There always was. He always loaded the full seven rounds the magazine would hold, jacked one into the chamber, dropped the magazine out of the butt and slid in an extra round. It was an ingrained pattern that he followed every time he loaded or checked the automatic. It gave him a total of eight and he preferred the odds that way.

Tentatively, he raised his head, trying to peer through the footwell of the Yamaha to get a clearer look at Mikkelitz. He instantly regretted the move. The other man was obviously waiting for him to do just what he did and a rapid double volley hammered into the far side of the Yamaha. He dropped facedown in the snow again. He didn't have a shot underneath the snowmobile. The angle was too shallow. And to get a better angle, he'd have to put his head up into Mikkelitz's line of fire. Unfortunately, Jesse had ducked first, leaving Mikkelitz with the tactical advantage in this situation. He could see. Jesse couldn't. He could keep his gun lined up in Jesse's general direction. If Jesse was going to get a shot off at him, he was going to have to give Mikkelitz the first shot.

And so far, the three that Mikkelitz had taken had come close enough to tell him that this was not a good idea.

He was tossing this around, trying to figure his next move when there was a heavier report and something slammed into the side of the Yamaha, rocking the machine on its springs. He recognized the heavier caliber shot of the .38 that he knew Murphy carried, in addition to the automatic. Another shot, another splintering of fiberglass and ringing of metal and the Yamaha rocked again. Then again. Three shots. And three to go.

Plus four in the Walther. Or five if Mikkelitz loaded it the same way Jesse did the Colt. Either way, too many to risk looking.

The .38 barked again and again Jesse felt it through the frame of the snowmobile. God alone knew what damage the jacketed slugs were doing to the machine. He could hear liquid dripping somewhere, hissing on the hot metal of the engine. And he thought he could smell gas.

Then again, this close to a two-stroke, you always could smell gas. Wham! The Yamaha vibrated again. They were carefully spaced, aimed shots. If Mikkelitz was planning to keep Jesse's head down, the plan was working. He could see the fine detail of the snow right in front of his face, feel the wet coldness of it against his skin. One more shot in the .38, he thought.

And there it was, slamming into the legshield at the front and, by the sheerest fluke, deflecting down and sizzling into the snow a few inches from Jesse's face. He flinched violently.

Silence, broken only by the rising murmur of the wind through the pines and aspens above them. He realized that the .38 had been firing in a definite rhythm, spaced shots, about five seconds apart. Now the five seconds had passed—and another five. And another ten. Jesse had to risk taking a look. By now, the .38 was probably fully loaded once more, so there was no way he was going to put his head up over the Yamaha. He inched painfully forward on his elbows, dragging himself to the front of the snowmobile.

From here, he could look around instead of over. And, being lower to the ground, he could drop back into safety a damn sight quicker. Tentatively, the skin on the back of his neck crawling, he edged his face around the front structure of the snow bike, raising himself slightly to get a clearer view of the slope below him.

And felt a chill hand clutch at his guts.

He understood now what Mikkelitz had been doing while he was firing those spaced shots into the Yamaha. He'd moved the few yards that separated him from Abby. He now held her in front of him, his left arm around her throat. In his right, he had the Walther again. He was watching the spot where Jesse had last been like a hawk, ready to fire if the deputy showed himself again. He didn't seem to have noticed the corner of Jesse's face, which was all that showed around the front of the snowmobile.

Infinitely slowly, Jesse eased the .45 forward. He shrouded the hammer with his left hand to blanket any slight noise and carefully eased it back to full cock. The wave-like sound of the wind in the pines drowned the faint snick-ick as the sear engaged.

Mikkelitz and Abby were thirty to thirty five yards below him—a long shot for a pistol under the best of conditions. With most of Mikkelitz's body screened by Abby, there was no way Jesse could take the chance of shooting. As he watched, he saw Abby reaching up with one hand and doing something to her other wrist. He frowned, straining to see what she was doing, and caught a flash of metal, realizing she had been handcuffed to a tree branch and now was undoing the cuff.

Abby sobbed softly to herself as she unlocked the cuff around the tree branch. That first sight of Jesse as he'd skidded to a halt on the access trail above them had brought a wild surge of hope.

Then fear had replaced the hope as she saw Mikkelitz realize who it was on the other snowmobile and bring the pistol up to fire. It had all happened so quickly, she wasn't sure if Jesse had gone to ground before the shot, or if it had knocked him off the snowmobile. For an awful few seconds, she'd thought he was dead. Then she'd seen movement above the saddle of the Yamaha and saw him duck back into cover as Mikkelitz fired twice more.

She'd been puzzled when he switched guns, slipping the automatic into his side pocket and bringing a short-barreled revolver out of a shoulder holster. Then he'd begun that carefully timed, carefully placed barrage of shots, all the while backing across the slope to where she was, trapped helplessly by the aspen. With the last shot, he'd dropped the revolver back into his parka pocket, replacing it instantly with the automatic. Then he'd bounded behind her, grabbing her throat in his arm, pinning her in front of him. He set the Walther down for a second and produced the key to the handcuffs, shoving it roughly into her free hand.

"Unlock it," he rasped in her ear, grabbing the pistol from the snow again. She'd tried to insert the little key into the cuff around her wrist and he'd rapped the pistol hard against the side of her face. Her jaw ached and her teeth buzzed where the metal had slapped her.

"Not that one. The other one," the voice in her ear snarled. She could feel his breath, hot against her neck. Hand trembling, she fumbled the key into the lock and unsnapped the cuff. Her arm, pinned above her head for the last ten minutes or so, dropped limply. For a moment, she considered tossing the key away. He seemed to read her thoughts.

"Go right ahead," he told her. "I don't need it to refasten it. You just need it to get yourself loose again."

Numbly, she realized he was right. He tightened his arm around her throat, set the gun down again and reached around for her to hand him back the key. It took only a few seconds, then he had the gun back—except now it was jammed painfully into the soft hollow under her right ear, grinding against the jawbone.

"Deputy Parker!" His voice was hoarse and loud, right beside her ear and she flinched with shock. He waited but there was no sign of movement from the other snowmobile. He called again.

"Parker! Look what we've got here," he yelled. Now Abby thought she could see a slightly lighter patch of . . . something . . . beside the front runners of the other snowmobile. She tried not to react but realized she must have made some involuntary movement of her head. Or maybe Mikkelitz just saw it for himself.

"Come on, Deputy," he called again. "I can see you there, playing peek-a-boo around the front of that old snowmobile. Now stand up and show yourself like a man."

"Don't do it, Jesse!" The warning was torn from her almost before she realized she was going to call it. Again the pistol rapped sharply against the side of her jawbone, and the arm tightened around her throat till she gasped for air.

"Shut up, whore," he grated in a lower tone, right in her ear. "You speak again and I'll blow your fucking head off, okay?"

She couldn't speak. The pressure on her throat was so tight that it was all she could do to breathe.

"Okay?" he repeated, rapping again with the pistol. This time, she felt some sharp projection on it tear the skin of her face, and warm blood started to trickle down her jawline. Still unable to speak, she gagged, choked and tried to nod. She could hardly manage that either with his arm locked around her throat. But the attempt seemed to satisfy him. He called to Jesse again.

"Now here's the way of it, Deputy. You make one move toward me and this is one dead TV star. Understand? I even think you're trying to move on me and I'll put a bullet in her pretty little blond head—mess up all this fine blond hair with blood and brains and bits of bone. You understand me?"

"Let her go, Mikkelitz." Jesse's voice carried clearly to them. Calm. Matter-of-fact. Unworried. "Just turn her loose and maybe we can talk."

The killer was taken aback for a moment at the use of his name. Then he laughed sarcastically. "So you figured that out, did you? But that doesn't mean you can start giving the orders. I'll decide what happens here." He lowered his voice and said to Abby, "That boy just doesn't know when he's holding a losing hand."

He allowed his grip on her throat to loosen slightly and she gulped air gratefully, her knees sagging from the shock and the fright and the near strangulation of his hold on her.

"Turn her loose," Jesse called again. "I'm warning you. I've got a bead on you here and I'll shoot."

"Well, you go right ahead," Mikkelitz offered. "You take your best shot, Deputy. And it had better be real good unless you want to chance hitting your little friend here."

Silence from up on the hill. Abby knew that Mikkelitz had called Jesse's bluff. The deputy's threat was empty. At this distance, he simply couldn't take the chance. Mikkelitz was right. The chances were that any shot from Jesse would hit her.

And suddenly, she remembered what had happened to Jesse down in Denver, remembered why he'd quit the Denver PD and knew he could never take a chance like this, even if she wanted him to. Mikkelitz laughed again. This time it was a derisive snort of triumph.

"No?" he called. "Not ready to shoot? Well, okay. Now I'll tell you how we're going to play this. You toss that gun of yours out into the snow where I can see it. And you do it NOW!"

Again, Abby flinched as he yelled the last word in her ear. Jesse didn't move, didn't show himself. She willed him not to throw the gun out. At least, as long as this impasse continued, she had a chance. Someone might come. Help might be on the way. But she knew if he tossed out his gun, there was nothing to stop Mikkelitz simply getting on the snowmobile with her and riding away.

The gun ground into the soft hollow beneath her ear again and she gasped with the sudden pain. Mikkelitz's voice had risen in tone. There was a higher-pitched sound to it now. "Now come on, goddamn it! You toss that gun out or we've got us one dead TV star! You'd better believe me!"

Gratefully, she felt the pain and the pressure ease as the gun was removed from her neck. Her relief lasted only a second or so, because suddenly she felt the muzzle pressed against the fleshy part of her calf and then, unbelievably, there was a sharp bang and a burning, searing pain and a mule kicked her in the leg, right where the gun had been. She sagged, her leg giving way underneath her, and tried to scream. But the arm was tight around her throat again and she could manage only a choked little moan. She felt the warm blood rush on her leg and realized, without fully believing it, that Mikkelitz had shot her simply to make a point.

"Abby!" Jesse's voice was frantic. He half rose from behind the snowmobile and she could see him clearly for the first time. She sobbed with the pain and the shock, then stumbled forward as Mikkelitz shoved her toward the Polaris, all the while staying behind her.

She understood nothing. She was centered only on the pain and the shock in her leg. For a few moments there was no reason, no thinking, no intelligence. Just her and the shock and the pain.

And in those few moments, she felt Mikkelitz clamp the other end of her handcuffs around the grab handle once more. And once more, she was trapped, without any means of escape.

Jesse watched helplessly as Abby was shackled to the Polaris. Mikkelitz had remained behind her throughout the maneuver. Now he sank to one knee so that Jesse's view of him was blocked by the little vehicle and Abby's body. There was still no chance of a clear shot. As he crouched behind his own snowmobile, wondering what to do next, he heard a faint metallic snick, then the unmistakable sound of the Walther's action being rapidly worked back and allowed to slam forward. He realized that Mikkelitz had loaded a fresh clip into the automatic.

Jesse knew that if he stalled much longer, the other man would carry out his threat to kill Abby. The sheer indifference, the way he'd placed the automatic against her lower leg and fired, was more than enough to convince him. It had been a totally casual, totally callous act. Assessing the situation, he realized that Mikkelitz had nothing to lose. He could break the stalemate by killing Abby and he'd still be on level terms with Jesse. If it came to a shoot-out between them, there was no telling who'd come out on top. Only one thing was certain: Abby would be dead. After that, it was an even money throw of the dice for Mikkelitz. He could afford those odds and the consequences. Jesse couldn't.

And as he realized it, he knew he was going to have to do as Mikkelitz said.

"So now," Mikkelitz was saying, "we all know I'm serious. So let's get rid of that gun I see there in your hand—and my, what a big gun it is."

Jesse remained irresolute. He saw Mikkelitz place the Walther against Abby's jawbone again, saw her wince and her eyes screw shut with the pain and the fear. There was a psychological element to the threat as well, he realized. As much as death, Abby would be in fear of the total disfigurement that would result from a bullet to that part of her face. Even if it didn't kill her, she'd be maimed and horribly disfigured for life.

"Come on, Parker." There was an edge in Mikkelitz's voice now. An ugly, angry edge because things weren't going his way. "Let's have that gun. And let's have it now!"

Jesse saw the hand holding the Walther drop a little, so the slug would angle up through the jaw, through the roof of the mouth and into the brain. A killing shot, he realized, then remembered that Mikkelitz had worked as a paramedic and so could be expected to have a working knowledge of human physiology. The gun-hand fingers flexed and he knew, without a shadow of a doubt, that the other man was about to squeeze the trigger. Abruptly, he jerked his right arm in an underhand toss, sending the Colt spinning away to bury itself in the snow.

Abby watched it land and disappear into the soft powder. Her last vestige of hope went with it. The adrenaline flooding her veins was working now to disperse the shock and the reaction to the pain. In the contest between fear and shock, fear won.

Earlier, she'd guessed that they were heading for the Storm Peak weather station. Somehow, she had to let Jesse know. Somehow, she had to give him the chance to catch up with them again. And if she'd guessed wrong? She thrust that thought aside. She had to be right.

The gun dug into her again, into her back this time, and she was propelled toward the Polaris.

"Pull that starter cord and get this motherfucker going," Mikkelitz ordered.

He was still close by her, still screened by her body. He couldn't be totally sure that Jesse didn't have some kind of holdout weapon. A lot of cops carried them, he knew—a little short barrel .22 in an ankle holster maybe. Or maybe one of those two-shot .38 over-and-under derringers they were making again these days, copied from the old .41 Remingtons they used to carry on Mississippi riverboats. Now that Jesse was disarmed, for a moment he'd considered just walking up there and letting him have it—a .32 slug right in the face. But he couldn't be sure that the deputy wasn't waiting for him to do just that.

He'd settle with him another time, he thought, when he was sure of all the angles involved.

"Pull, fuck you!" he screamed at Abby. She'd tugged on the starter twice. But there was no answering kick from the engine. No sign of life. Not even a stutter. He racked his brains. The motor had been running sweet as pie just before the deputy had arrived. He'd cleared the flooded carburetor and gotten her going. He'd . . .

Then he remembered. To clear the carburetor, he'd turned off the fuel tap, to stop further fuel flowing in on unsuccessful attempts. When the engine had finally fired, he'd neglected to open the fuel tap again. The motor ran for a few seconds on the gas in the carburetor and the fuel lines, then simply cut out as it was starved of fuel.

He shoved the reporter to one side, leaned past her and found the tiny lever. He twisted it through ninety degrees to allow the fuel to flow, thumbed the rubber priming pump two or three times to get things started. Then he shoved Abby back into position.

"Now pull!" he ordered her. She leaned forward, sobbing quietly, to seize the plastic molded handle on the end of the starter cord. She pulled once and this time the engine caught, stammered, then died. One more would do it, he thought exultantly. He slapped her again with the stubby muzzle of the Walther to urge her on. She stumbled, fell against the little snow vehicle, then dragged herself up again, her weight on her uninjured leg. She looked up the hill to where Jesse still crouched behind the Yamaha. She could see the fury of helplessness etched in every line of his face and she called quickly, "Jess! I'll always remember skiing the bumps with you!"

She cringed instantly, knowing Mikkelitz would hit her again. She felt almost triumphant when he did. She'd seen the puzzled look on Jesse's face. She knew that the message didn't make sense to him, knew that, because of its lack of sense, he would grasp the underlying meaning.

Or hoped he would.

"Shut up, bitch, and pull that rope," Mikkelitz ordered her.

This time, the engine fired, stuttered, recovered and settled into a steady throb. Mikkelitz shoved her against the snowmobile so that she was forced to swing her injured leg over the saddle. Then he swung aboard in front of her. He was turned back through forty-five degrees to watch Jesse standing on the trail above them. He quickly brought up the Walther and snapped off a shot at the deputy. Jesse saw the movement and dropped prone behind the Yamaha, which was exactly what Mikkelitz had intended.

He shoved the Walther into the shoulder holster that had previously held the .38, clunked the Polaris's drive into gear and accelerated away through the trees.

SIXTY-SEVEN

As the snowmobile's engine note faded into the trees, Jesse stumbled downhill through the soft snow to the spot where he'd thrown his gun.

The spot was easy enough to find. The heavy Colt had left a deep mark in the surface of the snow. The gun itself took a little more time. It had sunk about two feet deep. He retrieved it, scrabbling in the soft snow till he saw a glimpse of the blued metal, then digging it out. It was caked with snow and he'd need to clear it before he tried using it.

His breath coming in huge clouds in the frigid air, he made his way back to the Yamaha. The spreading, red stain of fuel underneath the machine looked like blood. There was a steady rain of drops coming from the little machine. He unsnapped the engine cowling clamps instead, letting the side panel drop clear of the engine.

His heart sank as he saw the damage the .38 caliber slugs had done. The gas lines were cut, of course. He'd already realized that from the flood of gas running into the snow. The other damage was more serious.

One slug had smashed the single spark plug to shards. Another had savaged the carburetor and a third had blown a section of the finned combustion chamber away. The snowmobile wouldn't be going anywhere without major repairs.

He cursed once, then set about cleaning the Colt while he tried to think of his next move. He brushed it clear of snow, dropped the magazine out and worked the action, catching the chambered round as it spun clear. He held the slide back with the lock safety and peered into the chamber, blowing into it violently several times and checking to make sure the barrel was clear of snow. Satisfied, he replaced the magazine into the butt and tried to shove the gun into his jacket pocket. It struck against something hard and unyielding. He replaced the gun in its usual positon, in the back of his waistband, and felt in his pocket. His fingers closed over the radio Lee had given him.

Mentally, he kicked himself. In his rush to get up the mountain and find Abby, he had clean forgotten that he had the radio on him. He groaned softly as he realized he could have reported seeing Abby and Mikkelitz from the gondola.

He checked that the radio was switched on, then thumbed the transmit button quickly, several times. No answer.

He tried again, knowing the action would cause an insistent beeping on any other communications unit tuned to the frequency he was on. This time, he heard a crackle, then Lee's voice, recognizable even through the tiny built-in speaker of the set.

"This is Sheriff Torrens." There seemed to be a lot of static on the connection, like a roaring background noise, he thought. He thumbed the talk button again.

"Lee, this is Jesse. He's got Abby and he's heading for Storm Peak. He shot out the motor on my snowmobile. I have no chance to catch him. It's up to you."

"I'm on my way," Lee told him. "We've got Ray Newton's chopper here. I'll be there directly, Jess."

Maybe it was the events of the last ten minutes or so that affected his thinking, but he didn't realize that she meant it literally—that she was already in the air, and only a few minutes away from the top of Storm Peak. He assumed she meant that she was leaving the office.

"Just get here as fast as you can, Lee." He switched off the radio and dropped it back into his pocket. An idea was beginning to take form in his mind.

He jerked open the carry pack at the rear of the Yamaha. The snowmobile was outfitted for use by the ski patrol and it had a certain amount of rescue gear packed in there. Along with an extensive first-aid kit and a harness for manually unloading passengers from the chair was a coiled, fifty-foot length of braided nylon rope. It was for use in case a skier went over a drop and rescuers had to reach him from above.

He slung the coil of rope over his shoulder, then scrabbled through the fiberglass cargo canister, tossing thermal blankets, bandages, and inflatable splints into the snow. Finally, his hand lit on a filled canteen of water. He hefted it experimentally, satisfied with the weight, then set off at a run, following the hard-packed access trail through the trees.

He could hear the hum and rattle of the Storm Peak Express chair-lift getting louder as he ran. He'd realized that the access trail he was following cut right under the path of the chair. And, from the top of the bank above the trail, the moving cable was not much more than fifteen feet above the snow. Farther up the mountain, the contours of the ground fell away and the height of the cable reached twenty or thirty feet. But here, where the trail had been cut and the bank piled on the uphill side, was one of the points where the chairs were closest to the ground.

He was breathing heavily when he reached the cleared path under the chairlift. He scrambled awkwardly up the bank and paused for a few seconds, his chest heaving. Quickly, he passed one end of the rope around his upper body, tying it in a quick release knot and loop-ing it around his chest. Then he gathered the other end and quickly tied in half a dozen figure eight knots, spaced about five feet apart, and starting around ten feet in from the end. Finally, he looped the end through the sling of the water bottle and quickly tied it off. All the while, the chairs passed above him in succession, fifteen seconds apart. It wasn't a lot of time for what he intended, but it would have to do. He realized he should have brought the K-bar knife from the rescue pack on the Yamaha in case things went wrong. But there was no time now to go back for it. He'd have to trust dumb luck.

He figured he should have plenty of that.

His eyes narrowed with concentration as he held the water canteen ready for an underarm throw. He swallowed twice, realizing, incon-gruously, that his mouth and throat were dry, and he had the means to take care of that in his hand. Then he threw, arcing the weighted end of the rope up, trying to lob it over the moving cable above him.

And missed.

The canteen, with the knotted rope trailing behind it like a banner, dropped back in the snow. He stumbled forward and retrieved it. He was conscious now of skiers on the chair peering down at him curi-ously. There weren't many of them. Most of the chairs were empty—further evidence, if any were needed, that Mikkelitz's reign of terror was having an effect. He waited till another chair passed by above him, tossed the canteen again.

This time he made it. The canteen lobbed up and over the cable, dragging the rope behind it. He glanced frantically at the next chair as it seemed to rocket up the hill, suddenly moving faster than he thought possible, as he heaved in on the end of the rope, tightening it, feeling it biting into his body under his armpits. The chair was almost up to him now. In a second or two, it would snag the rope looped over the cable and begin dragging it up the mountain. He pulled as much slack out of the rope as he could, then sprang high, driving with his legs, and stretching to catch the rope as far above his head as possible.

His hands closed around the smooth, thick-braided nylon. He started to slide down, then managed to obtain a proper grip at one of the knots. At the same time he was frantically jamming his feet together on the rope, searching for the purchase of another knot. He found it and hung, suspended from the cable. The rope stretched as the last of the slack went out of it and he sagged back down toward the snow. Then the chair caught the looped rope and suddenly he was dragged uphill from the bank where he stood and the contour of the mountain dropped the ground away from him by another ten feet or so.

Dangling and twisting like a fish on a line, holding desperately to the rope with his hands and feet, Jesse sailed up the hill, some fifteen feet below the chairlift.

Incongruously, he realized that he was now pursuing Mikkelitz using the reverse of the murderer's own original technique, dangling below a ski lift on the end of a doubled rope.

The thought didn't remain long at the forefront of his consciousness. Very quickly, his world became the agony of his shoulders and forearms and calves as he clung to the rope. He twisted one arm through it to give himself a little relief. But even with that extra purchase, he didn't know how long he could hang here. His shoulder muscles screamed with red-hot pain and his forearms were already beginning to cramp. Dully, he realized that they were the muscles that had taken the brunt of the work as he'd fought the snowmobile up the mountain. Now they were being asked to do double duty.

Vaguely, he heard someone shouting, realized it was a passenger. God alone knew what the people on the chairlift thought. Probably thought the Mountain Murderer was climbing up to get them. He spun slowly in the wind, the snow-covered pines sliding past him on either side. As he came around to face uphill, he saw one of the chair-lift towers looming closer, and felt a sudden chill.

The chair was designed to pass over the tower, as it was suspended from one side of the running cable only. The rope, looped over both sides, would jam as soon as it reached the point where the cable passed over the tower top. He had to get rid of the rope. Had to throw it loose. And he had two choices. Up or down. Get up to the chair above him, hang on to it and drop the rope, or slide back down to the snow-field below him.

And be stranded here, with no hope of reaching Abby in time.

Then he knew there was no choice. His muscles cracked as he began to haul himself hand over hand up the rope, gripping with his feet, reaching with his hands and hauling. He was spinning faster now, his own movement adding to the lack of stability. As he rotated, he could see from the corner of his eye the massive steel structure of the tower looming closer and closer.

He was inches from the chair now. He stretched. His hand brushed the metal of the footrest, fingers clawing. He touched again, then got a solid hold. He thanked his years of working in the mountains for the fact that he'd tied the rope around his chest in a quick-release knot. He tugged the end now and felt the rope fall loose. He tossed it away from himself, and grabbed for the footrest with his free hand.

He hung there now, swinging from the inverted T of the footrest. He jackknifed his body, legs searching for the other footrest, finding it, and coiling around it to take some of the weight.

Then the chair was bumping and clanging over the tower, and he could see the rope whipping up and over the cable, hoping it wouldn't catch and jam up the cable, bringing the chairlift to a halt.

It didn't. It slid smoothly over the greased steel, its end flicking in ever smaller arcs as it got closer to the top, then dropping away to lie coiled and lifeless in the snow below the cable. The chair, with Jesse hanging under it like some gigantic possum on a branch, sped up the hill toward Storm Peak.

He hung there for a minute or so, regaining his composure. Slowly, his breath and heart rate, which had accelerated alarmingly as he'd struggled to get the rope clear of the tower, dropped back to somewhere near normal. The strain on his arms was a lot less now, as his weight was shared by arms and legs. He felt he might be able to improve his position on the chair a little.

He heaved up and got a good right-handed grip on the safety bar above the footrests. He shifted his position so that his feet gave him some purchase on the footrest, and with a convulsive heave, hauled himself up and over the safety bar, to sprawl along the four-seat length of the chair.

The chair swayed alarmingly, the plastic bubble canopy rattled back and forth with the movement and he breathed a silent prayer of thanks for the automatic mechanism that tilted the bubbles back as the chairlift came into the loading area. If the canopy had been down, he'd never have got into the chair. He would have had to hang precariously below it all the way up the mountain.

He scanned to the left, trying for some sight of the Polaris. But the pines on either side of the chairlift loomed higher than the cable, effectively blocking his view. And it was then that the significance of Abby's shouted message struck him.

"I'll always remember skiing the bumps with you," she'd said. Yet Abby, in spite of the fact that she was an excellent skier, hated mogul skiing. Hated skiing the bumps. The only time he'd tried to teach her, when they were first married, she'd lost her temper with him and the mountain after the first fifty yards, and skied out of the mogul field to find a groomed run down the mountain.

He'd been teaching her in the Chutes—a series of narrow black diamond runs out on the limits of the ski area, just below the old weather station. And then, it all fell into place. Mikkelitz, Jesse was sure, was planning to head out into the wilderness area beyond the ski boundary. Yet he hadn't been carrying any of the equipment he'd need to survive there: cross-country skis, a pack, some kind of tent, food and survival clothing. So he must have stashed them somewhere at the top of the mountain.

At the weather station building. That was what Abby had been trying to tell him. That was where they were heading.

He reached into his jacket pocket for the radio. His fingers closed on nothing. For a moment, he felt panic as he searched the pocket, then the other side pocket of his jacket. Then he realized what had happened. The radio must have dropped out when he'd been hanging half-upside-down below the chair. There was no retaining flap on the pocket, nothing to stop the little radio sliding clear, unnoticed, and dropping into the snow. Come the spring thaw, he thought grimly, he'd have to come back up here and look for it.

It'd probably be here, along with the hundreds of poles, skis, gloves and personal items that the mountain crew found under the chairlifts every summer. More than once, he knew, crews had found brassieres, boxer shorts and panties. He took his hat off to people who could manage such acrobatics on a chairlift.

The top of the lift was in sight now and he knew what he was going to do. His gun was still firmly jammed into the back of his waistband and the deputy sheriff's star was secure in his shirt pocket. One or the other would be all he'd need to get a pair of skis and boots at the top of the chairlift.

The chair slid onto the slow speed circuit now, rocking as it decelerated down to an easy walking pace. He tossed back the safety bar that had served him so well, and came off the chair, hitting the snow at a run and moving to the right where the lift attendant was watching him through the window of the hut.

To one side, a ski patroller was also in position, monitoring the people on the chairlift as he'd been told. He frowned slightly at the sight of someone running from the chair, not wearing skis, then recognized Jesse.

"Hey, Jess," he began, a little puzzled at the deputy's grimly determined expression. "What's going down, man?"

Jesse could see the other man's Atomic slalom models thrust base down into the snow beside a tree. He pointed to the man's feet, began shucking off one of his own battered running shoes as he made his way toward him, hopping on one foot.

"Your boots," he ordered. "I need them. And your skis. Quick, Harry, get them off."

Harry grinned foolishly, convinced this was some kind of elaborate joke.

"My boots, Jess?" he asked, shaking his head, waiting for the tag line. He actually recoiled a few paces as Jesse's anger flared.

"Your fucking boots! Now!" the deputy yelled. A few skiers crossing toward Buddy's Run and the Flying Z stopped to stare at the sudden commotion. Still Harry didn't understand.

"Jesse—?" he began, but Jesse was in no mood for long-winded explanations. He balanced on one foot, the other one now shoeless, and got a hard grip on the ski patroller's parka.

"Harry, I need those boots. I need your skis. And I need them real fast. Now, for Christ's sake, give them to me!"

The urgency communicated, even if the man could see no reason for it. Shaking his head, he knelt, unclipping the fastenings on his right ski boot.

Jesse realized that he'd removed his own left shoe. He gestured to it. "Other one first," he snapped.

There was nothing to gain by having to stand in the snow in nothing but his socks.

Harry saw the sense of it. He removed his left Koflach and exchanged it for Jesse's beat-up sneaker. Jesse jammed his foot into the ski boot. He'd need it to fit the skis on. The ski bindings wouldn't attach to a normal walking shoe, of course. The boot was a little tight in the fit but he wasn't planning on wearing it long. He hurriedly snapped the lever fastenings into place. By the time he'd done it, the still puzzled ski patroller had the other ski boot ready. Jesse shucked off his shoe, tossed it to the other man and shoved his foot deep into the ski boot.

"Thanks, Harry," he said breathlessly, grabbing the skis from where they were rammed upright into the snow and dropping them flat beside each other. He stepped into the bindings, clamping his heels back down to lock them. The ski patroller had the stocks ready for him. He grabbed them gratefully.

"Thanks," he repeated quickly. "I'll explain later. Wait in the chairlift hut."

Then he shoved off with the poles, at the same time skating the skis, digging the edges in for purchase, and went gliding quickly across the firm packed snow toward the trail that led to the weather station.

SIXTY-EIGHT

For the first quarter mile or so, the slope was slightly downhill. Jesse continued to skate and to pole hard, building his speed as much as he could for the point where the trail started uphill again.

There were a few people out skiing. He passed them quickly. For the most part, they were taking their time, planning to turn off down Buddy's Run, or maybe to begin dropping down the slope a little as they worked their way over to the Ridge and the Crowtrack, the black runs that wound their way down through the trees to the flatter expanses of Big Meadow. One or two of them glanced up at the lone skier who whipped past them, working arms and legs to build his speed across the groomed snow. A computer programmer from Dallas grinned at his companion, a honey blond doctor's receptionist from Ohio whom he'd met the night before. He jerked his head in the direction of the fast-moving figure who'd just passed them.

"Extremist," he drawled. The blonde cocked her head curiously.

"Now where's he going in such a hurry?" she asked. Her companion shrugged.

"Guess he's taking the tough runs down through the trees," he said with a trace of envy in his voice. Those runs were way beyond his meager ability on skis.

None of this was noticed by Jesse. He'd hit the uphill slope now. The momentum he'd built up kept him moving easily for the first sixty or seventy yards. He was glad that the skis had been waxed recently and the snow itself was firm, without a trace of slush. Head down, he continued to pole and skate, creating a classic herringbone pattern in the snow as the pitch of the trail increased and he needed to set his edges out to the side to give him increased purchase. He moved his skis in a wide V-shape, stepping rapidly from one to the other. There was no longer any forward gliding motion in his progress. He was walking now, using the spread skis to gain purchase. His breath came in short, sharp explosions of mist in the cold air. A snowflake drifted down, swirling uncertainly past his lowered eyes as he plowed up, head down.

He glanced up briefly. There were more big, soft flakes spiraling down. The sky was a dirty dark gray and he could tell they were in for another dump. Which meant, if Mikkelitz did make his escape into the wilderness, as he assumed he was going to, there would be no trail to follow.

His thighs were burning with the repetitive skating motion. The boots, a little too tight, were painful on his feet. He gritted his teeth, lowered his head and concentrated on the savage rhythm of movement that he'd developed. Step, pole, step, pole, thrust, step. To an onlooker, it would have appeared easy and graceful. Only Jesse knew how much effort was going into it.

In spite of the cold, his shirt was already damp with sweat, and drops of perspiration were running into his eyes. He shook his head angrily to clear the salt sting. Just keep it going. Couldn't be more than half a mile to the weather station. Maybe less. Don't look up. Don't see how much farther you have to keep up this pace.

His upper body rolled from side to side and he was grunting in time to the movements now—a visceral, primitive sound that was dragged from him by the effort and the adrenaline and the need to keep going. To make it to the weather station before it was too late.

Now he was off the groomed trail, deep among the trees where the snow was softer and the going was much, much more difficult. He fought the snow, thrusting, stepping, dragging huge, gasping draughts of knife-cold oxygen into his lungs.

At last he had to stop. He stood gasping, shoulders heaving. The building was visible now through the trees, barely two hundred yards away. He could see the darker tones of the timber walls against the snow. His view was still partly obscured by the trees, and he had no way of knowing if Mikkelitz and Abby were already there. He waited till his breathing steadied a little, then listened. The snow was falling more heavily now, seeming to blanket out sound around him. He was listening for the high revving note of a snowmobile engine but there was nothing. He'd lost all track of time and a glance at the Seiko on his wrist meant nothing to him. He didn't know when he'd last seen them. Didn't know how long it was since he'd dangled under the chairlift like a hooked mackerel.

The ominous thought was forming in his mind that he also didn't know for sure that this was where they were heading. Abby's message may have simply been the confused words of a terrified, disoriented woman.

Maybe they were heading somewhere else. Maybe they had already been here and left. Maybe they were yet to arrive. He simply didn't know. All he did know was that he had to keep going now until he found out, one way or another.

It took him another hundred yards.

He plowed on through the soft, deep snow, wishing he'd been able to commandeer a set of cross-country skis. Then, without any warning, he was in the open, barely seventy yards from the old weather station. The trees receded behind him and the slope of the ground in front of him dropped away so he could glide forward once more. The skis made no noise at all in the fresh falling cover of snow, already several inches deep.

He skied forward carefully, aware that he was in the open now. Aware that if Mikkelitz were inside the building, watching him, he was an easy target—a dark figure against the white background. So far, however, there was no sign that anyone was in the building. The windows and doors that he could see were closed and shuttered, although he knew that, on the far side, there was a garage-type roller door that gave access into the storeroom and workrooms of the building. Now, as he came closer, he became aware of something just visible around the right-hand corner of the building—dark object that was gradually becoming covered by the falling snow. An object that didn't seem to be part of the building itself, didn't seem to belong.

And then he recognized it as the front section of the Polaris.

He let his momentum die and coasted silently to a stop. The building was barely forty yards away, with no sign of Abby or the man Jesse had been hunting for the past two weeks. He let the ski poles drop, shucking the retaining straps from his wrists as he did so, and reached behind his back to where the Colt nestled.

He felt its familiar weight in his hand as he brought it up to cover the building, easing back the hammer to full cock as he did so. He shuffled forward in the skis, then realized that, in spite of the present mobility they gave him, they could quickly become a liability—and a fatal one. Lifting his right foot clear of the snow, he angled the tip of the ski out to the right and stepped down with the base onto the quick release of the left binding.

The binding clunked open and he stepped free of the ski, keeping his weight on the right foot. Now he stepped back on the right binding and released that as well. Stepping free, he sank knee-deep into the snow, and started wading awkwardly forward.

Abby and Mikkelitz emerged around the corner of the building by the snowmobile. Abby saw him immediately. Her reaction was totally involuntary, torn from her by the shock of the moment.

"Jesse!" she called, and instantly Mikkelitz swung around, saw him and dragged her back as a shield in front of him.

Hindered by the deep snow, unable to shoot for fear of hitting Abby, Jesse began to blunder forward. He saw Mikkelitz's arm come up, heard the dull report of the Walther, strangely muffled by the heavy falling snow, then felt a sledgehammer slam into his right thigh.

For a few seconds there was no pain. Just a numbing shock and a terrific impact that knocked the leg from under him. His heart raced suddenly and his breath gagged in his throat as he was hurled sideways into the deep snow. Falling, he heard another shot and the angry crack of the bullet whipping over his head. He scrambled sideways in the snow, dragging the useless right leg with him, grateful now that he'd gotten rid of the cumbersome skis just a few minutes earlier. Another shot, and something zipped into the snow a few feet from him.

A few yards to his right, there was a snow-covered tree stump, all that remained of a pine that had been felled when the area was cleared. It reared some three feet out of the snow, its solid bulk offering protection. He switched his gun to his left hand now and lay on his right side, pushing with his left leg and dragging himself with his right arm into the cover provided by the stump. Lying low in the snow as he was, he couldn't see Mikkelitz or Abby. He guessed that the gunman's view of him was obscured as well, as the deep snow provided at least some shelter.

He reached the stump and lay back against it, breathing heavily. And now the first wave of pain from his leg hit him, like a red-hot torrent pouring through his body. He doubled over and groaned aloud with the agony. Of the leg itself, he could feel little. He was merely conscious of pulses of pain ripping through his entire being. And of the warm feeling of blood seeping slowly from the wound.

Gritting his teeth against the pain, he risked a look around the stump to see if Mikkelitz had moved. He was still in his original position, still with Abby held helplessly in front of him as a shield.

Obviously, Jesse figured, the killer couldn't be sure whether or not he'd hit him with that first shot. Or if he had, how badly he was injured.

Bad enough, the deputy groaned to himself. Each movement sent more pain tearing along his nerve endings.

For the moment, Mikkelitz seemed content to stay as he was, shielded by Abby, until he could figure his next move. Until he saw some sign as to whether Jesse was still in the game or not.

He glanced down at his right leg. The bullet had gone into the flesh and muscle. It seemed to have missed the bone. But there was a steady leak of blood seeping out of the entry hole. Steady, not pumping, so no artery had been hit either. He'd once heard that relatively minor wounds caused the most pain. He was grateful for the first fact, less so for the second. He unbuckled his belt and tugged it loose from the loops in his jeans, then quickly fastened it around his thigh, above the wound. He jerked it tight and fastened it again, noticing that the flow of blood seemed to have lessened.

That seemed to be the extent of the first aid available to him. The pressure of the belt somehow seemed to localize the pain of the wound. It still hurt like hell, but the constant waves of pain were lessened. Now there was just an insistent throbbing in his thigh itself. Using the stump for purchase, he dragged himself to a half crouch, resting his gun hand across the top of the old severed pine.

"Well, Deputy, you do seem to keep turning up at awkward times, don't you?"

He focused on the two figures by the side of the building, the Colt's muzzle wavering slightly. His voice, when he spoke, was a croaking rasp.

"Turn her loose, Mikkelitz. And drop the gun."

"Fuck you, Deputy. I don't think you're in any shape to do anything about it if I don't."

Jesse brought the Colt up to an aiming position. Even with the stump to rest it on, the sights wavered and trembled as he tried to get a clear bead on Mikkelitz. There was little of him to see, just his head. And at thirty yards, shocked and injured, with a handgun, Jesse simply couldn't take the shot. The odds were high that he'd hit Abby.

Or miss entirely.

"Turn . . . her loose," he croaked again. He kept his forefinger outside the trigger guard, desperately willing the sights to settle, knowing they wouldn't. Remembering another time, years ago, when a panic-stricken Tony Vetano had blundered into his line of fire.

And as that thought came to him, Jesse knew that he couldn't shoot, couldn't take the chance again. And he knew that by not doing so, he was condemning Abby to death.

"Not feeling so good, Deputy Parker?" Mikkelitz's voice was more cheerful now, as he began to feel on top of the situation. Now he realized that Jesse was injured, the whole thing took on a different look. Up until now, they'd been heading toward a dangerous standoff—one where he couldn't predict the outcome.

He had the major trump card in the deck—Abby. But, ironically, the card only remained a trump as long as he never played it. He could threaten her life to hold Jesse back. But if he actually had to kill her, there was nothing to stop the deputy coming after him. Had Jesse been fit and uninjured, Mikkelitz couldn't risk having him pursue him into the wilderness. Somehow, he would have to have killed him. And he knew that wouldn't have been easy.

But now, with Jesse injured and unable to follow him, he was firmly back in control. It wasn't exactly how he'd planned things. Originally he'd intended that the final killing would be Opie Dulles, the ski patrol commander who'd humiliated him. But this was even better. Abby was a celebrity—the TV reporter who'd told the world what a bang-up job Parker was doing. It was fitting that she'd be his last victim, and that Parker would be left to know how badly he'd failed.

He could see the way the deputy's gun wavered as he tried to aim. Could see the frown of pain and concentration as he tried to keep focused. He sensed that Jesse wouldn't dare shoot. So did the girl he was holding. She called out to the man across the clearing.

"Shoot, Jesse! Take the chance! I'm dead anyway!"

With a snarl of anger, he rapped the muzzle of the Walther along the ridge of bone above her eye. He was expert at finding painful spots for the short, savage blows he kept dealing her. The impact hurt, and the blade foresight cut the skin there, setting up an ooze of blood. In a low voice, meant for her alone, he rasped, "Shut the fuck up, you bitch, or I'll kill you here and now!"

Abby's head had sagged with the pain of the blow across her eyebrow. Now, she seemed to gather herself and raise her head. He felt her take a deep breath and knew she had submitted to the inevitable.

"All right, you bastard," she said, making an immense effort to be calm. "Go ahead and shoot me."

He didn't answer immediately, because he wasn't paying attention to her. He'd seen the involuntary movement from Jesse when he'd hit the girl. The big Colt .45 he was holding had jerked back up to an aiming position again . . . and then lowered. He smiled grimly when he saw it, then replied, "In my own time, sweetheart. I'll kill you when it suits me."

Then, in a louder voice, he called mockingly to Jesse, "You're really not feeling too good there, are you, Parker?"

Dragging Abby with him, his arm like an iron bar around her throat, he began to move sideways toward the parked snowmobile. The figure crouched behind the tree stump followed their movements—the gun in his hand trained at the ground somewhere between him and them.

"In fact," Mikkelitz continued, "I figure I could just mount up on this snowmobile and ride away from here and you could fire every bullet you own and you'd never hit me, would you?"

"Maybe he wouldn't," said Lee, stepping from the trees to the right of the clearing.

"But I might just give myself a chance."

SIXTY-NINE

The weather station had been deserted when Lee stepped down from the Jet Ranger. Crouching slightly, even though she knew the rotor blade was well clear of her, she moved away from the helicopter and waved Ray off.

The jet engine wound up to a whistling roar and the pilot lifted the aircraft up, swung to the northeast and headed, nose down, out over the snow-covered ranges of the wilderness area. She took out the comm unit and tried to contact Jesse once more. She'd already tried several times since his last transmission, without any success. She tried to tell herself that it simply meant the radio was malfunctioning, but she couldn't get rid of the thread of fear that whispered Jesse wasn't answering her calls because he couldn't.

There was an outside ladder from the rooftop helipad down to ground level. She climbed down now and stopped to listen. There was no sound, other than the surf of the wind through the pines. Then even that died and snow began to fall.

Jesse had said that Mikkelitz was heading toward Storm Peak and she assumed that he meant the top of the Storm Peak chair. It was half a mile away through the snow, but at least it was downhill. She unzipped the front of her sheriff's office parka, reached inside to her shirt pocket, where she found the sixth .44 Magnum slug she always carried there, and loaded it into the empty chamber of the Blackhawk. Then she re-zipped the parka and started out down the hill through the snow.

She'd gone maybe two hundred yards when she heard the whining buzz of the snowmobile, and caught a glimpse of metal and fiberglass as it roared up the slope toward the weather station.

The little snow bike was below her, on the western side of the slope as she headed down the crest of the ridge. It rapidly moved past her, then climbed to her level and swung toward the building. The quick glimpse of shining pale blond hair was enough to tell her that Abby was on the back of the snowmobile. She guessed the driver was Mikkelitz.

She blundered through the thick snow, back up the slope to the building. She'd barely gone fifty yards when she heard the two-stroke motor pop and splutter and die away. She redoubled her efforts, hampered by the fact that, with every stride, she sank at least knee-deep into the snow.

There was no sign of Abby or Mikkelitz when she reached the building. The Polaris was parked outside, at one corner of the station. She guessed they'd gone inside, but had no idea where. She stopped in the tree line and slowly circled the weather station. Her first instinct was to go crashing in. She considered the idea for maybe five seconds before discarding it. She had no idea where they were inside. She had no way of gaining access to the inside without making noise. By charging in, she risked not only Abby's life, but her own. Mikkelitz would have all the advantages on his side and Lee was too good a hunter to consider that acceptable. So she stayed inside the tree line, maybe forty yards from the building, and found a position to one side where she could watch the snowmobile.

Briefly, she considered the possibility that Mikkelitz might kill Abby while they were in the building. Then she shrugged. This was still her best course of action. Instinct told her that the killer would keep Abby alive until he was absolutely certain he was home free. That wouldn't be till he left the building and went wherever it was that he was headed.

If she was wrong, she was wrong. Getting herself killed as well wouldn't do Abby the slightest bit of good. So she waited, hunkered down in the cover of the trees, allowing the lightly falling snow to cover her shoulders and upper body, helping conceal her from any eyes that might be watching from the building. It was nothing new to Lee. She'd hunted since she was eleven years old, and if need be, she could sit here all day, legs drawn up, collar zipped right up around her ears, in the shelter of a wide-branched pine.

By positioning herself where she could watch the snowmobile and the door on that side of the weather station, she'd unknowingly placed the building between herself and Jesse. Accordingly, she had no warning of his arrival, was totally unaware that he was less than a hundred yards away when the door opened and Mikkelitz emerged, pushing Abby roughly in front of him.

He had a survival pack and a set of cross-country skis slung loosely across his left shoulder. As Lee watched, he let them drop to the snow, then, still holding Abby, moved to the Polaris.

Moving slowly and carefully, Lee eased the .44 forward, crouching low and holding a two-handed grip. She didn't have a clear shot yet. He was too close to Abby, and besides, there were several trees between her and the edge of the cleared space. She started to move forward now, angling for a better shot.

When all hell broke loose.

Mikkelitz suddenly lunged at Abby, grabbing her around the throat with his left arm and pulling her back against him, hard. Lee froze instantly. She knew he hadn't seen her. He was looking in a totally different direction. Maybe she'd made some noise. Or maybe . . . then Abby called something. Just one word that Lee didn't catch. And then Mikkelitz was firing at something on the downhill side of the building.

One shot. Then another two in quick succession. And as he fired, he dragged Abby back against the side of the station, keeping her between him and the spot where Lee was standing, wondering what the hell had gone wrong.

She brought the Blackhawk up again, hesitated. It was too long a shot under the conditions. The falling snow made vision uncertain and the light wasn't good. Add to that the fact that almost all of Mikkelitz's body was shielded by Abby's and the odds were simply too long. She'd have to move for a better position, she thought, and began to do so, angling forward and to her right.

Then freezing in place as she heard Mikkelitz call out and Jesse's voice answer him.

Shaky and little more than a croak maybe, but Jesse, nevertheless. She felt a thrill of hope that he was alive, realized that all the while she'd been unable to contact him by radio, she'd feared, deep down, that Mikkelitz had killed him.

Then the first surge of hope turned to cold fear again as she realized that Jesse was hurt, maybe badly. She could hear it in his voice as he called for Mikkelitz to let Abby go.

So could the killer. She saw his confidence growing, his certainty that he had the situation well in control and there was nothing Jesse could do to stop him. Realizing that the man's attention was riveted on wherever it was that Jesse was standing, Lee took advantage of the distraction and moved quickly forward to the edge of the tree line. She was maybe thirty-five yards from where Mikkelitz and Abby crouched against the side of the building. She stopped, set her feet a little sideways to present a narrower target to the gunman, and heard his final, mocking speech to Jesse.

And decided it was time she took a hand in things.

As she spoke, Mikkelitz whirled halfway around to meet her, dragging Abby with him. The gun in his hand was jammed hard up under Abby's jaw again as he backed up to the rough concrete wall behind him. For a moment, she saw the shock in his eyes as he realized things were sliding out of his control.

She held the Blackhawk loosely in her right hand, angled down at forty-five degrees. There was no point in wearing herself out by keeping it leveled at him. The gun weighed close to three pounds and it wasn't the sort of thing you kept at arm's length until you wanted it there. She could almost read the thought in Mikkelitz's mind as he glanced down at his own pistol—a Walther automatic, she noticed. With its three-inch barrel, he'd be lucky to hit her with any sort of snap shot, and to shoot at her, he'd have to take the gun away from its threatening position, jammed against Abby's throat.

She saw his eyes drop to the seven-inch length of the Blackhawk's barrel. He knew he was outgunned. Knew that, at more than thirty yards' distance, Lee had the advantage in firepower and accuracy.

He also knew she'd never dare use that advantage, as long as he had the Walther pressed tight up against Abby's head like this. He shook his head at the snow-covered figure by the trees.

"Jesus," he said. "You got any more of you out there in the woods?"

"You'll never know," Lee replied evenly. "Now why don't you do what Jesse said, and let the girl go?"

He shook his head savagely. "Oh no. Oh no. I don't think that's what's going to happen here."

Lee frowned slightly. The speech was rapid and jerky. Mikkelitz was teetering on the brink here. He could snap at any moment, and it would be the end of Abby if he did. And, much as Lee could have killed Abby herself for ruining things between her and Jesse, she knew she wouldn't stand by and see her murdered. She spoke again, keeping her voice calm and level.

"Mikkelitz, it's over. Now let Abby go and put that gun down. There's no need for anyone to get hurt here. Okay?"

"Oh no. It's not okay you see, Sheriff. You see, you have no idea, do you, why I've been leading you such a dance these past weeks, do you?"

She forced herself to speak calmly. "Well, we figured you wanted to get even with the town, seeing as how you were sacked from your job here," she replied.

She realized immediately that had been a mistake. Realized she should have left Mikkelitz his pretense of mystery. She saw his arm tighten around Abby's throat and the girl was jerked backward off balance against him. She let out a little cry. Lee had seen her gather herself while Mikkelitz and Jesse were talking, saw her summon her courage to face whatever was coming. Now she saw the last of that courage melt away like the last trace of snow in the thaw. Abby was sobbing helplessly as the gun pressed against her head.

"So you knew that, did you?" he asked savagely. Lee said nothing and he ground the gun against Abby's face, forcing another cry of pain and terror from her.

"Did you?" he shouted.

"Well . . . we guessed, I guess," Lee said carefully. She thought that maybe she was going to have to take a shot anyway, some time in the next few seconds.

"Well, aren't you guys just the smartest fucking pair of hick-town fucking cops?" he spat at her. Slowly, she began to raise the .44 to shoulder level. He saw the movement, shook his head at her in warning, looking meaningfully at his own gun, pressing into the soft skin beside Abby's eye.

"Don't try it!" he warned her. But she kept the long barrel coming up to the point of aim she wanted, eased back the hammer to full cock and held the gun there.

The blade of the foresight sat neatly into the rear sight groove, and the two of them, foresight and rear sight, locked together, wandered smoothly across the aiming picture she'd created.

No one can hold a handgun absolutely rock steady without any form of hand rest. The sights will always waver slightly across the sight-ing picture. The real skill comes in timing the release of the trigger to the moment when the sight is crossing the center of the aiming point. And the temptation for ninety-nine percent of shooters is to anticipate that moment and snatch at the trigger, pulling the shot off-line. Lee breathed evenly and regularly, watching the sights move in a small circle, crossing Mikkelitz's head, just taking in a part of Abby's, then circling back again. Her forefinger rested lightly against the grooved trigger.

She could make the shot. She knew it. But the gun against Abby's head would almost certainly be triggered by Mikkelitz's dying reflex.

And for just a fleeting fraction of a moment, Lee found herself wondering if that would be such a bad thing. She would have tried. She would have done her best. There was even a chance that Abby might survive. Maybe she should just leave it in the hands of chance. After all, she owed Abby nothing. And no one would ever know what she'd done.

"That you there, Lee?" It was Jesse's voice, sounding weak and full of pain. She remained focused on the sight picture, both eyes open, arm and hand holding firmly but not so tightly that the muscles cramped.

"It's me all right, Jess," she called. "You okay there?"

Mikkelitz's eyes snapped around to his left as Jesse spoke. From the way the gunman had to lean forward, Lee guessed that Jesse was momentarily out of his line of sight.

"Can't move much," he replied. "But I'll heal."

And in that moment, she knew she had to wait till the Walther was no longer threatening Abby. Maybe if she fired now, if she took the chance, nobody else would ever know what she'd done. But Jesse would. And she would. And she couldn't live with either one of those.

"So, Sheriff," Mikkelitz was saying. "We've got ourselves a stalemate here. So maybe you'd better just back off and put down that great big gun of yours."

"Or?" Just the one word.

"Or I'm going to kill this girl. I'll do it. Believe me. You know I will."

Lee didn't hesitate. "The moment you do, you're a dead man," she said flatly. She sensed that Mikkelitz was getting back to that dangerous edge of hysteria again as he saw no way out. She knew she couldn't crowd him. Knew she couldn't back down.

She knew all the things she couldn't do, she admitted to herself. It was just she didn't seem to know one thing she could do.

"Maybe. Or maybe I'll kill her and then I'll kill you too." Slowly, she shook her head, meeting his eyes above the gunsights.

"I don't think so," she said flatly. Mikkelitz considered the statement for a few seconds, then shrugged.

"Either way, one thing's certain, the girl will be dead. You want that on your conscience, Sheriff?"

It was the tone of his voice that convinced her. He'd gone past that jerky, almost hysterical tone and had now realized that there was no way out. And having realized that, he'd found a way to win.

To him, surviving didn't matter any longer. Winning mattered. And winning was simply a matter of making sure she lost. If Abby, whom they'd come up here to help, should die, that would be enough for him now. Sure, he'd take the chance on getting away after he killed her. But Lee knew that killing her was really all that mattered to him now, and she racked her brains to find a way to defuse the situation.

No ideas came. They were on a knife-edge, she knew. She considered setting her own gun down, but realized that, if she did, he was just as likely to kill Abby immediately, then try for her and Jesse—if he were still conscious.

The one element that was still keeping him from acting was the fact that her gun was trained steadily on him. There was still one last fiber of survival instinct within him that was stopping him from killing Abby.

How much longer it would last, Lee didn't want to think about. The silence between them grew, broken only by a soft whimpering sound that Lee realized was coming from Abby. Her arm was beginning to ache, extended like this, but she couldn't break the tableau. She didn't know what would happen if she changed the delicate balance that existed between them.

Then, in her peripheral vision, she saw movement. She winced in concentration as she just stopped herself from looking away from the sights. The movement came again and now she realized it was Jesse, on hands and knees, dragging himself through the snow, his big Colt in one hand.

She risked a quick side glance at him, moving only her eyes. His right leg, blood-soaked from thigh to ankle, was dragging stiffly in the snow behind him. He was still hidden from Mikkelitz's view by the corner of the building. But, as he moved slowly forward, he would soon be exposed. There was no chance that he could take Mikkelitz by surprise, wounded and slow-moving as he was, and for a moment, Lee wondered what the hell he was doing.

And then she realized. He was giving her the chance for one clear shot, and one only.

Then it came. As Jesse edged forward into view, Mikkelitz's gun left Abby's throat and leveled at the spot where he could suddenly see the injured deputy.

The Walther and the Blackhawk both moved to their final aim points at the same moment. Lee saw the killer's head in sharp focus as the sights moved smoothly across it, saw Abby's blond hair shining and slightly fuzzy on the edge of her focus picture and calmly, gently, stroked the trigger.

Her right arm shot up almost vertical with the savage recoil and the deep boom of the shot echoed from the weather station walls.

Abby screamed as the metal jacketed slug ripped past her face, barely three inches away, at supersonic speed, and slammed into the middle of Mikkelitz's forehead.

He was hurled back against the rough wall like a rag doll, dragging the terrified Abby with him as he went. His right hand spasmed and involuntarily tightened on the trigger of the Walther, sending one shot high into the air, to explode a clump of snow from the top branches of a pine tree.

He was dead when he hit the snow, and his left arm relaxed around Abby's throat, allowing her to roll away from him, weeping in shock and fear. She'd stared down the barrel of Lee's gun, mesmerized by the sight of it, as it appeared to aim right at her. She'd seen the brief flash in the fading light, waited for the bullet to hit her, heard the obscenely loud crack of its passage and the ugly wet smack as it tore through Mikkelitz's skull and savaged his brain. Felt herself hurled back with him.

For a few seconds, Abby was convinced that the bullet had hit her. That she was dead. That it was all over. And she buried her face in the cold snow and wept.

Until she felt Jesse's gentle hands on her shoulders, rolling her over, and his calm voice soothing her, and his arms going around her and holding her as he knelt beside her in the snow.

At the edge of the tree line, Lee stood immobile, the big, single-action revolver hanging loosely by her side as Jesse scrambled painfully toward the stricken woman in the snow. She watched in silence as the man she loved put his arms around his former wife and held the pale blond head against his shoulders. She saw his lips moving in soothing, tender words that were meant for Abby's ears and no others.

And, as she watched, the sheriff of Routt County felt the hot, sharp pain of the tears in the back of her eyes.

SEVENTY

Lee sat in her office staring, unseeing, at a note from Ned Puckett on the desk in front of her.

She sighed deeply, picked up the single sheet of paper and, for the tenth time that morning, tried to concentrate on its contents. Vaguely, she was aware that Ned was querying the use of town funds to buy meals from the Steamboat Yacht Club.

Equally vaguely, she remembered authorizing Tom Legros to do just that a few days earlier, when she'd kept the residents of Mrs. McLaren's boardinghouse locked in the Public Safety Building for eight hours. Unfortunately, when she'd lit out in Ray Newton's helicopter, and Jesse had radioed her to tell her Mikkelitz was on Mount Werner, she'd neglected to tell Tom he could let the guests return home. As a result, they'd had lunch and dinner supplied by one of the more expensive eating houses in town courtesy of the Steamboat Springs municipal budget, and Ned wasn't exactly delighted about the fact.

She looked at the letter now, realized she'd have to do something about it, crumpled it in one fist and tossed it at the wastepaper basket in the corner. She missed, thought about walking across the room to pick it up, then decided, the hell with it.

"I'll deal with it later," she told herself.

Three days had passed since the confrontation on Storm Peak. She'd recalled Ray in the Jet Ranger and he'd flown Jesse and Abby to the district hospital, where one of Mikkelitz's intended victims was still a patient. Lee had chosen to wait with the body, riding down in a convoy of oversnow vehicles she summoned by radio.

They'd found a diary in Mikkelitz's room, a chilling collection of random, wandering thoughts, all with a recurring theme of victimization and revenge. Reading the diary, it became obvious that Mikkelitz had ultimately planned to avenge himself on the man who had fired him—but this time, he wanted the whole town to suffer as well.

There were references in the diary to other events in the past, other slights and acts of revenge. It seemed that, previously, he'd been content to kill and slip away undetected. The Storm Peak killings represented an escalation in his thinking. It was as well they'd stopped him, she thought.

She'd passed the diary on to FBI headquarters. A phone call the previous day told her they had found unsolved murders in three states that might just be the work of Anton Mikkelitz.

She glanced out the window at the mid-morning traffic on Lincoln. The ski shuttle bus was pulling away from the curb, the racks on its sides more than half-full of skis. She smiled wanly. There'd been a hurricane of media coverage once word got out that the Mountain Murders case had been solved and that the killer himself was dead. For two days, you could hardly move along Lincoln Street without being stopped by TV crews, half blinded by the glare of their lights, or knocked unconscious by the sudden thrust of a microphone in your face.

The news teams had been bad enough. Lee had made an official statement to a bank of cameras, lights and tape recorders, then got the hell out of the room, followed by a hundred shouted questions. Later that evening, a producer from *60 Minutes* had approached her, wanting to discuss a story on "The dead shot who'd put the 'she' in sheriff," dressing it up to sound like a piece on women in new age law enforcement. Lee saw it for what it was intended to be—a sensational piece, emphasizing her role in killing the murderer.

Politely, she'd declined to be interviewed for the piece. The producer insisted. Less politely, Lee told her to fuck off.

That seemed to do the trick.

She felt no remorse about the death of Mikkelitz. She didn't glory in it. She didn't regret it. Rather, she accepted it. He'd chosen the path, she reasoned, and he deserved no better. Given the chance, she would have taken him into custody and seen him stand trial. As it was, she thought the way things had turned out made a more satisfactory conclusion. Mikkelitz may have been—in fact, almost certainly was—insane. But he was criminally insane and dangerous to all around him. This way there'd be no trial. No legal double-talk. No slight chance that he might find himself out on the street, free to murder once more. It had happened before, she knew, and more than once.

He was gone and she didn't regret it for a moment.

She'd been to see Jesse once in the hospital. He was recovering from the gunshot wound and a severe loss of blood. He'd been sedated and only half aware of her presence and she felt awkward, standing by his bed, holding his hand in both of hers. She kept remembering him kneeling in the snow beside Abby. Holding her. Comforting her. Lee had to admit it, they looked good together.

She'd seen Abby as well. The reporter was also in the hospital, being treated for shock, the gunshot wound to her leg—and for a whole face-ful of bruises and contusions where Mikkelitz had beaten her. They'd shaken hands, although Abby had seemed more inclined to want to hug her, and Lee had stood awkwardly while the other woman thanked her, the terror of the hours she'd spent with Mikkelitz still visible, deep be-hind her perfect blue eyes. Lee had left the hospital room a little more abruptly than the occasion warranted.

And now, today, the media had packed up and gone. The Mountain Murderer story was cold news and the tourists were slowly returning to Steamboat and Mount Werner, encouraged by the fact that accom-modation was available and special discount prices were being offered as local traders tried to save something from the season.

Today was also the day when Abby would leave the hospital and return to Denver. Somehow, Lee knew that Jesse would be going with her. And as she knew it, she shook her head angrily, knowing that Jesse and Abby, no matter what they had between them, were simply not as right for each other as Jesse and she.

She knew it. Was sure of it. Unfortunately, there was absolutely nothing she could do about it. Jesse and Abby, she knew, might last a few more years together. But inevitably, they would drift apart and break up again.

But this time, knowing Jesse as she did, he would be too proud to return to her. She smiled sadly as she thought about it. Would she be too proud to have him back if he did, she wondered? Then she admit-ted, no, she wouldn't. Pride was all very well. But it had no place be-tween two people who were so right for each other.

There was a tap at the door—a light double tap that she knew was Jesse's.

"Come in," she called, and he stood there, a little awkward, his weight not fully on his wounded right leg, smiling at her, tearing her heart.

"Just dropped by," he said, gesturing vaguely to indicate that he was here.

She nodded.

"Abby's . . . kind of . . . on her way back to Denver. Flying out of Hadley at one o'clock," he said.

She nodded again, and for the sake of something to do, glanced at her watch. It seemed appropriate, since the time of day had just been mentioned.

"Should be an easy run out to the airport," she said. "Road's clear, I guess."

Jesse walked to the window and looked at the traffic outside. "I guess so," he agreed. "Been no snowfalls in forty-eight hours, so I guess the road's clear."

Silence. Awkward, tangible. It stretched on, then Jesse finally said, "Abby would probably like to say good-bye, you know? And say thanks for what you did."

She made a dismissive little hand gesture. "No call for that," she said. "She already said all that and anyway"—she glanced around at the nearly empty desktop, looking for Ned Puckett's crumpled up memo— "I've got paperwork I've got to catch up on."

She thought she could just get through saying good-bye to Jesse. She wouldn't be able to bear it if Abby were here, thanking her. She was uncomfortably aware of how she'd been tempted to shoot Mikkelitz and take the chance that he might or might not pull the trigger on Abby. The thought had only been there for a microsecond, but it had been there.

"Just tell her good-bye from me," she added.

Jesse nodded two or three times. "I'll do that," he said. Then, after a pause, "I'm going with her."

Lee rattled open the top drawer of her desk, making a production of finding a felony report form and a ballpoint pen, keeping her eyes down and away from Jesse's as she spoke.

"I kind of figured you would be," she said. She looked up, felt herself smiling like a death's head. "I guess you'd better be going then." She looked quickly down, beginning to fill in meaningless details on the form.

Jesse frowned, looking at her, hesitated for a few seconds. "Yeah, I guess so. Be seeing you, Lee."

"Yep." Just the one syllable, bitten off, delivered head down, still writing. "Be seeing you."

He let himself out. She heard the door click softly shut behind him, finished writing her name in the space for "reporting officer," wrote after the name "Sheriff, Routt County, Colorado," then set the pen down and put her hand over her eyes and wept silently.

She didn't hear the door re-open. Didn't hear Jesse enter the office and stop, watching her shoulders shake with grief. She didn't hear anything until he spoke her name.

"Lee?" he said. "Are you okay?"

He'd gotten halfway down the corridor, wondering at her strange, over-bright behavior and her abrupt manner. Something was wrong, he knew, and he turned back to see what it was.

Now the hand dropped away from her eyes and he could see the tears running down her face as she made no effort to stop them. And the eyes, those gray, up-tilted eyes that he'd loved since he was seventeen, had a depth of sadness in them that looked fit to tear the heart right out of his chest.

"Jesus, Lee," he breathed, moving toward her. "What's the matter?"

But she stopped him, one arm flung up, palm out, as if to hold him back.

"Just go!" the words were wrenched from her. "Just go, please. Go to Denver with Abby and, for Christ's sake, be happy."

He frowned at her. Not understanding. "Denver?" he asked.

She nodded, the tears still running. "You said you're going with her. Just go! Now! Please, Jesse?" The last two words were a helpless plea and suddenly, he understood.

"I'm going with her to the airport," he explained. "That's all. I'm seeing her onto the plane, then I'm coming back here." He hesitated, then finished, "If you want me."

She stopped sobbing, choked in disbelief. "If I—" she started, couldn't finish the sentence, shook her head in wonder and tried again. "If I want you? Oh, Jesus God, Jesse, of course I want you, you damn fool!"

He grinned foolishly at her, relief and pleasure mixed in the expression. "Anyways," he said, "I figured if I stuck around for another eighteen years or so, with any luck, I might get you back into bed again."

She was out of her chair and around the desk in one movement and his arms went around her as she buried her face into his neck. He smelled the natural fragrance of her hair, felt its softness against his cheek, felt the press of her body against his and he kissed her.

She responded enthusiastically. So did his body, and she pressed herself harder against him, twining one leg around his to hold him closer to her. He winced. Luckily she'd chosen his left leg, but the movement sent a shaft of pain through his wounded right one as he set more weight on it. She didn't notice, so he didn't bother to tell her, afraid she might pull away if he did. Her tongue explored his mouth, found his, and he forgot about the leg.

Neither of them heard the door open as Tom Legros entered. He stopped, startled. His sheriff had her back half to him, her shapely, jean-clad butt was resting on her desk and she had one long leg twined around her deputy's. Their arms were around each other and their faces locked together.

Just a little embarrassed, Tom looked away from the scene by the desk. Neither of them seemed to have noticed his arrival. He wasn't quite sure how to cope with the situation. Maybe they had noticed him after all. Maybe he should say something. Tentatively, he cleared his throat.

Lee disengaged her lips from Jesse's by a few millimeters and said, rather indistinctly, "What is it, Tom?"

Tom cleared his throat again nervously. Still looking to one side, not looking directly at them, he rotated his Stetson in his hands.

"It's Miz McLaren again. Seems she's got another guest complaining about those boys on the snowmobiles. Wants to talk to you, but I guess—" He hesitated. He wasn't quite sure what he guessed. He continued.

"Anyway . . . what do you want me to tell her, Sheriff?"

Lee leaned back a little in Jesse's arms. She considered her reply for a few seconds, then, more distinctly, said, "Tom? Tell her, fuck her."

He leaned forward a little, not sure that he'd heard her right. "Tell her?" he hesitated apologetically.

"Fuck her," Lee repeated, a little more distinctly.

Tom nodded nervous agreement. "Tell her . . . fuck her. Yep, I'll do that, Sheriff. I'll . . . get on it right away." He backed apologetically out the door, closing it behind him. In the corridor, he took a deep breath, set his Stetson squarely on his head, and started back to the phone.

He figured he'd maybe paraphrase Lee's message, just a little.

AUTHOR'S NOTE

Steamboat Springs and Routt County are real places. Many of the shops, hotels and bars named in this book are real as well. The characters, of course, are all fictitious.

In addition, as authors sometimes do, I may have taken a few liberties with the organization of law enforcement agencies in the town to suit the purposes of my narrative. I hope the real-life law officers of Routt County will forgive this minor self-indulgence.

ABOUT THE AUTHOR

John A. Flanagan, now a full-time author, is a former advertising and television writer. His adventure series for young adults, Ranger's Apprentice, has spent more than five months on the *New York Times* bestseller list.

Background for the Jesse Parker series came from his many visits to the ski fields of Colorado and Utah. He lives with his wife, Leonie, in Manly, Australia, on Sydney's northern beaches.